Heather
Scotland
and two
kept pigs

marketable pies and pates was the beginning of a business that led to her catering for Orient Express tours on their trips to Penshurst Place, the stately home of Lord De L'Isle in Kent. During this time she started work on her first book, *Country Enterprise*, which was published in 1983. Of *Beauty* she writes:

'In pursuit of the commercial world of beauty I met many of its inhabitants and am grateful for their enthusiasm.

'My sons Alexander and Rex grow increasingly helpful. My daughter Joanna has stopped growing and is indispensable, as is my husband Jonathan and my best-spelling mother.

'Felicity Bosanquet at Yves St Laurent, Niki Stenning at The Burton Group and Julian Dodds at International Management & Promotion set me off on new tangents for which many thanks.'

923-8806

By the same author

Country Enterprise
The Business
Heritage
Honour
Heroes

HEATHER HAY

Beauty

GraftonBooks

A Division of HarperCollins*Publishers*

To my family, as always.

GraftonBooks
A Division of HarperCollins*Publishers*
77–85 Fulham Palace Road,
Hammersmith, London W6 8JB

A GraftonBooks Paperback Original 1991
9 8 7 6 5 4 3 2 1

ISBN 0-586-21077-6

Printed in Great Britain by
HarperCollinsManufacturing Glasgow

Set in Times

Prologue

Beauty is no inheritance

'The Waldorf?' Charles Benson, six foot something, American, Ralph Lauren stereotype, asked huskily.

Marie Sullivan, attractive, raven-haired, twenty-nine years old, leaned her head slightly to one side to hear his words over the clatter from the airport arrivals hall.

'I beg your pardon?' she asked. In her well-cut navy Simpson suit and softly draped cream silk blouse, she looked just what she wanted to look, a purposeful executive.

Her accent was English, with just a hint of Irish in the warmth of her vowels.

'Well, Marie, being a traditional American, I always stay at the Waldorf when I'm over in London. And I thought, since we sat together for the flight over from the Big Apple, we could share a taxi into London, and then, how about a drink? What's the time here?' He glanced down at his watch. It had three time-zone displays: New York, London and Tokyo. 'Just after nine A.M. OK, so no drink – how about a late breakfast? That stuff they served us on the plane was just so much cardboard. Even first class you can't get a decent plate of eggs.'

'I'm afraid I'm going straight to my office.' Marie kept her voice modulated and polite, but she was tired of being overpowered by the overuse of Eternity for Men, tired of being overpowered by the oversell. The plane had been packed, and she'd been too close to 'Chuck' for comfort.

'Yeah – Body Beautiful you said you worked for? I suppose your office is listed in the phone book?'

'I should hope so. We've a hundred locations UK wide. But I wouldn't like to leave you with the wrong impression. It was nice meeting you. But I'm afraid I am very busy. I'll take my case now.'

She reached towards the well-packed leather hold-all that he'd insisted on carrying off the plane for her.

'Now hang on there a minute, little lady.'

'Will you please give me my bag – I am in a hurry.'

'Look, I didn't waste my time chatting you up for all those hours just to get a sweet thank-you and goodbye. Jesus – I even bought you champagne.'

'And if you remember' – Marie smiled sweetly – 'you drank it yourself.'

As she spoke, the slender stiletto heel of her French blue Bally court shoe stabbed down firmly. She'd chosen her target perfectly – the soft, exposed side of her unwanted admirer's instep. It was only thinly covered by a dark cream silk sock, and nicely underlined by the low cut of his bottle-green Gucci loafers.

'Thank you so much.' She reached down and swiftly picked up her case.

The red, white and green silk scarf tied to its handle fluttered behind her like a pennant as she walked quickly away across the crowded concourse, leaving him bent over and swearing.

'Jerk!' she muttered.

It didn't do to be polite. She should have snubbed him from the start. There was a queue for taxis, which she didn't think it politic to join, so she followed the signs for the rail link.

Her feet began to hurt as she hurried towards the station. In normal circumstances she would have changed

6

into a more comfortable pair of shoes – with lower heels – for the flight, but she'd come straight from an important meeting and been late booking in. Still, the stilettos had more than justified their existence.

Chapter 1

Beautiful flowers are soon picked

'I see what you mean about the view.' Marie undid a brass catch and pushed up the sash-cord window between her and a Monet-coloured panorama of rooftops.

The frame moved easily in its grooves, the immaculate quality of the ivory paintwork contrasting charmingly with the grey stone sill. Marie breathed in, drawing the city-scented air into her lungs, savouring the magic mixture of life and money that was London.

Three floors below her the Covent Garden piazza provided an open-air theatre. An exotic mixture of sounds and smells drifted up on the chill air. Crowds of warmly dressed tourists meandered slowly, enjoying the early evening ambience; in the midst of them, a couple entwined in a passionate embrace were draped decoratively over a bench.

Close to the arcades, a Pierrot leaned theatrically against a cast-iron lamp post and a small crowd gathered as he began his mime. From her eyrie, Marie watched his painted face contort in a parody of joy and sorrow that elicited a smattering of applause. With a final flourish he clapped his white-gloved hands together, and a flurry of pigeons took flight, winging their way upwards until, on a level with the open window, they turned to wheel across the dove-grey sky.

Peter Burnet, the most promising junior partner in Lloyd Lloyd and Fraser's Mayfair office, broke the awkward silence in the room.

'I knew you'd like the flat,' he said. 'I've been keeping it under wraps until you came back. And it's a snip; the chap who owns it's strapped for cash – he'll accept whatever I say's a fair offer. Two hundred thousand and it's yours. You'll have a couple of well-fitted bedrooms each with their own bathroom en suite, and the kitchen/diner was done by Smallbone, so that's another plus. This drawing room's a good twenty by twenty-five and the ceiling's a good height; in fact, all the rooms are spacious. The market won't be stagnant for much longer. This time next year I reckon you'll have more than doubled your money.' His cultured English accent made the vowels soft and liquid.

Suddenly, despite the disorientation brought on by jet-lag, Marie was aware of how much she wanted him. They'd been lovers for more than two years, but she could still be as excited by him as she had been the first time they met. That was at Henley, where Peter was supporting his old school, Eton, and Marie was a guest in his employer's hospitality tent.

Marie had just signed up to buy a small chain of six leasehold lock-up shops spread around London. The total purchase price of one hundred and forty thousand pounds was a drop in the ocean for London's premier estate agents, but the partner who'd handled the sale reckoned Marie was in the market for more.

He'd been right. Body Beautiful, the skin-care company of which Marie was founder and managing director, now had one hundred and fifty high-street shops in the UK and Europe. Its most recently acquired locations were in the US. The company now had an extensive property portfolio, one that with the prospect of recession could well prove an embarrassment.

Marie turned away from the window. She wished Peter would make the first move and come and take her in his arms. She'd been brought up always to be the subservient female, never to make the overtures. That was why it took every ounce of her determination to function as a strong, successful businesswoman.

Peter was still looking hurt; all six foot two of him was taut with suppressed emotion. He was so handsome, she thought, with his classic English fair hair and blue eyes, that the stiffness of his face made him look like a fashion plate. But she wouldn't tell him that. He didn't like her to admire his looks – he thought it unmanly. She smiled, trying to make him smile too. He was like a little boy when he was upset.

She was so sorry that she'd forgotten it was his birthday, the ultra-important three-oh. But with the late flight back from New York, and the final meeting of her trip still needing writing up, the last thing on her mind had been the relevance of the date.

There was another, underlying reason for his remaining aloof. Two weeks ago, just before she'd flown off to the States, they'd had their first major row. It was over what he had called her 'prudishness'. For all his repressive education, Peter could be surprisingly inventive in bed, and he felt that she was too inhibited and didn't trust him enough. However vehemently Marie denied it, she knew that most of what he said was true. Her problems came from having been brought up to believe that to enjoy sex was a sin. It was an old-fashioned concept that as a very modern woman she was having old-fashioned problems overcoming.

Marie laughed suddenly and Peter raised one well-sculptured eyebrow in surprise. The idea that had come to her couldn't have been better timed. She was working on conquering her insecurities in the boardroom, and now, she knew, it was time to start tackling them in the bedroom.

10

'I just want to check something,' she said.

Before Peter could say anything, she'd stepped out into the hall, crossed quickly to the master bedroom and entered the eau-de-nil tiled magnificence of the en-suite bathroom. She was away for no more than a couple of minutes before coming back to him in the drawing room.

There were butterflies in her stomach at what she planned to do. The flat still belonged to someone else and she struggled not to think that the owner might come back at any minute. She walked over to the window and then turned her back to the view. To calm herself she looked once more round the room. It was possible to imagine it furnished in her own style; the purity of her Italian-designed furniture would be perfect against the existing oyster-silk walls. She would position her twin leather sofas to flank the Adam-style fireplace . . . but all that would come later. In the meantime, for what she had in mind, she was grateful for the carpet on the floor – it was wall-to-wall soft grey Wilton.

'The flat's not all I want.' Her Irish accent was hardly discernible – ten years in England had seen to that.

She breathed in hard, flattening her stomach. She'd gained at least four pounds from all the working lunches in America, and she just hoped it didn't show. Peter tilted her face back so that he could look into her eyes.

'I want you, Peter,' she murmured. 'I want you here and now.'

Peter smiled. 'It's been a long time,' he said as he took her in his arms.

He bent his face towards hers, but she put the flat of her hands against his chest and pushed firmly against him. He looked down at her, puzzled that she didn't want to kiss him. Then she took hold of the wide-cut lapels of his Gieves and Hawkes suit and slid his jacket off, and he understood.

'Can't you wait?' he asked. 'Is this to show me you've been saving it all up?'

Marie nodded – she couldn't trust herself to speak – and swallowed the saliva that was flooding her mouth.

'Come away from the window. We don't want to frighten the pigeons.' He ran his hands approvingly over her hips. The skirt she was wearing was straight and well-fitting.

He slipped the palms of his hands over the swell of her buttocks as she stepped towards him, moulding herself to his body. 'Have you thought about me?' He was nuzzling her neck, his voice low and caressing.

Marie nodded again and smiled up at him as she slipped her feet out of her shoes. 'I thought about you all the way here.' She laughed and the sound was low and warm in her throat. 'And I thought I'd surprise you.'

Her words were smothered by his mouth as her lips parted under his. He was so good . . . she ran her fingers through his short thick hair and arched against him, then as his hand began kneading her breast she pushed away suddenly.

'Go down for me, go on – on your knees.' She began pulling her skirt up. 'Please . . .'

He ran his hand up the inside of her thigh and over the top of her stocking, feeling the smooth, cool skin. It was silent in the flat, still and soundless apart from their breathing. Slowly he inched higher.

'Jesus Christ,' he exploded. His fingers moved swiftly into the warm wetness. 'You've got nothing on under here.' He pushed her skirt upwards, burying his face in the salt taste of her.

'Well, you didn't really think I'd forget your birthday, did you? I had a surprise ready for you all along.'

She moaned as his tongue began to work.

12

Chapter 2

Beauty unchaste, is beauty in disgrace
ALEXANDER POPE (1688–1744)

The Dark Blues – pop musicians to royalty – had their amplifiers turned up to maximum.

The four Oxford graduates had performed at the North Sussex Hunt Ball before and they knew that the revellers liked their music loud. The venue, as always, was a ragstone monastery belonging to an enlightened religious order. The generous donation that the hunt handed over for the use of their rambling property for one cold night in February ensured their continued enlightenment.

The lively music reverberated off the solid stone walls and crashed down on to the mêlée of dancers gyrating in the refectory. The brown-habited monks kept to their austere cells, well away from the frivolity. The father abbot didn't want them tempted by the bright young things in their off-the-shoulder ball gowns who were parading their wares before an assortment of males in black jackets or hunting pink.

Several of the smaller ground-floor rooms were filled to overflowing with hired-in gilt-backed chairs and circular folding dinner tables that were littered with the aftermath of supper. The quality of the food had been dismal, as usual, and the cognoscenti had eaten elsewhere, with friends, before coming on.

Damion Sullivan dabbed at the sweat running down off his brow. He prided himself on being fit, but the little raver he'd danced the last three numbers with seemed to be firing on an extra cylinder. It was a relief to be sitting one out.

'Bloody good band,' a deep female voice bellowed in his ear. 'Really get the feet tapping.'

Damion could just make out the words over the music, and nodded his agreement.

'Told you young Annabel was a goer.'

So that was the girl's name. Damion had a lot on his mind and he'd forgotten what she was called. He'd had to drive flat out to get down from town in time for the evening. His sister, Marie, had held him up at the office, trying to insist that he changed his mind about giving up his position of production director at Body Beautiful.

She'd used all her old arguments, and a few new ones now that she'd understood that this time he was serious. It hadn't worked, it never would. He was determined to make a go of it with a string of good horses. To be a success as a trainer was his one overwhelming ambition. He would be thirty-three next birthday and he had the feeling that it was now or never to take the plunge.

He watched Annabel for a moment as she danced with Fred, the whipper-in. She was shaking her shoulders so violently that she had to keep on hauling up the front of her dress, not that she need have bothered on Damion's account – he'd already had more than an eyeful at dinner.

Damion turned to face the woman beside him. Mo Beaumont had been their hostess at the impressive timber-framed manor house – her husband was, as the saying went, 'something in the city'. Mo was flushed with excitement and it highlighted the inevitable red veins that spread across the cheeks of a fox-hunting matron. He thought briefly of suggesting that she should use Body Beautiful's ultra-violet protective cream over the active moisturizer, but he hated talking shop.

The object of Damion's scrutiny was looking forward

14

to the dancing. Her dress was an old favourite, made from green brocade. It was good material in a serviceable boat-neck style that would stand up to any amount of tugging in the post-horn gallop. She looked what she was, he thought – a good sport.

'Fancy a dance, Mo?' he asked.

The sound of her name spoken in his soft Irish accent, combined with the appeal of his clear green eyes and dark wavy hair, made her blush like a girl.

'Rather.' She grinned, exposing almost as many teeth as her favourite hunter could manage. 'Hope they start playing something smoochy,' she added as she gripped Damion's arm firmly and negotiated their way to the centre of the heaving throng.

Once there she turned towards him and flung her arms around his neck, tipped her head back and closed her eyes.

'Heaven – pure bliss,' she murmured.

As Damion began to shuffle slowly across the floor, she pushed her ample pelvis against his narrow loins.

After a while, she began to move tentatively against him. Her words had been smothered by the din, just as she trusted her moment of passion would be hidden from her overweight, undersexed husband, whose existence she pushed firmly out of her mind. Damion was a beautiful man, and with her eyes closed she could enjoy his closeness while seeing the vision of him that she created regularly in her fantasy. He was wearing jodhpurs – they were pale cream ones that fitted like a glove and outlined the slim, long muscles of his thighs.

She pressed harder against him as she imagined the next part – the growing bulge that showed how much the beautiful young man wanted her. His chest was naked . . . Her head tipped back further as her breasts flushed with adrenalin. She imagined his nipples, hard and dark

15

in the soft, smooth skin stretched tight over flat, solid muscle. A silk stock was tangled loosely round his neck. They'd been so charged with longing that he'd ripped off his shirt, and it lay discarded on the ground behind them.

The music changed abruptly as the pulsing reggae beat gave way to soul. The gentle rhythm engulfed her and she laid her head snugly against the manly breast that for the next few precious minutes would be hers alone.

Damion grinned over her head at a friend trapped close to him in the crowd. Jeremy Gaines was a gentleman farmer, one of the new breed, who actually drove a tractor himself. Like Damion, he was clasped in the warm embrace of one of the older generation.

The middle-aged *grandes dames* of country life looked forward to the hunt ball for months. For most of them, it was their only chance of close physical contact with the possessors of the taut masculine bottoms that a hunt across country revealed in all their tantalizing glory.

At least now Mo had slumped against him, Damion had time to think. He ran his hands academically up and down her back. The muscle tone wasn't bad considering she was probably a size sixteen. But he damned her for interfering in his love life by asking him to join their party for the evening. He'd accepted without thinking, and that acceptance included being paired off with Annabel.

There was no way he could have cried off once he'd realized his mistake. Mo's husband had expressed interest in owning a steeplechaser; it would need training, and he could well be Damion's first owner. The training fees would be his lifeblood. Marie kept refusing to buy him out of the company, so he'd have precious little capital.

Mo trod painfully on his toes and he muttered an apology as if it had been his fault, then he went back to thinking about his problems. He'd left Rose, his groom, crying her eyes out because he'd been thoughtless enough not to realize she expected to go as his partner. After all, she'd wailed, she was always turning up at the hunt meets, qualifying his point-to-point prospects while he was at work in London.

Rose had thought that entitled her to an invitation – and for other reasons that he preferred not to consider while he was still clutched in Mo's iron grip. Mo, to whom the feelings of a groom were ranked as of infinitely less importance than those of a horse.

Rose Knowles was a fresh-faced country girl who'd been in love with horses from the moment she could walk. She'd managed to make a life for herself with them by having a gentle touch and a firm seat. Her family lived in a tied cottage on a farm close to Damion's picture-book cottage with its timber-built range of three stables and seven acres of well-fenced pasture. When she answered the advertisement he'd put in the window of the village shop, she'd seemed heaven sent, but now . . .

He felt a sudden stirring in his arms.

Mo whispered breathily in his ear, 'Don't dare risk any longer, darling. People will talk, you know . . .' Her voice tailed off and she looked up into his eyes with a happy, conspiratorial smile.

He felt he couldn't do anything else but give her one back. He squeezed her briefly against him and then led her off the floor.

'My God, what a super night!' Annabel was still full of vigour.

The pulsing music had finished long ago, and it was icy cold in the darkened parkland outside the monastery. Like a matador, the girl trailed her Laura Ashley black velvet cape along the ground. It left her shoulders bare, and her dark, bouncy hair cascaded in curls down her back and gleamed in beguiling contrast to the buttercup silk Renaissance-style dress that she wore.

She was very pretty – a highly bred animal with all the vibrant energy of youth. If it hadn't been for Rose, Damion thought, he might have felt tempted. She turned and came running back towards him, her breasts bouncing in the moonlight, and he stopped pretending to himself; there was no 'might have' about it, but he had no intention of accepting what was clearly on offer. He had quite enough problems already.

'I need a pee.' Jeremy Gaines' plum rich voice carried on the still night air.

He had an arm firmly around Mo, to whom he was distantly related. Their claim to be second cousins twice removed justified his solicitous attention, and the hand with which he fondled her buttock was there – as he would have said to anyone who questioned it – just for fun.

'Damion, O Damion,' Jeremy warbled in a voice made hoarse with drink. 'Wherefore art thou, Damion? Come on, me darlin', I need some male company. It's dark out there and I'm desperate to find something to piss against.'

Damion was also aware of an overloaded bladder. He stood still and stared out into the blackness – all they needed was privacy from the ladies. There were far-off sounds of hilarity as the last of the revellers came out into the night, but apart from that the almost empty temporary car park was silent. Jeremy tried a quavering imitation of an owl but quickly gave up. He needed all his powers of concentration to walk a straight line.

'There were trees behind the cars,' Jeremy said. 'I saw them in my mirror, when we parked.' He began to walk resolutely forwards into the dark, unzipping his fly as he went.

Damion kept pace with him. His head was swimming.

18

He'd eaten very little of Mo's mediocre cooking and drunk too much of her husband's excellent wine.

As it seemed to grow darker around them, Jeremy started to sing again. '"Queen Elizabeth sat one day,"' he sang to the tune he had learned fifteen years ago at Harrow, and then with a laugh broke into the school boy's version of the words. '"Watching her mariners rich and gay, suddenly all the springs gave way and there was . . ."' he continued.

They walked on to the sound of his singing until, with a sudden gurgle, the words stopped and he disappeared as if the earth had swallowed him up.

Damion was opening his mouth to call out when suddenly the ground gave way beneath him, and he was falling. They landed, huddled together at the base of a massive tree.

'Take your hand off my dick,' Jeremy bellowed as Damion pushed himself up to a sitting position. 'Where the hell are we?'

Within minutes the wavering light of a torch shone around, and Mo called out, looking for them.

When she found the two men, she began to laugh helplessly. 'What on earth are you doing down there?' she asked. 'And what is that you're holding, Jeremy? Put it away, dear boy. Whatever do the pair of you look like?'

The small yellow circle of light shook wildly.

'I'm going to have my pee.' Jeremy slowly stood, and balanced himself carefully, one hand against the tree trunk, the other still holding on to what he liked to think of as his friend Willy. 'Bloody silly place to dig a hole.'

Damion clambered out of the ditch, which was about four foot deep and appeared to go right round the base of the magnificent oak. The fall had sobered him, and suddenly Jeremy looked very silly sprinkling pee all over the tree and his shoes. The whole evening seemed a farce.

19

He shouldn't be squandering his time, he had to get on with his future.

'You've got a car phone, haven't you, Mo?' he asked.

'Absolutely, dear boy . . .' She shone her torch on his face and decided to shut up.

Damion held his hand out for the car keys, and Mo passed them to her guest, who a moment before had seemed as light-hearted as the rest of them – but suddenly looked uncompromisingly serious.

Rose's father answered on the third ring. He wasn't happy to be woken up and had to be persuaded to get his daughter to the phone. The girl's voice was wary, but clear – she hadn't slept at all. She'd seen Damion's abandoning her for the evening as an omen, and she hadn't stopped crying for hours.

'Rose.' Damion took a deep breath.

He knew that he didn't really love her – not with a deep, fulfilling passion that swept him off his feet – but he was very fond of her and, as his sister would have said, he had a soft heart. Ever since he was little, he'd hated to see anyone hurt needlessly.

'Rose,' he said softly. 'Will you marry me?'

Mo's voice was clear beside him. 'Rose? You don't mean Rose Knowles? Good God, Damion, you're out of your mind!' she said.

It was what they would all say. The simple country girl and the educated man of the world – it was all right for a fling, but anything more would be madness. But there was something they didn't know: the girl was expecting a baby – his baby.

'Will you?' he asked again, and felt a great surge of relief at the whispered 'Yes.'

Chapter 3

Beauty is potent, but money is omnipotent

'I haven't just left you in at the deep end,' Damion shouted. 'I've spoken to a firm of head-hunters . . .'

Marie slammed her hand down hard on her desk. 'Head-hunters?' She laughed bitterly. 'They specialize in replacing missing brothers, do they?'

'For Christ's sake.' It was as bad as Damion had known it would be. He slumped back in the overstuffed grey leather sofa that the office designer had called 'haute coutour'.

'Christ isn't going to help you, Damion. I could shake you. You're being so damned stupid. Can't you see that your position in the company is the only solid thing in your life? It doesn't mean you can't keep horses. Working as a chemist is the only way you can afford to feed them. Come on now.' She stood up suddenly, smiling conspiratorially, willing her brother to respond. 'You've had a bad patch, but let's just hug and make up. I'll even come down to the point-to-point on Saturday. I'll bring a hamper.'

'Don't mother me,' Damion roared. His face was streaked with red and sinews stood out on his neck. 'I'll live my own life. You're not the only one with ambition. I've given you years I could have spent setting up my own future, chucked up everything so far to give you a fair crack at yours. You knew it would end one day. Now leave it. There's nothing you can say. It's over for me.'

It was true, there was nothing more she could say.

Marie stood. She felt numb, she seemed incapable of thought. It was as if her mind had stopped functioning, and she could only feel the truth of what Damion had said. It really was the end of working together. She would be alone at the top.

'Come down on Saturday, anyway. It's the first of the season,' Damion cajoled. He'd thickened his accent and was smiling with the sideways tilt of his lips that always worked with women, his sister included. 'You're going from strength to strength. In next to no time you'll be my most important owner.'

'I'll never buy any horses for you to train. I won't encourage you.'

Damion shrugged and stood up. His eyes were narrow with anger, but his voice was level.

'Well, perhaps you won't need to,' he said. 'I've got a good reputation as a horseman in my neck of the woods. Perhaps the business will come rolling in once people realize I'm going at it full-time. I've already got a new owner bringing three horses in this week. His name's Berry Jopling. He's a South African who came over here because he couldn't stand their system. He's done more than well, and he doesn't want me penny-pinching with his animals.'

'The devil looks after his own.' Marie reached down and slammed closed the day book that had been lying open on her desk. 'I'm going to pack it in early, and I'm not even going to take any work home with me. I feel shattered.'

'I'm sorry.'

'No sorrier than I am. I'll have to catch up tomorrow, and then I'll have to start in on all the things you would have been doing.'

'It won't be as bad as you think. Nothing ever is.'

'Really,' Marie said sarcastically. 'You know what goes on inside my head, do you?'

Damion thought that he probably did. His sister had ability, the single-mindedness to pursue a goal. She could also make mountains out of molehills. He'd always said he'd leave the company if he found the right set-up, the ideal yard. He'd done her a favour by not looking too hard until the product range was under wraps.

'Look, sister mine.' Damion reached inside his jacket and pulled out a folder. 'This is the firm of head-hunters I told you about. They're called Capita. I heard about them just the other day through some chap I met in the pub.'

The expression on Marie's face showed what she thought of such an introduction.

'They're kosher, all right. I checked up on them. Four partners – you don't want a bigger company, otherwise the fact that they won't do any poaching from their existing client list cuts out too many possible candidates.'

'I don't have the money to employ head-hunters. I'll advertise, myself.'

'Can this be the same woman who was just telling me how impossibly busy she is? You don't have the time to do your own search. You'd have to do a lengthy, in-depth campaign to get the right person. We chemists don't just grow on trees, you know,' Damion finished, with a relieved laugh. Marie was starting to look human again.

'Your replacement might well not have the same qualifications as you do.'

'What?' The disbelief was clear in Damion's expression. 'You're not trying to tell me the business hasn't needed a chemist all these years? Do me a favour, Marie. I know you're mad at me, but don't pretend I made no contribution.'

'You made your contribution all right, Damion, and I'd never say otherwise. But would you be making the same contribution if you stayed on? You've said yourself that a great deal of your work recently has been administration rather than development. Our product line is pretty comprehensive. Sure we'll need new products in the future. But I'm not convinced that a full-time chemist will be needed to produce them. You know' – she looked at her brother appraisingly as if an idea had just come to her – 'if you could just give the company a couple of days a week . . .'

'No way.' Damion slapped the head-hunters' brochure down on Marie's desk. 'I'm out for good. From now on in, if I set foot in this building it's either to see how my fifty per cent is being managed.' He grinned. 'Or to take my favourite sister out to lunch.'

'How much do these people charge?' Marie ran the tip of her finger over the hard-gloss deep blue cover emblazoned with the gold script *Capita*. 'They look expensive.'

'They're all basically the same. One-third of the first year's salary. There are variations in the fee charged for a nonstarter. This lot charge a basic five thousand. That covers their expenses if you shouldn't fancy any of their applicants.'

'I should think five thousand would cover their expenses! And what kind of guarantee do I have that they'll get the right kind of people? They could just throw – '

'Hold on a minute.' Damion sat down again.

He wasn't going to get away as early as he'd hoped, but at least they were being civilized to each other. 'Included in that fee is a survey of your marketplace. They'll produce a profile of how your competitors see you. They will also produce details of salary levels among your competitors; how your competitors' companies are structured and any new developments that they believe you should be aware of. It's a bit like employing a firm of

24

surveyors to find out if you've got dry rot and finding that they're prepared to do all the legwork to find you an ideal home.'

'I can do without the sales talk.'

'I just want you to know that I haven't taken this step lightly. I know you're going to want a replacement, so I've done everything I can to find you the right route to getting one.'

Marie sat silently. It was typical of Damion to make her start to feel in debt to him when in reality he was producing one of the most difficult problems the company had ever had to face.

Damion's name was known. A lot of their PR had been on the basis that it was a brother-and-sister venture. Unfortunately it had not always been picked up that, unusually, it was the female member of the partnership who was at the business's sharp end. She would have to work hard to establish that fact. The bank wouldn't like it for a minute, and they were already unhappy about the level of their borrowings.

She frowned. 'I'm going to be totally calm about this, so don't you overreact, but I have to say yet again that for you to leave now would be a big mistake.'

Damion breathed in noisily but kept his lips firmly pressed together. He wasn't going to restart the argument.

'The timing couldn't be worse. We need more working capital – you know that as well as I do. The bank is going to be very suspicious if they see you abandoning ship and me going in, cap in hand, for another sizeable loan.'

'That's why it's going to be very important that you choose the right person to replace me. You've as much as said that my contribution to Body Beautiful is at an end. You can make the same point to the bank, say that you edged me out, if you like – I don't mind. Make it a plus point. You could even have my shares, if it suited. I could do with the cash.'

'Don't you even think of it. You know how I feel about those shares. They're the only solid thing in your life, Damion. You might not have enjoyed the years you put into making them worth something, but they are your only decent prospect for the future. I'll accept that you're giving up an active role in the company – apart from seeing through the final development of the massage glove. Don't forget you promised me that. And you'll accept that you hang on to those shares through thick and thin. There'll come a day you'll thank me for it.'

They parted apparently amicably, but Marie was certain it was only a lull in the storm. Damion's intentions had been clear enough. He wanted whatever money his fifty per cent of the company would bring in. He would put it into his training venture, where it would disappear without trace.

Marie stared sightlessly at Capita's expensive brochure. She couldn't afford to buy Damion out, and even if she could she wouldn't want to. If she owned a hundred per cent of the company, she would be totally at the bank's mercy – as if she wasn't already.

She laughed out loud in the empty room, her shoulders relaxed, and a surge of energy replaced the lethargy she'd fallen into. It was another challenge to face. Damion had been a prop that had not always been secure. Now she was, as she had been before, on her own.

'John Blake from Capita on the line for you.' Angelique's voice sounded clipped on the intercom. Marie had started the morning with a needless lecture on efficiency and the secretary was still smarting from it.

'John, I've been wondering what had happened to you. Have you any news for me?' Marie forced her voice to sound bright and on the ball, but she kept pressing her fist tight against her temple where a vicious pain was throbbing.

'Have I got news! Three excellent contenders. It says quite a bit for your profile that I've managed to drum that much interest up. After all, you're not as big as most of our clients . . .'

Marie closed her eyes. Capita's pushy executive had said that line once too often. If it wasn't that she was so short of time she'd go elsewhere.

'I think we'll progress from the bottom up – that's the C1 end of the cosmetics business I'm talking about, of course. As far as St John Aldridge is concerned he's very much flavour of the month. He took Pretty Face to the City and made a damned good job of it.'

'He's their financial director isn't he?' Marie asked. Capita had hooked a big one, and she was impressed. St John Aldridge was regularly quoted as an up-and-coming financial wizard. That he would consider working for Body Beautiful was remarkable.

'Absolutely.' Blake paused and Marie could hear him rustling pages, then he began again. 'Second on the list is Mark Moorman. You may not have heard of him – he's a highly qualified chemist, a product developer with one of the truly exclusive perfume houses. As a matter of fact, he's asked that I don't identify the company to you until after an initial meeting.'

'That's a bit petty. After all, you know who he works for.'

'Well, these geniuses have their funny ways.' The loud laugh was patently artificial and cut off instantly as the head-hunter continued his sale. 'Last, and in some ways first, I have Sarah Hatherleigh. Now she is definitely special, you're bound to know her work, the campaigns she's masterminded. That beautiful model wrapped in

27

nothing but brown paper, you must know the one. It's simply stunning – the concept, the photography.'

'The perfume it's selling is rubbish,' Marie interrupted. 'Besides, I don't need anyone in publicity or marketing. I do that part of the business myself.'

'But you're getting bigger, aren't you? You told me you were, and, of course, that is why people like St John Aldridge are prepared to give you credence. I have to say, it's on that basis that I was prepared to act for you. I mean – '

Marie interrupted again. 'Yes, we're growing quickly, very quickly. I'll see all three. I'm available . . .'

There was a brief silence on the line as Marie flipped over a few pages of her desk diary and then realized the impossibility of finding three consecutive free hours. Whenever she chose, she would have to cancel appointments, but she had to find someone soon. The strain of not having a replacement for Damion had affected her far more than she'd expected.

She coughed to clear her throat, and then said, 'Make it as soon as possible. Any morning. Tell my receptionist when you've got it fixed.'

It was John Blake's secretary who phoned back to suggest Thursday morning. Clearly John Blake himself did not speak to receptionists.

The man in the cream Galliano jacket tossed his carelessly folded copy of the *Daily Telegraph* on to the brass-bound oak chest in front of him. It looked messy beside the two immaculate piles of *Vogues* and *Elles*. He adjusted his position irritably on the kelim-covered banquette and looked ostentatiously at his watch. He'd waited nearly a quarter of an hour already, and he'd arrived right on time for his appointment. The girl on reception was working at a word processor and he had to clear his throat to attract her attention.

He called unnecessarily loudly across the cream-carpeted gap between them, 'You did tell her I was here?'

'Yes, Mr Aldridge, and I'm sure you won't be kept long now but I'm afraid Ms Sullivan is still on the line to New York.'

The girl's soft Jamaican accent was gently pacifying, as was her pretty, chubby face. She smiled at the visitor and then turned to run an efficient eye over the lights on her mini telephone exchange. There was a gentle rattle of glass as the red and green beads decorating the dozens of plaits hanging down to her shoulders collided.

After a few more minutes, Angelique added, 'She said you're to go in as soon as she's finished.'

St John Aldridge brushed nonexistent specks of dust off his bitter-chocolate linen trousers. He disliked West Indians. They made him uncomfortable, and he thought the girl's presentation coquettish in the extreme. The entire place showed it had a female in control, and he didn't like it. The only women he admired were those dedicated to the pursuit of classic beauty – their own beauty, which they worked hard and skilfully to enhance for the enjoyment of the male sex. If it wasn't for the possibilities that he thought the next hour or two could bring, he wouldn't even want to find himself in the same room as Marie Sullivan. She was nothing more than a jumped-up salesgirl who was trying to make a go of things in a man's world.

Marie sat back in her posture-sculpted leather chair.

Her desk was cleared and she had left the phone off the hook after her call to New York ended. There had been a spate of raids on her shops. They were all well positioned, in air-conditioned malls. Unfortunately, the welcoming, open design of their interiors had proved irresistible to the bands of young thieves who had forced her competitors to hire expensive security guards.

This was the first applicant the head-hunters had produced. She reread the word 'applicants' that she had written at the top of her jotter and crossed it out. It wasn't right. After all, the man waiting in reception had been approached on behalf of Body Beautiful – he hadn't applied for anything. Shaking her head at how effectively the nun who'd taught English grammar at the convent had managed to indoctrinate her, she wrote 'candidate'.

The fact that St John Aldridge was interested enough to come for an interview meant one of two things: either he was interested in a job as number two in a small but fast-growing beauty products company jostling for position in the maelstrom of international cosmetics; or he was using the approach as a useful way of getting inside her company's defences. Whilst sounding him out, she would have to be careful not to reveal too much of her own future strategy. Intercompany espionage was a daily fact of life in any business allied to the fashion trade.

She reached out and replaced the telephone receiver. There were another two interviews booked for later on in the day, and whichever two candidates she selected on the first sweep would have a final interview the following week; she didn't have time to waste.

'My record speaks for itself.' St John stretched like a satisfied cat.

There wasn't anyone to touch him in the industry. The day he'd qualified as an accountant he'd walked out of Coopers and Lybrand, who'd trained him, and into a job with Coty. After two years learning the rudiments of the cosmetics business, he'd moved on to Max Factor, where he had quickly worked his way up to middle management,

30

and then, making his most important career move to date, he had joined Pretty Face. He was now financial director of the third-largest mass-market cosmetics giant in Europe, the fourth in the world. It was acknowledged that he had masterminded them through a massive restructuring and diversification programme.

'You can understand that I'm constantly receiving approaches like yours,' he added smugly.

Marie nodded. 'But I assume you don't follow them all up. After all, you do have to leave some time to devote to your existing job.'

St John's face creased in the smile that his present co-directors had come to dread.

'Career,' he murmured. 'I have a career; jobs are for the workers. No, of course I turn down most of them. But I have to admit that your company intrigues me. The high profile you've achieved despite the relative smallness of your turnover, and the rather clever product range.' He gestured with a smooth white hand towards the glass shelves flanking Marie.

The whole product range was there: the distinctive shell-shaped flasks that contained as close as science could get to the top-name, top-price beauty products.

'We are growing very quickly. As you no doubt know, we're well established in Europe, and we've recently started up in the States. That's why whoever comes on the board to replace my brother should be able to join us within a month at the most.'

'Your brother,' St John mused. He dropped his lips on to the steeple he had made of his hands and his voice became muffled. Marie had to concentrate to hear him. 'Of course, he was the prime force, the company will suffer . . .'

'Damion was our chemist,' Marie interrupted. 'He was responsible for developing our range, and therefore extremely important in the formative stages. He is a highly talented scientist, and that's what his function has been in Body Beautiful, nothing more and nothing less. The company is mine. I started it, and I shall continue to run it as I see fit.'

Marie's voice had hardened as she spoke. As usual, it had been assumed that the man in Body Beautiful was the driver behind the wheel. She worked at calming herself and slowing her breathing. She had no intention of letting Aldridge rile her with a remark that she ought to have expected. 'As you say, your achievements speak for themselves. But what I still don't understand is why you are interested enough in my organization to spend an hour of your obviously precious time with me. I would have thought we were too small for you.'

'But you're not going to be small for long, are you?' St John sat forward in his chair and began to show the dominant personality that had given him clout in the money markets. 'I have reached a pinnacle in a mass-market company. In time I could progress to become chairman, if not of my present organization, then of something comparable. I'm forty-five and I estimate that it would take another ten years at least for me to achieve that move. I see that as ten years of dead, repetitive time. If I joined a smaller, fast-growing company, one that I could have a stake in – well, then my personal rewards would come that much sooner.'

'How big a stake are you envisaging?'

'I think we should discuss that at our next meeting.' St John rose elegantly to his feet. He felt that he was in command of the interview. By leaving early, he had proved his superiority. 'My time, as you have so rightly said, is valuable. Whilst having this exploratory talk with you, I am still loyal to my employers. Loyalty is a rare thing in our business, as I'm sure you've found.' He stretched his hand out towards Marie. 'À bientôt.'

Sarah Hatherleigh arrived right on time for her two o'clock appointment and Angelique showed her straight into Marie's office. The two women were practised at instant character judgements, and their dislike was mutual. The pink jacket that the second candidate wore over a straight black skirt was from Dior. The leather shoulder bag fastened with what looked like a snaffle bit was from Hermès.

'You've never worked exclusively for one company?' Marie kept her eyes on the typewritten curriculum vitae on her desk as she spoke.

'No, initially I was agency based. As you can see, I was with the big boys, but for the past two years I've worked freelance. And I'm doing very well, thank you.'

'Then why are you here.' Marie's face was deadpan.

The tight, upper-class accent of her visitor was off-putting, as were the long, slim fingers that were drumming a silent tattoo on a well-shaped knee. Ms Hatherleigh's pale blonde bobbed hair, wide-spaced blue eyes and full, red lips would turn men on like heat turned cream to butter.

'I'm not quite sure.' The laugh was just as artificial as the simulated indecision that accompanied it. 'I've admired your PR, even though I think I could do better. But it's clever, and very, very cheap for the amount of coverage you're getting. Let's just say that I was interested enough to come and find out more. You've still got a long way to go, and there aren't that many women who can make it all the way to the top on their own, so perhaps we should stick together. After all, the blokes do, don't they? The old school tie and all that. You don't mind if I smoke, do you? I didn't have time for lunch.'

Before she'd finished speaking, Sarah was already delving in her handbag, rummaging for the packet of Marlboros under a wad of Kleenex tissues that were there just in case.

Just in case her twelve o'clock appointment with the editor of the cosmetic industry's most influential trade magazine had led to a little hanky-panky behind the closed doors of his office. As it happened, it hadn't, principally because there had been a couple of subeditors in on the meeting and a gang bang didn't seem quite right for the middle of the day.

'You don't have to like someone to work with them,' Sarah said as she sucked on the nicotine-flavoured smoke, leaving a perfect red ring of Estée Lauder around the filter tip. 'But you do have to admire them. And there's one thing successful women have in common – the knowledge of how bloody hard it's been to get there.'

Marie was at her desk by eight-thirty. There were half a dozen letters that she'd intended to dictate the night before, when yet another argument on the phone with Damion had taken up the time she should have used to get them done.

Peter had arrived at the office punctually at seven to take her to see *La Traviata* and she hadn't had time to change. He hadn't been amused at having to wait while she quickly tried to effect a transformation. The recent stress had been bad for her skin, and the last thing she'd wanted to do was put on make-up, but she'd felt she needed it to cover the dark circles under her eyes.

Now she switched on her dictating machine and began straight away. The last of the candidates put forward by the head-hunters had cancelled yesterday's appointment and was due at ten. She hoped he was more suitable than the first two offerings.

34

'Date February the twentieth,' she began. 'To Monsieur Alphonse DuBois, Champs Élysée address as in file. Cher Alphonse . . .'

'Mark Moorman has arrived.'

The disembodied voice on the intercom surprised Marie. It was twenty to eleven, and she had given up expecting the final candidate. She laid down the sheaf of papers she had been working her way through. Her desk was littered with work in progress, and her instinctive reaction was to go out to reception and cancel the interview. But the man was well positioned in what was apparently an important couture perfume company, so she would at least have to see him.

Mark Moorman was a giant of a man. Well over six foot, he was fat and lumbering, his pepper-and-salt-coloured hair was unruly and grew low over his collar. His eyes were sunk into folds of skin, and his nose and mouth were indeterminate. His face was remarkable only in that there was so little to recognize it by. He wore a long, elderly raincoat over an expensive but ill-fitting grey flannel suit. A blue shirt that looked as if it might have been slept in formed a background for an unexciting red and black striped tie.

Marie offered her hand and Moorman shook it quickly, as if fearing some kind of contagion. In contrast to the rest of him, his hands appeared small and beautifully manicured; the nails, pink, filbert in shape, were almost feminine in their perfection. As Marie accepted his half-hearted apologies for being late she wondered if the three were really the best the head-hunters could come up with – for five thousand pounds.

There were quite a few charmers in the beauty business – she'd come across some herself. But she instinctively felt that both Aldridge and Moorman were women-haters. It wasn't a good start.

'You're very highly qualified, Mr Moorman.' Despite her instinctive dislike of the man, Marie was impressed by the string of letters after his name.

'A true scientist never stops learning, and I have few interests other than my work. You'll find I'm more than an adequate replacement for your brother.'

The voice, like the rest of the man, was carelessly assembled. It was an amalgam of accents – there was a west of England resonance mixed with a transatlantic drawl – and he had a habit of running his words together. His abbreviated life history showed that he had lived in several Arab countries and worked in the oil industry, before switching to cosmetics.

'We'll have to skip the formalities as I have another appointment at eleven,' Marie said. 'To save time, why don't you tell me how you would see a future position for yourself in my company.'

Ignoring her suggestion completely, Moorman started on the presentation he had rehearsed.

'The Body Beautiful range,' he began, 'almost covers the total spectrum of skin-care products. I have, of course, analysed the various items. They come close to their claims – which, as we both know, is remarkable in this business.' There was a pause when he might have smiled, but didn't. 'What you need is something unique. A beauty aid that takes you out to the forefront, something that is so amazingly effective that you leapfrog the competition. I have a formula that would enable you to do that.'

'This is something that you have not produced for your present employers?' Marie asked.

Moorman's last position had been product development director of Renoir, one of the world's élite perfume houses, a member of the exclusive group of twenty companies which accounted for over eighty per cent of total sales in a one and a half billion dollar industry. Presumably his present job was with a company that was somehow even more special.

'That is right.'

'But aren't you under contract to the effect that anything developed by you whilst in their employ is theirs? I have to say that I would expect you to sign that form of contract for me – should you be selected.'

'Selected!' He snorted the word. 'You can't afford to turn me down. And don't talk "contracts" to me. This is a filthy business we're in. Dog eat dog, or perhaps in your case I should say bitch eat bitch.'

'Mr Moorman, I really think . . .' Marie stood abruptly.

'Look at these.' He stretched his hands towards her, showing their smooth, shell-pink backs, then turning them over to reveal the delicately mottled palms. 'Go on, look at them. Five years ago they were ruined by acid burns from a foul-up in the lab. It took two years' physiotherapy to get the full movement back in them, and the skin was like paper – dry and splitting. My hands used to bleed when I washed them and the skin around my cuticles was so damaged that my nails grew crooked. They wanted me to have extensive skin grafts, but I knew better than any of them. Feel, go on, feel.' He thrust his hands into Marie's. 'They're softer than yours, aren't they? That's what my miracle cream did for me. Think what it could do for you – for your company, *our* company. Because that's the price. For making Body Beautiful into the most successful beauty company in the world, I want fifty per cent of the equity. You can't say I'm an unreasonable man; I'm suggesting equal shares, half and half.'

'That would never work – you know it and I know it.' Marie's head was spinning. If what Moorman said was true, his formula was worth a fortune. 'One of us would have to have a deciding vote to cast.'

'It would take at least three years' research for anyone else to get where I have. Think about it – three years ahead of the field with an exclusive product that would revolutionize skin care as the world knows it.'

'Why have you come to me with your offer?' Marie asked.

'Your people approached me just as I was about to go out and look for a suitable vehicle. I need an existing framework, and your profile is high, considering your size in the marketplace. Body Beautiful provides the ideal launch pad for my creation.'

Marie was still holding his hands, feeling the strange baby-softness. She let go of them almost grudgingly. There was so much on offer, and yet it would be such a price to pay. She would be letting go the control of her company. It was like being tempted by the devil.

'I'll let you know,' she said. 'I'm sure you will appreciate that there are other applicants.'

Moorman smiled, as if to a small child.

'Angelique.' Marie picked up the telephone the moment she heard Moorman leave the outer office. 'Get Damion on the phone for me. Tell him it's urgent, really urgent. And then you'd better get hold of Peter. Tell him I'll be late this evening. No, on second thoughts, tell him I won't be able to make it at all. Say something important's come up.'

She put the receiver down and waited for Damion. Could she contain a man like Moorman? She rubbed her palms together without realizing it. She could remember how amazingly soft his hands had felt.

The product must be something based on vitamin C, she thought. He must have harnessed its restorative powers and managed to counteract the peeling it could cause. A miracle cream – she had to find out from Damion if it was possible. If Moorman's claim could be substantiated, they would make a fortune. She could pay off the unsecured overdraft at the bank – that would help her to sleep at night.

If they relocated the production plant from Ireland to England it would mean that her father would no longer have a hold on her. Perhaps then their relationship would improve, perhaps she could even start to get close to her mother again. With the money rolling in, she could buy more sites in the States and work them into the projected franchise package there. That was what the City analysts had said would make the future flotation of Body Beautiful a cast-iron winner.

She got up to start walking about the office; she was so excited that she couldn't sit still. Only last night, Damion had been trying again to persuade her to buy out his fifty per cent of the company so that he could set himself up in a decent training establishment.

Fifty per cent. The even split had worked with her brother, but only because he gave way to her. He acknowledged that the company was hers and that it had been from its inception, and therefore her opinion was the one that counted. Moorman would never be like that.

She'd started at the bottom in the beauty industry, on the shop floor of one of her father's Irish department stores and going under her mother's maiden name of Morgan, through sheer ability she'd worked her way up to department supervisor. She'd been forced to move to England to escape her father's dominance, and had worked for John Lewis and finally Harrods before setting up on her own.

If Moorman joined Body Beautiful on the terms he wanted, they could never take a step forward unless they both agreed. Anything contentious would be a stalemate. She picked the receiver up before it had stopped vibrating from the first ring. 'Damion,' she said, but then closed her eyes in frustration.

It was Peter. He'd be furious that she couldn't make their date. She loved him, but it was proving impossible to see him as often as he wanted. As for him moving in with her, the thought was terrifying. She needed her freedom now, more than ever. She forced herself to smile, so that she sounded loving. 'Peter,' she said. 'I'm so sorry, but . . .'

Chapter 4

The maid who modestly conceals
Her beauties, while she hides, reveals
EDWARD MOORE (1712–1757)

'I'm sorry I'm late, darling. It just went on and on . . .'
Marie kissed Peter on the cheek as she shrugged her
shoulders out of her raincoat.

The waiter hovered, holding an oversized menu in front
of her the instant she sat down.

'I ordered you a G and T,' Peter said. 'But that was
hours ago and the ice has melted. You'd better have a
fresh one.'

Peter was red in the face, his voice thick with the anger
he so clearly felt.

'No, no, this is fine.' Marie was desperately thirsty and
would have loved a long cool glass of Perrier, but it didn't
seem the time to ask for one. She took a quick couple of
mouthfuls of the tepid liquid. 'Honestly, it's fine.' She
glanced quickly round the restaurant. It was full, as always
in the evening. There were dozens of people eating,
chattering. Montpeliano's was where Peter had taken her
on their first date. It was one of their special places, but
this evening she'd rather have been at home.

She couldn't keep her mind off the meeting she'd just
left – in the City, with her bankers. It had been really
heavy, with three of them ranged against her. She would
have to get a move on choosing Damion's replacement, if
only to bolster her numbers.

Peter glared up at the waiter and then stabbed down at

the menu with a finger. 'I'll have the grilled calf's liver with a tossed green salad. I'll start with the smoked salmon, and bring another bottle of this Frascati.'

Marie hastily scanned the menu. Even the thought of liver added to her feeling of nausea. Perhaps it was something she'd eaten at lunch, she thought – and then she remembered she hadn't had any, and there hadn't been time for breakfast. She would have to choose something sensible.

'I'll start with some minestrone, please,' she said, as she found to her relief something that appeared to be a plain grilled chicken. 'And then the chicken, and I'll have a green salad as well.'

The waiter whisked the menu from her fingers and flicked the starched white napkin neatly over her lap.

'And I'd like some – ' She was about to say 'Perrier' but remembered just in time where she was. '*Acqua minerale.*'

Every table was full, the tables close together. There were jovial foursomes, romantic couples – the atmosphere was happy and relaxed, everywhere except at their table.

'This is the second time you've been late this week,' Peter said crossly.

He was working at controlling his voice. He reached forward to take the almost empty bottle of wine from its wickerwork cradle and poured a splash into Marie's glass. He then emptied the remaining half a glass into his own.

He sipped before continuing, 'I just wish you'd say if you can't make it. It would save me a lot of embarrassment.'

'But I . . .' Marie started to say that she had tried to tell him she was too busy, and it was Peter who had insisted she come.

But there was no point in arguing, in spoiling the evening for both of them. She had so little spare time that it was precious. She reached across the table, taking hold of his hand. It felt stiff and unyielding in her grip.

'Can we start again,' she asked, softly. 'Can't we act as though I was on time. It's lovely to be together. Come on, look, I've drunk that disgusting G and T. That was my penance.'

'God, I've had a pig of a day.' Peter squeezed her hand hard. 'The atmosphere at that place absolutely stinks. If something doesn't let up on the interest front soon, we'll all be out on our ears.'

'Is it seriously as bad as that?'

Peter nodded and then drained his glass. He felt very much under pressure, but there were some things he wasn't going to reveal, even to Marie.

He glanced away from her as he said, 'I'm all right, I've got money to fall back on. But there are a lot who'll be on Carey Street. They've got high mortgages of their own, families. You know a half per cent reduction would do it. That and just a whisper that there might be another half to follow it in a couple of months. I think that would bring a lot more buyers and sellers into the marketplace. They'd see that prices won't remain stagnant for ever. They just need to see a bit of daylight to make the commitment. Christ knows how much longer they can keep up this squeeze.'

'It wouldn't hurt me if the rate dropped a bit,' Marie said with feeling.

She reached out for a breadstick, feeling light-headed from drinking the alcohol on an empty stomach. They were silent as the waiter brought them their starters and ladled freshly grated Parmesan cheese over Marie's soup.

When they were alone again, Marie asked, 'What do you know about a financier called Berry Jopling? The bank seem to think he's some kind of guru who can do

43

something about Body Beautiful's properties. Funnily enough he's just sent some horses to Damion's yard.'

'Funnily enough?' Peter squeezed lemon juice liberally all over his generous helping of smoked salmon. 'There's nothing much funny to be had from friend Jopling. From what I've heard he's an asset-stripper of the first order, and he's been making a few nice little killings on this depressed market. I should hold very tight on to everything you've got, if I were you.'

'Everything?' Marie felt the soup bringing life back into her.

'Everything – including your virtue. He's got a reputation as a shark in his personal as well as his business life.'

Marie wasn't really surprised. When she'd met Jopling she'd thought he was very attractive. Large, yet not fat, charming but not smarmy. He was obviously very well in at the bank. She had decided to jolly him along while she carried on doing just as she liked with her company. But she had realized it might be more difficult than that. And she hadn't liked their insistence that she talk to an advertising company they recommended. If she took on Sarah Hatherleigh it would spike their guns there, but she still hadn't made up her mind which two of her three possibles to interview next.

'Fancy some red wine with that chicken?' Peter asked.

Marie looked surprised, Peter didn't normally suggest red wine with chicken. She looked at the dish the waiter proffered and understood. The fowl had been cooked in a rich reddish-brown sauce. All her earlier nausea returned.

'If you would like to wait in the boardroom . . .' The lithe, six-foot, mini-skirted receptionist allowed her softly spoken words to trail off. Her eyes were unfocused but directed vaguely in Marie's direction.

There were windows running the full length of two opposite sides of the room. Ahead of Marie, white linen blinds took the edge off the sunlight that streamed in; behind her, the light was muted, the view of a central well that was lush with greenery. She placed her black briefcase on the highly polished maple-topped table and began slowly taking off her gloves. The door opened and she turned to face it.

'So sorry I couldn't come down to reception to greet you, Marie.' Cool, appraising eyes in a deadpan face made the point that the account director was so certain of her custom that he hadn't even considered wooing her as he would most prospective clients. 'Thought it might be a good opportunity for you to meet a few of the team. This is Peter.'

A tall, slim and eager young man in a red and white shirt immaculately folded up to the elbows nodded briskly.

'And of course, Dierdre. Marie Sullivan.' Julian Dodds, known as Jules to his friends, made the introductions.

He dispatched Peter to rustle up coffee and Dierdre to pull the blinds on the windows overlooking what he referred to as the 'atrium'. Meanwhile he took a seat on the opposite side of the table to Marie and stared at her appraisingly. After a disconcerting pause he asked, 'Now, just how do you think we can help you?'

'I thought I was here for you to tell me that,' Marie countered. She too was smiling without warmth in her eyes. The overture was clearly to be a jostling for pole position, and it was one that she had every intention of winning. It didn't matter to her that the advertising agency had a higher turnover than Body Beautiful – the director designated to deal with her account was hers to command, not vice versa.

'I think we can dispense with all the foreplay, don't

45

you.' Julian helped himself to three heaped teaspoonfuls of sugar and stirred it noisily into his coffee. He burnt up calories on presentations. 'You know all about us, and that's why you're here. We're big and we're beautiful. We've made household names out of tinpot companies who couldn't tell a hype from a hole in the ground.'

'I know all about hype, and I'll say it before you can – being from Ireland I also know all about holes in the ground.'

Julian laughed, and the sound surprised Marie because it contained genuine amusement. 'They said you were quick,' he grinned. Then in an instant the sign of humanity was covered. 'This will be the first meeting of many, so we have to get the ground rules straight. We will produce ideas for you, plan campaigns and implement them. I gather that in the past you've done your own thing. That's fine as far as it went, but from now on I have to know everything. No going off and giving quotes to the press without clearing it with me first, no change of image or product emphasis. From start to finish, we'll take you all the way you want to go. So just leave it in our hands.' He paused for a moment and then finished, 'the bank want it that way too.'

Marie sipped at her coffee. There was a niggling pain just above her left eye and she concentrated on it, willing her temper to calm down. They were trying to force her into a corner. It would cost her company a fortune to buy the services of Julian and his band, and she would be paying to be treated like an inferior being. It was clear that as far as the advertising company was concerned, her bankers were the client to be fêted.

'Peter has a rough outline of the campaign as we see it.' Julian sat back, tipping his chair so that his knees showed above the table, he dropped his head forward so that his chin touched his chest, and appeared to enter some form of trance.

'We want to make the image much clearer.' Peter turned in his seat to look earnestly at Marie. He'd put on thin-framed tortoiseshell glasses with lenses that looked like ordinary glass. 'At the moment you just come over as a range of beauty products. That's nothing special in the marketplace. We feel that you should tell the consumer what you're doing, make the point that your intention is to make them more attractive. We – '

'Is this the royal "we", or are you referring to your agency in general?' Marie interrupted.

Peter had the grace to blush as he answered, 'It's been gone through with your bankers. They feel the same as we do. It's a problem of identification. You have to tell the people what you're doing for them, and once they've understood that, the rest is easy. You've been trading as the Body Beautiful, and that's a negative image – it's too factual.'

'Beautiful People.' Julian sat forward suddenly. 'Says it all. Tells the punters what you're doing for them.'

'You're saying that I should change the name of my business?' Marie's horror made her choke on the words.

Her first, overwhelming emotion was one of pain. Body Beautiful was hers. She thought next of the costs that would be involved – the signwriting, the packaging, the origination design costs would be prohibitive. Then back to the beginning – the company was Body Beautiful. It always had been, it always would be.

'No,' she said firmly.

They looked embarrassed. Julian stared down at the table top as he said, 'It's been given the go-ahead.'

Marie stood up slowly and began gathering up her things. 'I'm sorry you've been wasting your time,' she said. 'My bank don't have the power to make that kind of decision – at least not yet. And I'm prepared to sweat blood to make sure they never have. Thanks for the coffee.'

She walked out of the building and on to the sun-drenched pavement. She felt better than she had in ages. There was no confusion now. There was only one thing for her to do. She had to get out from under. A load of the high-street sites would have to go. To get herself and her company out of the grip of a load of . . . She rarely used it, but the word 'shits' fitted the men who'd once been so very happy to lend, lend, lend, so perfectly that she almost said it out loud.

She stepped out into the road to flag down a taxi. She was smiling grimly as she gave her office address.

Marie stepped out of the taxi and handed over an uncreased, apparently unused, five-pound note. The fare was four pounds twenty and the tip was more than she normally gave, but she was inexplicably nervous about meeting Berry Jopling off her home ground and she felt it might bring her luck.

The lunch had been his suggestion, as had the venue – Langan's Brasserie. Marie had been there a couple of times before, at night with a crowd of Peter's friends.

He was there before her, and she felt relieved he wasn't the type of person who was late for lunch to make the point how busy he was. That would have made her angry, and she wanted him on her side. The timing was good – she had a meeting at three, so she'd have to be away by two forty-five at the latest.

The smart young woman who'd greeted her by the lectern led the way down the crowded restaurant. At a far table by the windows, Berry sat facing the room. He smiled in greeting and stood as she came towards him.

'Glad you could make it.' He came round to hold the

chair for her. 'Your secretary said you were generally booked for lunch.'

'Angelique likes to surround me with an aura of power.' Marie laughed.

She didn't want Berry to know she was so busy trying to get Body Beautiful back on the straight and narrow that lunch with anyone other than him would have been classed an unnecessary luxury.

'Like a drink to start with?'

'I would love a vodka and tonic.'

It was only a moment before the drinks arrived. She was breaking her unwritten rule of not having alcohol in the middle of the day, but she needed something to give her a boost. She'd been working since six-thirty.

Marie looked up at the brass heads displayed on a shelf on the end wall, and asked, 'Did you know him?'

Berry didn't need to look round to know who she meant. Langan had been a legend in his lifetime. He raised a hand to attract a waiter.

'My liver's probably grateful,' he said, 'but I regret to say our paths crossed very little. I've never been a regular here.'

'Then why – '

'Why did I suggest it today? Somehow I guessed it wasn't your neck of the woods, and your Angelique confirmed that. I thought we'd be easier on neutral territory.'

Marie studied her menu intently. He was too clever. The men she came across would never give their reasons the way he did.

After a few minutes, she said, 'The hot goat's cheese sounds nice, and the swordfish.'

'Bubble and squeak's more in my line. With the bangers and mash to follow.'

'Finishing with nursery pud?'

'Got it in one. So, are we ready to order?'

There was too much goat's cheese. Two large round pieces nicely browned on top, displayed on a bed of curly lettuce. She had to struggle to finish half her portion. Berry's dish was clean by the time she'd given up her attempt. He'd also eaten two bread rolls. She could see why he was so well-built.

'So, tell me, who's your idol, the one person in your line of business who you'd like to be?' Berry asked.

As he waited for her answer, he watched the wine waiter dealing with the white burgundy he'd ordered.

Marie took her time. The reason for the lunch was clearly for Jopling to find out what made her tick. The only business he'd talked had been peripheral. What she replied now could be important.

'Yves Saint Laurent,' she said finally. 'And that's not cheating because although he was originally a clothes man, his beauty line is probably the most widely distributed in the world. And the packaging is superb, the image clear and well-presented. But that's not why I chose him. You see, the truth is that I'm not an artist. I'm a worker. I've worked to develop my lines, and to get the organization to market them. My basic motivation is that I want to succeed. I think Saint Laurent's motivation is that of an artist who wants his creations displayed and appreciated.'

'He certainly has the traditional artistic temperament. He's very highly strung.'

'So they say, but I'd swop my artisan nature for his artist's neurosis any day. Or at least, that's what I'm prepared to say because I know it can't happen.'

'So.' Berry held his fork like a short spear and stabbed down at a mangetout. 'You tell me you are a worker, and of course if I'm considering putting money into your business, that is a trait I would admire. You must also

50

consider you are safe in implying that you are not artistic because I have already expressed admiration of your product line – after all, that's why I approached you in the first place. Well played.'

The sautéed swordfish suddenly tasted dry and Marie laid down her fork. 'Helping me dispose of my properties isn't the same as putting money into my company. And the answer I gave you was quite true. Of course I slanted it to gain the best advantage I could, but that's only reasonable. Why don't we stop waltzing round each other and get down to brass tacks?'

'Waltzing, now that's an interesting idea. I should think you do a mean lambada.' He smiled as he wiped his lips with a damask napkin. 'More wine?'

Marie shook her head. She was beginning to feel angry and already regretted that she had begun the meal with a drink.

'I visited Pierre Bergé in Deauville last year,' Berry continued as if she hadn't just abandoned her lunch in irritation. 'They'd just finished the dacha in the grounds. It's all wood and stained glass, icons and ottomans. It's quite beautiful – Soviet-Moroccan-Austrian, Bergé calls it, but it works.'

'Designed by a team like that, it would have to, wouldn't it?' Marie had read about the *faux*-Russian hunting lodge that Bergé and Saint Laurent had helped design for the grounds of their lovely Deauville home. She had thought at the time how similar the concept was to Saint Laurent's couture, where he so brilliantly mixed contemporary culture with exotic influences and then used his unique style and cutting ability to develop an art form that clung to the bodies of his beautiful models.

'They've even planted birch trees behind it to add to the atmosphere.'

They seemed for a moment to have found a safe area

for conversation. The waiter cleared their plates, tsking over Marie's scarcely touched fish. When she declined a dessert he sniffed audibly. Berry ordered treacle tart and they both requested decaffeinated coffee. Marie thought it was probably the first sign of an awareness of personal frailty that she had detected in her host.

Marie regained the pavement outside the restaurant at two-thirty precisely. She would be early for her appointment at the Savoy, where she was meeting a potential Middle Eastern agent. He would inevitably be late.

'No taxi?' Berry had joined her, she had left him paying the bill on the excuse that she had another meeting to get to.

She shook her head. 'I'm going to walk.' She began to stride away, back towards Bond Street.

'All the way?' Berry called after her.

'All the way to where?' She turned to face him. He seemed to know all her moves, and the anger she had subdued at lunch flared.

'Well, Abdullah always hangs out at the Savoy and he said he was meeting you this afternoon. At three.' He paused, and smiled. 'He'll be at least forty minutes late, so you'll have plenty of time for a leisurely stroll.' A taxi pulled up to answer his raised arm. He was still smiling as he drove away, leaving her standing.

Angelique was momentarily tempted to listen in as she put Berry's call through to Marie. He'd called in personally the other day, to make the lunch appointment, and she thought he was a real hunk. She liked her men big and impressive and she just loved the twinkle in his eye.

'Marie?'

Marie made a point of taking a few seconds to reply. She still wasn't sure how she felt about the man who might just turn out to be the saviour of Body Beautiful.

'Berry, you've beaten me to it. I'd been going to call you to thank you for lunch yesterday. It was delightful. I must make a point of going to Langan's more often.'

'Perhaps you'll manage to eat a bit more of their food next time. I'm not sure you didn't upset the chef.'

She could hear the taunt in Berry's voice, and she felt obliged to make an excuse.

'It was all that goat's cheese to begin with,' she said lightly. 'Next time I'll go a bit lighter on the hors d'oeuvres.'

'And next time I'll go a bit lighter on the psychoanalysis. Am I forgiven yet?'

This time Marie's pause was involuntary. Yet again he'd managed to take her by surprise.

'I should have expected it,' she said.

'But you did. And your answers were prepared accordingly. I'm sorry that you didn't like me pointing out that I appreciated your tactics. I promise not to do it again. I thought perhaps this time a spot of the exotic. Do you like curry? We could go to Veeraswamy's, and if you eat up quickly, make a show as well.'

'I beg your pardon?' Marie felt her face stiffen. The man was insufferable, acting as if he owned her.

'Well, tonight's as good as any, don't you think? Angelique seems to reckon you've got nothing on that won't keep . . .'

'Angelique is not employed to act as my social secretary, and I'll thank you not to go asking my staff about my private life. The only relationship you and I have going is business, and that's just how I like it. I appreciate that there may well be other questions about Body Beautiful shops that you'd like to ask, but I think you'd be doing us both a favour if we meet in office hours next time. In my office or yours. I'm not being obstructive and I wouldn't like the bank to think I was.'

'That's what this is all about, isn't it? If we hadn't met through the bank then you wouldn't be being so damn awkward.' Berry's voice was getting louder. He was close to shouting down the phone. 'The only reason you're refusing a date is because you're mad that the money men reckon I might be able to bale you out.'

'A date?' Marie's voice was ominously cool. 'How very quaint. I haven't heard that expression since I was at school. No, Mr Jopling, I'm not turning down your invitation because of the manner in which we met. I'm turning it down because we have very little in common except the ambition to make money. To that end I will be glad to meet you again. Since you and Angelique clearly find it pleasurable to converse, perhaps you'd like to fix a convenient day and time with her. She has my diary right now.'

Marie flicked the switch that transferred him back to reception and then she slammed the receiver down hard. She swore venomously and she ended up, to her own surprise, using words more suited to her brother's stables than her sophisticated office. Then, inexplicably, she thought, she burst into tears.

'And I thought you didn't test your products on animals.' Berry laughed.

Damion's hand suddenly became still as he stopped the wide, circular sweeping movement with which he had been massaging the rich cream into Beauty's flank.

He paused before speaking, trying to control the surge of anger. Eventually he said, 'I would never experiment on Beauty. She's the creature I love most in this world.'

There was a loud clatter as Rose threw down the feed bucket she had been carrying into the box, and Damion began once more to apply the green-tinted ointment.

'Sorry.' Berry grinned self-consciously. He was aware

54

that he had sparked Damion into saying more than should have been said. 'What's in that stuff anyway?'

'Avocado mainly. The oil makes for a good shine on the coat. She could eat it if she wanted.'

Damion held a handful of the cream close to the horse's nose. She sniffed at it and then breathed out heavily, clearly disdaining to prove his point.

'And will my horses always get such tender loving care?'

'Of course. I've always believed in massage, for animals and people. It firms the muscles, improves the circulation and the appetite. Improves your sex life too, if that's of any importance.' He felt his good temper returning and laughed. 'I'll give Rose a good rub-down later. How about a drink now?'

They crossed the yard together. Berry wanted to ask about Marie, to find out if she'd got a replacement for Damion in the business yet, but he thought he'd wait until they'd had a drink or two. Damion was too touchy to ask right out.

They were sitting companionably in front of the newspaper-laden coffee table when Marie herself walked into the sitting room. She had come from upstairs. There was a towel wrapped round her hair and she was wearing a blue-checked dressing gown that was obviously Damion's. Clearly, she had expected her brother to be on his own.

Berry stood up quickly, he was still clutching his glass of whisky and soda, so he raised it in mock salute. 'I didn't know you were here,' he said.

'That makes two of us.' Damion stretched his legs out in front of him and drained his glass to the bottom. 'You might warn me when you pop into my humble abode to make use of the ablution facilities. I might have bundled Rose off to her parents and had a floozie in here.'

Marie remained where she was in the doorway. She

55

had been going to curl up on the settee with the Sunday papers. Usually Damion would have stayed out in the yard for hours. She said, 'I parked round the back of the barn, so I don't suppose you saw the car. My hot water's packed up.' And I was on my own because Peter has gone off in a huff, she would have added if Berry hadn't been there.

'If you want food you'll have to cook it. In fact, you could cook it for all of us.' Damion's voice quickened.

It would be a good idea for Marie and Berry to have lunch in the cottage, then Rose could join them, and he wouldn't need to apologize to her for the remark about the horse. He was sorry that she'd heard that.

'Why don't we go down to the pub?' Berry asked. 'I quite fancy something like shepherd's pie. Come on, Marie, I'll buy you lunch. It's the least I can do to make up for the last time we talked.'

Damion looked at his sister inquisitively. He hadn't heard anything specific about that.

Marie turned quickly to hide her smile, then she said, 'I'll have to dry my hair first,' and ran up the stairs.

It was early evening as Marie drove back into town. The sun was still warm and she had the car window down. It had been a lovely afternoon. After lunch at the pub they'd walked down by the river. The air was crisp and clean and Damion had been more relaxed than he'd been in ages.

Berry was good for him, she thought. As well as providing the prospect of income for the yard with a dozen or more horses, he brought Damion out of himself. It was just a shame he was involved with the bank; she'd have to warn her brother to be careful what he said about the company.

She turned up the volume of the radio as she drove over Waterloo Bridge. The Thames looked beautiful, blue and serene. There were several white-painted pleasure boats out on the water, it really felt like a Sunday. She parked easily and blessed the fact that it was the weekend. As she walked the last few yards to the flat she passed Peter's yellow Porsche.

For an instant she considered not going inside. She didn't want to face him in one of his moods; it had been such a happy, uncomplicated afternoon. There were children squealing on the roundabouts, the air smelt of frying onions and hot dogs, and suddenly the country seemed far away.

In the flat, Peter had left an enormous bunch of red roses on the hall table. In the sitting room he was lying asleep on the settee. She went up to him quietly. He looked like a child in sleep. The irritable lines that had recently marked the centre of his forehead were wiped out. He was breathing softly. She leaned over him and suddenly his hand moved towards her, clutching her wrist and pulling her close. He smiled without opening his eyes.

'Where the hell have you been?' he asked, but he didn't really want to know the answer as she bent to kiss him on the lips.

Chapter 5

O how can beautie maister
the most strong!
EDMUND SPENSER
(1552–1599)

'This marquee's awfully grand,' Marie said admiringly.

She stood at the very centre of the elegant contraption that had been erected on the *manège* behind the stables.

'It's costing me an arm and a leg.' Damion grinned good-naturedly. 'And that doesn't hurt too much, considering it's an arm and a leg I don't have.'

Marie turned quickly to look at her brother. He thought suddenly how proud he was of her. She looked stunning in a pale pink suit, nipped in tightly at the waist, and with a puffball skirt. Her hat was a great wide rose-coloured disc that perched on her polished hair. He decided she was pretty enough to be a bride herself, but it was a shame about her temper. Judging from the look in her eyes, she was all set to blow.

'What does that mean?' she asked forcefully.

'It means that as of today I have not actually got the wherewithal to pay for this glorious shindig. But as of the day after tomorrow I will have. So you can eat, drink and be merry with the rest of them tonight, me darlin', and shed a tear for me in the church. Since I'm your only brother, it goes without saying that I'm your favourite. Now come on, don't you feel a tear coming on, a sniffle, just a – '

'And how exactly are you expecting to come by this windfall?' Marie asked softly.

She knew her father would never put a penny towards the wedding he'd so bitterly opposed. Rose's parents would certainly never be able to run to such splendour. She wanted to know how it was to be paid for and she had no intention of being put off by Damion's banter. He was continually bemoaning how stretched things were at the yard. To have made such a fuss over the wedding was an unnecessary extravagance.

Damion tapped the side of his nose with a forefinger. 'Not in front of the staff.' He nodded at the florist who had just swept into the tent, her arms full of sugar-pink peonies. 'Fanny!' he called out. 'How beautiful you look, just like a bloom yourself.'

Damion swaggered away from Marie, relieved to have temporarily escaped from her questioning. He'd been stupid to have made the arm and a leg remark; now his sister would nag away until she wheedled the truth out of him. The unfortunate truth was that she wouldn't like it when she heard it.

The inside of the stone-built village church of St Nicholas was a picture. It was almost overflowing with wedding guests, most of the men in morning suits and the women almost without exception in wide picture hats. It was very 'county' and the accents were those of the royal enclosure. If it hadn't been for Damion's unsettling comments earlier, Marie would have been thrilled for her brother. The best had certainly been made of a bad job.

Rose came down the aisle looking the perfect young bride. Her dress was soft cream taffeta, with low scooped neck, wide flounced skirt and short train. Damion's mother had sent the veil from Ireland. The colour of buttermilk, it had been worn by Sullivan brides for a century and a half. The scalloped lace edge that swept the red carpet on the floor had been worked by an ancestor who had spent her five-year engagement plying her needle with dexterity. The dress itself had not been sent over. With its eighteen-inch waist it would have been an impossibility for the buxom Rose, who was, after all, several months pregnant.

Damion looked beautiful, Marie thought. She felt the tears stinging her eyes at his proud stance, the way he held his head so high. He was a fine match for any woman, so handsome and so clever, if only he'd give up the horses. But he was doing more than the honourable thing in standing by the girl. He was making the grand gesture, and there were dozens of racing's grandest families represented in the tiny Norman church to see him do it. It was just a shame that his parents weren't there as well.

The photographer shooed the guests together outside the church. The bride's veil blew in the light summer breeze; ladies held on to their hats and gentlemen tilted theirs to a racier angle. The two bridesmaids grinned self-consciously. They were Camilla and Josy, Damion's two other grooms. In pink flower-sprigged lawn, they looked feminine and vulnerable. The ushers were jostling for Josy's attention; Peter Raleigh, Damion's ex-flatmate in London, had already staked claim to Camilla.

The caterers had laid on a magnificent spread. Starting with chilled vichyssoise at their tables, guests went on to a served buffet from tables almost literally groaning with dressed serpentine salmon, baked ham, glazed Norfolk turkey and dozens of assorted salads.

It was as she queued for her dessert that Marie saw Berry. He must have arrived late. He was escorting a stunning blonde. Tall and slim, she was quite obviously dressed in haute couture. Her skin glowed with the unique patina achieved by a winter house in Gstaad and a summer one in Cap d'Antibes. She held very lightly on to Berry's arm. With a start Marie moved forward in the queue. She had been staring, and that was unforgivable . . .

Unforgivably what, she asked herself, and when the inevitable answer was 'embarrassing' she blushed furiously. To make things worse, inevitably Peter hadn't been able to make it. Saturdays were an estate agent's nightmare.

The speeches were short and witty. Damion's longest-standing owner gave an excellent impromptu address in lieu of words from the bride's father, who had succumbed early to the flowing champagne. The best man ended on the happy note that he had the honour to declare himself godfather of whatever variety of little Sullivan arrived. There was a great laugh at this. Damion had never hidden what he termed the little 'bonus' that his wedding to Rose would bring. Guests began drifting away at six, many of them going back to neighbouring hotels to change for the evening reception that was scheduled to begin at eight.

Marie changed in the cottage. All of the bright young blades had made a point of asking her for a dance later. She surveyed her reflection in the bathroom mirror. The Anouska Hempel that she had splashed out on was shot maroon. It made her skin look like cream, her dark hair gleam with hidden lights. She arranged the off-the-shoulder sleeves to perfection. She wore starburst earrings and her eyes sparkled in their reflected light.

If Peter hadn't been coming down for the evening, she would have driven back to London. She felt out of place, as if she didn't belong, and it was all because of a willowy blonde with probably less brain than a pea.

She stuck her tongue out fiercely at her reflection. Damn Berry Jopling, damn Peter, damn her brother for worrying her about how he was going to pay for the reception. Damn men in general.

'We come to company vehicles.' Berry Jopling leaned back in his chair.

The boardroom table gleamed opulently in the light of a dozen brass wall lamps. Green leather folders at each of the twelve director places were reminders that notes were expected to be taken. Berry liked to see his fellow directors – the minions, as he referred to them in the privacy of his own thoughts – showing their own initiative by taking written reminders of special points. The man who waited for the transcript of the minutes, albeit only a scant half an hour in general, was the man who was going slow.

'I have here the results of a survey I've had done. This will interest you in particular, Patrick.' Berry stood up to distribute the typewritten sheets that had been stacked beside him.

Patrick Oolay smiled tightly. It would be something to do with the time it had taken him to get into the office that morning. It had been damned annoying to be late for the board meeting, and he didn't need Jopling's caustic comments. After all, it wasn't his fault that the few miles he had to drive in from his mistress's flat in Stamford Hill had taken him just under an hour. The worst he'd managed before was forty minutes.

'You'll see I've gone into the BMWs.' Berry paused at Patrick's place and was amused to notice the smile, which he quickly eclipsed by adding, 'And the Hondas. Please read quickly, gentlemen. I know your time is precious.'

'But this is preposterous!' Patrick spluttered. 'I wouldn't be seen dead on a motorbike. I ask you, a motorbike. Is this meant to be some kind of joke?'

There were several other exclamations of surprise mingled with one or two of delight.

'You don't mean to say that you're behind the times, Patrick.' Berry smiled. 'You do have a Filofax, I trust?'

Oolay nodded briefly. He couldn't trust himself to speak, he was so angry.

'And you have seen the Coke advert – the one where the good-looking young guy gets his woman in the office, astride one of these power machines? Then you should be delighted that you'll be one of the first with the next indispensable status symbol. Alexa Lacham of Mocheck, the Honda dealers in Fulham, had one of her chaps time a few routes I suggested. It may interest you, Patrick, to know that the journey from Stamford Hill to the office took fifteen minutes. My case rests. Oh, and by the by, I've chosen the BMWs. They'll cost about £6,000. That's for a high performance K100RS. Despite the charming Alexa, I couldn't resist the company.'

It had been policy for top Intel executives to have BMWs for several years.

'I can't possibly come into work dressed up in black leather, looking like something out of . . .' Patrick Oolay searched his mind for a suitably derogatory reference and failed.

'I think it's an excellent idea.' Bob Manders, the finance director, had known about Berry's plan and wholeheartedly approved it. 'And so should you, Patrick. You'll save on your tax, because your car will be commensurably smaller. Let me see.'

They all waited while the highly qualified accountant ran an eye down a list of names and figures in front of him.

He looked up, directly at Patrick to say, 'You would have had a £20,000 car, so with £6,000 off for the bike you'll be down to something around the £14,000 mark.

You'll still have something big enough to get the wife and kids in.'

The board meeting ended swiftly. In general there was agreement that the motorbikes would be a good idea. Bob Manders had found an interesting article on biking for leisure and stress reduction and he promised to have copies circulated.

As was his habit Berry remained in the boardroom while his secretary typed up her notes. He was to take delivery of his own motorbike that afternoon. He took the specification sheet from under his papers. He'd decided to spoil himself.

The Norton FI was an awesome machine. It took three seconds to go from 0 to 60 mph, and on an open road its top speed would be 145 mph. He'd tried it out at Brands Hatch, and having started by frightening the living daylights out of him, it had ended making him fall hook line and sinker in love with its all-black livery and forward-leaning handlebars. At £12,700 it would cost the same as a GTi car.

Chapter 6

A thing of beauty is a joy forever;
Its loveliness increases
JOHN KEATS (1795–1821)

Honour Montford straightened her back, lifted her chin and prepared to greet her guests.

She was nearly seventy years old, but her eyes were bright and there was something about her that still seemed young. The excitement she felt at the great stone house of Pencombe being alive again made her able to believe for a moment that all the years since the last war had been a dream.

There were vast flower arrangements on the long oaken tables running down either side of the great hall, and a multitude of fine beeswax candles burning in the wall sconces. She could almost imagine that her mother was still dressing upstairs, that her brother William was some-where organizing the staff, and that Eddy, her other brother, dear beloved Eddy, who was the only one in reality still left on this earth, was young and well again.

'Tom, dear.' Honour leaned forward, offering her cool cheek to the tall, fresh-faced young man so obviously ill at ease in his evening clothes. He was her cousin's son. 'How handsome you look – just like your grandfather. He would have been so proud.'

There was a long queue of guests, all waiting in line to shake hands with Honour, the venerable matriarch of the line of Montford. They all knew that she had been the one member of the family to stick, through good and bad times, to the family home.

Honour's twin sons, Carl and William, should, in the natural course of events, have taken over the running of the estate. But Carl had died in a car crash only a year after his marriage and no one knew where William had gone. It was over ten years since he'd left Pencombe; he'd gone away after a family row during which all his past hurts and grievances had seemed to meld in one great, solid, insurmountable obstacle between him and his mother. She didn't expect ever to see him again.

In a few months the house would become, finally and for ever, the property of the National Trust. The ball was a last gesture, a defiance in the face of the inevitable.

'No, no, I'm not upset. On the contrary, I'm very pleased. This way there will be a positive future for the house.' Honour nodded her head as yet another distant relative expressed sadness that the Montford family would no longer have a stately home to call their own.

It had all taken so long that she was resigned now. And after all, there was no one capable enough to carry on when she was gone.

'I'm Marie Sullivan. I don't think we know each other.' The young woman was almost the last of the guests to arrive. She extended an almost hesitant hand, and then smiled. Her face showed intelligence and interest, and her long, fitted gown of dark-green velvet emphasized the paleness of her skin and the greenness of her eyes.

Honour's pulse quickened so that for a moment she felt faint. 'You're James's girl,' she whispered.

'Yes.' Marie smiled again. The old woman hadn't let go of her hand and she was surprised by the strength of grip in one who looked so frail. 'My father's name is James. But I'm afraid I don't know what our connection is with the Montford family. My father hasn't ever talked about you, or about this beautiful house. I came because your invitation seemed so intriguing. "Time that old feuds should be forgotten", that's what you wrote, isn't it? Well, I hope that it won't upset you, but as far as I'm concerned, whatever this feud is I'm not aware of it.'

'How nice.' Honour smiled. 'It means we can start afresh. We're cousins, several steps removed, of course, but blood will out. Did you bring your brother Damion with you?'

Marie shook her head. 'No, I'm afraid he's very busy these days. He's into horses.' Actually he had reacted very strangely to his invitation. He'd been so dismissive that Marie thought he must know something of the so-called feud, but he maintained he didn't.

'What a pretty girl you are.' Honour linked Marie's arm through her own and started to walk through the throng around them. 'I like pretty things around me. They're warm and they give me life. So, you don't know a thing. Far be it from me to resurrect old grievances best forgotten. Come and meet my daughter-in-law. You'll like her.'

A hired butler smiled obsequiously as he proffered a tray of champagne glasses to Marie and she reached out to take one. As her fingers closed on the thin stem, a voice that amazed her by its strength shouted very close to her ear.

'That tray is a disgrace.' Honour pulled herself up to her full five foot three. 'It belongs in a kitchen. Take it out of here at once, and,' she called after the swiftly departing servant, 'don't fill the glasses so full, you're slopping champagne all over the place. What exactly do you do, my dear?'

'I have a company that produces cosmetics, skin-care products,' Marie answered automatically.

She felt bemused by the lights and the chatter and the old woman who seemed out of another era. A couple of hours ago she'd been dressing in the calm comfort of her Covent Garden flat; now it seemed a lifetime away.

'Now, here's my daughter-in-law. I'll leave you two alone – you don't want an old lady . . . Thomas!'

Marie almost choked on her drink as the amazing voice that somehow issued forth from the thin, pale, aristocratic lips once more gained the attention of the room.

Lucy Montford had dark, thick hair, clear blue eyes and a happy, smiling mouth. She was in her early forties. Her cheeks were reddened more by the exertion of dancing than rouge, and her eyes were simply made up. Marie found herself analysing the woman's cosmetics because she was so taken aback by the warmth of the welcome.

'I'm so pleased you came, so pleased.' Lucy kissed Marie on the cheek in greeting and a faint drift of Chanel Number Five lingered for a moment. Like the make-up it had been lightly applied. 'I had hoped that your brother might have come too.'

'He's very busy at the moment.' Marie found herself apologizing for her brother.

'I understand he's a keen horseman, isn't he? My daughter's fiancé said he'd come across him out with the East Kent. Do you hunt yourself?'

'No. I'm afraid I don't really agree with it. I always seem to feel bad about the fox.'

'Vermin – you mustn't take their side. They kill my chickens, you know, and not just for food. They do it for sport, and that's what makes it seem so bad.'

Marie smiled wryly. 'But that's just like the fox-hunters. They hunt for sport too, don't they?'

Lucy laughed. 'I told Gee you'd be clever. You do know that's what we call her? Honour is always known as Gee in the family. Come on, I'll introduce you around.

There are some fun people here and there amongst the old fogies, but I'll take good care to keep away from the fox-hunters. I don't want you to think we're all far too bloodthirsty.' Lucy linked arms companionably with her guest and began their progress through the crush. She turned suddenly and whispered, 'They don't really catch many foxes, you know.'

Marie smiled. Gee had been right – she did like Lucy, very much.

'You know, you have beautiful hands.' Berry placed his own wide masculine hand on the desk top beside Marie's.

'I should have, I work hard enough on them.' Marie laughed self-consciously. 'It wouldn't be good for my image to have chipped nail varnish.'

'It's not the gloss you've put on them that makes your hands special, it's the length of the fingers, their slender-ness.' He was speaking softly as he placed his palm over her hand.

She quickly sat back in her chair, breaking the contact between them.

'If I didn't know better I'd think you were coming on strong.'

'Would you mind if I was?' Berry's eyes were a fath-omless blue.

Marie was so surprised that she found herself wonder-ing how she would react if he did make a pass. She'd assumed that the blonde at the wedding was a permanent fixture. She was silent for almost a minute.

Then she said, 'I never mix business with pleasure.'

'Perhaps you're missing a lot that way. Who do you meet that isn't to do with your business? I know the hours you work, there can't be room for another interest in your life.'

'I don't need another interest.'

'So.' Berry removed his hand abruptly. 'We have another Coco Chanel in the making, do we? You see yourself as one of the great women moguls. Running your empire single-handed from your ivory tower, keeping everyone at a distance, using acquaintances for company if and when you feel a fleeting need.'

'And what in your experience makes you such an expert on women moguls?' Marie asked wryly. 'Or would that be telling secrets out of school?'

'I admire women with power – most men do – as long as they're not in my way.'

'There's an old-fashioned feminist description that fits you to a tee, Berry.'

'You can call me any names you like, Marie, and I'd probably enjoy it. Because I also admire a woman with spirit.'

'Then you can admire me for bringing our conversation back to the business in hand.' She pulled a sheaf of papers in front of her and began turning the pages. 'You've had a chance to look through Body Beautiful's property portfolio. Have you come to any conclusions?'

Berry pulled his briefcase on to his lap and opened it to take out a thick bound file. 'You mean, apart from the fact that all your valuations are way over the top? They're at least six months out of date.'

Marie remained silent.

'There's a lot of lightweight stuff in there, short leases, secondary locations.'

'Six out of the top forty on the list are secondary, the rest are prime sites. As far as the veracity of the value of the properties is concerned, you can see the name of the firm I used, and the date.'

It was Peter who'd done the most recent valuations, and she'd asked him to be kind.

'Let's not beat around the bush.'

Marie raised a clearly defined eyebrow. It was her visitor who was throwing in all the unnecessary verbiage.

'Four million for the lot. That's present-day values plus a bonus of two hundred thousand for a neat package.'

'You're joking!' Marie laughed as she spoke, letting out some of the tension that was building inside her.

'I never joke about money. I have a breakdown of my offer here.'

Berry laid the A4 folder down on the desk between them. He looked Marie directly in the eyes as she waited, willing herself to keep control.

'I can let you have ten days,' he continued. 'Then, I'm afraid, my offer lapses.'

'I can give you your answer now,' Marie snapped. She was furious. She'd wasted well over a week getting her strategy right for a man who was so obviously prepared to believe she was an idiot.

'Suit yourself. This would get rid of everything at once for you. Otherwise I'll take a bit of time, shop around for some offers. It doesn't need someone as intelligent as you are to work out the interest you could end up paying by not accepting my offer.'

There was a hard knot of stress in Marie's stomach. If it really came to the crunch then she would be lucky to clear the four million.

She stood up and held out her hand. 'Ten days, you said. Thanks, but I don't need it. We'll stick to the valuations. Obviously I'll be happy to sell at those prices.'

When Berry had gone she left the 'in conference' button on her intercom switched on. She didn't want to be disturbed while she compared his valuations with hers. After checking through eight of the properties, it was obvious that he had known what her figures were all along. Each of his offers was exactly seventy per cent of hers.

71

There were only two people who could have revealed her figures. She reached out hesitantly for the telephone. Whoever she called first would have to be whoever she suspected more. She began dialling Damion's number while she tried vainly to convince herself it was more likely to have been Peter.

'At last!' Sarah Hatherleigh dropped her capacious Hermès handbag on to the floor and then folded herself into a chair.

Marie carried on writing. She did it deliberately, knowing that it was a device to intimidate and despising herself for being so petty. She heard the PR specialist rummaging in her bag, and then the sounds of a cigarette being drawn from a packet, and finally lit.

'God, that's better. What a day!'

A new silence fell. At last Marie laid down her pen, straightened her papers and sat back.

'You got my message?' Sarah asked, one well-shaped blonde eyebrow lifted languidly. 'My portable phone was playing up this morning, and I had to cadge a call on some messenger's very outdated equipment.'

'Yes, I got your message. Fortunately I didn't have a lunch engagement, but I do have an appointment at two,' Marie said.

She looked at her watch. She had twenty minutes. It wouldn't take that long to make her mind up, it was virtually settled already. She couldn't work with the woman on the other side of the desk. They would have no common ground. It had been dislike at first sight and it hadn't changed.

Marie had decided that she wouldn't take Moorman on. However tempting his new product was, it was essential she kept all the Body Beautiful shares in family ownership. She felt that especially strongly since Berry

Jopling had come on the scene. That left St John Aldridge and Sarah Hatherleigh. At least with Aldridge on board the bank would find the company less vulnerable to attack. He'd know any financial wrinkle there was.

'You're very good, you know.' Sarah's Sloane accent quickened suddenly. 'I've admired your strategy from the start. At least, the start as far as I know it. I'd like to hear the real origins of your business someday. It would be interesting to see if there are any angles you've missed. The old rags-to-riches bit is hackneyed, but it still works. And of course you're Irish – that's a great help in the States. That is where you're going to expand next, isn't it?'

Marie nodded. 'I think we might be wasting each other's time. As you know, I do all my own PR work. John Blake was very insistent that I should see you, but you're obviously as busy as I am.' She let her words hang for a moment. Her lips were curved in a polite smile, but she could feel how stiff her face was.

'I saw Moorman sliming his way along Bond Street the last time I was here. He doesn't usually leave his dismal cellar in daylight. He's bad news – I should keep clear of him, if I were you.'

'Who does he work for?' Marie regretted the question as soon as she'd asked it.

'God, he's not acting the shrinking violet is he? Let me give you some clues: probably the second-best-known exclusive perfume brand – in Europe, that is. Packaging deliberately timeless, spends oodles on advertising – well, who doesn't? Present company excepted.'

So, as she had thought, Moorman did work for the really big guns, John Blake hadn't oversold him. And they'd released a new perfume only a few months ago that was presumably due to Moorman's talents. It didn't matter; she wouldn't ever change her mind as far as the shares were concerned.

'He's a clever man, our Moorman. Too clever really. I think he has problems.' Sarah tapped her temple suggestively. 'I saw him in a temper once and I can tell you it wasn't a pretty sight. So that's dismissed one on your list.' She smiled then, and it seemed for the first time to contain genuine warmth. 'Who else can I stab in the back, and all this on an empty stomach.'

'I don't understand why you seem so keen to join Body Beautiful. You have a very successful company of your own, and obviously a lot of freedom.'

'Oh, yes, I'm very successful. Only – what's that phrase – something about it being lonely at the top? Don't get me wrong, I'm not just looking for company. I'm just a trifle bored at creating such wonderful growth opportunities for organizations I don't have a stake in. I get well paid on a consultancy basis and lots of praise, but it's no longer enough. I want to feel I'm creating something concrete. That was what I said when Capita approached me, that I would be interested if I had a stake in the company. I've proved I'm effective. If I worked with you, then you would be free to concentrate fully on the company itself. Publicity in this business requires full-time commitment. If you carry on the way you are, you're not giving your best to your own company. That doesn't seem logical to me.'

Marie leaned back in her chair and breathed in deeply. Both Sarah and St John had intimated they would want some kind of stake in the company. A modest percentage might be feasible. It was true that not having to spend time generating publicity would benefit Marie's work on other fronts. Could she let personalities affect her business judgement?

'I think we should schedule another meeting,' she said

74

slowly, contemplatively, 'one that leaves us more time. Do you want to handle that through Capita?'

'What, via the super-cool John Blake? No, I think we'll just handle this direct. He'll get his cut if we do get together, but there's no reason for him to be in the middle for everything. Look' – she flicked through the pages of her scarlet Filofax – 'I'm free first thing Thursday morning. That gives us both a few days to think things over. Nine on the dot?' She laughed. 'And that means there won't be any meetings before that to run over time.'

'Nine it is.' Marie stood up and walked round her desk. 'I'll look forward to it.' They briefly shook hands.

Marie tried Damion's number again. He should be home by now. If she phoned the minute the interview was over, it would be a reason to talk. She was desperate that the gulf between them shouldn't grow too wide. After four rings the answerphone cut in and she slowly put the phone down.

Damion sat very still as the phone rang. He listened to his own voice coming over the loudspeaker and heard the click as the caller disconnected. It would be Marie.

He sipped at the brimming glass of Irish whiskey and stretched his feet out to rest on Fang's ribs. The dog opened one sloe-coloured eye, and then went back to sleep. Soon he began twitching, chasing rabbits, as Marie always said. It was cold in the house. There were dirty dishes piled high in the kitchen sink and a litter of old newspapers spread around the sitting room. Rose was out in the tack room with a bar of saddle soap and half a dozen bridles. The work of the yard had to come first.

Damion nudged Fang again. 'The wife's right, you know, old chap,' he said. 'It's a dump we're living in.'

The dog got grudgingly to its feet and then stretched, the bristle around its muzzle catching the last low rays of sun that had managed to penetrate the unwashed windows. Damion tipped his glass up and drank quickly. A glow of warmth spread through him. He stood up and stretched, then he and the dog made their way down the yard.

The contrast between the orderly tidiness of the tack room and the mess of his home had never seemed more marked. Rose was vigorously rubbing at a snaffle bit. 'That Rags is an absolute pig, there's grass stains all over this, and that kid Polly hasn't got the strength of a mouse. She should keep his head up. He stuffs himself when she takes him out, and then it's up to me to make sure he doesn't keel over with bloat. One day I'll stuff a few handfuls of bran into her fat little face and see how she feels.'

'She's a paying customer, or rather her mama is, so I'd appreciate it if you spent more of your energy on that bit, and less on the vitriol.'

'Vitriol?' Rose looked up quickly, her face flushed and her damp curly hair sticking to her temples. 'Vitriol's another thought.'

Damion grinned and then turned away. There were still times when he and Rose got on all right, but she was too immature for marriage, and he understood that now. She wanted their house to be a cosy little nest but she couldn't understand that it was something that just didn't happen overnight. It all came down to money. They had to have more. That was why he'd taken the pony liveries.

He adored his horses, doted on them, but ponies were something else. They were as evil as their overfed mounts, and as such he was happy to accept the livery fees they brought in, but not prepared, as Rose for once agreed, to expend too much sympathy. He walked back out into the yard, dusk had come quickly, and the lights were on.

Outside each of the twenty boxes the wire-encased bulbs spread a small yellow circle in the shadows.

Beauty whickered. Her head was out of her box, hanging over her door, and she tipped it up imperiously to summon her master's attention. Her eyes rolled briefly, showing the clear blue white. The warm, sweet smell of her came towards him. The outside bell rang shrilly. It would be Marie again. Damion pressed his nose against Beauty's, blowing softly against her velvet skin. One, two, three, four, and then the welcome silence as his answerphone gave its message. There was a sudden clatter as Rose lead Wellcool out into the yard. She would exercise him in the *manège*.

It would be her last job of the day, because it was Damion's turn to do evening stables. He kept his face averted as she mounted, and then with a sharp tap of the whip cantered up the lane. He hadn't wanted to talk any more. He kept wondering what the others would be saying about them later on in the pub. Since he'd taken to drinking at home he'd started fantasizing about what the locals thought. That he had got one of the grooms in trouble was probably no more than they'd expected. That he had now married her. That was something else entirely. He just hoped he was getting the sympathy he thought he deserved.

There was a mouse in the feed store. It scuttled swiftly over the zinc-lined grain bins and disappeared under a piece of wooden skirting. Damion bent to survey the minute crack through which the little creature had made its escape. He'd put a trap out later. It would be a humane one, and once he'd caught the grain thief he'd take it out for a drive in the country, get a mile or so away before giving it its freedom. That was something else he did that made the locals think he was touched in the head.

Chapter 7

Beauty and folly are often companions

Several dozen bottles of Lanson champagne were standing in the bottom of the maplewood jacuzzi. A scant inch of water lapped beneath the pristine labels.

'The bloody ice has melted.' Peter's cultured tones were harsh with annoyance. 'I told you to keep on topping it up.'

The thin young man on the receiving end of Peter's anger remained silent. He was dressed in the well-known regency-green livery of Bunty's Capitol Caterers; his long dark hair was pulled back tightly at the nape of his neck, making an elegant pony tail. Slowly, deliberately, he raised one eyebrow.

'Don't look so damned insolent. I've a good mind to see you fired.' The colour in Peter's face was rising. 'This isn't a bunch of plebs you're catering for tonight, you know. Christ knows why Bunty has to employ a load of drama-school amateurs like you.'

Most irritatingly, he did know. Forty-year-old Bunty, ex-Roedean, Swiss finishing school and disastrous marriage to aristocratic wimp, liked her men young. And thin. The fatter she got, the narrower their hips had to be to excite her.

The situation at Lloyd Lloyd and Fraser, as far as Peter was concerned, was becoming worse. The 'squeeze', as it was called, meant that everyone still fortunate enough to be employed in the property sector had to pull more than their weight. That, combined with the fact that the value of his investments had taken a dive, seemed to Peter to call for some drastic action.

A technicoloured sunset added expensive highlights to the terracotta stone of the grandest department store in the world. The golden *Harrods* signs glowed opulently against their bay-green background. The usual summer evening parade was reflected in highly polished windows. A sprinkling of international couture-dressed creations walked, or rather strolled, amongst the inevitable crowd of back-packing youth crowding the pavement. The elegant poseurs almost, but not quite, eclipsed the mannequins on display.

Walton Street, tucked behind the 'shop', its white Georgian houses bathed in the most becoming tone of salmon pink, was at its very loveliest. A silver Lamborghini passed slowly between the closely parked ranks of top-of-the-range executive saloons interspersed with the nannies' Renault Fives; it cruised the nearby streets for several minutes before finding a space to park.

'Roger!' Peter greeted his first guest effusively. He felt happy now. There was fresh ice clustered around the racing-green bottles in his bathroom, and he himself was fresh and crisp in a new white silk shirt and maroon Armani trousers. He smelled strongly of Yves Saint Laurent's Jazz.

They began to arrive in droves, a succession of taxis disgorging the model girls that a friend at an agency had laid on and the twenty prime male targets who were top of Peter's summer hit list.

The party began to swing. Trays of miniature delights circulated with the champagne. Tiny barquettes of smoked salmon and quail's eggs competed for attention with cornets of Parma ham stuffed to overflowing with black seed pearls of caviare.

'I've said it once, and I'll say it once again. You really know how to throw a good party, Peter.' Gerry Bowen-Smythe, florid-faced secretary of the National Culture Club, waltzed past his host. In his podgy hands he balanced an overflowing glass of champagne, a high-piled caviare canapé, and a Balkan Sobranie cigarette.

The red-damask-lined reception room echoed to the strident sound of male laughter and the high-pitched giggles of beautiful young girls already earning more than their parents ever had. The nonstop drinks and canapés were costing a small fortune, but if there was one thing that Peter could rely on, it was that old commodity – money – for turning a gathering into a celebration.

'This is the kind of atmosphere I'd like to get going at the club.' Bowen-Smythe had again cornered his host. 'The mix of people you have here is just right.'

And so it was, the potent mixture of young and avaricious with middle-aged and wealthy had raised the decibel level so that it began to build upon itself and the air of excitement became doubly intoxicating.

The forty guests and attendant staff filled the ultra-designed space that stretched almost thirty feet from the front-facing white-sashed windows with an 'almost' view of Harrods, to the elegant French doors leading out on to a Yorkshire-stone patio that in turn led on to the garden.

Close to the swagged red velvet drapes, a strategically placed floor-to-ceiling gilt-framed mirror reflected an extraordinary garden vista. An avenue of cypresses had been cunningly planted so as to transform London into Tuscany. The trees were subtly graded in height: the ones closest to the house well over six feet, the ones screening the far wall half as tall. The false perspective was further intensified by a narrow pond, wider close to the house, that tapered almost to a point at the end of the view.

The property was well worth the thousand pounds Peter had paid to hire it for the night.

The Italian theme was complemented by ornaments inside the house. Almost hidden by guests, a splendid marble bust of Caesar stood to one side of a Renaissance fireplace, the fresh wreath of laurels around his neck echoing other touches of greenery amongst a wealth of decorative objects that were all either gold or white. *House and Garden* would have called it a room decorated in the Empire style. But which empire, taking into account the final touch of fleurs-de-lis on the wall-to-wall carpet, even the most inspired of journalists might have found difficult to say.

'Everybody happy?' Peter said at least twenty times.

He was circulating. Champagne bottle in one hand, his glass in the other he was being the efficient, charming host. He had filled his own glass half-full nearly an hour earlier and the level had hardly dropped, despite the ritual glass to lips that he performed on each fresh encounter.

Five to eight. It was almost time to start on the next phase. His punters were warming up nicely. There were three Harley Street doctors, a couple of dentists and, finally, several euphemistically titled financial consultants about the room who were probably the least likely to have a dabble in his project.

Bowen-Smythe was twice welcome. First as the cosignatory of a new management account that had been given to Peter by the National Culture Club. They wanted him to negotiate for, buy and then renovate a lodge that adjoined their Belgravia premises. Peter had seemed an ideal choice; after all, his expertise in the property market was shown by his position in LLF and his father had been a lifelong member of their club. The second reason for Bowen-Smythe's welcome was that he had recently come into an inheritance. It was nothing too spectacular, a scant twenty thousand, but Peter would be more than happy to have it invested in his scheme.

'Ladies and Gentlemen.' The impressive majordomo with a parade-ground voice called the gathering to order.

The handsome, exceptionally well-preserved fifty-year-old plastic surgeon who was the very top of Peter's list of prospects, smiled like a cat with the cream. With the ease of practice he slid an immaculately manicured hand gently over the firm round buttock of the six-foot blonde sixteen-year-old beside him. She grinned with real pleasure. She liked doctors; they knew the right buttons to press.

'Ladies and Gentlemen.' The last whispers died away. 'I give you your host, Peter Burnet.'

Peter raised his hands to stop the ripple of applause. 'Please, you mustn't give me praise. My psychiatrist says it's much better for me if I'm beaten – preferably with a little leather whip . . .'

There was a satisfying titter of laughter from the girls.

'I promised you a fun evening, and so far I can see – ' he made a show of peering round the room – 'you're all making the best of the opportunities on offer. So much so, in fact, that I'd like to announce the sudden engage-ment of . . .' He let his words die off in the general laughter. 'Enough of the foreplay. Dinner, my friends, is served.'

The staff had their instructions and the half a dozen liveried waiters who'd been on hand in the drawing room ran ahead of him, out of the door that led into the hallway, and across to the stairs that led down to the basement. Peter followed, and after him, like the children of Hamelin, trailed the guests.

The focal point of the dining room was a magnificent twenty-foot table made of thick planks of honey-coloured wood bound together with wide bands of polished brass. It was flanked by rough-hewn benches. At either end stood massive oaken thrones carved with an abundance of heraldic symbols and modern, tapestry-covered seats that pulled together the basic colour scheme of the room.

Ochre hessian lined the walls, burnt sienna paint had been dragged on doors and skirtings, and the carpet's rough, almost homespun texture accentuated its many tones of brown. Dark Elizabethan blues and reds glowed from half a dozen medium-sized oil paintings that were picked out by concealed lighting. A handful of Grecian sculptures were highlighted by strategically placed down-lighters. There was the barest glimpse of kitchen through a far door, merely an impression of heavy wooden units and a workmanlike black and white tiled floor.

There were name cards at alternate place settings. The men of the party had been carefully positioned according to rank. It would have been naïve of him, Peter thought, to have predetermined which young model sat with whom. He'd been right; within minutes the gathering around the table was settled to its own satisfaction and a dozen or more animated conversations broke out.

The three cooks working in the kitchen were female, in their middle twenties and, from the practised ease with which they chopped, sautéed and whisked, professionals. One was dark-haired; the green and gold badge on her brilliant chef's whites proclaimed her as Celia. Her partner at the work surface had long blonde hair pulled back severely from her round, almost childish face. Her name was Claudia. The two worked well together, dove-tailing their movements neatly, even in the unfamiliar workplace. A third girl, Tansy, was working at the cooker, her hair tucked up into a chef's hat.

'Ready?' Peter was bouncing on his heels, all ready to roll.

'You're sure you want us to come in with you?' Celia queried. She was deftly folding whisked egg white into a stiff, mint-green cream.

'We'll do it just as we rehearsed.' The natural pompousness in Peter's voice didn't seem to offend any of the girls. They maintained a clearly inborn sang-froid.

'Here.' Claudia handed Peter a wide silver salver. It was loaded with cream porcelain shells artfully filled with seafood and garnished with rosso leaves, strips of marinated avocado, and slender slivers of black olives that were scattered like the petals of some fabled flower.

The girls each took another platter, and the four of them advanced in line to the dining room. They began serving the guests as the waiters whisked starched damask napkins on to laps and poured chilled Pouilly Fuissé into the first of the five glasses ranged at each place setting.

Each course of the meal followed the same pattern. Peter and the three chefs served the food. They paid attention to the guests, smiling and coaxing to gain the maximum effect from the spectaculars on offer. After the *fruits de mer*, there was a chilled summer soup the texture of velvet and the colour of cream, with the flavour of almonds. Home-made tuiles with just the slightest hint of cheese in their crisp aftertaste completed that course.

The entrée was baby lamb chops garnished with a mousseline of tongue and served with steamed fresh vegetables. In the Continental manner, cheese was served next, including a bomb-shaped creation with a centre of garlicky butter. The home-made biscuits that accompanied the board were rough in shape and texture. Their raw oatiness provided an admirable foil for the bland richness of what had been a predominantly French selection.

Dessert was based on the pistachio parfait that had been receiving its final touches at the beginning of the meal. Fresh Scottish raspberries had been sieved into a sauce to pour over ice-cream-filled meringue nests. The perfect chewiness of Aga-baked egg and sugar complemented the minty freshness of the ice and the tart, soft fruit. By the time coffee was poured – from several cafetieres – there were very few able to take up the offer of cream and sugar, although almost everyone accepted one of the hand-made mints, white or green, that shimmered on silver bon-bon trays.

An amiable hush had fallen on the room. The eminent psychiatrist categorized it as that unique stage of fulfilment enjoyed after one form of gratification whilst strength was gathered for the prospect of another.

That was how Peter had planned it as well. He stood up from his place at the head of the table and smiled. There was no need for him to tap a bottle with a spoon or resort to any other time-honoured method of attracting attention. For the next half an hour at least, they were all his. Almost silently, an electrically controlled silvered screen unrolled itself to cover the wall behind him.

Peter stepped aside and the concealed video player clicked into action. An instant vision of emerald greens and verdant motion filled the screen. Brown hands reached into focus to twist unripe fruit from the stems. Groves of avocados burst into life in the apparent security of Knightsbridge.

'Ladies and gentlemen,' Peter announced, 'I present the most dynamic property investment it has ever been my pleasure to encounter. You all appreciate the benefit of this exotic delight.' He gestured to one side of him.

Tansy stood beneath the downlighters, her hands stretched out before her, cupping and caressing the swollen green fruit with a gesture that was surprisingly sensual.

'To whet your appetite further,' Peter continued, 'I can

reveal that every single course of our banquet tonight contained the versatile avocado.'

The sell went on. The groves were in that golden land of opportunity – Spain. Where tourism was fading, agronomy was growing.

The enthusiasm was there, Peter could sense it. He went on, linking the investment in the groves to Body Beautiful. They'd heard the gossip that made Marie Sullivan and him a feature. They'd heard it because he'd made sure they had. It meant that every Body Beautiful shop was a reminder to them – invest in this, and they were investing in the high street as well as the farm. Beauty products as well as food products – it would be bound to weather the current economic downturn. It was all so very plausible.

Later, much later, Peter bid his guests good night. Each one of the prospects had been given a thick, leather-bound portfolio. As well as containing an impressive flow chart and projections of the scheme, there was a glossy hand-scripted menu of the evening's fare.

Bowen-Smythe signed his twenty grand away before he left to go home to his two-bedroomed terraced villa in Fulham.

Feed them and fleece them, Peter mused happily. It worked every time.

The three girls loaded the Miele dishwasher and put the left-overs in the American fridge-freezer to chill. Caterers, professionals, throw nothing away but the dishwater. Peter sat in the dining room going through the results of the evening. He ticked six of the names on his list, and beside Bowen-Smythe's name he put a cross. One positive and half a dozen potentials – not bad at all for an evening's work.

Later, he lay sprawled out on the king-sized bed in the

master bedroom. He was absentmindedly fondling Tansy. His hand up her blouse, he was kneading her full bouncy breasts. She had come upstairs first, but on an earlier occasion that he had employed the threesome, he had got the distinct impression that her preference was for females. This evening, however, he intended to get his money's worth.

When the remaining two girls joined them he issued an ultimatum: when he was paying the bill he expected full participation – from everyone.

In a short while he was very satisfactorily positioned in an athletic carnal montage. The scenario was his to command.

He shouted his instructions in the king-sized bed in the king-sized room, and looked forward to a king-sized future. The revel carried on until nearly dawn – perhaps, Peter thought as he slipped finally to sleep, that showed the true value of the humble avocado.

Chapter 8

*Every woman would
rather be beautiful than good*

'What I'd like are your first thoughts,' Marie said. 'This test is much more effective if you don't edit your response.'

Sarah looked down at the typewritten lists on the sheet of paper on the desk in front of her. She couldn't believe she was seriously meant to complete it.

She laughed as she said, 'I've never been asked to do anything like this before.'

'Then it'll be all the more illuminating, for you as well as for me.'

'But I don't understand why you want it done. What's it called, a "Cleaver" did you say? What's that meant to be? Some kind of pun on "axe"? If I fail then you could say I'm axed. But I haven't even got the job yet.' Sarah laughed.

The truth was, Marie still wasn't convinced that she was prepared to let Sarah into her company. The choice was down to the woman, or St John Aldridge. The finance director had suggested Marie should join him for a few hours on his boat at the weekend. She was hoping that seeing him in a nonwork environment would make her feel easier at the thought of having him in the boardroom.

The Cleaver tests were something Marie had considered using a few years ago. In the end she'd discarded them and decided to trust her own judgement in choosing whom she employed. But in this instance her judgement was being affected by the fact she didn't want to let the publicity out of her own hands.

'This first block,' Sarah persevered, 'gives me the choice of being "persuasive", "gentle", "humble" or "original". From what you've said I assume I'm meant to think the word that's most like me is "persuasive" and the least' – she paused for a moment to consider and then went on firmly – 'is "humble". Although God only knows I wouldn't put me down as "gentle" either.'

'If those are the words you chose, then go ahead and start filling it in. There is another, slightly different one for you to have a go at when you've finished.'

'Do you give these tests to everyone applying to Body Beautiful for a job?'

Marie frowned. She just wanted to get this stage over and done with, and nodded abruptly. She felt she couldn't do anything else.

But Sarah still wasn't prepared to commit herself to paper. 'Have you done one of these?'

'Yes,' Marie said shortly.

She had done one for fun, as had Damion, and they'd laughed at the results. Marie's had read as if she was a megalomaniac, Damion had appeared gay. That was a couple of years ago.

Marie picked up her pen and said, 'I'll get Angelique to run the results through the computer, so the sooner you begin . . .'

It was a lie that Angelique would check the results. Marie had long ago misplaced the grid that gave Mr Cleaver's instant analysis.

There was silence for several minutes. Marie worked steadily through the pile of correspondence on her desk. Sarah ticked her way down three columns each containing six blocks of four words. She was beginning to get annoyed.

The words forced you into a corner. With a choice of 'willing', 'poised', 'agreeable' or 'high-spirited' it seemed silly to have to pick one as being least like her. Her pen hovered over the space beside 'agreeable', but she couldn't tick that as being 'least'. She considered 'willing' – she'd have to appear that. In publicity you were expected to lick the backside of anyone who mattered. 'Poised' – well, that was an essential too, she had to look the part. That left 'high-spirited'. She ticked the 'least' space beside that. It was silly, but it bothered her, she felt she'd let herself down.

'How's it going?' Marie didn't bother to look up. She'd checked her watch, and Sarah had taken ten minutes so far.

'On the last one.' Sarah laid her pen down.

She was going to take her time. It was obvious Marie Sullivan wanted to rush her, but the managing director of Body Beautiful wasn't going to get it all her own way. If the job hadn't been so appealing, so much what she wanted for her next step, she'd have told her what to do with it long ago.

Marie reached out towards her phone and then abruptly changed her mind. She wanted to see the self-description chart that the woman had filled in. She got up and walked over to where Sarah sat.

'Just a minute.' Sarah looked for the last time at the final choice.

She could be 'restless', 'popular', 'neighbourly' or 'orderly'. For the least like her she ticked 'neighbourly' – she thought it sounded homey, and she certainly didn't have to be that. Now for what was most like her, she could choose 'popular' or 'orderly'. She thought fleetingly of the row she'd had that morning with the man who'd shared her bed last night. He'd said she was a selfish bitch, without a friend in the world. 'Orderly' – the kitchen at her flat was a tip. 'Restless' – her pen hovered for a moment and then put a tick beside it.

'Finished? Good. Now let's see.' Marie scanned the columns quickly. 'You've ticked the right number of spaces. And "ticked" is the operative word. Didn't you notice it says to put a cross? I see that you've put yourself down as "accurate" in this last column. You might like to rethink that.'

'For heaven's sake . . .'

'In this business it's often the little things that count.'

'Look, why don't you just come right out and say it's no go? You obviously don't want me working here.'

'That's not true. I haven't made up my mind yet. If I had, I wouldn't be wasting my time this morning.'

But she was wasting her time and she knew it. She was procrastinating over what was a simple yes-or-no decision. She shouldn't be giving Sarah a psychological test, she thought wryly, she should be giving herself one.

Marie didn't get back to the flat until gone ten. She found a note from Peter attached to the fridge door. It said, *The monkey's gone out to find a few nuts in the jungle.* He'd used the china-banana magnet to hold the scrap of paper. She smiled briefly, and then made herself a ham and lettuce sandwich. There was plenty of food for his supper if only he'd bothered to look.

She would have liked some company; that was why she'd agreed he could stay at her flat for a few days whilst he had the builders in at his own place. Their relationship had become very much an on-off affair. Perhaps, she thought, it suited them both that way.

Clutching a glass of French wine, she carried her sandwich and Sarah's analysis sheets through to the sitting room. She'd skimmed through the self-evaluation test in the cab on the way home. Sarah came over as domineering, confident and lacking in compassion – nothing that wouldn't be an asset in her job. The self-actualization sheet might be more revealing.

There were nine important subjects involving the applicant's life listed, and within each category were six words to be marked from five downwards in descending order of importance.

The aim of the test was to highlight priorities in the major issues. 'Personal values' listed 'power', 'ethics', 'beauty', 'wealth', 'compassion' and 'truth'. Marie tried to remember what she had put down as her first choice – she thought that it had been 'power'. It certainly would be today.

She slowly bit into her sandwich. Sarah had put 'beauty' at the top of her list. That could well be true, or it could be that she thought it was a clever answer. Marie tossed the sheet down on the coffee table. This wasn't getting her anywhere. What was needed was a firm decision.

Peter came back just after midnight. He called out as he stepped into the hall and closed the door behind him. He felt good, he'd met up with some pals in a wine bar close to his office. They'd talked shop and then compared women. As bedmate of one of the highest flying women in town he'd definitely come out on top.

The sitting-room lights were still on but there was no sign of Marie. He had a quick look in the kitchen. The lights there were off and a plate and glass were on the drainer. He could hear running water and he grinned. He loved it in the shower. Walking on tip-toe across the thick pile carpet of the hall and into the bedroom, he began to hum softly. He undid his tie, and then began unbuttoning his shirt.

In the bedroom the sound of the shower was quite loud. Marie couldn't have heard him come in at all. He stepped out of his trousers and draped them over the back of a chair. He was getting a hard-on; he turned sideways to look at his reflection in the full-length mirror on the wall. He patted his flat, muscled stomach and admired the already more than right-angled erection. 'Up, up and away,' he sang softly. He had reached the bathroom door before he remembered about his socks. Marie always teased him if he left them on.

The etched glass screen gave him a tantalizing picture. Arms uplifted to the shower, dark tousled hair, her head tilted back, allowing the water to run over her breasts, Marie gave Peter all the stimulation he needed for the final forty-five degree elevation he wanted. He opened the glass door with a shout, Marie spun round with a look of shock on her face and he stepped in beside her, folding her in his arms.

'You frightened me half to death!'

He could feel Marie's heart beating against his chest and he pressed himself against her. Her earlier look of dismay turned to amusement.

'What on earth have you been up to to get yourself in that state?' she asked.

'Watching you through the door.' He began nibbling at her ear.

She tasted soapy. Holding her to him, he turned them both around so that the warm water streamed down his back.

'Hey, I'll freeze.' Marie tugged playfully at his hair. 'Let me back under the water.'

'You don't need the water to warm you up.' He clasped her firmly under the buttocks and lifted her up.

He felt the enticing tickle of her hairs rubbing up the ultra-sensitive underneath of his penis, and then she was positioned perfectly. Slowly, with infinite care, he lowered her on to him.

She drew her breath in sharply. The sudden sting of soap entering her softness was almost instantly covered by the overwhelming sensation of heat.

'That's good,' she murmured. 'That's so good.'

Peter bent his knees until her feet just touched the ground. Then he began to move, rhythmically, slowly to begin with and then with increasing speed. Marie came almost immediately, and then a second time, climaxing just as Peter lifted her feet off the ground with his final thrust.

Marie had left the Cleaver tests on the table beside her bed. Peter, in his satiated state, wrapped in a white bathrobe, with wet hair standing up, looked nearer twenty than thirty. He picked the sheets of paper up and waved them at Marie, laughing.

'You're not serious, you aren't actually using these things, are you?' he asked, disbelievingly.

'They're very good, very reliable.'

'Oh sure, they're very American too.'

'What's wrong with that?'

Marie had sat down in front of her dressing table. She was slowly rubbing moisturizing cream into her skin.

'Nothing, I suppose, if you want to run your company that way. If you want to be all crackers and milk.'

'I do. I'd like nothing more than to succeed as much in the US as I have over here.' Marie watched the flush of anger spreading up her neck. Peter could be infuriatingly insular.

'Just as long as you remember to keep some time for me in your transatlantic travels.'

The tone in Peter's voice was light, but he increasingly regularly brought up the major bone of contention between them. In reality he wanted Marie waiting at home for him, the little woman. But he also revelled in her image. He'd even been pleased by the *Financial Times* coverage which had more than hinted at her exposed position on high-street property.

'Do me a favour and flick through that top sheet, will you?' Marie began putting cream on her hands and arms. 'Tell me what you think of the traits it shows.'

'*Jawohl, mein Fuehrer.*' Peter flopped back on the bed. 'It says "best use of free time" here. Your victim's marked, "pursue the arts" – very noble. Mind you, she could have put "helping children", then she would have sounded a right bimbo.'

'What would you have chosen, Peter?' Marie turned round to look at her lover.

She suddenly wondered if she really knew him at all. She accepted the surface version, the hail-fellow-well-met image, but was it real?

'"Board of Directors", that's what I want, although I don't see why that's classed under "best use of free time". That's what I want for the dreaded six-hour day.'

Marie laughed. 'You do know the rest of the world grinds on for eight hours.'

'Now, you know I don't like it if you take the micky. Look, this is getting interesting, it says "career enrichment" – you can choose from "spiritual growth", "charitable works", "exercise authority", "personal investments" . . . what the hell's "analysis of research"? The final one's "freedom of expression". I'll have that. Then I could tell Trodgers to fuck off. Yes, that would do nicely. Common little Trodgers can fuck off and then I'd have his place on the board of directors.' He lay back on the bed. 'Christ, I'm tired. You know I've got to tell you, you're a really good fuck.'

Marie laughed self-consciously. She could never get used to what she thought of as his schoolboy forthrightness.

She said, 'You're not so bad yourself,' but he didn't hear her.

His eyes were closed, his breathing had become deep and regular. Like a child he had fallen instantly asleep. The robe had fallen open, and the parts of him that he proudly referred to as his 'tackle' lay exposed. It seemed innocent, vulnerable. Slowly Marie stood up and let her towel fall. She slipped her night dress over her head. It was oyster silk, a straight tube with slim coffee-coloured ribbons over the shoulders.

'Get into bed, Peter.' She stroked his face to wake him gently. 'Come on, just wake up for a minute, you'll sleep better in your pyjamas.'

Peter stripped off the robe and slipped naked under the soft, down-filled duvet. Marie got in beside him, but she kept to her own side. She didn't want to get entangled in his embrace. He liked to throw his arms around her shoulders, drape a leg over her legs and then breathe loudly close to her ear. She found it suffocating.

She would have to come to a decision about Sarah or St John, she thought, waiting for sleep. If only Damion would change his mind. If only he hadn't found that damned stable yard. She'd been really unlucky that her brother had found just what he'd been searching for when it was the most awkward time for the company.

Peter turned in his sleep and came closer to her. She turned on to her side and moved right to the edge of the bed. It was uncomfortable, she felt she was balancing on the edge of a void. And she no longer felt even slightly sleepy. Slowly, carefully so as not to wake Peter, she sat up. She didn't want him to prove his virility again. At that moment she wanted to be on her own, somehow she had to think clearly.

There was too much pressure on her, with the bank wanting the company to reduce its property commitment.

They had introduced Berry, saying they thought he could help dispose of some of the 'superfluous' sites. So far his role within the company had been unofficial, and she wanted it to stay that way. She didn't want them putting anyone on to the board of Body Beautiful.

After an hour of directionless thinking, Marie knew that she either had to get up and make herself a hot drink or accept that she was never going to get to sleep. She silently got out of bed and went into the kitchen. She was pouring the hot, chocolate-flavoured milk into a mug when she heard Peter going into the bathroom.

'Make one of whatever you're having for me too, will you? Plus plenty of sugar. I need some energy,' he called out. 'And then hurry back. Percy's feeling frisky again.'

They made love slowly, with the requisite amount of tender, exploratory care, for the second time in a few hours. It was just past three when Marie faked her orgasm so that she could get it over and done with.

With Peter draped over her she thought she'd never get to sleep. She got hotter and hotter. But when the alarm rang stridently at ten minutes to seven she had to fight her way up from some bottomless pit of unconsciousness.

It was Friday, and she'd promised Sarah a decision by that afternoon at the latest. She'd go straight to the office without any breakfast – she couldn't face Peter being the cheerful, indulged lover.

'If you'd like to come through now, Marie.'

Marie laid down the newspaper she'd been pretending to read. She took one last look round the featureless regional radio reception area where she'd spent fifteen long minutes waiting. The pretty girl in the floaty summer dress who'd brought her a glass of iced water when she'd arrived led her through a word-processor-littered outer office and then to the door of the sound studio. This was a watershed. If Marie decided to appoint Sarah Hather-leigh, this would be the last publicity interview she arranged herself. If she appointed St John Aldridge she would be busier than ever escalating the PR side of the business herself.

Marie could see the man who would be interviewing her. He looked cool in a short-sleeved white shirt. His short fair hair was ideally suited to the black headphones he wore like a badge of office. A last flutter of nerves surged in Marie's stomach. She wondered if all the hours she'd spent awake last night working out answers to the kind of questions she imagined she'd be asked had been wasted. Everything was now in the evidently capable hands of Martin Bailey.

'And that was' – Martin Bailey spoke smilingly into the microphone in front of him and glanced quickly down at the neatly written list in his hand – 'Lonnie Donnegan and "Last Train to San Fernando". Just time for one more quickie before the two o'clock news and then, as prom-ised, I'll be talking to Marie Sullivan – a young lady who's making a very big name indeed for herself in the beauty world.'

He flipped the switch that dropped the stylus down on to the already spinning disc. The dulcet tones of a jazz clarinet filled the studio.

'Hi!' Martin extended a hand and smiled briefly at her. 'Won't be a . . .' He went back to flicking switches and running a trembling finger down the margin of his notes.

Marie forced herself to look slowly around. Two of the back walls were covered in pale grey panels studded with hundreds of tiny holes. Another was taken up almost entirely by a wide clear pane of soundproofed glass. On the other side of it, the girl who'd shown her through sat talking into a telephone. Suddenly aware of scrutiny she looked up and, catching Marie's eye, smiled absently.

'Keep playing, keep playing.' Martin's plea to the record made Marie quickly turn back to face him. 'Sorry, it's only the third day I've ever done this. I'm standing in for Steve, he's on holiday. I think we're ready for the . . .' The news bulletin had begun, and it would last only a couple of minutes. 'Oh, my God, I've forgotten to check your voice level. Look, just say a few words, will you.'

Marie stared at him. She couldn't think of anything to say. The grey, felt-covered mike in front of her was a threat, and she was aware of how hot she still was – the journey down had been appalling.

'Just say something,' he told her, looking down at his controls.

'It's been so hot, I mean,' Marie was aware that she was talking too fast. She was almost choking on her words and her voice was too high. She coughed, and saw the look of irritation that crossed Martin's face – she'd obviously mucked up his levels. Suddenly she thought how funny it all was. She'd been dependent on a total stranger's ability to see her through the interview and he was more panicky than she was.

It was ridiculous, she could stand on her own feet.

An 'on air' red light flashed on on the wall above the door.

Martin's lips parted in a nervous smile and he leaned forward to speak into his mike. 'So, it's five past two on a gloriously hot, sunny afternoon and what could be nicer than to get the deckchair out, put your feet up and listen to what made Marie Sullivan, high-profile founder of Body Beautiful, into the international success she is. Marie, thank you for agreeing to come on our programme.'

'Thank you for inviting me.' Marie surreptitiously wiped the moist palms of her hands on her skirt.

'So tell us, you're obviously an amazingly busy lady,

how do you manage to give up an hour in the middle of a Friday afternoon to come all the way down to Canterbury to talk to us?'

Marie laughed. 'I sneaked out of the back door of the office. I couldn't resist the thought of an afternoon in the country.'

'And who could in this glorious weather?' Martin was succeeding in speaking with the warmth of a professional DJ but the look on his face was apologetic.

Marie wondered if he was apologizing for his earlier confusion or the heatwave that had made her hour-and-a-half drive a nightmare.

'So, this new product range you've announced – it's a selection of sunscreens and creams – it couldn't have been more well-timed, could it?'

'I must admit that when we went for an August launch we were hoping for some sun, but I think this might have gone a bit over the top.'

'"Sunkissed" – it's a pretty name.' Martin held up the sample bottle that the station had been sent. 'And it's a very pretty package. How would you describe it? It's a shell, certainly, but it's not the same as your usual products.'

'It's a periwinkle shape – at least that's what I used to call that long, thin spiral shell when I was a child. My brother and I were brought up in Ireland. We used to spend hours and hours on the beach picking up seashells and then take them home and stick them all over card-board boxes and glass jars. We used to think we were making works of art. We weren't, of course, but the shells themselves were quite beautiful. That's why we chose their shapes for our beauty products.'

'You mention your brother. I think I remember reading that he's left the company. That must have been very upsetting for you.'

'Damion was only ever in the company to develop the product line. He is a very talented, highly qualified chemist, but his first love has always been horses. He is setting up a training establishment but he'll still be on hand to give advice as and when we need it on future products.'

'You say, "we". Who exactly does Body Beautiful consist of? Tell us some of the personalities.'

Marie blinked. He might not have had much practice as an interviewer but he'd instantly hit what the bank saw as her weak spot.

'In a business like ours the products are the stars,' she said brightly.

'And that kind of clever answer is no doubt exactly why you're such a success today.' Martin laughed.

He reached out to flick the switch to let the music play, and a muted version of Frank Ifield's 'I Remember You' filled the studio.

'Great, that was great. Let's . . . hang on. Now what the hell? What do I do now?' Martin's hands were hovering above his controls. 'I don't know what to do!' He was looking frantically through the window to where the girl was still talking animatedly on the telephone.

At last she looked at him. Marie had turned round in her chair too. The girl was looking perplexed. She took the receiver away from her ear so that she could listen to the broadcast that was coming over a speaker in the office. She shrugged her shoulders and mouthed an 'OK'.

Martin shook his head. 'Something's wrong, it's not playing loud enough in . . .'

Sudden horror showed in the girl's face. She dropped the telephone in her hand as if it was red hot. She put her hands to her mouth and then stabbed a finger towards Martin and then Marie. By then Martin had worked it out for himself. He reached forwards to flick a switch, then

101

sat back slowly in his chair as the music from the record on the turntable came up to full volume.

'It was your mike,' he said. 'I'd left it switched on. At least you didn't make a fool of yourself. It was only my voice they heard. Sorry.'

'There's so much for you to do, isn't there? I'm sure I couldn't cope at all.'

'I've done a load of stage work, and some television, but I have to tell you that this is the most nerve-racking thing I've ever done. It's totally up to me, totally. If I make a muck-up then there's dead air, absolute silence. Or, of course' – he grinned tiredly – 'the listeners get too much of a good thing, me talking and a record playing at the same time. Christ knows what I said just then. Here we go again.'

The record was ending. Marie sipped at the glass of lukewarm water in front of her. She thought fleetingly that she must remember to stress the naturalness of her products and the positive good that even the suncreams did for the skin, and then she was on air again.

The traffic leaving Canterbury on the London road was a long, fume-shrouded snake that curved uphill ahead of Marie. She wound down the window beside her. The radio was crackling with interference, so she turned it off and as she did so glanced down at the telephone, but decided not to call the office.

There was a magnificent view of the cathedral in her rear-view mirror. She'd have liked to spend some time in the city. She'd had a quick Diet Coke after the interview, but the touristy coffee bar hadn't given her any local atmosphere. She leaned back against the car seat. The drive to Pencombe should have taken her about an hour, but in this traffic there was no guessing how long she'd be.

At least the car was an automatic. She kept her foot lightly pressing down on the accelerator and was able to let her thoughts wander. She was pleased at the soft-sell she'd managed to get over, and in closing his interview Martin had given her products quite a strong push. It had been satisfying to be able to talk about the natural plant bases of many of their lines and to expound, yet again, her own business ethics. There was no reason why basic beauty products shouldn't be available at a reasonable price. Yes, she'd agreed, in a way she was doing a similar job to the Body Shop, but her customers had a wider choice, more freedom. Not everyone wanted to follow the back-to-basics concept. Buying Body Beautiful, they could experiment with new lines at a fraction of the price of the great international companies' products. It was always a difficult message to get over.

The last thing Marie wanted was a lawsuit slapped on her by one of the market leaders. She'd been careful to say that all Damion did was develop products as close to the newest on the market as his own research and copyright would allow him. And that it was fun to think that you could pamper yourself with skin treatments similar to those used by the Hollywood stars.

The slightest breeze touched her forearm on the car windowsill. She adjusted her position slightly so that it ran in a cooling line under her arm and inside her blouse.

She really did want to call the office. Checking in the rear-view mirror, she noticed that the creep in the car behind her was eyeing her with a 'come-on' leer under his mirrored sunglasses. Drop dead, she thought irritably. The minute there was some space ahead of her she'd manage to leave him behind; the engine under her bonnet was infinitely more powerful than the one under his. She began to smile at the thought, and her jaw clenched in her aggression towards the nameless slob.

The thought amused her until the motorway opened out before her. After a quick check behind, she pulled out to the third lane and with the needle of her speedometer firmly on seventy overtook a succession of slow-moving lorries. The mirrored glasses kept up with her until a long steep hill took the impetus out of his aged Ford Cortina engine. She wouldn't take much over an hour and a half to reach Pencombe after all.

Lucy had quickly become a friend. It was tragic that she'd lost her husband after only a year of marriage. They'd married very young, and she could have been no more than twenty-two when she became a widow. It looked as if her daughter, Fleur, was going to follow the tradition of becoming a bride in her early twenties. Fleur was such a pretty name, Marie thought, and it suited the girl perfectly; she had violet eyes, short curly brown hair and a heart-shaped face. She was a busy, happy creature who adored an older, handsome man known to all as Benjy. Benjy's only fault in Marie's eyes was that his life was spent in pursuit of foxes. He was a master of the local hunt, and the owner of a few hundred acres of the best hunting land in the county. He had made his money in the city and 'retired' at thirty-seven to a life of rural luxury. Two years later he had become engaged to Fleur, granddaughter of the house of Montford. The only possible future blight on Fleur's far horizons, as far as Marie could see, was disillusionment at having achieved everything too soon.

Chapter 9

Beauty draws more than oxen

Sun sparkled on the gently undulating waters restrained by the inner harbour at Ramsgate in Kent. It was the setting for one of the most exclusive marinas on the south coast, and boasted massive traditional stone quays, complete with great iron rings big enough to tie the *QE2* to. The time was nine o'clock, early morning to those on the multitude of moored yachts, but already a crowd of brightly shirted tourists sat on municipal benches, eating ice-cream cornets and gawping at the playground of the rich.

St John Aldridge bounced energetically up through the open hatch on the foredeck of his forty-foot twin-screw diesel yacht. The sharp salt breeze tugged through his hair and the champagne air washed his eyes bright blue. In moments he felt more alive than he had all week in town.

Slooki was St John's private passion. He loved the pure, sleek lines of her hull, the gleaming wooden decks. He knew every inch of his beloved craft. And this was the best way to appreciate her, a hard drive down from town in the early hours, and a few hours of oblivion spent, alone, in the duvet-covered double bunk.

To step out of the masculine atmosphere of the main cabin into the shiny new day was worth all the hard work it had taken to pay for – and continue to afford – the ultimate in marine luxury. Elegantly dressed in aquamarine sea-island cotton short-sleeved shirt and slub linen cream shorts, St John perched lightly on a brightly polished chrome rail to think out his approach to the day.

The main decision was how to handle Marie Sullivan. Should it appear pure business, or business with pleasure? It was most delightful to feel able to relax over the next step in his future. John Blake at Capita was being most helpful. The fact that the chemist, Moorman, had been turned down because he'd asked for fifty per cent of the shares was highly useful information. As was gossip about Damion Sullivan. Approached properly, there was no reason to believe the brother wouldn't part with his share of the equity. The minute Marie parted with even one per cent of her shares, Body Beautiful would be ripe for picking. That was what he loved about the beauty business, the succulence of the prizes on offer for the bold.

St John tipped his face back to catch the sun. He had applied a generous helping of moisturizer over a sun guard before coming on deck – he was a great believer in caring for his skin. Personally he preferred the smell of YSL's Jazz, but on the boat he felt Kouros more appropriate.

He stood, hands on hips, swivelling lightly on the balls of his designer deck-shoed feet, as he surveyed the panorama. There were several hundred other pleasure craft moored either side of the wooden pontoons crisscrossing the inner harbour. The breeze played a tinkling melody on a myriad halyards, and fluttered an army of coloured pennants.

The financial expertise that paid for his more than satisfactory lifestyle had been inherited from his father. As a child St John had enjoyed all the privileges of private education traditional for the son of ex-pats living it up on an oil company salary. His parents had now retired to Portugal. They owned a comfortable villa in Val do Lobo, where they golfed all day and played bridge all evening with a coterie of other wealthy English people. He visited them every Easter.

There were a few more chores to be completed before his visitor arrived, so, armed with a wicker basket he'd brought back from Portugal last year, he set out for the shore. It required a good sense of balance to walk well on the swaying pontoons. Today the wooden slatted walkway rocked gently on the oily water of the harbour, but when the wind was up it pitched and bucked.

Only a week ago he had seen a woman from one of the smaller boats trip and fall into the murky water. She'd lost her purse – credit cards and all. Worse than that, in St John's opinion, she'd had to suffer the indignity of a stomach pump at the local hospital. The harbour authorities tried to enforce strict no sea-closet evacuation laws. But they were nowhere near as devious as the rich, who for some perverse reason, were determined to dump their own shit on their own doorsteps. The lock gates to the inner harbour opened twice a day but it would have taken several months of flood tides to cleanse the water.

The security guard on duty at the head of the stone steps leading up to the harbour wall greeted St John by name. Enzooed in his wire cage, the guard was the regulation six foot tall, in his early twenties, and fancied he was good-looking. He wasn't sure which way *Mr* Aldridge jumped. He'd seen women come down as guests to the *Slooki* – well-dressed, expensive women. And he'd also seen men, mostly young, tanned, and spoilt. He wouldn't mind being spoilt, and he was prepared to do whatever it took to achieve that state of grace.

Marie wished she hadn't agreed to spend her first free Saturday in ages going down to Ramsgate to see St John Aldridge. She'd spent the night at Pencombe, and woken to a perfect day. To have to get into the car and drive

107

right across Kent again had seemed a waste of precious time.

St John's directions were immaculate. Marie gave her name to a security guard and walked down the harbour steps and on to the pontoons. She was glad she'd worn trainers. The strange motion of the floating wooden walkway was disconcerting. The guard had told her to walk straight on until she reached the fourth branch off to the left.

There was such a solid presence of wealth in the white-and-chrome vessels tied up on either side of her that it was hard to believe the present state of the economy. Most of the boats were occupied and several couples were enjoying a leisurely pre-lunch drink on board. It appeared that the requisite gear for husband-and-wife teams – or at least what Marie assumed were marital alliances – was blue and white Breton jumpers and spotless white jeans. The men were mostly grey-haired, the women wore headscarves.

St John was waiting for her. His dark glasses were fashionable wrap-arounds; they, and his clothes, looked very expensive.

Marie had chosen to wear a peach silk shirt and matching trousers. It wasn't a nautical outfit, but it made her feel glamorous and, she thought, look dynamic. She pushed her sunglasses up on her forehead and accepted the hand her host extended.

'May I say you look quite delightful.' St John gestured for Marie to sit on the red leather-covered banquette that went round three sides of the rear well of the deck. 'If that sounds too much like me buttering up the boss, then you'll have to blame the heavenly weather.'

Marie smiled and slid the dark glasses back down her nose. She hadn't realized before that St John's act was a bit too precious.

'I didn't know this place was s . popular,' she said.

'Do you mean with us sailors, or with the hoi poloi?' St John indicated the crowds thronging the harbourside. 'Sometimes I think I'd rather be moored in some hidden-away little spot, where everyone's one of us – Bosham, somewhere like that. But it's so handy for popping over the Channel from here. And much, much nicer than Dover – that's not my type of place at all.' He busied himself opening a bottle of chilled white wine.

'Do you come here a lot?'

'As often as I can – at least once a month in the summer, even if things are really hectic. It's just close enough to town for me to be able to drive down for the day. But it's also far enough away so that I feel I'm getting a real break. Of course . . .' He paused and smiled winningly as he handed Marie her drink. 'If I join Body Beautiful I might just have to give *Slooki* up altogether, for the first year or so. Until I get things really under control.'

They had lunch on board. The china was very Thomas Goode, and the food very Greek; St John said he had ordered it from a restaurant in the town. There was creamy taramasalata with hot pitta bread, and strong-tasting black olives, followed by an aromatic stew of vegetables, then stuffed vine leaves and grilled quail. Dessert was fresh fruit – figs and peaches – with thick sheep's yoghurt. The conversation, Marie felt, was like the yoghurt – strained.

'That was delicious,' she said. 'That restaurant must do a great trade catering for all these boats.'

'Well, I suppose we all like to think we've a touch of the Onassis in us.' St John laughed.

As the meal progressed and the level of retsina in the bottle decreased, his laugh had become a strident bray.

Marie glanced pointedly at her watch. 'I really mustn't keep you much longer. We've talked over most of the relevant points.'

She'd gathered that he wasn't too concerned about the size of his stake to begin with. As long as he started out with five per cent, he'd be content to base further share acquisition on his measurable performance.

'You don't have to rush off to another meeting, do you?' St John sounded almost panicky.

'Not exactly, but . . .'

'There's something I'd really like to show you.'

Marie struggled to control her face. For one mad moment she thought St John was making a pass – that what he wanted her to see was a very personal part of his anatomy.

They drove in silence. It wasn't an awkward one because St John had turned on a Verdi tape to play at full volume. It was much easier than talking. He was clearly nervous.

Marie sat back on the soft leather upholstery. If she'd had to guess what car St John drove it would have been an XJS, and she'd have been right. She let the music wash over her. For a man whose business image was hard as nails, she had the feeling that St John had a vulnerable soft centre. She was concerned about how effective he'd be in ten years' time. She didn't want an ageing smoothie spending more time worrying about his appearance than his job. Whoever joined Body Beautiful had to have business longevity.

They slowed as they entered a small village and drove at a crawl between terraced red-brick cottages with white latticed windows. St John had turned off the music.

'Peter Rabbit land.' He laughed, glancing quickly at his passenger. 'Isn't it charming?'

110

Marie nodded. 'It's almost as pretty as the village where my Kentish cousins live. Just look at those flowers.'

Hanging baskets almost hid the windows of the small, end-of-terrace pub. There was a profusion of blue lobelia cascading amongst purple and pink geraniums and fat white daisies.

Ahead of them, while the council road curved sharply to the left, an obviously private drive led straight into parkland. They drove between high wrought-iron gates and on to a wide gravel drive littered with pot holes.

'Dene Park.' St John said the two words reverentially. 'Fate chooses some houses to heap with blessings; this is one of them. This drive was first cut through the fields in the fifteenth century. That was when a well-endowed yeoman built a modest timber-framed farmhouse for himself and his family. As his family grew, so did the house. In the 1800s it was ideally positioned for the amorous pursuits of the Prince Regent. The famous architect, Henry Holland, was given carte blanche to transform the already sizable property into a jewel in the garden of England. He encased it in a Georgian shell, adding an immaculate façade of cream plaster containing twenty of the new and fashionable long windows. A magnificent pediment graced the front door, and a final touch was added by a great curve of windows on the west elevation, overlooking the park.'

'You sound like a guide book.' Marie laughed awkwardly.

As St John continued his monologue they reached the property. It was as lovely as the description had painted it. Pink roses in formal beds broke the wide expanse of lawns, twin yew hedges formed an alley leading to a stone fountain.

'The locals say the Prince's gallant grey charger is

111

buried at the end of the yew walk. It's supposed to gallop the park on misty nights.'

Marie followed St John's example and got out of the car. She followed him up to the royal-blue front door and watched as he performed an elaborate security ritual to open it.

'You have to admit,' his voice echoed back as he walked into a large dark panelled hall, 'it would make the ultimate beauty hydro.'

Marie was so taken aback that she stood still on the wide stone steps. St John was advancing further into the interior without her. It was unbelievable. She'd given up a whole afternoon to be dragged out to the middle of beyond and given the hard sell for what, in the depths of rural Kent, had to be a white elephant.

'Hey!' she shouted. She leaned forward to shout again through the open door. She didn't want to go into the building. There were dust sheets on the furniture and a smell of damp reached out towards her.

What an odd way to make her mind up, she thought. She turned to look out over the rolling parkland. She had to wait for St John to drive her back to Ramsgate. Perhaps the writing had been on the wall all along and she'd just been too stubborn to see it. Sarah Hatherleigh was very good at publicity and Marie Sullivan was very good at marketing. Together they should make a great team.

Honour ran the tip of her tongue along the gummed strip on the edge of the envelope. She was still undecided as to whether she should post the letter or not, so she laid it down beside the silver bowl of roses on the hall table.

She stared for a moment at her reflection in the gilt-framed mirror. Lucy had recently had it brought through from the west wing to hang in the hall. The pale blue eyes that looked thoughtfully back at her were just like the

112

eyes in the portrait of her mother, Isabella. Dame Laura Knight blue, that's how her brother Eddy had once described them. Like the blues of Cornwall, he'd said. He'd grown quite poetical in his old age, before the stroke. Now, Honour thought sadly, he was just a vegetable. The blue in her eyes faded to grey.

The letter was to the National Trust. She was deliberately slowing down her dealings with them, nit-picking at the small print in the agreements that were really quite straightforward. If only Lucy hadn't seemed suddenly so certain that they could keep the house in the family. It was seeing how Marie had built up her business that had provided Lucy with the final spurt of enthusiasm. That and Marie's conviction that they could seriously make a go of the hospitality business. The two younger women had spent Friday evening discussing possible menus for discerning London executives.

Honour picked up the letter and carried it out into the garden with her. There were a lot of visitors enjoying the afternoon sun, certainly more than last year on the equivalent Saturday. The physic garden was clearly proving an attraction and the book called *The Pencombe Herbal*, which they'd had printed privately during the winter, was selling surprisingly well. Lucy had edited the handwritten manuscript that was found amongst Victoria's papers. Victoria Jones, Honour's aunt, had been the writer in the family, the one whom Fleur wanted to take after. There were several copies in the library of Victoria's first novel *Heritage*. That had been based on the story of the Montford family's early years. After that, Victoria had produced nearly a dozen other books. Honour had read them all so often that she knew them almost off by heart.

It was strange that she'd forgotten about the herbal, though. Isabella, Honour's own mother, had compiled it during the early years of the war. There'd been a garden party at Pencombe where contributors had donated money to the church roof fund for the privilege of adding their personal herbal remedy to the collection. It had done nothing since the war years but gather dust, until Lucy rescued it from oblivion. Now proceeds from the sale of copies went into the income of the property. It felt reassuring to have Montford ancestors contributing to the upkeep. Lucy had used that fact as yet another reason for keeping the estate in family ownership.

'Gee!' Fleur's call made Honour start. She'd been daydreaming and hadn't noticed the girl walking up the gravel-lined path towards her. 'Gee, have you seen Dibs? I want to give her these flowers for the dining room, but I can't find her anywhere.'

They were having a celebratory dinner that evening. Fleur's fiancé, Benjy, had finally got planning permission to convert an outlying block of dilapidated farm buildings into housing. He was going to use the money he made to renovate the stableyard close to his home.

'Have you looked in the buttery?' Honour asked. Dibs was the woman from the village who came in to do the cooking. That evening was also to be a trial run of some of the recipes she thought would be suitable for the executive dinners.

'Yes.' Fleur sounded exasperated. 'And the girls there said that she was getting some tarragon for the chicken, so I thought . . .'

'You thought she'd be in the herb garden,' Honour finished for her. She reached out to take the bunch of bluer-than-blue delphiniums that were about to trail on the ground as something else took her grandchild's attention. Fleur was looking intently at a cluster of pink and red hollyhocks at the back of the flower border beside them.

'They're wonderful,' she breathed. 'Just think how they'd look against the stone walls, in a great tall vase between the suits of armour. They'd really look something else.'

'They can be admired for a lot longer if they're left growing in the garden.' Honour handed the girl the envelope she had been carrying. 'I'll go and find Dibs and you can pop into the village with this for me. I want to catch the post, so be a dear and do it now.'

Would the National Trust leave the garden as it was, Honour wondered, or would they find it too labour-consuming? She'd visited several of the gardens that the Trust owned locally and they were all very beautiful, but there was perhaps a certain similarity of style. She stood admiring the hollyhocks that she'd saved from Fleur. The truth was that she would rather not give up her control at Pencombe. One day she would have to, whatever happened, but she still felt very well. With the warmth of the afternoon sun making her body feel supple and ache-free it was easy to imagine that she could go on for years.

Dibs was coming down the path towards her. There was certainly another couple of years before she need make up her mind. Honour gave the delphiniums to the cook and then went on towards the herb garden. She would give a hand serving the short queue of would-be purchasers; she liked talking to the people who took the trouble to come and visit her lovely home. Dibs went back to the buttery and told the girls that she hadn't seen madam looking so sprightly in ages.

Fleur held tightly on to the end of the lead rein; it was a soft, red cotton one that had been bought many years ago when she had ridden a black Shetland pony called Geronimo. The pony had long ago been handed on to another family with small children and now the rein did service as

115

a dog lead. On the end of the rein, Archie, the family's wire-haired fox terrier, lunged despairingly. He was longing to join the other hunt dogs as they were bundled unceremoniously into the Land Rover. Fleur kept calling him to heel, but he was frantic and she might as well have saved her breath.

The hunt met in the pub car park on the south side of the village. Pink-jacketed riders mingled with the humbler black; damson-bloomed chestnut hunters stood shoulder to shoulder with immaculate greys. They were all milling round, the riders downing the stirrup cup dispensed by the white-whiskered publican. The green wellington'd younger element amongst the foot followers were keeping an eager eye out for the expected antis; the inevitable scuffles between the opposing groups could add an extra dimension of excitement to the meet.

The event was a treat anyway, because it was out of season. Today's purpose was to provide film footage for a documentary on hunting. A pair of cameramen and several technicians were working hard at not getting beneath the horses' hooves. The local bobby had taken up a strategic stance beside the phone box, and several small boys with mongrel dogs were clustered round his panda car.

Normally Fleur would have been riding too, but her shoulder was still aching from a fall she'd taken exercising an overexcitable four-year-old gelding, so she'd told Benjy she'd follow on foot. Now, with the sky a soft dove-grey breaking to show an underlying blue, she wished she'd doused herself with embrocation and gone with him.

The fox had come out of a copse, low on the valley side. He was elderly, past his prime, with a shabby, mangy orange coat, but he had all the cunning of his years. He was making for the railway embankment, where there

116

were intermittent patches of dense bramble providing good cover for a couple of miles and, more importantly, there was a network of drains.

Benjy was well ahead of the field, and the cameras. He knew where their quarry was headed. There had been problems on the railway line before. They'd lost a hound the previous year, a good bitch as he remembered. It wasn't going to happen again. He was riding Cavalier, his second horse. Squire had gone lame earlier that morning; the vet would probably be up there now. He stood up in his stirrups, gaining vital height as he surveyed the land.

The hounds had split into two groups and Fred, the whipper-in, was with the leading pack. They were making for the stile leading to the footpath that ran beside the railway fencing for a good hundred yards. For some inexplicable reason there was a low point in the British Rail fence there. The hounds could jump it with ease.

Benjy's immediate concern was for the portion of the pack making for the drains. Any fox worth its salt would know their value – half-flooded, and clogged with a tangle of weeds and barbed wire, they were an escape route for a bone-thin fox, and narrow deathtraps for the wider-boned hounds. Benjy swore as he saw the hounds push their way through a gap in the wire netting and begin streaming up the slope. The safest way for him to get after them was by riding back to where Fred had created a gap in the wire. The fastest way was to jump the five-bar gate that British Rail had put in further up to allow for emergency access to the track. With Squire he wouldn't have thought twice, but Cavalier was still a bit of a novice.

The lead hounds were out of sight, over the top already. Benjy took a wide approach, letting his mount see the obstacle clearly. He sat in deep, jerking the reins to get the horse back on its haunches, building power under the saddle. There were five strides to go, four, three . . . They soared effortlessly over. It was a pity Fleur hadn't seen that, he thought. She was odd about Cavalier, saying he was an unlucky horse; there was some nonsense she'd thought up about the colouring of his eyes. He kept up the impulsion as they breasted the embankment. The hounds were in a gaggle down below him and he pulled sharply on the reins, reminding the horse to watch its speed. It wouldn't do to canter down amongst them.

There was a warren of rabbit holes around them. Benjy muttered under his breath at the size of it. The local farmers had a court action going against BR for not taking reasonable measures to effect control. On some of his own fields, the rabbits were grazing more than the sheep. Cavalier tossed his head irritably. There was a heavy smell of diesel fumes on the air, a glint of sun shone oilily off the metal rails. They began the descent at an angle.

Deep in the drain the fox turned. It was being forced to meet its pursuers face to face – the end of the drain had been blocked. The hounds nosed their way in. There was a tingling sensation in the air, a soft vibration. In the distance a train was coming, making the rails hum like live things.

Cavalier scented the danger. His ears flattened, but Benjy didn't notice. He was watching a signal beside the track as it flicked from yellow to green. He swore out loud a fraction of a second before Cavalier slipped. The tussocky grass tugged around the horse's fetlocks as it scrabbled for a hold on the sliding earth.

The fox leaped forward, teeth flashing, snapping its way to freedom that was no longer even to be glimpsed past the throng of brown and beige bodies blocking out the light. Benjy swayed in the saddle, gripping with his strong calf muscles, using words soft and low, struggling to calm his mount as the train came into sight.

118

There were animals on the line. The driver of the train didn't have to think twice, he reached up and pulled the horn. He was nearly on them. Once, twice, he pulled the lever. Cavalier reared in terror. Benjy pulled at the reins, desperate to keep the horse from tipping over and going under the spinning, clattering wheels. There was a rush of air that man and beast felt as a physical assault. They were falling. Benjy's strength had pulled them away, bending them towards the sandy earth, away from the flashing silver wheels, the prospect of instant death.

The girth snapped under the final assault, and as the saddle began to slip beneath him Benjy clamped his feet under the animal's soft belly, frantically trying to keep his balance. His struggle gained him precious seconds as the final coach of the train thundered past. The new gust of air that hit them made Cavalier squirm like an eel.

Benjy threw up his arms as he fell, twisting frenziedly in the air, trying to avoid the rails. He hit the ground so hard that all the breath in his body was expelled in a shout. He gulped in, striving for precious air at exactly the same time as his neck flicked viciously and his head hit a thick, grease-covered metal bolt. There was a moment of searing emptiness in his lungs, then a vivid, multicoloured, piercing pain, and, finally, darkness.

Chapter 10

*Take away from our hearts that
love of the beautiful and you take
away all the charm of life*
JEAN-JACQUES ROUSSEAU
(1712–1778)

Marie smiled wryly. She was beginning to relax. The superb standard of food and service given by the Savoy, combined with Berry's amusing charm, was working miracles. It was odd that the first thing to bring her peace of mind since the tragic accident at Pencombe was a dinner meeting she hoped would help her business. She had accepted Berry's invitation because she realized he was the lesser of two evils. If he kept to his declared intention to help dispose of some of her sites, he could act as a buffer between her and the bank.

She had to get alongside the financier, she understood that now. The bank was becoming ever more insistent that she dispose of most, if not all, of the high street sites. Truthfully she would like nothing more than to be able, overnight, to get her products into the big stores, preferably on a shop-within-a-shop basis, but failing that, simply on the counters. But there were a lot of market forces working against her and, in the depressed retail market, the fact that her whole product line was a straightforward 'take-off' of other, higher-priced brands, was the biggest drawback of all.

She was able to look genuinely at ease as she replied to her companion's question. 'Damion was never my Monsieur Bergé, never the business brains behind my artistic abilities,' she said firmly.

Berry gestured at a hovering waiter to leave them alone. He took the half-empty bottle of Bollinger from the champagne bucket and topped up Marie's glass himself. 'Perhaps he was more your Mademoiselle de la Falaise, your right hand, your inspiration?'

Marie laughed happily. It was fun to be able to make silly, frivolous conversation with someone who totally understood her references.

'It's as well I know all about the Yves Saint Laurent legend,' Berry continued. He seemed to be able to read her mind, as well as being able to join in with her in-jokes.

'I think you probably know more about him than I do,' Marie said. She indicated the splendour of the room around them, the highly organized bustle of the Riverside Restaurant. 'I can only pop in and out of this kind of environment. I travel a fair bit, and get to France several times a year. But London is my home, my headquarters, and I spend most of my time here in my office. I have the feeling that you're far more the international socialite. After all, you told me you know the great man himself.'

'Know is too personal a word. I "know" Pierre Bergé, and through him I have met the maestro. But I'm not amongst his friends. I think to achieve that status I'd have to have a touch of the artist in my make-up, and that I certainly can't lay claim to.' He tipped the last of the champagne into his own glass. 'We'll have another bottle of the same, I think, so that we can toast your idol. I gather it went very well for him last week.'

'You mean the Paris show?'

Berry caught the eye of a passing waiter and ordered more champagne.

Marie paused until she had Berry's attention again and then continued, 'Yes, I gather it was brilliant. Your friend Monsieur Bergé must have been delighted. I was touched by his saying that when there is no longer an Yves Saint Laurent the couture house will close.'

'It was also a nice opportunity for him to make disparaging remarks about some of his competitors. What was it he said? Something like, "Look at Chanel without Mademoiselle Chanel, and Dior without Christian Dior. It is more than a nonsense. It has no integrity. It is a sham." I tried to remember the quote exactly. I thought you'd appreciate the cleverness of it.'

'How nice of you to be thinking of me in Paris.' Marie laughed. 'I would have thought you had someone with you to take your mind off business.'

'Yes, I had someone with me.' Berry suddenly looked serious. He reached over the table and laid his hand gently over Marie's. 'But that didn't take my mind off you.'

'Berry.' Marie slowly pulled her hand away. She had absolutely no intention of allowing the relationship to develop into an intimate one. 'I think you should know how I feel. I have a rule – a golden rule – never to mix business with pleasure. I broke it once, a couple of years ago, and things have gone very wrong. It just proved how right I'd been to begin with. I can't do business with you and become personally involved.'

'That's easy.' Berry laughed although his eyes had become cold. 'We'll just give up the business side of our relationship tomorrow. No, let me rephrase that, we'll give it up tonight. Timing in these things is of the essence. More champagne?'

Marie shook her head. 'No, thank you. I think I've had more than enough already. You still haven't said what we're celebrating.'

'No, I haven't, have I. And now I'm not going to. It was strictly business. I'll play by your rules.' He reached out and took her hand again. This time so firmly that she couldn't remove it from his grip.

Marie felt the colour rise to her cheeks. She didn't like to feel trapped. 'It has to be business between us – you know that. The bank made it more than clear that you're to be involved in Body Beautiful. A little flirting has been fun, but that's all it has been. Please don't make things more difficult than they already are.'

'I don't take no for an answer. You can find that out from anybody I've worked with in the past. We're very much alike, you and I, in that we can get a lot of the thrills and spills of the chase from our working lives, but there comes a time when work stops. I want you.' His grip tightened. 'I've tried the traditional English gentleman's way – nice food, nice wine and a nice line in chat. If that's not how you want to play then it's all right with me. But make no mistake, Marie, we belong together, in the boardroom and in bed.'

'I'm not an asset.' Marie pulled her hand free. She felt choked by her anger. 'You can't strip me like some company you've taken over.'

The smile touched Berry's mouth but not his eyes. 'What a clever pun to produce under pressure. But then you are clever, aren't you? That's a great part of your appeal.'

'I'm so pleased to hear it.' Marie stood abruptly. 'Because it's my cleverness that you'll be dealing with. I shall ask a representative of the bank to be in on our next meeting. I think they should see what, if anything, they are getting for their money. Because you are being paid a retainer, aren't you? As well as the percentage of whatever property deals you fix up for my company. I do so hope this meal gets covered by the expenses they give you. I wouldn't like to think you'll have to pay for it out of your own pocket. Especially since you won't get what you so clearly expected out of it.' She left Berry sitting at the table.

Walking swiftly between the tables of chattering, elegant diners, she went out towards the wide green-carpeted stairway that led down to the rear exit of the hotel. Two men in white dinner jackets were paying off a taxi. She waited on the pavement until they had finished and then, ignoring their studied attentiveness as they opened the door for her, stepped into the dark interior of the cab. She could feel hot tears ruining her make-up. The driver had to query the address she gave him twice. She could hardly speak; she had never felt so humiliated, never.

'Give us a smile, luv. Go on, show us some teeth,' the photographer shouted.

From his vantage point, balanced on a three-foot-high ornate cast-iron litter bin, he was way above the other twenty or so camera-decked members of the press assembled on the Thames Embankment. The traffic beside them had slowed to a crawl as fascinated drivers craned their necks to get a view of Marie posing on the car roof. Beneath her elegantly high-heeled feet, a mirror-polished white stretch Jaguar, the latest cult vehicle, attracted almost as much attention as she did.

Marie's cheeks were aching. The smile she had fixed on for the photographers felt like a grimace. They'd only been about a quarter of an hour taking shots, but it felt like for ever. Sarah had achieved a spectacular turnout for her first photocall, and the weather had also obliged by being brilliant.

'Over here, Marie, over here,' they were all calling to her, each wanting an exclusive, special shot.

Her legs were trembling with the effort of balancing on the shiny surface. If she fell off, as she thought she might, they'd be delighted. A short sharp breeze from the river

124

beside them blew open the wrap-round skirt of her navy suit to expose a thigh clad in five-denier porcelain lycra. The cameras clicked like an orgy of crickets.

'Three more minutes,' Sarah called out from her position by the stone wall that kept pedestrians from falling in the river.

Body Beautiful's new PR director looked ice-cool in a mint-green skin-tight dress that owed much of its inspiration to a cheong sam. Many of the photographers began winding up, removing lenses and filters. A young man Marie recognized as a trade journal photographer stepped forward. He'd been biding his time.

'Nice smile, please,' he asked, and received just what he wanted. 'Nice. Now just tip your head down a bit, chin in. Nice.' He wound on and took a couple more shots then politely thanked Marie.

'You can get down now,' Sarah called.

It was going to be easier said than done. In the excitement of clambering up on to the car, she hadn't had too much of a problem, except trying not to show her underwear. This bit, however, was going to be tricky. She bent slowly and slipped off her shoes. The *Sun* journalist surreptitiously reloaded his Nikon.

The dove-grey-suited hired chauffeur who had come with the limo looked about eighteen years old and lacking in any sort of initiative. He stood a good six feet back from the side of the car and watched as Marie slowly edged her way forward. As her feet touched the chrome rim running around the top of the windscreen he called out:

'My boss ain't gonna like it if you muck up the wipers.'

Marie glanced over at him. The river was glinting, and a group of Japanese tourists clustered at the entrance to the river boat where she had earlier given her prepared press release on the new Sunkissed range. Her toes felt the slipperiness of the glass.

She looked over at Sarah. Why on earth didn't she do something? Angelique and the other helpers had gone back to the office the minute the photocall had started. Someone had to give Marie a hand down, but she didn't feel like asking for help in front of the still assembled press.

'Here.' The young man who'd asked so nicely for his photo came forward, holding his hands up. 'Hang on to me.'

Marie reached towards him. Her legs were trembling in earnest now. The *Sun* photographer had come up close behind her would-be gallant. Her hands clutched convulsively as she started to slide. With a small cry she launched herself off the roof of the car towards the pavement. She caught the sensation-seeker from the tabloids with the point of her elbow. His camera flew sideways and out of his hands, the woven strap around his neck almost throttled him and he swore fluently.

There was an ominous tearing sound as Marie landed, but a quick check didn't show any damage to her skirt. She smiled as she straightened up. The soles of her feet hurt from hitting the pavement. Her knees had jarred painfully, but her dignity was still intact. She turned and retrieved her shoes from the roof of the car and slipped them on.

'Thank you, boys!' she called out.

She walked slowly back along the covered gangway to the dining salon she'd booked for the morning. Only in its deserted calm did she rub hard at her elbow. The initial numbness had worn off, and it was throbbing from the collision with the photographer. She heard the clatter of high heels as Sarah approached and turned to await

126

her. An expression of fury replaced the smile she'd worked hard for so long to keep.

'I don't care what you say, it was still worth a try.' Sarah pouted at her reflection in the mirror, then slowly and carefully applied Estée Lauder's most vivid red lipstick in a perfect outline.

Marie was still furious. She glared at the image in the opulent plate-glass behind the marbled basins provided by the management of the Residence, London's latest in venue.

'You should have told me what you were up to,' she said. 'I might have broken my leg jumping off that damned car.'

'But you didn't. And if you hadn't knocked the camera out of that guy's hands we'd be looking for a front-page shot of you tomorrow.'

'A front-page shot of my Janet Regers, you mean.'

'Just be glad you were wearing some. That reminds me.' Sarah turned quickly away from the mirror. They were alone in the powder room. 'Be an angel and go and lean against the door.' She was pulling her skirt up, wriggling to ease the tightness of it over her hips.

Marie looked away in embarrassment at the sudden exposure of nakedness. Sarah was running hot and cold water into a basin. She reached out for a miniature pearl-shaped soap and rubbed it quickly into a lather between her hands, then she spread her feet wide apart and began lathering the short crinkly hair that proved she was a natural blonde.

'Jesus, that stings,' she said.

'Why on earth are you . . .?' Marie couldn't think of the words to finish her question. She'd thought that nothing Sarah could do would have the power to surprise her, but she was wrong.

127

'Going out on the town.' Sarah's voice came out in gasps as she splashed cool water on to the glistening hairs. 'Always remember the Girl Guides' motto, Marie, and be prepared. I've got an idea, or let's just say, a hope, that my date might be a tongue man.'

As Marie made a face expressing her disgust, Sarah shook her hips, spraying droplets of water around the room.

As Sarah looked vainly for a towel, Marie suddenly laughed convulsively. 'Now this I've got to see,' she spluttered.

Unexpectedly, the door behind Marie opened a fraction, stopping abruptly when it hit an obstruction. Marie leaned back and it closed again.

'Won't be a minute,' she called out.

Sarah directed the hot-air dryer downwards and stood on tiptoe in front of it. With a giggle she pressed the button to turn it on. Hot air blew on her belly button. She stretched higher on her toes and felt the air just where she wanted it. 'Mm, that's nice,' she murmured, and tipped her head back in a parody of ecstasy.

'Don't be revolting.' Marie laughed. It wasn't sordid, though, she thought. Sarah was so without shame it was funny.

'True feminism,' Sarah said as she rubbed the palm of her hand briskly over the springing hairs to help them dry, 'is a state of mind. Independence is what it's all about. No man is going to tell me what to do. At least . . .' She paused and smiled at the thought. 'Not unless he's imaginative enough to come up with some variation even I haven't tried yet.'

They went back into the kelim-strewn bar together. Berry was waiting. He was holding flowers, a bouquet of white roses. Marie began to smile. She'd not been looking

128

forward to going home alone after such an enervating day.

After her upset at the Savoy she'd come to understand that it had been her fault, she'd handled it badly, been too overwrought to start with. She welcomed the chance to get back on speaking terms with Berry. For once she wouldn't tell Angelique off for telling the man she so approved of where to find her boss. Marie let him kiss her on the cheek and then watched as he greeted Sarah in the same way.

'Can I get you a drink, Marie?' Berry glanced almost imperceptibly at his watch. 'We've got time before the ballet.'

Marie felt momentarily disconcerted. She was still wearing the severely businesslike suit that she'd chosen for the press conference; it wasn't what she would have chosen to wear to the ballet. Sarah's dress was more suitable for that.

'What did you say we were going to see?' Sarah was looking up at Berry, her head tilted to one side, every inch the attentive female.

There was a moment's awkward silence and then Marie heard herself say, 'No, no, I won't have a drink, thanks. I've still got a lot of paperwork to clear off my desk.' She left the restaurant in a daze.

All Sarah's preparation – she had a vivid visual memory of her standing in front of the basins, shaking her hips, sending the water flying. The things she'd said – she'd been talking about Berry. Sickness was sour at the back of Marie's throat, and she wanted to vomit. The bitter taste of bile flooded her mouth. And she would have gone with him. She had the sudden, awful realization that she would have spent the evening, probably even the night, with him, if he'd asked.

She flagged a passing taxi aggressively. 'Bastard,' she

muttered. 'Rotten bastard.' She flopped down on to the shiny leather seat. Her suit would crease, but it didn't matter. Her breathing was loud, as if she'd been running. Her jaws were clamped tight and she was trembling with rage.

Trembling.

The word reminded her of the way she'd felt on the roof of the car. Sarah had thought they would get better coverage if the elegantly dressed Ms Sullivan could be photographed slipping and sliding off the extrovert's Jaguar. It was ridiculous. Sarah's view was that Marie's image had become a bit too perfect. To appeal to the woman – and man – on the street she had to appear more approachable. Showing her knickers to the press would certainly have made her that.

Covent Garden had never seemed more a place for lovers. The soft evening light made pools of shadows that were populated with clinging, whispering figures.

Tears of anger stung Marie's eyes as she hurried upstairs to her door. The flat was empty, silent. Two red lights glowed on her answerphone but she ignored them. Going straight to the fridge, she took out chilled vodka and a half-bottle of tonic. She poured a generous measure of spirit into a tall, straight-sided glass. She paused for a moment and then slopped in some more. There were no bubbles in the glass as she poured the tonic. The drink tasted flat and lifeless. It also made her feel sick again.

She turned on the television, hopped all four channels and then tried cable. There were game shows, movies, nothing that interested her. But she couldn't bear the thought of silence. Eventually she left it tuned to a sports channel. The mindless drone of sports cars chasing each other round and round a sun-scorched track lulled her almost as much as the effect of the drink.

*　*　*

Sarah tilted her head provocatively. 'But I know all about little boys at school. I'm sure you must have done it sometime or other.'

Berry laid down his knife and fork and waited until the wine waiter had reverently filled his glass to within half an inch of the rim and then departed.

He took one sip, and answered, 'It seems to excite you, the fact that I might have, as you so coyly put it, "experimented" with members of the same sex. I hate to disappoint you, but no, I didn't – not ever.'

'I love the way you say "members".' Sarah's voice was deliberately breathy, but the expression in her eyes showed she was simply winding him up.

'Are all convent girls as wicked as you?' he asked.

'Certainly, just the same as all public-school boys are suppressed homosexuals.'

'Touché!' Berry laughed and ran the tip of his forefinger over the back of her elegantly manicured hand as it lay on the table top between them. 'You're a maniac, you know that, don't you? I thought the maître d' wasn't going to let us in to begin with. I know it's top fashion what you're wearing but . . .'

'You think he hadn't ever seen a tit before?' Sarah looked down at her wide-open cleavage in feigned amazement. 'It's not all that shocking. I mean, it's only one of them at a time, and it only escapes if I move my shoulders.' She shrugged experimentally and one perfect browny-pink nipple slipped into full view.

'Your dress looked quite innocent when we first met this evening, I think you must have lost a button during the ballet. And you're putting me off my food. I'm not giving this the attention it deserves.' He pushed the wafer-thin slivers of duck breast around on his plate and the blood-red juices merged with the coulis of blackberries.

Sarah began eating calmly and methodically. 'Just you

tuck that beautiful protein away inside you, my sweet. You're going to need all your energy tonight. You wouldn't want to disappoint a lady, would you?'

At Sarah's request they went back to Berry's flat. She said that it was too early in their relationship for her to invite him into her 'sanctum', as she called her home. But it was really because she would have to get a firm of cleaners in before she asked him back. There was a specialist company called Skivvies who would tidy up her chaos, bring the Colefax and Fowler luxury back to its former glory. If things progressed happily, she'd give them a ring.

'You have a beautiful home,' she murmured, her lips close to his, her breath, sweet with their final cognac, touching him like an arousing caress.

'It's dark, you can't even see it.' He'd closed the door behind them as she put her arms around him, holding him so closely, guiding his hands down the hard, slim outline of her body, and there had been no time to turn on lights.

'I can tell by the smell.' She had her lips close to his ear. Her tongue flicked quickly, sending stabs of longing.

He wanted to touch her breasts, to fondle what had been turning him on all evening, but she knew that, and turned and twisted in his grip, moving her pelvis against his growing hardness, but always keeping her breasts beyond his reach. It was driving him crazy.

'Come on, big boy. My, you're beautiful, really beautiful.' Her words were muffled, but her hands were active. She was feeling the size of him, making him grow until it was a physical pain – the restraint of his clothes and the pressure of her pubic bone against him as she moved in a rhythm that made his breathing loud and all sense of time and place disappear.

'Now,' she cried.

Her hands were in his hair, pushing him down until his mouth closed on the hardness of her nipple. She was moaning, striving against him. For an instant he couldn't breathe, and it heightened his desire. He was gasping for air as he fumbled with his belt. She stumbled back against the door, pulling at her skirt so that he could touch her, feel how hot she was, how ready for him.

He entered her standing up. She was on tiptoe as he thrust backwards and forwards, and instantly she was at the edge of release. She dug her fingers into his back, urging him, goading him into furious activity. They climaxed together, his savage roar of achievement mingling with her cries.

'That was very nice.' Sarah sat demurely on the beige suede sofa. She had tightened the top of her outfit so that it seemed no more than a moderate décolletée.

'Nice?' Berry almost choked on the word as he put down the tray laden with coffee percolator, cups, cream and sugar. 'I can think of a lot of words to describe what happened between us a short while ago, but I don't think "nice" even comes into it.'

'It will get better.' Sarah leaned forward, her face hidden from him as she busied herself pouring the coffee.

Berry silently shook his head. She'd been explosive, literally screaming with passion. Now she seemed like a different person.

'Cream?' she asked. 'Sugar?'

They sat in a silence that neither of them would have described as companionable.

Eventually Berry said, 'Do you have a boyfriend – someone regular?'

'No.' Sarah shook her head emphatically. 'I don't believe in making a habit of anything. Been there, seen it, done it. That's my motto. I'm a very self-contained person. Sex is for . . .' She paused for a moment and then finished, 'I was going to say for fun, but it's more serious than that. Sex is for real. It's the only time I get down to what I am, that I'm not acting. I wouldn't fake it for anyone, and that's what having a "regular" would require.'

'You don't think that within a loving, caring relationship you wouldn't find you'd have to fake anything?' Berry thought, as he asked it, that his question sounded stuffy, but he was disconcerted by her attitude.

'No, I know I would. I don't like hurting someone I'm fond of. It's easier with strangers.'

'I'm a stranger?' Berry's voice registered astonishment. They had only met a few times, perhaps, but they'd spent several hours together that evening before eventually making love. He had felt they were becoming close, that they were at the start of a relationship that could mean a lot. He felt used. It was the first time in his life he'd ever felt that.

'You don't know much about the beauty business, do you.' Sarah stated it as a fact, not a question. 'There are a lot of women in it who have the same outlook on life as me – and a lot of men. We work all day extolling the perfect face, the exquisite body. We're in the marketplace of sex. A beautiful breast, a smooth, silky buttock – girls can make good money with assets like that. The punters look at their pictures, and for a moment imagine it's theirs to fondle. Sex is sensation, it's pleasurable, an extension of what we're spending our lives selling; only an idiot isn't going to get their fair share.'

'Does Marie believe that?' Berry's face showed his disbelief.

'Thanks for the coffee.' Sarah ignored the question, and put her empty cup back on the tray and stood up. 'I'll get a cab back. Your doorman can hail one for me – don't

134

bother about coming down.' She leaned forward and kissed him on the cheek. It was an empty gesture, more social than emotional.

'Nice?' Berry repeated the word. He suddenly felt lonely. He was aware of the silence of the surrounding flats, the hollowness of the building, the void of the night. He wasn't tired, he wasn't elated, he wasn't feeling any of the emotions he normally experienced after sex.

Sarah smiled suddenly, it was like an echo of how she'd been earlier, when they had been so much more at ease together. 'Well, it was more than nice. And since we're still strangers we can look forward to it being more than nice again, and again. Until we get close to being friends, and then it will have to stop. It's just as long as you know the ground rules, Berry. That way neither of us gets hurt.'

When she'd gone, he cleared up the coffee things and thought about going to bed, only he wasn't tired. He loosened his tie. Something had made him put it back on afterwards.

Afterwards . . . The word stayed with him. There wasn't even a rumpled bed to show where she'd been. He walked over to the computer and flicked on the power. The hum of the machine filled the silence, green letters flashed across the dark screen. He sat down and began touching the keys, his mind switching into gear. It was as if the evening had never been.

Chapter 11

What ills from beauty spring
SAMUEL JOHNSON (1709–1784)

Spent grains of coffee floated slowly downwards in the thick brown liquid beneath the steel mesh disk.

Marie stared intently at the cafetiere in front of her on the kitchen table, resting her chin on her hands. Her head was going to burst. She was aware of the brain in her head as a soft painful lump colliding at every possible opportunity with the inside of her skull. Three aspirins had done nothing to dull its effect. She blinked slowly and carefully, and another spasm of pain shot through her temples. Her lips were dry, the taste in her mouth a mixture of too much peppermint toothpaste and too much hangover. It couldn't get any worse, the coffee would have to make an improvement.

The telephone rang shrilly, creating more waves of pain. One, two, three rings and then the answerphone cut in. It was Sarah again, her voice unnaturally high through the loudspeaker. She left the same message as she had every hour, on the hour, since eight o'clock. A far-off clock struck midday.

So, Sarah said she had something important to tell her. So, Sarah said she was convinced that Marie was at home, listening to her leaving messages. There would be no danger of her coming round to check her suspicions, Marie knew. She would be tucked up, nice and cosy, in bed with Berry.

Marie concentrated once more on the activity in the

coffee pot. It would require a great effort of will for her to press down the plunger, pick up the glass jug and pour.

The banging on the front door of the flat woke her. Her shoulders were painfully stiff, her neck had been twisted uncomfortably as she'd slumped forwards on her folded arms. The coffee in the jug in front of her looked lifeless, a cold bitter brown. There was a flurry of knocks on the door; someone was determined to attract her attention. She blinked a couple of times, and then ran the back of her hand over her mouth. She felt awful, in need of a bath.

'I knew you were here.' Sarah swept past Marie and into the living room. 'Christ, this place smells like a brewery.'

She walked quickly over to the windows, opening them wide and letting hot, diesel-fumed air in.

'It's Saturday,' Marie complained.

'That's never stopped you calling me into the office. You haven't changed your clothes since yesterday.'

Sarah stood, hands on hips, looking, Marie thought, disgustingly fit. She was wearing tight denims and a long, loose white shirt. Her blonde hair was fluffy, newly washed, her cheeks glowed with health.

'Coffee?' Marie gestured vaguely towards the kitchen.

She couldn't pull her thoughts together. It was ages since she'd had too much to drink. She couldn't actually remember ever having had a hangover on her own before.

As if reading her thoughts Sarah said, 'Drinking alone is the one vice I don't allow myself.'

The word 'vice' triggered a sudden memory of the way Sarah had looked at Berry. It sobered Marie more quickly than any coffee.

'I'm surprised to see you,' she said acidly.

'You needn't worry, I didn't stay over and have break-fast with lover boy.'

Sarah went through to the kitchen. She put the dregs of vodka back into the fridge, the empty tonic bottle in the flip-top bin.

The sound and smell of fresh coffee grinding inspired Marie to follow her through.

'You're too hung-up about sex.' Sarah began laying a tray with side plates, cups and saucers, some bread and cheese. 'It's probably your Catholic upbringing. You could have gone one way or the other, of course. A lot of ex-convent girls end up on the game.'

'You never told me you went to a convent.'

'Naughty, naughty.' Sarah picked up the tray and carried it into the living room. Marie followed. 'Now, go and get out of that revoltingly creased suit and have a shower while this coffee draws. You might feel human then, and hopefully look it.'

They talked business over lunch. Sarah had brought the press cuttings they'd achieved from the press conference. It wasn't a bad result. The *Express*, as promised, had a picture. The caption just touched on the fact that the occasion of Marie Sullivan showing off the new Jaguar was a product launch of her own. The *Mail* hadn't done anything yet, but they might pick up something next week, Sarah said, but without much hope in her voice. The *Mirror* had a picture that showed a lot of leg and the caption *Sunkissed chairman says sunbathing's just the ticket*. It took Sarah to point out the superimposed parking meter at the side of the Jag before Marie worked it out. The late edition of Friday's *Evening Standard* had the best picture. Marie was looking straight into the camera, her smile natural and relaxed.

'That was taken by the guy who helped you down off the car,' Sarah said. 'I thought it would be good so I contacted a pal at the *Standard*.'

'But . . .'

'But you were using up my time giving me a bollocking afterwards? You'd be surprised how effective I can be, Marie, even with you scratching my eyes out. Which brings me right back to my reason for dragging you out of your vale of despond. Lover boy's all yours, sweetie. I don't like screwing with someone whose mind's only half on the job. And don't look at me like that. We're all grown-ups here. Didn't your little Irish boyfriends ever go off and have a snog in the bushes with one of your friends? I bet you didn't hold it against him for ever and ever.'

'That's not the same.'

'Of course it's the same. I'm single, you're single, Berry's single. What do you think I'm going to do if he takes me out for a good time – give him a peck on the cheek at my front door?'

Sarah was tempted to go further, to put Marie out of her misery by saying that Berry had asked about Marie's views on sex – after making love to Sarah – and she had the feeling she'd just been a surrogate. But she wasn't that much of a goodie-two-shoes. In any case, she wasn't sure yet if Marie was right for Berry or vice versa, and in her strange way she was becoming fond of them both.

'Ms Rendle,' Angelique announced.

She stepped aside to let the journalist in the navy pinstripe trouser suit walk into Marie's office. Over the visitor's sharply sculptured shoulder she made a face at her employer. Ms Rendle was a number one bitch. Angelique could sniff them out a mile off.

'Please, take a seat over there.' Marie indicated the informal group of cream upholstered chairs close to the window. 'I won't keep you a minute.'

She skipped through the last few paragraphs of the letter Angelique had just typed. It was to be delivered by special messenger. She signed it, put it into an already addressed envelope and then stood up. Smiling briefly at her visitor, she walked over to the door and walked into reception to put the letter in the out tray.

'Sorry.' Marie stepped back into her office and closed the door behind her. 'Would you like a coffee?'

'I don't drink coffee.' Ms Rendle's voice was low, flat and very American.

The journalist looked thirty something. Her square face and Slavonic cheekbones were accentuated by her hair. Baby-blonde, it was severely cut in an ultra-short bob.

'Tea, or something cold?' Marie smiled.

She was beginning to sound like a waitress in a fast-food restaurant. Any minute now she'd be saying 'Have a nice day!'

'Since we're already five minutes late' – the journalist looked down at her large, round-faced watch as she spoke – 'I think we should get right on with the interview. As I said on the phone, I'm doing a piece for *Vogue*. Information I obtain from you may well also end up in *Harpers & Queen*, and several other publications. I'll take notes as we speak, but I would also like to make it clear that I have a recording device in my bag.'

Marie watched the woman gesture at the efficient-looking black leather grip she carried. Everything she said had been delivered in the same monotone. Not a trace of expression touched her skilfully under-made-up face.

'I understand,' Marie said and sat down.

The emotionlessly delivered introductory paragraphs may have been the journalist's stock in trade, but they had sounded ominous.

'This new range of sun creams you've brought out . . .'

'You're referring to Sunkissed?'

'Yes.' Ms Rendle paused for a moment, apparently struck by a new idea. 'The name is rather misleading,

140

wouldn't you agree? *Sunkissed*. I don't think by any stretch of the imagination the sun could be said to "kiss". Modern research proves conclusively that the sun's rays are harmful, you might go as far as to say deadly.'

Marie said slowly and carefully, 'The name Sunkissed was chosen to reflect the appearance of how we believe healthy skin looks after our products have been used in the sun. They are very effective. We have a full range, right up to a total sun-block lotion with a protection factor of twenty-four.'

'Protection factor.' The journalist stared down at her pad as she scribbled a few hieroglyphics. 'And what exactly is that protection factor a measure of, Ms Sullivan?'

'If you are the experienced fashion and beauty journalist that you represented yourself as on the telephone, Ms Rendle, I'm sure you're just as well aware what they are as I am. But just for the record, the factors are calculated on a cream's ability to delay reddening of the skin in strong sunlight.'

'I wanted to make sure that we're talking the same language. So I am quite correct in saying that your creams offer some protection against ultraviolet B – that is, UVB. Those are the rays that make the skin turn red. It is that very reddening that has acted as a limiting factor to sunbathers in the past. You are agreeing with what I say, aren't you, Ms Sullivan?'

'Yes, but if you'll . . .' Marie could feel herself being backed in to a corner.

'If you will just let me finish my line of questioning. I mean, this is an interview that you want to give? Just tell me if you want to call it a day here and now.'

Marie slowly shook her head. The device in the woman's handbag was recording everything. If she threw the journalist out now she would be on a hiding to nothing.

'So, let's recap, shall we? Anyone who uses your Sunkissed range of products can sit out in the strongest midday sun for several hours without apparent discomfort.'

'Depending on the factor they use, it is certainly possible to enjoy quite intense sunlight without burning.'

'And you have a product that you label as suitable for children, I believe. Including babies, I seem to remember.'

'One of our sun-block products – a soothing lotion – is specially prepared to be used on quite small children, yes. We do have a warning on the container that all children should have their heads covered in strong sun.'

'So, in this idyllic world that you would like us to believe in, young mothers and babies can safely cavort on pale golden sands whilst tanning themselves to a deep bronze. In fact, you are encouraging mothers to let their children and babies out in intense sunlight that they themselves would never have been exposed to when young. Cigarette packets have to carry government warnings. I'm surprised that these so-called sun-care products don't. Would you agree to that, Ms Sullivan, if you were asked to? Would you print a health warning on every bottle of your Sunkissed range?'

'I think you should come to the point. I agreed to meet you to discuss Body Beautiful's latest product range. This isn't a discussion.' Marie wanted to go on, to say this is a hatchet job, but just in time she remembered the tape recorder. 'What exactly is this interview meant to achieve?'

'Do you know that in Norway skin cancer is the commonest cancer in women aged between twenty-five and thirty-four? Do you know that between one thousand

142

and two thousand Britons die of skin cancer every year? Please, answer yes or no – these questions aren't just rhetorical. Do you know that twenty-two-year-olds are coming into skin clinics with malignant melanomas – which are killing cancers.'

'UVB is the radiation associated with skin cancer. As I have already said, the protection factors are based on the reddening ability of ultra-violet B.'

The journalist smiled for the first time. She had gained the very quote she was looking for.

'That theory is years out of date,' she said smugly. 'You can't really expect me to believe that you seriously support it. You're just talking commercially.'

'Our sun products are on a par with many other market leaders – Piz Buin, for example. Our buyers know that they are getting the same high-quality creams and lotions at half the price of other name brands.'

'I find it very interesting that Piz Buin is the example you have picked. Their factor twenty-four, billed as a total sun block, has only a factor four protection against ultraviolet A. It's UVA that does not reveal itself by burning. We have no real idea of how deadly it may be, but we do know it's what gives life-long sunbathers that lined and sagging look; those glitzy rhino hides.'

'Tell that to Joan Collins. She's got the best skin of any woman her age, and she's a devout sun worshipper.'

The look on the journalist's face showed just what she thought of Joan Collins, and it wouldn't have been printable in *Vogue*.

'Ms Sullivan, I am as well aware as you are that Britain's sun-screen industry alone is worth sixty-five million pounds a year.'

'If you are trying to imply that I would do anything to make money, including risking the lives of people who buy my products, then you couldn't be more wrong. All that we have done is to produce a range of skin-care products that, used according to the instructions on the package, can help almost anyone to get an attractive tan. And, whatever you think, millions of people want to look tanned. There will inevitably be some people who stay out in the sun for far too long, and there I believe our products can minimize the self-inflicted damage. We also produce an emergency cooling gel. We don't lay any written claim to this but in many cases it can avoid serious burning, even after quite severe over-exposure.'

'I find it interesting that your first excuse, that you're just doing what the others are, is just the excuse that was used at Nuremberg. And as for the rest of what you've been saying, well, it's just so much garbage, isn't it?'

Marie stood. 'I'm not going to give you the satisfaction of throwing you out of my office. But neither am I going to give you any more of my time. There is a press release pack for Sunkissed available in reception.'

The journalist opened her bag to put away her note pad.

The soft hissing of the recorder sounded quite loud in the silence. She was pleased with the interview. Mark Moorman had inspired her to have a crack at the head of Body Beautiful; he'd said it was imperative for the company that their new sun range was a success. And he'd explained to her that it, like almost all the other similar ranges on the market, was vulnerable to attack. He'd been right. Just as he'd been right to stress the Sunkissed baby-care product – she'd get some good column inches out of that.

When Marie was once again alone in her office, she went back to her desk. From a thin, red file she extracted a single sheet of paper. It was a photocopy of a letter Marie had torn out of a newspaper, from Dr Jack Ferguson of the consumer products division at Boots

Pharmaceuticals, and it contained several numbered paragraphs. One had been ringed in Day-Glo. Marie reread it slowly.

> Sunbathers using mainly UVB sunscreens can expose themselves to massive doses of UVA radiation, much greater than would normally be expected with unprotected skin. This could be up to twenty-five times the normal UVA exposure, depending on the protection factor and the sunscreen ingredients used.

The journalist's timing had been impeccable.

Marie had drafted an open letter that detailed the advances that her own company's research facility had made and the levels of UVA protection her products would contain next year. She'd wanted to release it to the press, but Sarah had advised against it.

Dr Ferguson's remarks and the list of effective UVA protectants would soon be public knowledge. So far, all of the information about the industry's next year's products was strictly confidential. That was the basis on which several of the companies sharing the largest slice of the sunscreen market were cooperating on UVA research.

A few months ago, left to her own devices, Marie would have acted on her intuition and revealed everything. But she could no longer behave so impulsively. If her new range was to get into Boots and the other important high-street outlets, she was going to have to take a more moderate line.

If the market leaders felt that revealing how much attention they were paying to research would mean admitting their doubts about their present products, journalists like Ms Rendle were going to get a lot of column inches.

* * *

'I thought I'd got up early this morning.' Marie laughed. 'But this is what I call dedication to duty.'

'I couldn't sleep.' Fleur looked up from the pink and white flower arrangement she was working on. 'Every time I started to drift off I'd think of everything that has to be done this morning.'

It wasn't the whole truth; since Benjy's accident she'd been desperate to keep busy. It was the only way to stop thoughts running on and on.

The chill of the stone buttery floor began to penetrate Marie's thin-soled shoes. She shivered and pulled her navy cardigan closer around her shoulders. She was wearing a cotton dress which would have been warm enough in the main part of the house, but where the thick stone walls of Pencombe hadn't been Victorianized with plaster the atmosphere was damp and chill.

'At least you're dressed for the part,' she said.

Fleur was wearing an old pair of denims and a big baggy scarlet jumper. She had thick red-and-white socks and trainers on her feet.

Trestle tables had been put up along two adjacent walls, and a further square made up of four tables stood in the centre. Marie thought that at least they would have plenty of room to work. It was a strange way for her to spend a Sunday, helping out with one of the executive lunches, but as they said, a change was as good as a rest.

Several buckets of multicoloured dahlias were ranged under the table Fleur was working on. She had pushed a litter of leaves and stalks to one side to give her room to concentrate on a domed centrepiece, which was almost finished. Half a dozen other similar arrangements lay on the table beside her.

'You must have been in here for hours. Would you like a coffee or something?'

Fleur nodded. She couldn't speak because she had put

146

a bunch of wire flower pins between her teeth. It was only now she had almost completed the table centrepieces that she had established a satisfactory method.

The small scullery off the buttery had flaking white-washed walls and a scrubbed wooden drainer beside a chipped butler's sink. It also had an electric kettle, several assorted elderly mugs, and a jar of instant coffee. Marie stamped her feet as the kettle began to hiss. She was actually looking forward to the day. It would be totally unlike anything she had ever done before. She would have no time to worry about her own problems.

Honour joined them as they were finishing their coffee. She was dressed in a blue and pink Liberty print day dress, her hair immaculately pinned up in a French pleat.

'Your arrangements are lovely, Fleur.' She sounded very matter-of-fact. There was no surprise in her voice at how long her granddaughter must have been working, although it was still only twenty to eight. 'The pair of metal torchères will need some tall flowers. I think I'll go and cut some gladioli, and ivy would work well, it can curl down the stem.' Her voice drifted away as she picked up a pair of white-handled secateurs from the table. 'You have finished with these, haven't you?' She didn't wait for an answer but walked out of the room, leaving a faint scent of eau-de-cologne and talcum powder.

Fleur began to giggle. 'It's all right, Granny, I didn't mind getting up at four in the morning to do the flowers, honestly.' She spluttered with laughter.

Marie quickly shook her head. She'd heard Honour's footsteps stop. They stood silently, guiltily, until the sound of feet on the stone flags started up again.

'I'll help you finish these.' Marie picked up several dahlias and began snapping their stalks short so that they would fix firmly into the oasis balls that Fleur had already put into low white plastic bowls. Several earwigs fell out of the flowers and ran across the table top.

'God, I hate those little buggers,' Fleur said feelingly. 'One of them got inside my jumper earlier, and they bite, you know. You should have seen me jumping up and down trying to get it out.'

A man's voice surprised them. 'I would have liked to see that.' They hadn't heard Benjy's approach. He wheeled his chair swiftly towards them, manoeuvring around the trestle tables with ease. He glanced at their empty cups. 'Like a fresh cup of coffee?'

'And fried eggs and bacon.' Marie grinned. 'With fried bread and tomatoes.'

'A spoonful or so of baked beans,' Fleur added. 'Followed by lots of hot toast and butter and thick-cut marmalade. But in the meantime.' She bent swiftly and kissed Benjy on his cheek. 'Black instant coffee out of a chipped mug would be heaven.'

The chef arrived at ten. He was over six feet tall, well built and spoke with a strong Scottish accent.

'So, Robert.' Honour put her glasses on. Then she sat down behind her desk so that she could read the letter of introduction that the man had brought with him. 'The agency tells me you have worked at Claridge's and Gleneagles.'

'That's correct, madam.'

'It seems we're very lucky to have you to cook for us today. Do you enjoy catering for this kind of event?'

'I certainly enjoy the opportunity to visit such a beautiful home as you have here, madam. But to tell the truth, I'll feel a lot happier when I've seen where I've to cook. I have my own knives with me, of course, and my whites, but not much else. I'll be using your equipment – the agency did make that clear, I hope.'

'Yes, that was all made perfectly clear. We do have a facility for catering for the public already. You can use that if you'd prefer it to the buttery. As it's a Sunday the girls won't have much to do in it until later. You can leave your jacket here and we'll go down there now.'

Robert MacKenzie followed Honour as she had requested. He stayed what he seemed to think was a required five feet behind her so that every time she asked him a question about the menu she had chosen she had to pause and turn round. By the time they had walked the long corridor from the front office to the garden door and crossed the courtyard to the arch-topped gate that led to the gardens, Honour had given up her attempt at conversation.

Yellow rambling roses grew up the sandstone walls of the single-storey building that had been converted to a simple restaurant. Honour held the handrail and walked carefully down the four steps that led to the open door. It was the only concession she had made so far that morning to her age. She could hear the chatter of the serving girls as they laid tables for lunch. Not that they were expecting much trade. The average for a Sunday this late in August was twelve lunches. The tourists had got into practice by now, and brought their own picnics. It was hardly worth while opening for, but teas were much better – they often topped the fifty mark.

'Good morning,' Honour called out and the chattering stopped immediately.

There was a muted murmur of replies and the four fresh-faced country girls smiled shyly. Then, seeing the strange man behind madam, there was a great deal of blushing and surreptitious straightening of green-and-white-checked uniforms.

'Mr MacKenzie might be using the kitchen in here this morning, and he will also be using the buttery. You can give him any help he needs until the house opens and the visitors start to arrive, then you must attend to your own jobs.' She turned to face the chef. 'As discussed with the agency, I have two uniformed waitresses arriving at eleven. They will lay the tables in the dining room and serve, of course, but I've no doubt that they'll have some time to help you, should you require it. And there will be several members of the family on hand should you need to know where anything is. Some of the raw ingredients that you requested have arrived already and they have been placed in the buttery. If you'd just like to have a quick look at the kitchen here, I'll take you over and then leave you to get on with things.'

The restaurant kitchen was reached by walking behind a twelve-foot Formica counter topped with glass-fronted showcases, rush baskets of cutlery and a very modern-looking till. It was a room some twenty feet long and ten feet wide that had recently been tile lined from floor to ceiling. Stainless-steel tables ran along two walls. On another, catering ovens stood on either side of a commercial dishwasher. At the far end of the kitchen was a double sink with wide draining boards, in front of a window that looked out over a blank wall fronted with black plastic dustbins.

Robert relaxed. He could function very well indeed in such an environment. There was even a very effective-looking Ventaxia. He laid down the canvas holdall carrying his knives and whites and walked quickly back into the restaurant. He wanted to bring his raw materials over at once.

The buttery was everything that he'd hoped it wouldn't be. The sole cooking facility was two Baby Belling cookers. They each had two small boiling rings on top of a scant foot-square oven. They were ideally suited to a bedsitter existence, but not catering for twenty high-powered executives. Several wooden trestles had been covered with plastic table cloths.

Robert walked swiftly to a large cardboard tray overflowing with fresh vegetables and picked it up. 'I'll get on then,' he said. His accent seemed, if anything, to have thickened.

Marie was on hand to see the waitresses in at eleven o'clock. They were two older women from the village. In their late fifties, they had identical permanently waved iron-grey hair and hard Kent accents. With pursed lips they looked around the buttery. They'd only ever served in the restaurant before. They looked at each other and then back at Marie without saying anything.

'And this is the way to the dining room.' Marie spoke brightly, determined to ignore their obvious disapproval.

A doorway beside the sinks led to the narrow, twisting stairs that were the service route to the upstairs dining room.

'Up there? You're not expecting us to serve up there?'

Marie stopped on the third step and turned slowly to face the women. 'This is the way you reach the dining room. There aren't many stairs, about twelve or fourteen I suppose. Then it's all on one floor.'

'I'm not carrying hot food up those stairs. And you're not either, are you, Maisie?' The taller of the two women folded her arms over her pouter-pigeon bosom and stood still. 'No one's going to do that for you. It's not right.'

'You come from the village, don't you?' Marie deliberately kept her voice very level and low. 'These are the stairs to the dining room the family uses every Christmas. Service always comes from the buttery. You must know that.'

'We were told it was a business function, not family. We expected to be working in the restaurant, or possibly'

– the spokesperson for the two paused to add emphasis to her words – 'even in the great hall. We wouldn't have minded that. It's cold, and the floor's uneven, but at least it's on the flat. No one said anything about stairs. We don't do stairs.'

'Just wait there a minute, will you.' Marie walked quickly past the two women. There was no point in wasting time trying to change their minds. Even if she did, they would make such a performance of using the stairs that everything would be ice-cold by the time it got to the table.

The girls in the restaurant kitchen were busily chopping and slicing and there was an air of happy bustle. Two of them agreed to serve at the executive table. They grinned and nudged each other and Marie realized how young they really were, probably not much more than seventeen. She asked for, and got, another volunteer. It would be safer to be overstaffed.

The two older women walked slowly over to the restaurant where, with obvious bad grace, they began helping the chef prepare.

By twelve o'clock a great pan of fresh vegetable soup was simmering gently on top of the stove. A small mountain of julienne strips of carrots and cucumber was ready for adding at the last minute, as was a heap of chopped parsley and chives. The soured cream was in the fridge. The fishmonger had delivered the fillets of sole as ordered. Robert had deskinned them and then rolled each strip around a firm cherry tomato. The neat rolls had been fitted into a shallow earthenware dish, dotted with butter, scattered with slivered lemon peel and then sprinkled liberally with a good white burgundy. They were about to go into the oven.

Medallions of venison were marinating in a mixture of red wine and herbs. They were to be pan fried at the last minute. Several steamers were ready loaded with ribbons of turnips and courgettes. A macédoine of fresh vegetables was gently sweating in a deep frying pan, it would be served in the castellated pastry cases that were baking nicely in the fan-controlled oven. Dessert was a flummery of raspberries with heart-shaped vanilla mousses topped with thick local cream.

Robert's face was florid; in comparison with the snowy white of his uniform it looked almost purple. He was smiling contentedly as his performance came together.

Fleur had left her change of clothes in the front office. The executives would arrive at twelve-thirty to go straight in to drinks in the attractive tapestry-hung stone-walled room they called the queen's boudoir. They would be served by William, the general factotum who so admirably fulfilled the role of family butler.

Fleur was balanced on one leg, struggling out of her narrow jeans, when she heard the sound of a coach on the gravel. They must be early, she thought, and began to struggle harder, and then she heard the second coach. She was overtaken by a chilling calm. Dropping her trousers entirely, she shuffled over to the window so that she could look out on to the sweeping drive in front of the house.

The neat sign displayed in the closest coach windows said it all. It was a Garden of England tour. But it was Sunday. Fleur held tightly on to the cold stone windowsill. They always came on Thursdays. She felt sick, the most awful nausea swept over her. There was something she remembered, a message she had taken.

'Please, God,' she whispered and closed her eyes. Perhaps they were a mirage, perhaps when she looked again they'd be gone. But they weren't.

It was the twenty-sixth of August. That was the date the woman had said on the phone. Fleur remembered it quite clearly now. They'd changed their day to the Sunday because of the coming bank holiday. They would fill the restaurant. They were booked in for a three-course meal. It was a regular booking, it was precious. The Montfords always did everything they could to make the tour a good one.

The first middle-aged visitors were straggling towards the house. They would expect their guide to be ready to take them round, before their one o'clock lunch, preceded by a glass of sherry.

'Oh, God,' Fleur muttered. She pulled up her trousers and thrust her feet back into her trainers. It was speed that mattered now, not glamour.

Chapter 12

Beauty may have fair leaves, yet bitter fruit

'Berry!' Marie opened the door of her flat wide, in amazement.

The usually suave South African was soaked and dishevelled. Also, to judge from the way he was leaning against her door post, he was drunk. It was just past four on Saturday afternoon, and she hadn't seen him for over a week.

'Will you no do a favour for a poor wee soul,' he quavered, his voice far higher than usual and interspersed with snorts of laughter.

'For heaven's sake.' Marie gripped hold of his jacket sleeve and pulled him inside the flat. 'You're drunk out of your mind and you reek like a brewery. Where on earth have you been?'

'With ma friends, dearie.' Berry stood, swaying slightly, his legs placed wide apart to help his precarious balance.

'Stop speaking like that. You don't sound a bit Scots – at least I assume that's what it's meant to be.'

'I'm an Irishman,' Berry said determinedly. 'And it's quite official, I've been rebaptized.'

'That explains the water.' Marie started tugging at his jacket. 'This has to come off, it's in a terrible state. Who on earth got you in this mess?'

Without any warning Berry sank abruptly to his knees. 'Marie,' he said very seriously, 'I don't like to upset you, dear girl, but you've suddenly grown a great deal taller.'

'For goodness' sake let me get your tie off before you pass out. Come on.'

Marie had had experience of drunks before. In her teens she'd helped to hide her brother's excesses from their parents.

Berry reached out and grabbed her around the waist but she easily managed to twist out of his grip.

'You're a disgrace,' she said furiously. 'And why on earth did you have to come to my door like this?'

'Damion said –' Berry stopped speaking so quickly that he belched. He sat, his head moving slowly from side to side. Even in his drunken state he knew he'd made a mistake.

'Damion said,' Marie repeated slowly. 'So, this is his doing, is it?'

Berry lay down on the floor. He snuggled his cheek into the soft pile carpet and drew his feet up to his stomach.

'You'll ruin your trousers,' Marie said, but she didn't bother to say it loudly.

Her visitor had already closed his eyes. He was going to sleep on the floor in her hall, and there wasn't anything she could do about it.

She eased a pillow wrapped in a towel under his head and then laid a blanket over him. With luck he wouldn't be sick on the carpet.

He slept until gone eight. Marie was in the kitchen baking herself a potato in the microwave when she heard him moving about. She turned the oven off to hear what he was doing. When she gathered he was being sick in the bathroom she switched it on again. Ten minutes later he came into the sitting room, where she was laying the table.

'Sorry.' His face was the colour of wet plaster. His

saturated hair was dripping water down his neck and on to his shoulders. He had nothing on but a bath towel wrapped around his middle and he was shivering.

'You'll catch your death of cold.'

He has a beautiful body, she thought. Well muscled, with smooth, soft skin. She crossly handed him a travel rug to wrap around his shoulders.

'I . . .' Berry rubbed a hand across his forehead. 'I've cleared up in the bathroom.'

Marie made a face. She didn't want to talk about it, and she was disconcerted. They didn't know each other well enough for any of this. 'Do you want some coffee?'

'Please.' Berry slumped down heavily in an armchair.

Marie almost snapped at him to take care, her furniture wasn't built for crashing down on to, but instead she glared at him. It would be a waste of her energy to get seriously angry; he probably wouldn't remember anything in the morning.

Later, when he was sipping a cup of scalding black coffee and had the blanket draped round him, Marie sat down. 'So, you were with Damion,' she prompted.

'We went to a funeral.' Berry's voice was regaining some of its strength. 'I'm not sure exactly where, but it was somewhere in Kent. A funeral of one of Damion's other owners. An Irishman.'

'It wasn't a man called Danny, was it?'

'That's right, Danny Walters.'

'I didn't know he'd died.' Marie was surprised. 'He hadn't been ill, had he? I've met him a few times. He always seemed very fit, and he was very nice, quite charming, in fact. That's a pity – he can't have been all that old.'

'He was forty-seven, but what he didn't achieve in years he'd more than made up for in living.' Berry carefully placed his coffee cup down on a small wine table.

157

Marie quickly got up and put a mat underneath the saucer. She was sure it wouldn't leave a ring but she wanted to let Berry know she hadn't forgiven him for turning up drunk on her doorstep.

'That sounds like the kind of logic Damion comes out with when he's had a few too many,' she said.

'It's logic in anyone's language. Danny had a wife, three children, four mistresses, and three horses in training with your brother. I think even you'd agree that was living life to the full.'

'Four mistresses? Yes, that is a bit excessive, isn't it? Even for one of Damion's friends,' Marie said sarcastically.

'The women probably finished him off. I mean, they weren't just casual affairs he was having. He was obviously keeping all of them happy. Each of them turned up at the funeral complete with their families. I've never seen anything like it. There were five separate groups round the graveside. The vicar couldn't decide where to look. And Danny had good taste – they were all attractive-looking women.'

'So you got drunk at a good old Irish wake.' Marie sounded caustic.

'Five good old Irish wakes, to be exact. Damion had met all of the women, you see. Danny'd brought each of them in turn to see his horses. And, of course, now Damion's got no idea who's going to inherit the animals, so we'd got to go to each of them.' He sounded pleading. 'You do understand, don't you?'

'I still don't understand why you came here to me.'

'You seem determined not to understand anything I do or say.'

Marie stood up. 'Your clothes are dry enough for you to dress now.'

Berry slumped lower in the chair. Damion had told him

158

that a crisis brought out the softer side of his sister, so it had seemed a good idea to call on her for some womanly affection. He wasn't getting it, and he had a growing suspicion that men and women defined the word 'crisis' differently.

'I only got back from Rotterdam early this morning.' He thought it was worth one more try for sympathy.

Marie started to walk towards the kitchen to get Berry's clothes from the tumble-dryer, but Berry carried on talking, so she paused in the doorway.

'I went straight from the airport to see Damion. He'd left a message for me at the office during the week to say there was trouble with my colt, Oberon. He'd had a bad bout of colic.' Berry was sitting forward in his chair, trying to look serious, in command of the situation. He didn't want Marie to get really mad. He didn't feel up to it, having counted on getting a nice warm bed for the night – with company. 'I was going to go home and get some sleep as soon as I'd checked up on the horse. But when Damion said about the funeral, I thought I should go. Danny was a nice chap.' The last line sounded a bit lame, he realized, but he still felt too nauseous for anything clever.

'Well, I hope you're feeling better now.' Marie looked and sounded glacial.

She walked back and then picked up the empty coffee cup. Damion on his own gave her trouble; Berry was doing the same. United, they would be far worse, and she felt they were ganging up on her. She didn't like it.

'You can let yourself out when you've got dressed again,' she said. 'I'll leave your clothes in the kitchen and you can help yourself. I'm going out, and there's no point in waiting for me – I've no idea when I'll be back, but it'll certainly be quite late.' She walked through to her bedroom to change.

159

She would go out, go to the cinema; she was damned if she'd act as his nursemaid. And she was damned if she'd spend any longer with him dressed like a modern-day Tarzan.

It had been quite a while, she realized suddenly, since she'd slept with a man.

'Meet me in that little coffee shop behind Smith's Gallery.' Marie's voice sounded strained and Damion didn't know if it was a distortion from his mobile phone or something more.

'I'm not sure what time I'll make it. Why don't I just call at the flat?'

'No,' Marie replied quickly. 'Not the flat. I'll explain later.' She didn't want to tell him on the phone that Peter was staying there, and why.

'Suit yourself. But don't blame me if I keep you waiting. The horses always come first, you know that.'

'You've got help with the horses.' Marie's voice was sharp. 'I'm not suggesting for one minute that you should neglect them to come and see me, but this is important. Very important. Three o'clock this afternoon, at the coffee shop.' She put the receiver back on its cradle. Damion was impossible. He never did have a logical sense of priorities. She only wished she knew what she should do about Peter. He'd promised her that he wasn't hiding from the police, that it was just a misunderstanding between him and some investors in a foreign farming venture, something to do with avocado groves. But the fact that he couldn't go to his own home had to mean that whatever trouble he was in was serious. She didn't want to be involved. She didn't want to go and get his passport for him. The intercom beside her buzzed.

'Berry Jopling on line one for you,' Angelique said.

Marie thought for a moment. She didn't want to speak

160

to anyone, let alone Berry. When she heard his voice on the line, she said, 'Hello. I'm sorry but I'm in a meeting just now. Can I call you back?'

'No need, I'll pick you up from your office at six-thirty. We've got something to celebrate.' There was a loud click as he disconnected.

She stared at the phone. He was such a chauvinist he was unbelievable. She pushed the button on the intercom. 'Angelique, did Berry Jopling ask you if I was free tonight?'

There was a definite pause and then Angelique, sounding very positive, said, 'He's very nice, you know. Good-looking, and rich and available. And he's not stuck up like some I could mention.'

Peter's abrupt manner always offended her.

Marie didn't want to leave Peter at the flat on his own. He'd said he wasn't going out, not even to get a meal, so she'd been going to cook him something. Their relationship might be a thing of the past, but she didn't like letting him down.

Damion sipped his cup of Darjeeling tea with a slice of lemon and looked around the coffee shop. It was very arty. The rough-plaster white walls were hung with a selection of brightly coloured silk-screen prints. The one nearest him appeared to portray a camel with three humps, or perhaps two camels, one in front of the other. He stared hard, trying to distinguish how many legs there were, but the purple and orange lines merged into each other. On the far side of the refrigerated display counter a yellow Dodo glowed against a vivid green.

'Bit of a connoisseur, then?' The thick Scottish accent of the waiter who'd brought his tea obliterated the Frenchness of the noun. The young man, in laid-back apparel of open-necked, printed shirt worn loose over a pair of cut-down jeans, sat down easily on the empty seat at Damion's table. 'The bloke who does these is a bit weird. He won't give them titles. The tourists always ask, so I've named those camels *Life Intended*. Clever, don't you think? And of course, the minute the plebs realize that the creatures are actually screwing, they can't bring themselves to look at the other prints. I don't think he's sold any since I've started here. A connoisseur like yourself, of course, could pick the lot of them up for a song.'

'What song did you have in mind?' Damion asked, pleased that he'd found an entertaining way of passing the time. He'd managed to make it to the coffee shop by ten past three, and now Marie was late.

'Oh, I don't know, say a hundred each. There are eleven of them scattered about. You could probably pick the lot up for a thousand. Just think what they'd do on the walls of the old baronial home. I'll ask the bloke if you want.'

Damion stood up abruptly. 'You're late,' he said to Marie as he leaned forward to kiss her.

'Sorry.' Marie seemed abstracted. 'I didn't know you knew Simon.' She smiled a greeting to the young man who had hastily vacated her chair. 'You haven't let him sell you anything, have you?'

Damion shook his head.

Marie put her handbag on the table and began to take off the short-sleeved white linen jacket she was wearing over a neat navy blouse. 'Be an angel, Simon, and get one of your minions to produce some lovely iced orange for me, and a date slice would be nice.'

The young man left them and Damion watched him go in surprise. 'His minions? You mean this is his place?'

Marie nodded. 'It's a gold mine. He turns over these prints of his goodness how many times a week. He even

162

manages to sell them as a set every now and again, but that's only to real suckers. Usually it's one at a time, and for fifty pounds they're probably not that bad a buy. The frames are quite nice anyway.' She stretched and then yawned.

'Your sex life looking up?' Damion laughed. 'You look exhausted.'

'I am exhausted. Peter had me up most of the night.'

'Please! Spare me the hundred and one positions.'

They paused as Simon laid Marie's drink down in front of her. He winked to Damion as if implying that he hadn't really seen him as a sucker.

Marie sipped at the rich fruit juice. 'He's in some kind of trouble. One of his investment schemes has run into difficulties and there are several very irate investors after him. He's had to take leave of absence from his job and he says he can't go home.'

'So he's holed up with you?'

Marie nodded.

'But I thought the two of you had broken up?'

'We have. Truthfully I'd happily not see him again. I know that's over-reacting, but he wasn't good for me. I was always trying to make myself something I wasn't for him. Even this morning I found myself worrying because I wouldn't be there to cook him dinner. As if he can't look after himself. But it's not really his fault. It's mine. I should never have worked so hard at pleasing him. A relationship either has to work with the two of you being yourselves, or it's not worth carrying on.'

'Very profound, my little sister. And I much appreciate your sharing your pearls of wisdom with me, but in fact' – he looked down at his watch – 'I'm not sure that your heartrending confession is a good enough reason for me to be neglecting my business. At this very moment the vet will be – '

163

'Oh, damn the vet!' Marie pushed her glass away. 'Can't you understand how difficult all this is? I have to be able to function. The company's on a knife edge. But I'm stuck with Peter until I get hold of his passport. It's at his flat. I daren't go and get it myself. If it somehow got into the papers that I'd been helping a possible confidence trickster, it would give the bank just the excuse they need to call me in.'

'The perils of fame,' Damion said dryly. 'Confidence trickster? You sure about that?'

'No, of course I'm not, or I'd just kick him out and tell him to stew in his own juice. But I have to give him the benefit of the doubt. And of course I can't afford to be seen to be involved.'

'You want me to do it?' Disbelief made Damion's voice rise and Marie put her finger to her lips. 'You want me to go and get that poncy idiot's passport so he can do a runner. What if I get myself in the papers? It wouldn't do my image much good. "Trainer in brush with law" – something like that. I can just imagine what that would do for me. Sorry, old girl. He'll have to get someone else to do his dirty work.'

'I was wrong to ask you.' There were sudden tears in Marie's eyes. She reached out for her brother's hand and squeezed it tightly. 'I'm sorry, I wasn't trying to imply it wouldn't matter so much for you if it came out. I wasn't thinking clearly. Everything's so confused just now. I don't know where to turn.'

'Berry Jopling!' Damion almost shouted with relief. 'That's who you want to turn to. He's been trying to get on the right side of you for long enough. This is something he can do. He must have a positive cluster of employees just right for a little breaking and entering.'

'They wouldn't need to break in.' Marie opened her handbag and delved inside. 'I've got his key.'

164

'Then what are we waiting for? Come on, let's give him a ring and get things rolling.'

Damion put a five-pound note down on the table to cover the bill, then he stood up and began sorting through the coins in his pocket for a tip. Then he remembered who'd served them and decided to leave nothing.

'No, no. You needn't bother to stay with me any more. You've produced the bright idea, and that's all the help I needed. I'll do the donkey work.'

'You don't want me to phone him for you?'

They had reached the narrow cobbled pavement beside Smith's Gallery and Damion held Marie's jacket as she put it on.

'You said you were expecting the vet.' Marie wasn't looking at her brother as she spoke.

'He'll be gone by the time I get back. Now, why wouldn't you want me to phone Jopling?' Damion stood still, ignoring the fact that Marie was walking away from him. 'But of course' – he raised his voice so that it carried to her – 'you're going to be speaking to him anyway. He's got his wicked way at last. And you told me . . .'

Marie turned and hurried back. 'Stop it,' she said. 'It's nothing of the sort. It's just that I am already seeing him tonight. It's none of your business, anyway.'

'That's a good one.' Damion began to stroll on in a leisurely fashion. 'I'm the one whose assistance you so imperiously demanded. Suddenly it's none of my business. You're unique, Marie. I just hope Berry doesn't find out exactly how unique before I've had a chance to convince him what a brilliant trainer I am. It'd be a shame if he took his horses away because my sister played him up.'

Marie remained silent. She'd be nice to Berry, but she couldn't forgive him for having made love to Sarah, and for turning up drunk on her doorstep. And she certainly wouldn't sleep with him just to keep Damion's stables full.

Chapter 13

The autumn of the beautiful is beautiful
FRANCIS BACON (from the Latin)

'What the hell's that row?' Benjy demanded.

Fleur stepped quickly out of his way as he propelled his wheelchair violently across the highly polished floor.

The drawing-room windows were open wide to let in the fine morning air, and the sound of helicopter rotor blades thrashing the rhododendron hedge was almost deafening.

Fleur took a quick step towards him and then stopped. She was standing beside the marble-topped fireplace, her face reflected in the overmantel mirror. Her expression was unnaturally calm, and she was controlling her emotions with all the strength of character she had inherited from her grandmother.

There was a sudden silence as the engines of the machine shut down and her voice sounded strangely loud, 'It's someone coming to see Gee. A man called Berry Jopling. She wants to discuss the estate with him – he's in property.'

Benjy spun the wheelchair around to face her. 'Jopling? I know that bastard's reputation. He's an asset stripper. Your grandmother can't let herself be taken in by – '

'Gee asked him to come down. It's something to do with pension funds that buy up woodlands.'

Benjy was in such a foul mood. It happened more and more, and she hated it. His temper seemed a hundred times worse now that he could no longer ride it out of himself.

The dogs had started barking, making the kind of clamour that they usually reserved for the time when the milk tanker drove up the lane to the home farm.

'I doubt if even she'll be strong enough to resist his bite if he feels like sinking his teeth in here. If she wanted to talk to someone in property she could have talked to the company buying my farm.' Benjy was pale with anger.

He felt his own position was being threatened. Gee had been coming to him for advice recently. They'd gone over the accounts together, and she'd even said that she felt there was some daylight at the end of the tunnel now. To bring the whizz-kid Jopling down was like slapping him in the face.

'I'm going,' he said abruptly, and wheeled himself out of Fleur's sight.

She wished she could have told Benjy in advance of the visit, but Gee was certain that he would try to cancel it. And she was right. Why, Fleur wondered, why did her grandmother have to put so much faith in a man she'd only read of in the *Financial Times*? If what Benjy thought about him was true, it could well have been a case of inviting the robber baron inside the keep of their castle.

'So, what do you think so far?' Honour carefully placed her hands on the top of the five-barred gate and looked out over the green and gold panorama before her.

Berry turned his back to the distraction of the view. 'I think you have problems. And I think that the solution to those problems probably lies very close to home. So close, in fact, that you're not going to like my answer to your next question.'

'I'm too old to hold off asking questions for as small a reason as my possible discomfort, Mr Jopling.'

'Why do I have the feeling that you use your age as a bargaining tool, Miss Montford?'

Honour laughed happily. This man, in under an hour, had come closer to seeing through her motives than the family had. What was it he had said, that she wanted to prepare the estate for entry into the twenty-first century?

She laughed again, and when she turned to face him she felt almost girlish; there was nothing she couldn't accomplish. Age was no barrier, she'd overestimated its importance. It was brainpower that mattered. She had it, Fleur would possibly have it when she matured, but Lucy was a gentler, slower thinker, and the quick mental agility of her own two sons no longer counted.

'I should have called the family "the firm", just as the Queen does,' she said. 'It's a clever way of reminding its members that they have obligations to each other and to the unit as a whole, don't you think?'

'To call yourselves a company may be a better idea. A company with limited liabilities. Whatever you do, there will be some rocky times ahead. You have to develop strength and increase your capital position. You must get rid of some of the dead wood – and you can take that literally; the woodlands that I flew over are still decimated. That isn't good for you or the country.'

'It's an expensive job, reafforestation.'

'If you can't afford it then you should turn the land over to someone who can. Can't you see that you're simply wasting assets? Morally, you should consider the welfare of the land as a whole.'

'The last thing I expected from a man publicized as an asset stripper was a sense of moral obligation,' Honour said softly.

There was no other sound than the soft wind in the oaks behind them, the occasional far-off bleat of a late-born lamb.

'Moral obligation can be made into tangible assets. Publicity never hurt anyone, and good publicity is worth a lot of money. Let's say you established some kind of enterprise centre, and funded it by selling those woods to a pension fund. You could tie up a deal with a forestry company, complete with all sorts of figures and projections, include in the scheme the fact that the public must be allowed reasonable access, and in essence what you're doing is turning an area that is at present nonproductive into productive timberland.

'Ecologically that's sound, visually it's sound, and the estate meanwhile will benefit with an injection of much-needed cash. You have to be as productive as you can possibly be on the finest land that you possess. But let's be clever about this – when I say as productive as possible, I don't mean by the heavy use of chemicals. Make the land organic and you'll get a premium on the crops, and it's another good reason for visitors to want to walk your green and pleasant fields. Then they pay to go round the house, and enjoy a decent meal in the village.

'That's what you want, isn't it? The ideal vision of rural England. Well, it can be yours, if you're a bit radical and ruthless. You can't go on maintaining picture-book cottages for a few elderly tenants. Sell off the pretty stuff, and if your conscience insists, build a few old people's homes – you'll probably get the local council to chip in. There are deals to be done. The important thing is that you must be in a strong position to face the vagaries in the market that are to come.'

'The market?' Honour turned to face him. 'And which particular market do you see us in?'

'The leisure market, pure and simple. Even when you produce your organic crops, you're going to be catering for the family whose leisure occupation is eating what they consider good wholesome food. You're not producing something to satisfy the mass, quick-food market. Whatever you do, you're not in there able to fight those boys.

'Just do what you're best at, what a family like yours has proved its worth at. Provide quality. Quality goods that the public will pay a premium for, and that includes your tours round the house. Don't ever skimp – you've got to have more flowers than Cliveden, reek of a more personal history than Hampton Court ever could offer. Make sure the scones offered in the house and the village are simply dripping with cream, and the strawberry jam comes from your own organic gardens. You want to create an island of perfection.' Berry turned to look at the view. 'Christ, to do anything less in a spot like this would be a sin.'

Much later, as the helicopter lifted off the verdant lawns, he was able to look forward to his evening. He'd been so sure the meeting with Honour Montford would go well that he'd already booked Marie for a celebratory dinner. This time he was going to take things slowly. In fact, he wasn't even going to make a pass. He was content to let that side of things take their own course for a while.

'That could expose Peter to more trouble.' Marie carefully laid her silver fork down on the Limoges porcelain plate.

The Kensington restaurant they were dining in was very formal, very elegant and very French. They were both speaking softly so as not to be overheard.

Berry didn't look up from studying the highly artistic presentation of his fillets of sole in gooseberry sauce as he replied, 'I'm not interested in his welfare, I'm interested in yours. You can't afford to be involved with a swindler.'

170

'I'm still not sure.' Marie crumbled the bread roll on her side plate.

Her *soupe de poisson* had given her an appetite, but the conversation had become too serious for her to enjoy the vol-au-vent of sweetbreads that had earlier seemed such a good idea. She didn't want Peter to get into any more trouble than he already was. Berry had agreed to get hold of his passport, but he wanted to hold on to it for twenty-four hours so that he could check if Peter's Spanish venture was going to be investigated by the fraud squad. He'd also said he didn't think she should go back to her flat until they knew one way or the other. To her surprise he'd made it perfectly clear that he thought she should spend the night at an hotel – alone.

'Let's change the subject, shall we?' he said. 'I want to talk about Body Beautiful. I think it's about time we had a few more cards on the table.'

'I think you've seen all mine, I've been perfectly open with you.'

'Really?' Berry's voice rose sarcastically. 'I'd say you've been perfectly secretive with me. But despite that, I do have some interesting information for you now that I've finished my survey of your company. It's very much a question of the bad news and the good news, but with judicious pruning, you can come through this crisis relatively intact.'

'I assume it's my bank who've funded your "survey", as you call it.' Marie could feel her temper rising.

In the long run she would be the one carrying the bill for all Berry's activities.

'Certainly. I don't do anything for nothing, and in this economic climate anyone who does is a fool.'

'Do I get to see your report?'

He shook his head briefly. 'No way. But I'll tell you all the juicy bits.'

'How kind. Are you sure you're not breaking a trust talking to me about it at all? I mean, we could spend the next hour or so discussing the cricket, or the weather . . .'

'Or the beauty business.' Berry pushed his plate away and a waiter came hurrying to remove it. 'You should be right at the top of it, Marie, not struggling in the middle. You had a brilliant idea, and you're a very capable lady, but it's time for you to accept that your marketing strategy is wrong for now. You've got to get rid of *all* your stand-alone sites.'

'I don't believe in going backwards.' But she did.

She would like nothing more than to get back into all the department stores, just as she'd been five years ago. But admitting it was like admitting she'd been wrong, and she didn't think she had been. It was just that the market had changed, the recession had bitten harder than she had ever imagined it could. And now the established brand names were ranging against her. They didn't want her competing.

Berry carried on as if he hadn't heard her. 'Your problem is in getting back to a position where you aren't carrying a dead weight around your neck. Body Shop has taken the high street for the moment. You have to accept that, because you don't have the capital to get out there and compete in every shopping precinct. You can't afford to wait for customers to come in droves to your door. Ergo, you can't keep up the property side of Body Beautiful. What you need to do is get outlets that don't cost you exorbitant interest and rates, and keep on persuading the public that they are desperate to buy your products. That way you are going to get a whole lot of retailers on your side. Department stores are going through a lot of problems worldwide, and you're fortunate that so far the UK hasn't been that badly hit. But you've got to look further – think about a tie-in with other types

172

of retailers already out there on the street. You won't be alone in that, but get in early and it's a good strategy. Meanwhile, you still have to appreciate the clout of the big boys, the Estée Lauders, for example.'

They stopped talking to choose a dessert from the trolley. There were several ornate gateaux, a bowl of oranges in caramel, individual mousses and bowls of fresh fruit. Berry had a slim slice of what looked like an upmarket chocolate fudge cake and Marie went for a vanilla cream.

'Estée Lauder, Clinique, Aramis, Prescriptives and now Origins – all owned by the family Lauder – yes, I appreciate their clout, Berry. And before you say it, with Damion on board, Body Beautiful once had a claim to be a family firm as well. After all, he may not have a stake in the company, but my father does oversee the plant in Ireland.' She stared sightlessly at the ornate silver candlestick on the table in front of her. So much had changed with her brother leaving the company.

Berry said nothing. He couldn't have spoken, even if he'd wanted to. He'd suddenly thought of another way that Marie's company could be the foundation of a dynasty. He himself had every intention of ending up with a substantial proportion of its shares. What was more natural than a husband-and-wife set-up? He suddenly regretted that he'd become involved with the Montfords. It was all closing in on him and he had no intention of giving up his bachelorhood.

'We're all selling dreams.' Marie picked up her spoon and began eating the sweet flavoured emulsion garnished with crystallized kumquats. 'Whatever anyone claims, Vaseline is still about the most effective moisturizer there is. But we are part of a multi-billion-pound industry claiming to produce just what the consumer wants – the promise of youth. All those ad-men-invented slogans are just to give people hope. That's what firms their faces – a bit of confidence. And the by-product of using any of those creams – massage. You rub anything regularly on your skin and you're going to improve its muscle tone.'

'I take it that's not for publication?'

'Very funny. You're obviously serious – as you say yourself, you're being paid to look at Body Beautiful – so you might as well know the facts. In practice, the only things that can affect my face, or yours, are moisturizers and sun blocks. Mix those up in different proportions and you've got just about any product in the market. Skin consists of three layers, first there's the outer horny layer, then the epidermis and under that the dermis. As we get older, the dermis gets thinner and the skin sags and wrinkles appear. So it's logical, isn't it, that to be anti-ageing a skin cream would have to reach the dermis. They don't, and in the US at least there would be hell to pay if they did. Any substance penetrating that far would be classed as a drug and that wouldn't suit a cosmetics company at all. So there you have it: I'm selling dreams. I know it and now you know it. Probably most of my customers know it too, but they'd rather not believe it. Hope of a perfect face is like reading your horoscope – it makes the day go a lot better if the future looks rosy.'

'Your horny layer looks pretty good to me, if you don't mind the use of the word. What do you use on your face?'

Marie laughed, and had the grace to blush. 'I use everything that's going. At least I've got an excuse. Every new product that comes out on the market has to be tested, doesn't it? And after all, I may be wrong, we may all be wrong, and I'd hate to be one of the wrinklies unnecessarily.' She dabbed her lips with her napkin. 'Now, having put a generous measure of Yves Saint Laurent on their table linen, I'd better go and find myself a hotel room. I think you're right, and yes, please will you find out whatever you can about Peter.'

Berry drove her to the Waldorf and escorted her into the foyer, where he chastely kissed her on the cheek. He went home to ponder why he hadn't told her that he was going to buy the woodland at Pencombe, and spent a restless night exorcising any lingering thoughts of setting up a family dynasty with Body Beautiful.

'She's beautiful,' Sarah breathed.

'She should be, she's called Beauty.' Damion laughed as he swept the soft-bristled body brush over the horse's shining flanks.

Sarah stood silently. A ray of yellow evening sunlight had found a way through the high barred window of the stable, and a myriad golden specks of dust danced like tiny dervishes caught in a spotlight. The warm, sweet smell of fresh hay mixed with a deeper animal scent.

Damion started to whistle tunelessly through his teeth. It was the age-old professional groom's trick to avoid breathing mouthfuls of dust. He soon got into the rhythm he preferred, three long, strong sweeps of the brush, then a quick, short rasp across the upright teeth of a metal curry comb to cleanse Beauty's loose hairs from the bristle.

'She loves it, doesn't she?' Sarah asked.

The question didn't require an answer. The horse stood contentedly, her brown eyes wide and placid. A fly touched her neck and she shivered briefly.

Damion had begun working on one of the front legs, running the brush in a downward spiral. The physical effort was taking the tension out of his muscles. He felt hot, but not uncomfortable. He was wearing a green and beige checked short-sleeved, open-necked shirt and thin beige cord trousers.

Sarah had come down to Damion's stables to see how it would look for a publicity shoot. The buildings were fine, the animals ideal. Normally, Sarah knew, she would have found herself thinking disparagingly of her host's attire. She would have ridiculed the well-worn leather jodhpur boots the trainer wore, and his plaited rope belt.

Instead she was uneasy about her own clothes. The high Mandarin collar of her apricot silk blouse seemed suddenly restricting. Her own trousers, white and tight, seemed not quite right – tarty was the word that sprang to her mind. And yet the clothes that the girl grooms in the yard were wearing weren't that different, just less stylish, cheaper.

'Where's everyone gone?' She was aware of the sudden peace.

The clatter of buckets had died away. No one was sweeping outside the boxes any more.

'Tea,' Damion said.

He was bent double, working around the animal's feet, and his voice was harsh. He looked up abruptly, his green eyes staring intently into Sarah's.

'Our tea's not like the tea you'd have at home, Sarah. This is a proper meal, a fry-up, or beans on toast, and plenty of cups of tea, finishing with some bread and jam. They'll take half an hour, forty minutes, at least.'

'Why haven't you gone with them?' Sarah asked.

There was something about his eyes that gave her an answer. Her throat was suddenly tight and she was aware of saliva flooding her mouth, making her voice sound thick.

Damion stood up. He paired the body brush with the curry comb, face to face, so that they fitted snugly. Sarah watched his every move. He turned to the horse and whispered soft words. He stroked Beauty's neck and the animal whickered softly, aware of the tension in the man.

176

'Why?' Sarah whispered.

Damion stepped towards her. His face was stern, and there was a look close to anger in his eyes. He put a hand on her shoulder and his grip was firm, managing. She whimpered without knowing why.

She reached out for him and her hands were trembling. It was airless in the stable and she was struggling for breath.

He cupped her face in his hand and she felt the roughness of his fingers against the smoothness of her skin. He tilted her chin and her head fell back. Her lips parted and he buried his face against her shoulder, pressing his body against her. She could feel his need and the heat of him through her clothes. He was fumbling at her waistband, and suddenly he seemed vulnerable. She had to help him, hold him.

'Take them off.' His voice was muffled against her skin. 'Take the bloody things off.'

She felt for the button, then the zip, and all the while she was murmuring to him, making unintelligible sounds that spurred him on. He had unbuttoned her blouse, was holding her breast in his hand, was squeezing, kneading. She wanted to melt in his arms, wanted him to lift her up . . .

They lay down on the straw together. He pushed the hair back from her eyes. He wanted to watch her, to see the change in her. He pushed her legs flat, running his hand over her smooth thighs, swiftly over the damp curl-covered mount that she pushed up at him. He ran his hand over her stomach, using the same caressing sweeps as he had used to soothe the horse.

He bent to kiss her and she bit at his lip, making him pull back swiftly. Then he kissed her again, forcing her mouth open, bruising her lips against her teeth. His tongue flicked in her mouth and she felt hollow, empty. She wanted him to fill every part of her.

I knew, I knew, she exulted. She pulled him on top of her, writhing against him, clutching his sides with her knees. *Ride me, ride me, for Christ's sake*. She was drawing his tongue deep into her mouth, pushing his hands downwards.

He thought of his wife. He struggled to put her out of his mind, but the same picture of her kept intruding. She was so young, so misshapen, so helpless. He forced himself up, on to his knees. The woman lay spreadeagled on the straw. Her blouse was open, her breasts swollen, dark-nippled. Her flat white belly stretched down to a dark sweat-dampened triangle.

He stood and a look of near panic crossed her eyes, but he couldn't back away, not now. 'Stand up,' he said.

She stood slowly, aware of her nakedness and the sudden chill of fresh air on her overheated skin. He stepped back, and began, at last to unbuckle his belt. 'Turn around,' he said.

She shivered as she waited, the soft blonde down that ran down the centre of her back catching the light.

'Touch your toes,' he said. He saw her shoulders stiffen. She moved, as if to turn back to face him, but then she bent.

He entered her from behind and she gasped at his size. There was pain, a hot, searing pain, and then suddenly he was moving freely and she gasped with pleasure. She spread her feet and then went up on tiptoe, seeking with every movement to make it easier for him as he was overtaken by the rhythm. She reached back blindly for his hand, drawing it round to rub at her swollen clitoris. She was panting, sweat running down between her breasts, concentrating with every ounce of her being. She was so close, so very close.

178

He came, holding her tight against him, leaning back and lifting her off her feet whilst he was still deep inside her. All her weight was taken on his hand and she cried out as she climaxed and the surge of power flooded through her.

Chapter 14

Beauty is the flower of virtue

The sound of upbeat dance music filtered through from the ornately mirrored Café Royal ballroom to the throng in front of the bar in the French Empire annexe.

Men in traditional black evening suits mixed with others in ultra-fashionable dinner jackets of richly textured velvets. There were young women in short slender sheaths of vivid colour, and older ones in long, heavily embroidered designer gowns. There couldn't have been a dress in the room that had cost less than five hundred pounds, and many were well into the thousands.

Marie's party had already met up. She had left the office early to change into her multicoloured Zandra Rhodes. She had arrived at just past seven-thirty, Damion and Rose and Jeremy Gaines a few minutes later. Jeremy had been delighted to be asked to 'make up the numbers'. Peter had left the country, so far, according to Berry, not wanted by the police.

They'd shared a bottle of champagne by the time Sarah arrived with a beautiful young man who looked like a minor film star. Paul Debonio, as he was introduced, bent his perfect perma-tanned features over Marie's hand. His sun-streaked blond hair fell forward in an attractive quiff that he flicked back with aplomb. He was at least six foot two tall and made Sarah, in a midcalf tube of shimmering white silk, look slight and delicate.

'It might be an idea to go through to our table.' Marie

sipped at her second glass of champagne. 'It may well be that the Simmonds are waiting there for us.'

'Did I forget to tell you' – Damion was scanning the crowd around them as he spoke to his sister – 'the Simmonds couldn't make it after all. But I had a bit of luck. I met an old friend walking along Regent Street this afternoon. He'll be coming in their place.'

His accent had thickened as it always did when he was 'fabricating'. It was obvious from the way Damion wouldn't look at her that he was expecting Marie to be annoyed.

Sarah broke away from them briefly to talk to someone she knew. Rose accepted a cigarette from Paul, and sucked the smoke in hungrily. The red lace A-line dress she was wearing would normally have hung flatteringly loosely from her bust, but now it felt uncomfortably tight. She was well over seven months pregnant, and although her well-developed stomach muscles had held everything in for the early months, now there was no disguising her condition and she'd had to buy a pair of maternity jodhpurs. If the dinner dance had been a couple of weeks later she would have had to buy something specially, instead of squeezing into something she already had.

They made their way towards their table. On the gilt-framed table plan in the hallway outside, they were down as *The Body Beautiful Party, Table 14*. They were in a good position, on the first ring encircling the dance floor, and almost directly opposite the band. As it had said on the invitations, it was Georgie Fame and the Blue Flames. Paul had a firm grip around Sarah's waist. As they walked across the floor, he began swaying his hips to the Latin American beat and she laughed. Marie envied her publicity director, who was obviously relaxed and looking forward to the evening.

And why not? There wouldn't be many speeches, just

a couple of self-congratulatory monologues – hopefully short – on the standards sought and attained by the recently formed League of Responsible Employers. Body Beautiful had been happy to join the association; before long the linked-hands symbol that member retailers were entitled to display on their doors would become a valuable aid in recruiting good staff.

Marie had had to do very little to comply with the organization's rules. The company already did basic on-site staff training and had an occupational pension scheme. It was about to allow suitable candidates the chance to get involved in day-release training. That would be an investment they would only recoup in the long term, but for staff relations it had been a good move.

Another couple were already sitting at their table. The man had his back to them, and cigar smoke hung wreath-like above his curly dark hair. The first impression was that he was a big man, with broad shoulders and a thick neck. The woman with him was checking her make-up in an expensive gold compact. She had regular features that applied artistry had made into a stunning face. Her well-shaped creamy-skinned shoulders were revealed by an off-the-shoulder green satin dress and drawn-back long blonde hair. Sarah made an instant judgement: she was either a rich man's daughter or a hooker.

'Tommy!' Damion bounded forward with apparent delight. 'I'm so glad you made it.'

The man stood up and turned round to clasp Damion against him. 'As if I'd miss a chance of an evening on the town. Marie . . .' He reached his arms out, an easy smile on his lips. His face matched the rest of him. It was large, his colouring florid. He seemed a man of the great outdoors.

Marie walked slowly towards him. There were a lot of people watching, she couldn't create a scene, so she had no choice but to walk into the embrace. She hardly heard Jeremy's jocular asides not to handle 'his' goods too much. Tommy Docherty. She felt cold inside. This was the man she'd left Ireland to escape. For a moment she could no longer remember the overwhelming longing she'd had to win her independence, to set up on her own. Damion had suddenly brought back into her life the man who was the reason she'd left her home and her country.

The master of ceremonies walked up to the microphone, the members of the Blue Flames slipped off their chairs and went off for something to eat. Guests were to go through to their tables. Dinner, it was announced, would be served in five minutes.

They took their seats. Marie sat between Jeremy and Paul. Directly opposite her the girl Tommy had introduced as Samantha was gazing in apparent adoration at her escort. The Irishman had his head tilted towards his companion; his charm was obvious, even from a distance. A waiter poured white wine. Marie picked up her glass and sipped without tasting.

'Ex-boyfriend?' Jeremy asked. He didn't sound amused. He'd had a 'thing' about Marie for quite a while, and hoped he might be in with a chance now Peter had cleared off. 'If you can tear your eyes off him for a minute you might notice that your sister-in-law's looking decidedly groggy.'

Rose struggled to her feet. Having been very pale she turned quickly red. She looked despairingly at Damion, who had his back to her as he talked animatedly to Tommy across the luscious Samantha.

Sarah was quicker to act than any of them. She put her arm protectively round the girl and steered her through the tables and out to the cloakroom.

Damion looked uncertainly after her. 'What's that all about?'

'Your wife got a bit hot,' Jeremy said. 'There's not much air in here, is there?' He looked deliberately at Tommy's cigar.

'I'd better go and see if she's all right.' Marie stood up. 'Look after everybody, will you, Jeremy.'

'There aren't that many left.' He laughed.

Damion should pay more attention to his wife, Marie thought as she made her way between the tables. She knew several of the people she passed, and smiled, adding a quick greeting where appropriate. She'd reached the open space just in front of the large swing doors leading on to the landing when she felt her elbow taken in a firm grip.

'You're not going to escape me that easily,' Tommy said. The charm had fallen away from his voice. 'I haven't come all this way to have you snub me in front of your friends.'

'Let me go.' She tried to pull away, but he had hold of her too firmly.

He was forcing her to walk towards the lifts.

'I'm going to see if Rose is all right,' Marie said forcefully. 'Let me go now.'

'Certainly not.' He smiled broadly at a couple coming out of the lift in front of them. They'd heard Marie's loud protest. He lowered his voice and put his mouth close to her ear. 'Take it easy, we're just going to have a little talk. I'm owed.'

Marie stepped into the lift. She felt furious, but calm. She wouldn't let the fear he'd once inspired take her over now. 'You can let me go. I'll listen to what you want to say. We can go into the bar on the ground floor – I don't want to leave the building, I have to get back for the speeches.'

'All right, my dear. I'll let you carry on your act a bit longer. I won't spoil your little shindig.'

There was an empty table in the bustling bar. Marie sat on one of the surrounding red-velvet-covered chairs as Tommy went to get some drinks. He had his back to her, obviously convinced she wasn't going to try and leave.

'Cheers!' He raised his glass of malt whisky.

'What do you want?' Marie ignored the glass of dark brown sherry he'd put down in front of her.

'What did I always want? I want you. You should never have left Ireland. You belong there. Your parents are getting old; your place is with them – and me.'

'I don't need you telling me what I ought or ought not to do.'

'You need somebody.'

'There really is no point in this.' She reached out for her silver sequined evening bag, which she'd put down on an empty chair beside her.

Tommy took her hand. This time his grip was gentle; it was words that he was going to use to restrain her, not force. 'Damion owes me thirty thousand pounds,' he said.

Marie subsided in her chair.

'And I'm not alone in this – I offset half of it with other interests. They're not as patient as I am.'

'You mean he's been gambling again? After everything he promised.'

'He's addicted to it, Marie. Nothing you can say or do will stop him. It's in his blood, as is the fact he'll always be a loser.'

The traffic in Wardour Street had slowed to a halt. Marie leaned forward on the seat of the taxicab she had taken from Charing Cross. She tried to see if there was any movement in the queue ahead but a large lorry blocked her view. In any case, she had plenty of time in hand for her appointment. It was just that she was so worked up she couldn't bear to sit still. Whatever happened in the next hour would affect Body Beautiful's future, and that was her future too.

She kept thinking back to when Peter had left. She'd spoken briefly on the telephone to him; told him he should have left the flat by now, left it for ever. It had taken Berry a whole twenty-four hours to find out that her one-time lover wasn't yet in serious trouble with the police. But the odds were stacked against him.

She hadn't wanted to spend a second night at an hotel so she'd gone down to Pencombe. The atmosphere there had been fraught. Honour was selling the woodlands to a speculator, and there had been so many arguments that she was refusing to talk about it any more.

Marie opened her handbag and took out a lipstick. The mirrored case of her Clinique eyeshadow reflected the tense expression in her eyes. She closed them briefly, willing herself to relax. It wouldn't do for her to go into the meeting looking strained. She shouldn't have put so much black eyeliner on, she decided, and began to soften the hard outline with a touch of grey eyeshadow.

'What number Oxford Street was it you wanted, luv?' The taxi driver's shouted question startled Marie.

'Two hundred and ten. I'm sorry, but I don't know which end it is.'

'That's all right, ducks. I reckon it's got to be near the old Palmolive building. That was one hundred and sixty or thereabouts. I'll just stick my nose out at the end here, and we can see which way to go.' The cabbie was young, with short curly red hair and big pale brown freckles up the back of his neck. 'I'm pretty sure it'll be a block or two back towards Marble Arch, but we can have a look-see. I asked myself, when you got into the cab, if you'd like a nice scenic trip down Oxford Street, but you didn't strike me as a tourist, so I thought, no, let's do this the

186

quick way. You been down to the country, then, luv?' He was looking at Marie in his rear-view mirror as he spoke.

She nodded. 'Out near Tonbridge. It was beautiful. In this weather it's the only place to be.'

'You're too right. Never known business as bad as it is right now. Too much traffic on the roads, London's coming to a standstill.' They caught the amber traffic light and turned left. 'Hang on, here we are. Now you give a shout if you see a number before I do.'

The cabbie was right. A few hundred yards up Oxford Street, towards Marble Arch, Marie caught sight of a simple concrete portico bearing the numbers 214.

'If you'd just like to take a seat, Ms Sullivan.' The smartly dressed secretary gestured towards one of the twelve Georgian chairs arranged around a prestigious oval-topped mahogany table. 'Mr Sanderson will be with you shortly.'

The boardroom had apricot-painted walls, a large sideboard that matched the table and chairs, and several Persian rugs scattered on a fitted camel carpet. There were no pictures on the walls. A large wire screen looked as if it could serve as an instant display area. The atmosphere was one of functional comfort. Male voices came from what appeared to be a one-way-glass wall behind Marie.

She was no longer nervous. It made good business sense that an organization such as The Gear should buy the twenty-five retail outlets Body Beautiful wanted to dispose of instantly. A bulk buy would make sense to them – they would get a substantial discount on unit prices.

Body Beautiful would have the chance to retrench its capital position. With cash in the bank – or at least a far smaller overdraft – Marie would feel free to bargain hard for store-within-a-store slots. That was how she'd started off. Then she'd been determined to get high-street sites of her own. Good, solid, C1 locations. And now, she wanted to turn the clock back.

'Ms Sullivan.' The managing director of the ultra-trendy The Gear was forty something, five foot ten, dark hair going grey, and hiding behind the thickest-framed horn-rimmed spectacles Marie had ever seen. 'Let me get you a drink – tea, coffee?'

'A coffee would be nice, thank you. It's wonderfully quiet in here. The noise of the traffic outside is unbelievable.'

'As long as it's all potential customers seeking us out, the more chaos on the roads the merrier.' The narrow lips pursed as if they wanted to smother what might have been taken as a joke. 'You had a look inside our shop a couple of doors along, I hope. It's quite something. The decor . . . well, why don't you tell me what you thought.'

'Most impressive.' Marie smiled. 'Ideal for your market.' She hadn't even seen the shop, but it was bound to be 'ideal' for their market. After all, that was the name of the game.

'We're spending two million on refurbishing this year. That's new shop-fittings; solid wood display stands; brass rails; smoked glass. American dummies for all our windows – you wouldn't believe how much more expensive they are than the English variety. But the hair's real, all the joints move, they're lifelike. Our customers deserve the best.' His voice had swollen with an almost evangelical zeal. He paused as if challenging Marie to contradict him.

'I gather that you're riding out the recession better than most of your competitors.'

'We like our publicity releases to sound positive.' He bent his chin towards his chest and looked over the top of his glasses. His eyes were a watery blue. 'But of course

188

we, like every other high-street retailer, have suffered, and will continue to do so for some considerable time to come.'

'You must be pleased that you established your market position before things got bad.'

They were silent as the secretary brought in coffee on a brass-rimmed tray – two porcelain cups full of pale brown liquid. It was too late for Marie to say she took hers black.

'Well, Ms Sullivan, pleasant though it is to have a little chat, I think we should get down to business. I did ask my deputy to make certain that you, Ms Sullivan, have the authority to do a deal for your company.' He paused meaningfully. He had laid a heavy emphasis on the 'Ms'.

Marie smiled brightly, subduing her desire to spit out the over-creamed coffee. 'You've had a chance to see all the details your company requested on my properties?'

'Absolutely.'

'My last conversation with your deputy was to the effect that you are interested in purchasing our high-street sites. They are available for occupation as and when you require, subject to a minimum timescale of three months and a maximum of one year. Any locations that you do not require until after the three-month period I will undertake to rent from you at a fair market rental less twenty per cent for my willingness to vacate on a month's notice.'

'You are implying that you would expect us to complete on all the properties by the end of the three-month period.'

'That is correct.'

'I have to say I'm certain that my board would not agree to that. We are not in the rental business. Now, there are ten properties on your list that interest me particularly.'

Marie was aware of a sinking sensation in her stomach. Ten, possibly twelve of the properties were easily saleable. The others were marginal high-street locations and in a depressed market could hang around for years. 'We will not split the properties. The agents are under instructions to make that clear. I myself have continually repeated that point in dealing with your deputy. However . . .' Marie paused as if she was thinking, but she had had this suggestion in hand all along. 'I can understand your unwillingness to complete all the purchases by the third month. I may have a possible compromise.'

An hour and a half later Marie stood to shake hands. Her opinion of the man hadn't altered from the first impression he had made. He was, in the time-honoured phrase, a male chauvinist pig. Still, he had finally agreed to exchange contracts on all twenty-five sites by the end of the third month.

The Gear would proceed to immediate completion on twelve of the shops, the other thirteen would be completed as and when they required possession, with the whole having passed into their hands at the end of twelve months. Body Beautiful could carry on trading in the thirteen shops for the payment of a nominal rent – twenty per cent of ten per cent of the purchase price of each unit. That covered the interest The Gear would have to pay on those properties at that stage.

Marie walked back to her office. When the deal was finalized she'd have a crack at getting them to stock her body range; it fitted in perfectly with the concept of getting away from the straightforward department store.

She felt she was floating on air. She'd done it. Talk about last-minute reprieve. The bank could take a running jump, Berry could . . . She realized then how charged

190

with adrenalin she was. The thought of Berry had made a pulse beat in her throat. She wanted him, she wanted him physically. It was the first time she had seriously admitted that to herself.

Chapter 15

Beauty, strength, youth, are flowers but fading seen
GEORGE PEEL (1558–1597)

An assortment of expensive cars was parked right next to the rope barrier that was keeping the paying public off the three-mile point-to-point course.

Damion's silver-blue Range Rover was just to the left of the final fence, Berry's racing-green Bentley was beside it. The tailgate of the trainer's vehicle was open wide, displaying several elderly wicker hampers piled, apparently haphazardly, inside. There was a full bar, complete with spirits and mixers and dozens of glasses, tins of sweet biscuits, a couple of truckle cheddars and a whole brie, gingerbreads from Fortnum and Mason's and a giant jar of patum peperium next to several packets of Bath Olivers.

In the Bentley's boot, in what appeared to be studied abstemiousness, there was only one commodity – Veuve Clicquot. To make up for the lack of choice there were four full cases.

'Berry! Over here!' A slim, red-haired woman of well-preserved middle age shouted loudly enough to attract his attention.

Berry acknowledged her with a wave, but remained where he was, talking to the owner of an elderly grey Mercedes that was parked in the second row of cars.

Damion mockingly tipped the brim of his well-worn deerstalker for the umpteenth time that afternoon. He greeted all the men he recognized, however vaguely, and

192

all the attractive women, however unknown they were to him. He was in his element dispensing hospitality to the point-to-point aristocracy, the owners and occasionally the jockeys of the over-oated animals that were desperate for the opportunity to hurl themselves over the immaculately made brushwood fences.

It was a glorious day, the sky high and clear, a washed azure blue. The green countryside around them had as much richness as a mild late spring. There was an enormous crowd. Several thousand cars stretched back across the fields that had been turned into temporary car parks. In a far corner there was a small fair where gypsy-like men hawked silvered helium balloons, and a yellow and red bouncy castle wobbled like a giant jelly.

The crowd was culturally divided into the cognoscenti and the masses but across the board there was a plethora of Barbours and denim jeans. Green wellingtons, it appeared, were de rigueur footwear for anyone, male or female, between the ages of fifteen and twenty who couldn't rustle up a pair of Reeboks.

'Damion,' the red-haired woman wailed, 'I can't get lover boy's attention at all and somebody has to open the bubbly.'

Her full-length hunting-green Barbour coat accentuated the colour of her long wavy hair. She had darkened her eyebrows to an unnatural black, her eyes were heavily made-up, her cheeks artfully rouged to enhance the prominence of her cheekbones. Her friends called her Vix. It was short for the Vixen.

'Now you're not trying to tell me that you haven't pulled the odd cork in your time, Vix?' Damion put his arm lightly around the woman's thin shoulders. He could feel the tension in her. 'Just relax, come and have a drink off me. I've got the lot, Scotch, vodka . . .'

'I'd love a gin.' Vix giggled like a young girl. 'Champagne gives me wind anyway. I just thought, since you said I was to chat your punter up, that I'd better wait for him.'

'That's definitely not your style, old girl.' Damion gave her a quick squeeze and then began rummaging in the back of the Range Rover. 'As I remember, you never were one to wait for a man.'

They were laughing companionably as Rose came up. She was wearing cream maternity jodhpurs and black jodhpur boots, her green army-style jumper was flecked with hay. The saddle that she carried over her arm was polished to perfection. She trailed a leather headcollar and lead rein over her shoulder. Her face was flushed and shining with sweat.

'Like a drink, Rose?' Damion spoke over his shoulder, and without waiting for her reply poured a gin and tonic.

'Rainbow's lame and the vet's no good. He's half-pissed already.' She looked in disgust at the glass in her husband's outstretched hand.

'You mean he won't run?' Genuine anxiety showed up a myriad lines around Vix's eyes. 'Fred told me to be sure to back him, he was certain he'd win a packet.'

'Fred will still do all right.' Damion sipped at the drink he'd poured his wife. 'For a huntsman to have a BMW like his means he's sharper than the average.'

'He's got private means,' Vix hissed.

'What a delightfully old-fashioned phrase, "private means". Who's it being used about?' Berry asked as he joined the group. He reached into a case of his champagne and pulled out a bottle. 'If it's a woman, point me to her. I've just lost fifty quid on a bet with Bill Bomane.'

'He didn't catch you with that beetle trick of his, did he?' Vix's face had cleared miraculously, and she was wide-eyed, full of charm. She reached out a thin hand and

194

laid it on the Harris tweed sleeve of Berry's jacket. 'What a babe in the wood you are. Next time you go socializing, take me with you. I'll save you a fortune.'

'You mean it was a fix?' The disbelief on Berry's face made even Rose laugh.

The man who was the yard's most valuable owner might be the darling of the financial pages, but when it came to simple country wiles he was an infant in arms.

Rose turned to go back to the collecting ring and Damion put a hand out to restrain her. 'Don't go,' he said. He kept his voice low. He didn't want the others knowing that Rose had refused to help him dispense his hospitality.

'I have to. The girls are expecting me.'

'They can do anything that needs doing. Christ, they're not even our horses you're getting ready.'

'Their owners are our friends. Oh, I beg your pardon, I've got that wrong. They're my friends. I said I'd help and I keep my promises. You don't need me here.' She felt out of place.

She was young enough to be the Vixen's daughter. She couldn't understand why Damion had been so eager to get the woman close to Berry.

Damion turned his back on his wife. He was furious, it was important for him to cement his relationship with the man Jopling, and important for him to pick up some more owners. The day was ideal for it. Not too hot, yet fair. Anyone with any interest in the horsey scene would turn out. He had noticed the Warners walking the course earlier. They were a local family reputed to be going into ownership. He'd try and catch up with them after the next race.

The public-address system whistled and coughed and then vibrated with the old Etonian tones of Percy Fingle as he announced the runners for the next race. Berry used his gold Cross pen to tick them off on his card. He'd get Vix to provide him with a good tip. Damion had said that she had inside information.

She obviously expected him to squire her to the big dinner party Damion was throwing that night. Presumably she also expected him to take her to bed afterwards. There had to be some way it was going to cost him – she was that kind of woman. But he didn't think she would expect coin of the realm. It would be something more subtle. More likely, he realized, it would be Damion to whom he was to feel indebted.

Berry looked over at the trainer. He was deep in conversation with a lovely young woman dressed in what were obviously designer tweeds. She had small, perfect features, her long blonde hair was only partially restrained by a Sloane velvet headband. She'd flashed a look at Berry as she approached. It was clear that she'd recognized him from the papers, and equally clear that she approved of what she saw in the flesh. Her escort, who stood politely to one side, was a wimp all the way from the toes of his elastic-sided boots to the top of his regulation brown hat and back down to his sharply receding chin.

'How about a potter down to the bookies?' Vix asked. She'd seen the direction Berry's attention was taking; the Honourable Amanda Saunders was a spoilt brat, and her brother Simeon, who was with her, was a fag. 'Let's try and win back your beetle money, shall we?'

Berry patted her hand as it rested on his arm. He was in an excellent mood. He liked variety in life, and it was so wonderful all the exciting goods that were on offer. He had no intention whatsoever of giving up playing the field.

'It was good of you to come, Marie.' Rose was standing disconsolately outside her kitchen.

196

Damion had employed caterers for the après-point-to-point feast, just as he had employed a team of professionals to clean up the cottage. There were crates full of hired china blocking the way out of the back door. A short fat girl kept dashing backwards and forwards to the van parked outside. Each time she returned she was carrying some more food.

'I can't imagine what all this is going to cost.' Rose tried to push stray wisps of her hair back into the French pleat that had seemed to complement her straight, but bulging at the front, navy grosgrain dress.

'Damion is convinced he'll get some more clients from this evening,' Marie said soothingly. 'You must try and enjoy it, Rose. Entertaining is going to be an important part of your life from now on.'

'I hate it.' There was so much vehemence in the girl's voice that Marie was momentarily silenced.

Damion was so sure that this was the way to win custom for the yard and Marie was inclined to agree with him. She had tried hard with her own appearance; she thought she should look ultra-feminine and give Damion the chance to shine in their relationship. After all, a lot of the guests would know he was once an active director in Body Beautiful. For once she would play up to the preconceived idea of male dominance that always irritated her so much. It would be a proof to Damion that she did still love him, even if he'd upset her beyond all measure in baling out of the company, even if . . .

'You do know, I suppose, that only three rings of your cooker are working?' A tall, hatchet-faced woman in chef's whites strode out of the kitchen. She glared down at Rose as she spoke. 'There is no earthly way I can produce the menu your husband selected with such limited facilities.'

Rose put a hand to her mouth. She'd forgotten about

the fault with the cooker. She cooked so little that it hadn't seemed important. She looked desperately at Marie. 'I can't. I just can't face all of this,' she cried, and then ran away up the stairs.

The woman began deliberately untying her apron. 'I can't work under these conditions.'

'But I'm sure you can.' Marie stepped into the kitchen. 'You're a professional, I'm certain you're more than able to cope. Now, what can I do to help?'

It transpired that a couple of glasses of Damion's excellent burgundy did the trick. The chef, nicely mellowed, decided that a salad would be a better idea than hot vegetables and began slicing and chopping accordingly.

Damion had worked hard at the seating plan. Berry had been seated between Amanda and Vix. Marie, who was opposite him, was not amused. The man she fancied despite herself had the anticipatory look of a Jack Russell about to be put to stud.

Amanda turned her lovely face to look at her neighbour. 'But you simply must come over and see our little piggies,' she said. 'My beloved's absolutely gaga over them. They're Vietnamese pot-bellied ones, and I think he must be so fond of them because they remind him of all that Oriental travelling he used to do.' Her voice, high and breathy, had a tendency to lisp. Damion had revealed earlier that her husband – who, as usual, was away 'on business' – was almost sixty.

'From what I remember of her "beloved",' Vix breathed in a stage whisper that travelled the full length of the table, 'the pot-bellied bit's going to remind him of his own reflection in the bathroom mirror. He once informed me that he hadn't seen his little pinkie, as he used to call it, in years.'

198

'My husband says he never knew you,' Amanda's voice rang out.

'Then you've turned your husband into a liar, my dear. He "knew" me all right, socially and biblically. I always think it's so sad when a man has to deny his past.'

'Now, now, Vix.' Damion sat back in his chair. He had a glass of good wine in his hand, an excellent meal on his plate. He'd enjoyed the salmon mousse they'd started with and he was smiling as he wagged a finger at his most outspoken guest. 'You don't always have to live up to your name.'

Berry bit into a succulent piece of lamb and concentrated on the fine flavour. The Vixen's hand was almost vice-like on his upper thigh, her nails digging into his skin. Compared to the gentle pressure of silken thigh from the girl on his right, the older woman's sexual approach was almost violent.

Simeon coughed politely before anything he said. Marie would have liked to pat him on the back or hand him a glass of water, but it was clear that the affectation was too deeply seated for sarcasm.

'Understand you're fearfully high-powered,' he said.

Marie stabbed her fork into a softly yielding new potato. 'I don't know about fearfully.'

'Can't stand the City more than twice a week meself.' Simeon was wearing a monocle. Suspended by a thin black ribbon, it hung like some insignia of honour from his jacket.

'I try not to go to the City all that often myself,' Marie said grimly. The only reason she ever had to go there was for finance. It was a sore point. 'The effective work I do is in the West End.'

'But the crowds!' Simeon's voice had risen in horror. 'I mean, Knightsbridge is just about all right, but Oxford Street – well, I haven't been there in yonks, absolutely

199

yonks.' He returned to his lamb cutlets, fastidiously trimming every minute fleck of fat from meat.

'So much of what we are is based on what we were.' Vix blew out the sweetly perfumed smoke between her pursed lips.

The heavy four-poster suited her slight body. The sheets were lace edged, the pillows plump and square. The room was small; there was space only for the bed and an antique tallboy topped with a collection of brass candlesticks. A dozen flickering candles provided the only light. Her home was seventeenth century, a pretty timber-framed house on the outskirts of the village. One of a pair, it was approached by a long brick pathway that meandered between dense borders of sweetly scented flowers. The Bentley was parked on the verge outside; in the morning it would be the subject for comment of the faithful on their way to matins.

Berry sat back, comfortably propped up on the multitude of pillows. The smooth linen sheet was pulled up to his waist, and it was the only thing that covered him. The woman had made love with an abandon that had less to do with technique and more to do with desperation, but in mind and body he was satisfied. The frantic coupling had made a suitable ending to what had been an enervating evening. He smiled reminiscently. Marie had been so strange, so different, all frills and perfume, and she had been livid with him for being the centre of the other two women's attention. He smiled again. It meant that, after all, he was getting to her. She'd soon give in, they'd have a quick fling and he'd be able to get her out of his system.

'What are you thinking?'

Vix's sharp question almost caught him unprepared, but he hardly paused before he rolled on to his side to face her.

'I was thinking how you English always have the power to surprise me. Today, or I suppose now I should say yesterday, was an education.'

'The rich at play.' She shrugged her shoulders, and there was a pout at her mouth. 'At least the nouveaux riches. When I was younger . . .' But she didn't finish her sentence. Instead, she lay back against the pillows and stared, unseeing, at the fantastic patterns in the smoke floating above her.

'Have you ever married?' Berry asked softly.

'Twice. And it didn't get any better, it got much, much worse. This is preferable. However long the night sometimes seems, it's an improvement on a lot of what has gone before. I don't want anyone to own me. Not ever. It's a pity, isn't it, that we don't get a practice go. I mean, I think I'd do quite well now. I've learned enough of the ropes to get by. I wouldn't mind turning the clock back to be twenty again and have it all ahead of me.'

'Like Amanda?' Berry instantly knew he'd said the wrong thing.

'That slut?' Vix stubbed her cigarette out aggressively on a delicate china dish on the bedside table. 'I would rather come back as a worm. At least they serve some kind of useful purpose, even if it's only feeding the birds. Men!' She spat the final word.

'I'm sorry.' Berry reached out and ran a finger over the back of her hand as it lay on the bedcovers. The veins were standing proud, pale blue under the thin white skin.

'I wasn't even asked to their wedding,' she said. Her voice was strained, as if she was forcing her words out against her will. 'Two years of my life that man had, when his first wife was so ill. We did everything together, everything. Christ, I even cooked for him. You can have no idea what a sacrifice that was on my part, acting the loving hausfrau. And then she died, and he went through

201

all the motions of grieving. I was to go away, so that there wasn't any talk. And I accepted it, I went off to the Continent. I kidded myself I needed a break; the last few months had been difficult – he'd needed constant comfort, constant bolstering up. I came back in the autumn. He married that sly bitch at Christmas.'

'You would have made him your third?'

'No!' She laughed, suddenly happy, delighted by Berry's naïvity. 'Good God, no. How on earth could I marry a man who'd cheated on his dying wife? I just wanted him to ask. I just wanted the chance to say no. What a baby you are.' She turned towards him, moving under the covers until their bodies touched. 'Come on, baby, come to Mama.'

'So, you think Body Beautiful's American fiasco is due to their urban crime problem?' The banker's tone was acid.

'I think "fiasco" is a bit heavy,' Marie replied.

She was sitting very upright on a hard leather chair. It was one of a pair on the supplicant side of the prestigious partner's desk. The atmosphere in the dark panelled room overlooking St Paul's Cathedral was extremely unpleasant.

'Well, I'm afraid that I don't.' Nigel Bonsoigne's expression made it abundantly clear that he was most unhappy. 'We were expecting a high dollar revenue, not a deficit. And it really doesn't matter what caused the problem, whether it was the fees for these security guards you say you had to employ, or simply not enough sales.'

He shifted in his chair to make himself totally comfortable. He was about to embark on the lecture that he gave all good customers who had suddenly turned bad.

'I disagree,' Marie said, forestalling him. 'We've identified the cause of our problem in the States and are taking steps to deal with it. We're certainly not alone in suffering

202

heavily due to the vandals in the malls. I am negotiating for more "shop-within-a-shop" positions. It was being in our own premises that left us exposed to the security problem.'

'And what about those mall sites? If they are such a security risk you're not going to find them easy to dispose of. They're costing a considerable sum.' He turned the pages over in front of him, although he knew perfectly well the outgoings of Body Beautiful, USA.

'It will take three months for us to get established "in store". That will be quite long enough to pass the other leases on.' Marie felt like crossing her fingers as she gave what she knew to be an over-optimistic forecast.

'Three months?'

The silence became oppressive.

Marie was tempted to say how well they'd done in the past. How the bank had been more than happy to extend their overdrafts when business was booming. But she didn't say anything. She thought it more politic to wait and see what the parchment-faced banker was going to say.

'How do you intend to trade during that time?' It was the obvious question.

'We have plenty of stock over there.' They had more than enough for the disappointing rate sales were going at. 'It's just the day-to-day running costs, the wages, the utilities.'

'Utilities – why, you sound quite American.' He seemed scathing. 'Do you spend much time over there yourself?'

It was a dangerous question. Marie could sense the banker was poised to strike. She tried to hedge her answer. 'I was there quite a lot to begin with. It hasn't been so necessary for me to go in person recently.'

'But you'll have to do your own negotiating with the department stores. That, after all, has been one of your hallmarks – the fact that you like to do your business face to face.' He almost sneered. He disliked dealing with people who worked at having a high profile. 'When you're spending all your time in America, what will happen to your company's interests here?'

'There's very little I can't do on the telephone. I have an excellent new director who can handle anything that needs dealing with on the spot.' For a moment Marie wondered if Sarah's charms would smooth the passage with the bank. 'As you know, all the distribution is carried out straight from the factory to the shops.'

'My wife says that your products are going out of fashion.'

Marie couldn't think of anything to say in reply that wasn't offensive. The remark was so bitchy that she thought he must have made it up himself. She forced herself to smile as she began the 'sell' that she'd worked out – it wasn't a spectacular success. Even with the promised sale of twenty-five of the UK sites in hand, her position was far from secure.

Nigel Bonsoigne Esquire didn't let the fact that he liked his friends to consider him a gentleman interfere with his work. He was delighted that he had at last forced the entrepreneurial Marie Sullivan into such a tight corner that she had had to assign a second mortgage on her flat to the bank. It gave them a much tighter hold on the equity in the property than her personal guarantee provided. Most importantly, it stopped her increasing the size of her first mortgage with Lloyd's Bank without his own bank's permission.

Marie went back to the office undecided whether to feel like laughing or crying. She'd won a reprieve – that was the most important thing, and it was essential for the company – but she felt totally on her own now. She could no longer feel that the flat was anything other than part of the overall situation.

Damion had done well to get out of the company. There was so much to sort out. The American shops were draining the moderate profits they were making in the UK. Europe needed more attention; there was a wealthy marketplace waiting to be tapped, but it had to be worked. There were only so many hours in her day. She'd always been careful to run her company with as few staff as possible.

It cost her more to have her goods delivered by carrier than it would have if she'd had her own fleet of trucks, but she felt that she saved on her own time supervising a chain of employees. She'd divided her 'empire' into regions and appointed managerial heads in each area who hired and fired the workers under them. And managers were all they were – there was no one of executive calibre among them. In theory it was very cost effective; in practice she needed more help at the top, and now there was no way she could afford it.

It was gone half-past five by the time she'd made her way through the traffic chaos around Eros. In the end she'd abandoned her taxi in the jam and walked. Sarah's raincoat was still in the cloakroom and she felt a surge of relief at the thought of some company.

She knocked on the door to Sarah's office and went in. There were sheets of artwork spread all over the desk and drifting on to the floor but Sarah was nowhere to be seen. Marie went to her own office. She was feeling more and more annoyed at having given in on the second mortgage. She kept running through the meeting at the bank, trying to work out what she could have done differently.

She pushed open the door to her office and stood still in surprise. Sarah was standing looking out of the window. On the desk behind her were two glasses and a bottle of Jameson's whisky. Sarah turned slowly round.

'Well, you're Irish, aren't you?' she said, gesturing at

the bottle. 'Now, don't tell me . . . Looking at you, I guess things didn't go all that well at the bank. Let me make your day. What do you want first, the good news or the bad news?'

'I have to make a quick call.' Marie picked up her phone and began to dial. There was a problem with her suppliers of glass jars. She got put straight through to their managing director and started trying to calm him.

Sarah sighed loudly, she'd gone to stand looking at the Hockney print on the wall above the leather sofa. It was the picture of red arches – very Spanish, very hot. She could do with a holiday.

'Pure shit,' she said out loud.

Marie cupped her hand over the telephone mouthpiece. She frowned briefly at the interruption and then continued to speak smoothly. 'It's just been a minor hiccup with our cash flow. Another couple of weeks will see us through. As you've said yourself, we've done a lot of valuable business with you in the past.'

Sarah sat down heavily, then stretched her legs out in front of her and kicked off her shoes. Her feet were agony. Just on five it had started to spit rain. With the combination of tourists wanting to get back to their hotels and skiving executives wanting to catch the early train home, every taxi that cruised past had been full. She had had to walk back to the office from the Waldorf, and her heels had been too high, their elegant pointed toes too narrow.

Two hours with a freelance journalist who had demanded a nonstop supply of Bloody Marys and gorged herself on cucumber and smoked salmon sandwiches had seemed like a life sentence. The miserable bitch should have been fat, Sarah thought, but presumably the acid that ran through her veins in lieu of blood burned up the calories.

206

'Certainly you can come up and collect the cheque by hand, although I think . . .' Marie was having to struggle to keep her voice friendly. The supplier of glass jars was coming on very heavy. 'Two weeks today.' She nodded abruptly and put the phone down.

Sarah didn't give her a pause to catch her breath. 'So what would you like, the good news or the bad news. Don't bother to answer, I'll start with the good news – there isn't any.'

'Please, it's been a long day. Spare me the sarcasm and just tell me the worst.'

'They're after you for using animal testing.'

'They?'

'The press, that glorious reason for my being. Today's little baggage was just the tip of the iceberg. They reckon they've got you bang to rights.'

'That's – '

Sarah held her hand up. 'No, don't bother to deny that you persecute poor baby bunnies. There's no point because a denial isn't enough. The bottom line is that substances you use were once tested on animals, and that's gold dust in the hands of a clever journalist.'

'Why us in particular? I could name you half a dozen other top brand names who are far more at risk than we are from this sort of smear campaign.'

'You're going to have to do just that to get us off the hook. The only thing I can think to do is to provide this cow with so much ammunition on some other poor schmuck and persuade her that we're not big enough to bother about. As to why she started on us in the first place, well, I think we can both make an educated guess at that.'

'Mark Moorman?'

'Got it in one. Supershit himself. Come to that, I think I might have trodden on him as I scampered back to my

207

burrow.' Sarah made a production of peering at the sole of her shoe.

Marie stayed silent. If they could just hold on until the money started coming in from the sale of the shops to The Gear, then there was every chance. Bad publicity would trigger the bank; she was convinced of that.

'More, you have to give me something. The woman will need an angle.'

Marie sat with her head in her hands. She was walking a tightrope trying to keep raw supplies coming in despite the bank's new stringency. To provide a good story for the gutter press was almost impossible. And she was hungry. Her stomach began to rumble aggressively, and she closed her eyes to try and think more fluently. She had to have something to eat, she'd never make it through to the evening. It was the thought of food that gave her a clue. 'I've got it! How about the LD5O test? That's being forced on us by the EC. Since their 1976 cosmetic directive, all new active ingredients have got to be animal tested. The LD5O is disgusting. They force-feed a group of animals until fifty per cent of the creatures have died. It's bureaucracy gone mad. Under the list of active ingredients they include simple things like water, lemon juice and honey. The animals don't die from poisoning, they die because their stomachs become so distended.' She no longer felt hungry.

'But that's revolting. That's torture.'

'That's a damn sight worse than anything anybody can dredge up about my company. You tell your journalist to have a go at the organizations that make the rules. And tell her about the advances that this industry is making on testing. How about the experiments on egg membrane, the artificial skin cultures, and in-vitro testing, as well as the work with human guinea-pigs. This industry doesn't contain all that many monsters any more. She should go digging for dirt in the food industry.'

'She gets most of her work on the beauty pages. What goes in a meat pie won't interest her readers.'

'It will if they rub it on their faces. They'll probably catch cowpox or something similar. Don't I remember reading that they put udders in meat pies?'

'Now who's been reading the gutter press?'

Marie smiled wanly. 'Whatever we decide, you'll have to implement on your own. I'm going to have to go to the States and see if there's any substance in that franchise offer. So, what do you think our chances are with this journalist?'

'Of us buying her off with dirt on another company, or sidetracking her on to the EC? Well.' Sarah held her long, tapering fingers close to her face and intently studied her rose melon nail varnish. 'Unless the information we come up with is so juicy that it's libellous we don't stand a cat's chance in hell. Nothing you've said is that good. I could try a straight money offer. But I think it will have to be a real biggy. She strikes me as a five-figure lay.'

Marie laughed. Things couldn't get much worse and she needed a break from the tension. 'If someone offered me five figures for a quickie, you know today I might just be tempted.'

'Serious?'

'No, not serious, but it might be nice to have the offer. Just once. It's kind of the ultimate chauvinist compliment, isn't it? It would be good to be able to throw it back in their faces.'

'And I thought you liked to make your money on your feet. Not that, at the kind of money you're talking, you could expect the missionary position.'

The two women laughed. It had been a difficult day for each of them.

Chapter 16

Beauty is but skin deep

'We have a problem on costings for the body glove.'
Damion unbuttoned the cuffs of his white sea-island
cotton shirt, loosened his tie and leaned back in his chair.

There were only four of them in the generously sized
room that could have seated a dozen. Marie, Damion and
Sarah sat at one end of the mahogany table, Angelique
had taken a chair to one side, against the wall. On her lap
she held a shorthand pad. The atmosphere was thick with
cigarette smoke. Damion had come into the board meeting with a new packet of twenty, and he and Sarah
between them were down to the last one.

Sarah had just finished her presentation of suggestions
on how to combat the spate of magazine articles on the
dangers of UVA. She had spelled out how badly Sunkissed had been affected: sales were forty per cent down
on forecast.

Damion blew a thin stream of smoke out of pursed lips
and then continued, 'For Forma Plastics to produce the
design we wanted, with holes punched in the rubber to
look like the Elancyl product, is going to cost twenty
pence more than their first estimate.'

'Was it definitely an estimate?' Marie didn't look up
from the note-pad in front of her as she asked her
question. 'Are you sure it wasn't a quote?'

Damion laughed but he didn't sound amused. 'They
might be a small company, but they weren't born yesterday. And we were pushing them for an idea of price. It's
not really their fault.'

'Is it too late to go to someone else?'

'Everyone else was a lot dearer than Forma, anyway.' Damion looked purposefully at Angelique as she dutifully noted everything down in the minutes. Both his sister's question and his answer were just for the record. The closer they got to the edge, the more it seemed necessary to prepare the minutes for critical eyes.

'Why can't we just put the cost of our starter set up by twenty pence?' Sarah asked. 'Everything we do is a lot cheaper than the direct competition. What's the Elancyl mitt and soap cost on the shelves?'

'Eleven pounds something depending on where you buy.' Damion sounded resigned. However often Sarah had the Body Beautiful ethic explained to her, she kept on trying to narrow the price differential between their 'copy' and the original product.

'And Body Beautiful's massage kit is just under eight pounds. I don't see the problem. There's plenty of room for the extra cost.' Sarah had the feeling that the brother-and-sister team were subconsciously determined to see problems for themselves.

'The Boots system is seven pounds ninety-five,' Marie spoke in a monotone. 'It has a solid mitt, i.e. no punched holes, and the soap doesn't go inside – you rub it up to a lather on the skin first and then massage. The kit also contains a cream for after-use. We intended to produce a much closer alternative to the French brand, but still keep it right beside the Boots in price. We wanted to shave an extra five pence off our original costings, so to go twenty pence the other way certainly isn't on. What's a solid glove going to do to the figures?' She addressed her question to Damion.

'Knocks fifty pence off, but I'm just not happy about it as a concept. No way does that become a direct replacement for the Elancyl. Everything else is smack on. We're using ivy extract, and the soap and the gel are just as stimulating as theirs. Even the little plastic carry bag is practically identical. Everything was the same except that our mitt would be Mediterranean blue and white and the cream would be in one of our white shell tubes. It was so right, we'd be competing for price at the Boots level, but providing a product that competed with the top of the range in design. Shit.' He banged his fist down on the table. The soap and gel were the last products he'd developed before leaving the company full-time. He'd actually been excited about getting it on line. For the first time in ages he'd been happy to come up to town. Then the call from the South Coast suppliers had put the cat amongst the pigeons.

'How about international prices, Damion?' Marie had her pen poised above the checklist of questions she had compiled several years ago for this stage of development in a product.

'We're fine all over, it's just here in the UK that it doesn't work.'

'That just shows the worth of good old Boots.' Sarah laughed.

'Look, just whose side are you on?' Damion's voice was like ice. 'This product is damned important to us. If I can only get the soap inside the – '

'Hang on.' Marie stared at the mock-up packs on the table. 'How's our price on replacement soap?'

'Fine, spot on. But then that never was going to be a problem. The soap and gel are produced in Ireland, under our own control.'

'So the only problem is with the starter kit?'

Damion nodded.

'Then put in a smaller bar of soap. You can use the shallow moulds we had made for the glycerine soap. They're still at the plant, aren't they?' Marie struggled to

212

put enthusiasm into her voice. She felt nothing like her usual elation at finding the solution to a problem. 'No one sees the size of the bar inside the mitt in that pack, so you can easily knock off that twenty p.'

Sarah reached out and picked up the Elancyl product. She slid back the plastic zip and pulled out the green and white massage glove. 'You're right. It wouldn't make any difference at all on the shelf. You couldn't inset a loofah-type face as an alternative, could you? That's what I'd like to rub on my behind, especially if the soap came through it.'

'There are several loofah mitts on the market you could use.' Marie spoke abruptly. She was concerned to preserve a distance between Sarah and Damion.

'But none with a solid handhold,' Sarah persevered. 'It would make a big difference to the pressure you could use.'

Damion leaned back further in his chair, tipping the front legs off the floor. 'I wouldn't mind exerting a bit of pressure for you,' he drawled.

'You needn't write that down.' Marie turned to Angelique, who without looking up had reversed her pencil and rubbed out the last few shorthand characters.

'Right.' Damion's chair crashed back on to four legs. 'We can go ahead on that basis. It's over to you then, Marie. All problems solved.' He began gathering his papers together.

'Hold on a minute,' Marie said quickly. 'There's something else I want to discuss.'

Sarah sighed loudly. She wanted to get away early, she had a dinner date with a Harley Street plastic surgeon. She thought he was well worth cultivating. After all, one day even her face would react to the pull of gravity.

'We have to have executive cover for when I'm in America.'

Damion closed his eyes. When he opened them his face had closed down, his lips were narrow and firmly closed. There was an uncomfortable silence.

'Damion.' Marie's voice was taut. 'We can't just let things slide when I'm away.'

'You told the bank that there wouldn't be a problem. That you had everything organized, and anyway you'd be available on the phone. You managed to convince them it would be OK.'

Marie slammed her hand down on the table. 'So Berry does carry tales. My God, I wouldn't have believed it. How cosy for the pair of you – a little horsey talk, a little company gossip. What a couple of little tittle-tattlers you are.'

Colour flushed on Damion's cheekbones. He was angry at what his sister had said in front of the other woman, but he was also angry with himself. He'd made a bad slip.

'Come on then.' Marie's voice had risen. She was leaning forward, glaring at her brother. 'How are you going to try and wriggle out of that? Or aren't you even going to bother to deny it?'

Sarah sank down in her seat. She didn't want to be there, and she certainly didn't want to listen to a family row.

'May I join you?'

Marie looked up from contemplating her plate of rapidly cooling pasta. The typically American luscious cream sauce was congealing at the edges. An exuberant green salad sat untouched in its white porcelain bowl. 'I'm sorry, I didn't catch what you said.'

A woman was looking down at her. An overdressed, over-made-up woman in her mid-fifties. Despite the eccentric multitude of purple and green necklaces and

214

scarves that adorned her well-cut white trouser suit, she seemed somehow pleasant and charming.

'I thought, as it seems we're the only two women eating on their own in the hotel this evening, it might be a good idea for us to combine forces.' She was already pulling out the chair opposite Marie as she spoke in a definite New York accent.

'I wasn't hungry,' Marie felt constrained to explain. After all, she was visiting the woman's country.

She pushed the untasted plate away from her and picked up her wine glass. The half-bottle of white burgundy that she'd ordered was empty. She felt light-headed; she hadn't eaten since lunch.

'You're English.' The statement was made with a smile. 'I should have guessed from how you look.'

Marie glanced down. She was wearing an Armani jacket, and loose trousers in aubergine gaberdine that went well with the soft cream jersey top she'd bought on a business trip to Hong Kong. She'd thought she looked international.

'I won't bother with an hors d'oeuvre, I'll catch you up on the main course. And why don't we share another bottle of that wine you're drinking? It looks pretty good to me.'

They talked – or rather Martha Devine, as she introduced herself, talked and Marie answered in monosyllables – until Martha's order of minute steaks arrived. There were two of them, and the American woman insisted on passing one over to her companion. She fussed until the waiter had brought a fresh plate, and more salad, and finally a hollandaise sauce.

Marie tried a small piece of the succulent meat and suddenly regained her appetite.

'Had a bad day?' Martha asked, her head bent forward

215

in concentration as she speared an awkwardly shaped piece of olla rosso lettuce.

'You could put it like that.'

The potential American franchise deal had been nothing more than pie in the sky. The credit check she'd run on Simon Morin had proved he was nothing more than hot air. Sears department store had turned her down flat on a shop-within-a-shop deal. They didn't want her products undermining the sales of established brands. A call to her London office had proved, as she'd suspected, that Sarah hadn't managed to call off the press hounds.

Angelique had given her nearly a dozen names of callers who urgently needed dealing with. One of them was a police detective who said he was following up a claim that body cream on sale in Body Beautiful's Parisian shop had been contaminated with acid. It was the first Marie had heard of it. He had apparently been quite unpleasant when Angelique said her boss was out of the country.

Martha asked what line of business she was in. The older woman was a good listener, and before long Marie was telling her some of her problems – not all, but enough to produce a clear picture of someone working under stress.

'What you need is a holiday,' Martha said, as Marie paused in her monologue to eat the last of her steak. 'I've been in business myself. God knows, it's advice I never would have taken at the time. But in retrospect you can put problems in perspective. Even a few days can make such a difference. You need to get away from interruptions. Then write everything down, all the things that are going against you. You might need a decent bottle of Scotch to get through that. And then you take a fresh sheet of paper and write down all the things that are good. It makes a lot of sense. It was a shrink who told me to do that, after my husband died. It was excellent advice, even if it did him out of hours of therapy. He must have been some kind of nut.' Her hazel eyes, outlined with green eyeliner, were astute and yet kindly. 'Let's talk about something else while we have a dessert.'

After a leisurely look through the menu both women ordered strawberries Romanoff.

For the first time Marie noticed their waiter. He looked like Tom Cruise, and the similarity was obviously being encouraged. He ceremoniously served them their desserts. Giant crystal goblets were reverentially piled high with succulent scarlet berries scented with orange and brandy. Martha smiled self-indulgently at the steady stream of thick cream that was poured over her berries. Marie declined the topping and the beautiful young waiter left after giving her a look of total desolation.

'That boy could make a fortune selling his body.' Martha laughed. 'But I don't think he needs me to tell him that. Not that sex is such a good way of earning a living these days. It was in my heyday, of course. Tell me, have you ever been to an Indian brothel?'

Marie shook her head. 'Not as a customer, or an employee – or come to that, even as a madam.'

She had a sudden thought. Could her companion's one-time business have been running a high-class bordello? She wanted to giggle. She knew it was because she'd had too much to drink, even though the food was beginning to make her head clearer.

'My dearest Richard was very wild,' Martha said wistfully. 'But we were such chums, much more than simply husband and wife. He wanted me to go everywhere with him. He even wanted me to work alongside him, so he took me into his company. It was a very successful real-estate operation in Florida. I'd never done anything like that, but I'd always been a snappy dresser and I love people, so I got along famously. And then there were the vacations. Those glorious days of freedom. My God, what fun we had.'

'Do you have any children?'

'No. No kids. We were each other's babies, I guess. And Richard was quite a lot older than me. He didn't want to share me. It was as if all along he knew how short a time we'd have together.'

The waiter returned to serve coffee. He'd brought a small silver bon-bon dish piled with petit fours. Marie was now desperate for sugar. She ate a chocolate-dipped fresh lychee followed by a white-chocolate-covered pistachio. Normally she wouldn't have taken either delicacy, but she could feel herself burning up the calories.

'So – let's get back to the brothels.' Martha put her half-empty porcelain cup down on its saucer. 'There's this part of Bombay, Kamatipura it's called, where the girls work out of cages. You walk down this amazing crowded street and on either side of you the hookers are calling out from behind blue-painted bars, like they're in a prison. There are girls on the upper floors too. They hang out of the windows, and the abuse they yell at the customers who don't come in, well you'd have to speak the language to understand it, but even if you don't, you certainly get the message. And the noise, and the smell.' She paused a moment to wrinkle her nose in disgust. 'I can still remember it. A mixture of squalor and passion. Incense and mustard oil, garbage and cheap perfume, all overlaid by that musky smell of lust.'

'You're putting me off this last petit four!'

'It was enough to put you off anything. At least, it would be today, but then I was young. And Richard had had me suited up like a boy. We had an Indian guide with us, of course, otherwise I don't suppose a couple of

Westerners would have got out of there with their wallets.'

'Did your husband . . .' Marie stopped. She couldn't think how to phrase the question she wanted to ask.

'Did he partake of the services on offer? No, no he didn't. At least not that night. I do sometimes wonder if he didn't go back, without me. But I don't think so. You see, we were very much in love. It was just that he'd been such a man of the world before we met. He needed his titillation, and I didn't mind. It was such an adventure.'

Marie sipped her coffee. She would have liked it stronger, but at least it was scalding hot. 'What were the girls like?'

'Very young – that was my main impression – and cheeky. They didn't seem at all abashed, or unhappy. They would call out at the men passing by. Sometimes they'd bare their breasts, some even pulled up their skirts and waggled their bottoms at the potential customers. But it was all kind of impudent. I'm talking about the ones I saw, of course. Richard said that there were some real tragedies. Perfectly respectable girls who'd been kidnapped and taken hundreds of miles away from their families. Forced to give themselves to a succession of total strangers. That took the tawdry glamour off what I'd seen for a while. But then I wondered, was that really true, or was it a story some of the girls made up for their clients? I'll never know, of course.'

'You should write a book,' Marie said. 'A young relative of mine is just dying to be a writer, but her problem is she hasn't lived enough. She's always saying what a struggle it is for her to find something realistic and interesting that she could write about. I don't think you'd have that problem.'

Martha laughed. 'I'd just have a problem knowing what to leave out.'

* * *

It had rained during the night, and the straw lay sodden on the field. It was heaped in long, fat rows lying parallel to the line of copse that ran on either side of the ditch separating the ten-acre field from the Pencombe parkland. From where Fleur sat in the office, looking out through the windows of the Place, the men working on it seemed like toy figures.

It would require effort to get the straw back into a condition to take the match. They used two tractors that morning. The one driven by Sam, Dibs's husband, working the headlands, chopping the outer-lying straw into short stalks and then ploughing it in so that the fire couldn't take a hold on it. The second, driven by the flame-haired youngster they all called Carrots, flailed the straw, driving flat out up and down the rows, once covering the whole field, and then a second time until the driver stopped, got down out of his cab and tested his work. If the weather held they'd be ready to go by the afternoon.

They had been assigned the task of burning the stubble. In a year or so the practice would be banned, and then it would all have to be chopped and ploughed in. Samuel reckoned that was a shame. He always said there was nothing like a good burn-up for getting rid of the bugs. Carrots didn't care much one way or the other. At twelve they drove their tractors back to the farm. The sky was high, grey to blue, with vast banks of white-edged clouds sitting motionless above the skyline.

The farmhouse had been painted a friendly pink. The men washed standing side by side in the scullery, sharing the bar of soap at the deep butler's sink. Gwen, the housekeeper, was busy in the kitchen. The men came in shifts, never more than three at a time. There were eight single men staying at the house. The married ones had cottages in the village, and most of them took lunch at home, but with Dibs working at the Place, Samuel ate at the farmhouse.

Each of the 'lodgers' had a comfortable bed and plenty of good wholesome food. It all ran to the plan Honour had laid down twenty years ago. It meant that jobs at the Home Farm were sought after; good men came asking, having heard of the occasional vacancy by word of mouth. There wasn't the usual throughput of labourers.

The lunch was bacon roll – thick knobs of gammon cooked in a suet crust – with fresh vegetables from the garden: boiled floury potatoes and flavourful runner beans. There was plenty of gravy, all of them liked that, and a slab of wholemeal bread to wipe the plate. Gwen served as well as cooked and the atmosphere was one of family, an old-fashioned family, where the men tended the land, and the woman tended the men. For pudding there were stewed apples, windfalls from the orchards. The thick yellow custard had been made with milk from Daisy, the house cow.

When Samuel and Carrots had finished they left the table to sit on either side of the fireplace, where they started to read the papers over a cup of tea. Almost immediately there were voices coming from the scullery. The sound of boots being kicked off in the hall. The second contingent for the bacon roll.

The men took a can of paraffin back to the field. It would take only a sprinkling, but without it they'd find it hard to get their job started. There was no wind to catch them out, but they left their tractors a field away – farm rules; that way you didn't get caught out. At the very centre of the top of the field they set the fire, kicking a heap of straw loose, then pouring a steady stream of clear, inflammable liquid on to the pile. They screwed the can up tightly and Carrots took it back to the tractors, striding out in his elderly market boots. Keeping the can out of harm's way was another farm rule. Every new man was told of the time it had been broken. The explosion had cost a man half of his hand and, worse than that, his cosy berth at the farmhouse.

It took half a dozen matches until the first tentative wisps of smoke burst apart to show a heart of flame. A solid orange core of heat crackled and spat. They wiped the palms of their hands on their trousers and nodded briefly to each other. The next time they met it would be over. As the crackle turned to a roar, so the excitement in the men became tangible. From now on each man was on his own, responsible for an ever-increasing, all-engulfing line of flame.

There was a knack to it. Pulling the rake just so as it tugged at the burning surface, walking slowly enough to let the flame bite and yet fast enough to keep out of trouble. The line of orange grew, the flames were two feet high, three. Suddenly they were the height of a man, leaping, leaving their roots at times to cavort in the smoke-filled air.

A gentle breeze shivered the tree tops of the copse and stirred the short-cut chaff, and then it reached the flames. With a roar it was off. The burning wall galloped forwards, faster than a man could run, six feet, twelve, but then the breeze died away and the flames subsided.

Two fields away sheep grazed. The shepherd drove up to them in his Subaru, stopped and got out to check his flock. He watched the burning for a while, seeing that the men had fired the top and both sides of the field. Now they were working their way along the bottom. Soon they would meet and the circle would be complete. The shepherd turned away. He had other animals to check.

Thick, greasy brown smoke billowed up into the clear air, and with it went clouds of steam, pure white, the last dampness. The men were shadows, darker grey shapes moving purposefully. Where the flames had been, the stubble was black and crisp. In places small puffs of steam, like immature geysers, littered the suede black. There was a final aggressive flurry as the fire reached the fertile band that stretched across the lower half of the field. It was the upper limit of the autumn flooding, the strip that received the lighter-weight silt, the precious fertilizer swept down from other farms upriver.

The circle was complete. They stood for a moment, side by side, surveying their handiwork, but there were boundaries to check. It wouldn't do for a stray spark to mar the perfection of their job. They walked back up the field, each proud of their side. By the time they reached the top there was nothing left but a small ring of flame in the very centre. It was a sight to watch – the flames seemed to burn brighter, there was more urgency in the crackle and hiss.

The smoke billowed thicker; there was only a suggestion of orange at the base. Within a few minutes there was no orange at all, and then almost instantly the tall billowing smoke subsided, falling down on itself. Tufts of white steam persevered as the men walked down the field, through the centre, sweeping with their eyes, left and right, looking for any stray spark of flame. It had been a job well done. The glow of satisfaction matched the warmth through their leather-soled boots. Only an idiot wore wellingtons for burning.

It was done. Close up there were small patches that had been missed; only from a distance, where Fleur still watched, was the field an even black, but it was a good result. They walked companionably back to the tractors. It was three o'clock – a cup of tea was more than justified. The kettle would have been left gently burbling on the Aga, there would be home-made cake in the tin.

Gradually the birds flew back, inspecting the change in

their habitat. The bravest dropped down on to the warm earth but it would be a while before the worms poked their heads up again. A little later there was a shower of rain, enough to dampen even the most obstinate unfound spark. The men celebrated with a second cup of tea.

Marie pulled her raincoat more tightly around her shoulders. It was no longer raining, but the air still felt cool and damp. All around her the fields of Pencombe were coloured with the tints of autumn.

'He once compared me with Chanel.' She linked her arm through Lucy's as they walked together towards the still blue waters of the lake. 'He seems to think I want to end up like her, alone and unloved.'

'So.' Lucy pushed the wind-blown hair back from her face. 'Berry Jopling's talking about love already, is he? I saw him at the point-to-point. He's a beautiful man, and they're thin on the ground, unfortunately.'

Marie stood still. It was a classic English scene. The fields reaching down to the edge of the lake were lush and green, the water rippling like velvet. 'He's not my type,' she said softly.

'I wish I'd met him when he came down here the other day.'

'Berry came here – to Pencombe?' Marie looked amazed. 'But why on earth would he . . . ?'

'I know we're not meant to talk about it, but it's him Gee's selling the thousand acres of woodland to. She intends to use the money it brings in on the rest of the land – she's planning to go organic.' Lucy laughed. 'It'll take her at least seven years, but she's given up letting time be a problem to her.'

'Is she getting a good price?' Marie asked anxiously. She was trying to remember if she'd ever said something

224

that Berry might have found useful. She couldn't bear the thought that she might have left Honour exposed.

'She's delighted with the deal she's done. And so's the agent, especially considering the state of the market. I gather your Berry Jopling said he was particularly fond of this part of the country.' She smiled knowingly.

'He sleeps around.'

'Wouldn't all men, given half the chance? I know we're all meant to be terrified of Aids and all that, but it doesn't seem to have made much difference.'

'Is that from personal experience, or from the gossip columns?'

Lucy laughed and then she looked serious. 'If you like him, then I think you should go out and get him.'

'He slept with Sarah.'

'Your publicity director? That's nothing. You told me yourself that everybody sleeps with her.'

'He also slept with that woman they call the Vixen.'

'I don't like her.' Lucy's face looked suddenly pinched. There was a man she was very fond of, and he knew the Vixen too.

Marie wished she hadn't mentioned the woman's name. She went back to talking about Sarah. There was nothing there to upset Lucy.

'Sarah's an odd person,' she said. 'She's been very good for my company. I could never have weathered the last few weeks and kept on stirring up the publicity we need.'

'I read a play by Ustinov once,' Lucy said, apparently irrelevantly. 'In it there was a good fairy, and four colonels. An English colonel, a French colonel . . . I forget the others. The point is that the good fairy looked like a goodie-two-shoes but she wasn't really underneath. I mean, she was human, you had to read that into her character. He's a very clever writer, you know.'

'What on earth are you talking about, Lucy?' Marie

stooped to pick a dandelion clock. She began blowing at it, sending tiny gossamer-borne seed heads bustling across the grass.

'I'm saying that you mustn't always judge by appearances. From everything you've told me, Sarah's a good example of that. Sexually she's a slut, businesswise, you assure me, she's a genius. It's like the fairy, you see – a mixture. Most people are.'

'According to Berry Jopling I'm not. I'm a potential female mogul, and that's very much a single-stream occupation.'

'Gee thinks you're bored with your work. She says you ought to have a proper holiday, get away from it all. Dashing down here on the odd Sunday isn't enough of a break.'

Marie laughed. She breathed in deeply, the fresh, clear air making her realize how tired and stiff she felt. 'A holiday. You're the second person to tell me I should take a break. My God, how I'd love to do absolutely nothing for days, other than . . .' She tipped her head back, letting the sun on to her face.

'Other than what? Go on, you nearly said what you really want to do.'

Marie shook her head suddenly, pulling her arm from Lucy's. She had shocked herself with the realization of what she wanted. 'Let's get back to the others. I can't stay for long. I want to drive over to Damion's before I go back to London, and I've brought some stuff for Fleur. I have to fetch it from the car.'

They walked back silently towards the house. Lucy felt that she had triggered something in Marie. She was sure that Berry was just the right man for her friend, but she was worried that pride might well keep the two of them apart.

The pride would be on Marie's side. She was always so

226

determined to prove that she could do everything the men could – more than that, she had to do better. That was a mistake, Lucy believed. There was no need to beat men at their own game, just play with them on equal terms.

Damion was in his element. He rode with his stirrups long, sitting deep into the horse's back. His Donegal tweed jacket was soft with wear but hung with the unmistakable look of excellent tailoring. His jodhpurs were pale stone, his boots polished to chestnut. His hair blew free, unrestrained by any form of protective hat, and Marie touched her head at him and frowned.

There were half a dozen of his horsey friends mounted on the best animals that Damion's stable could offer. They were all in jeans – apparently they had not expected to be offered a ride. Marie shook her head curtly at Damion's suggestion that she should join them. As the group clattered off down the yard on the way to the bridle path, she went into the house.

There was a smell of cooking and the sitting room was almost unrecognizable. There were flowers in a bowl, cushions on the settee. Rose was singing in the kitchen. It was almost time for her baby to be born and she had become suddenly house-proud. It was a scene of domestic bliss. Marie bit her bottom lip between her teeth. She had come to talk over the results of her American trip with Damion. Now she felt undermined. The few words they had managed to exchange before he'd mounted up had finally convinced her of his passionate desire to sell up the business. Now she also felt vulnerable, and cut off from the new life that her brother was making for himself.

Chapter 17

Too bright, too beautiful to last
WILLIAM CULLEN BRYANT
(1794–1874)

'Departure gate nineteen.' The plastic smile of the girl on the booking-in desk flashed on and off as efficiently as departure times on the computer screens behind her.

Marie had only hand luggage. She could get everything she needed for a night away from home packed into the capacious Hermès leather hold-all that Peter had once given her. As always, she had a brightly coloured silk scarf tied to its handle. That way she could easily identify it, even at a distance.

She was an organized traveller. She had packed three pairs of knickers; one bra; a travelling kit of miniature skin-care bottles from her own range; a stretch-jersey black dress with scooped neck, elbow-length sleeves, below knee length, and depending on accessories, it could take her anywhere. The bulkiest individual item in the case was the roll containing her costume jewellery. For the past couple of months she'd been collecting chunky smoked plastic. She'd put together several pairs of large, dynamic earrings; one short and one long necklace made from inch-square chunks; and three thick bracelets. All the pieces looked like rose-washed ice.

The departure gate for Guernsey was at the end of a long corridor. Marie walked out into the light drizzle towards the airport bus waiting to take the passengers to the plane. Several business-suited men were already seated. She settled herself and looked out through the

228

rain-streaked windows. A bright yellow bowser bustled about, its driver in yellow oilskins. With a jerk the bus set off. It was almost full. The last arrival hadn't bothered to take a seat; a bulky man, wearing an open, beige raincoat, he strap-hung in front of Marie. Drops of wet from his coat began to drip on her feet and she tucked them further under her.

Why had Martha been so insistent she go to the island? She tried to concentrate, to ignore the smell of damp clothing, the inane chatter of two expensively dressed women who were loudly describing to each other, in intricate detail, the designer wear they'd bought in London to impress their Channel Island neighbours. Martha wasn't the type of woman to underestimate the difficulties Marie was in. To ask her to give up two days of the working week, it had to be important. Marie had almost convinced herself of that. There was, however, a small niggle of doubt. She'd so misjudged Peter, perhaps she was wrong about the American woman.

The plane was only half full, and to Marie's relief the seat beside her was empty. She wasn't in the mood for small talk with a stranger. The take-off was quick and efficient, Marie was lulled by the stewardess performing the inevitable lifejacket ritual; then she stared out at a grey sky until her in-flight breakfast appeared. She bit hesitantly into a cheese-and-ham-filled croissant. It had looked dry and hard, and it was. After a while the plane began to bucket. It was quite small, seating only forty or so. Marie preferred to fly in big aeroplanes. She hadn't had anything to eat before leaving home, and that had been a mistake. She could smell the coffee that was splashing around in the cup on her tray. Beside the white plastic cup was a small plastic tumbler filled with a few segments of canned grapefruit and a sprinkling of mandarin oranges. Marie picked up a plastic spoon and began to try and cut the grapefruit into manageable pieces. It was impossible. She tried the croissant again, taking small bites, and interspersed them with sips of the Marmite-flavoured coffee. The plane tilted, and glancing out of the window beside her, she saw down through a break in the cloud to a sparkling blue sea. It was dotted with grey-rocked islets circled with bright white spray. It was going to be a fine day after all. She handed the tray back to the air hostess and reached for her handbag to check her make-up.

Martha was waiting for her. Looking larger than life in the small terminal, the American was dressed to go to a garden party. Marie glanced down at her watch. It was only nine-thirty.

'Marie!' Martha waved enthusiastically. She was the only one in Arrivals, but she still acted as if she had to catch Marie's attention.

There was a short queue, and they only had a few minutes to wait before they got into an airport taxi. It was warm but windy and Martha had to hold on to her wide straw-brimmed hat. A strip of red silk ran round the crown and then through two holes at the back so that it could be tied in a pussy bow.

'It's nice to see you,' Marie said. 'You look fantastic.'

'And this, Marie, is our abode for the night.'

The taxi turned sharp right off the main road and pulled up outside the glass façade of a small hotel overlooking a quiet, leafy park. They'd left behind the sugar-pink and yellow Victorian terraced housing that had flanked their trip from the airport, and entered a business area of indeterminate fifties and sixties design.

'It's nothing like as ordinary as it looks.' Martha laughed. 'And it's reasonable, has en-suite bathrooms, excellent food, and most important of all . . . But I'm not going to spoil your surprise. Come on in and freshen up.'

Marie's room was a large double. Green hessian-covered walls and pink and green floral bedspreads gave the room a pleasant, calm atmosphere. Wide, double-glazed windows provided a relaxing view of a sandstone terrace smothered with climbing geraniums in ornate terracotta pots. She could just see the corner of a mosaic-lined swimming pool. The hotel was larger than she'd first thought. There were two wings at right angles to each other. All the rooms overlooking the pool area had wrought-iron balconies. Compared to the blank, unimaginative front of the hotel it was exotic, almost Moorish.

She washed her face, cleaned her teeth and reapplied make-up. Martha had suggested she should dress up a bit, and so she changed into her black dress, put on the shorter of the two necklaces and the matching stud earrings. The effect was day-time glamour. She wasn't prepared to go quite as over the top as her American friend.

A taxi took them to St Peter Port. The capital of Guernsey was crowded with tourists, and bright with sunshine. Having threaded their way through the slow-moving traffic, they at last pulled up outside the Body Beautiful shop. To Marie's amazement it was decked out with flowers; wicker baskets crammed full of giant white daisies spilled out from the doorway and on to the pavement. Pink rosebuds climbed up strategically placed trellising and were strewn amongst the shell-shaped bottles of the entire Sunkissed range that was on display in the bow-shaped windows either side of the Georgian green door.

Inside the shop, four young female assistants stood to

one side of Tonie Marchant, the enthusiastic thirty-year-old manageress. All of the staff were wearing necklets of flowers – pink and white lilies sprinkled with gypsophila. Tonie held two more garlands in her hands, and with a smile she presented them to the new arrivals. 'Quick,' she said. 'We've been warned that they're on their way.'

Marie turned to look questioningly at Martha. She had no intention of showing her employees that she didn't know what was going on.

Martha concentrated on manoeuvring the flower arrangement over her hat. When it was arranged to her satisfaction on her lightly padded shoulders she said, 'The shop looks marvellous, doesn't it, Marie? The girls have done wonders. And I'm sure it will all show up beautifully on the television. Producing your own little Guernsey flower festival is an excellent way to celebrate five years on the island. I'm sure you'll get very good coverage. How many newspaper journalists are turning up after the radio interview?' She addressed her question to Marie. 'Four, is it, or five? I can't remember.'

Marie slipped the flowers over her head. 'The more the merrier.' She smiled brightly as she went forward to congratulate Tonie on her five years' stalwart service. She would have to slip out later and buy a suitable memento. In the meantime she would accept all the publicity Martha had set up – and just hope to heaven that it was good. At least on the mainland the UVA fuss seemed to be dying down. There was a new health scare about pigmeat that was taking up column inches.

The press conference was a delightful surprise – nothing that was going to help dispose of any more locations, but the action of a friend. She sniffed back sudden tears. Since the American trip she'd spoken with her on the phone. It had been a help, talking out the situation with a sympathetic listener. The fact that the Gear deal was going through had bought her some time, but it was urgent now that she could dispose of the rest of the sites, and get her products out on other shelves. She was determined not to end up another Sock Shop.

The television crew consisted of a bright young man with the camera, another bright young man with the mike, and a third bright young man without technical paraphernalia, but with the all-important clipboard – he was to conduct the interview. It would go out on the six o'clock news. Marie's whispered question to Tonie elicited the fact that this team was from the commercial channel. BBC were booked to come later, when the coachful of romantic writers was due to arrive.

Thirty-five blue-rinsed lady writers of romantic fiction were attending their publisher's sales conference, which was being held on the island. Tonie had thought it a good publicity stunt to have them descend en masse into the twenty-five by fifteen foot beauty boutique. When it actually happened the chaos threatened to ruin the flower arrangements, and for a few minutes all the Body Beautiful employees – Marie included – had to run around putting the flower baskets out on to the already crowded pavement. It made excellent footage for the BBC local news.

By lunchtime, Marie had done the two TV interviews, one radio slot and five newspaper 'quickies'. No one had mentioned UVA. A good part of Guernsey's appeal for the essential tourist was the sun; they weren't out to upset anyone. Marie felt tired but exhilarated. All the problems of the last few weeks had slipped to the back of her mind.

'Lunch!' Martha swept into the shop and gripped Marie firmly by the arm. 'We have to keep our strength up.'

They went back to their hotel. Martha had straightened her make-up in the taxi, inspiring Marie to do the same. The older woman declined to answer any questions as to

233

why she had chosen Guernsey to set up her publicity coup. She said, however, that she was prepared to accept Marie's congratulations – and thanks.

The hotel dining room was opulent and spacious. Musk-rose pink walls were set off by sage velvet-covered chairs. The style was pure Louis Seize. Rococo gilt mirrors reflected ornate candlesticks and shining silver tableware. It was a room to challenge any of the great London hotels. Most remarkable of all the decorations, however, were the flowers. On each table there were exuberant arrangements of roses and lilies. The blooms had been arranged with generous artistry, and they would have graced the drawing room of any stately home.

At the far end of the room, four oval-topped French doors led out on to a broad patio. Between the wooden-framed glass doors, tall, white marble torchères formed elegant stands for massive arrangements of hydrangeas. The long-branched flowers had been dried, and their resultant colours – soft, muted greens tinged with pink – echoed the décor to perfection. Hanging from the ornate plaster cornicing, a thick ropelike swag of dried moss and bronzed leaves encircled the room.

'It's quite lovely,' Marie breathed.

'It's empty,' Martha replied.

They went to a table for two that was close to the windows. A French-speaking waiter came to take their order. The menu was long and complex. Martha chose to start with an aubergine pâté served with home-made cheese straws, and then, to follow, pan-fried free-range chicken with a mixed salad. Marie ordered consommé de volaille and a main course of monkfish à la grecque with green beans.

Martha sipped contemplatively at her glass of Perrier for a while, and then said, 'I'd really like to put you into this afternoon cold. I think it would be interesting to see how you respond to the challenge. But I know from what you've told me that your company's in trouble and this is all too important for you. I shan't play any more games.'

'You mean there's even more to my trip than this absolutely manic morning?' Marie laughed. Her consommé was delicious, the room, despite being totally deserted, was charming.

'This morning was just a bit of image-building for you. It may not even be necessary, but I like a bit of forward planning. Tell me, have you ever heard of Oliver Candelle?'

Marie shook her head.

'He's one of the richest men on the island. Come to that, by any standards, he's pretty wealthy. And Oliver enjoys his money. He likes to indulge himself. This is his place.' Martha waved her fork in the air to indicate their surroundings.

'He owns this?' Marie looked around the room again. 'It's a bit odd, isn't it, how the entrance so belies this grandeur?'

'Oliver was always somewhat odd himself. I've known him on and off for more years than I care to remember. And I've done the occasional bit of business with him. He's hard, but fair. He's also a sucker for wanting to know people in the public eye. What's that expression that says it all? Something I heard the other day? A star-fucker – yes that's it, Oliver is a star-fucker.'

The startled expression on the waiter's face as he silently cleared their hors d'oeuvres proved that his command of English covered the colloquial.

Martha carried on unabashed. 'And, no doubt, to try and atone for being such a naughty boy when he was younger, since his heart attack, he's become very much a family man. It's his wife who does the flowers here, and you have to agree that they're pretty much something. She also provided me with the arrangements for this morning's bash. In the past couple of years, Oliver has bought up several of the island's flower growers, so now he's one of the largest producers, and his eighteen-year-old daughter wants to join Mummy and Daddy in the business. Being a wealthy man to begin with, he wants to make even more money by sending his women out into the wide world. That's figuratively, of course. They won't actually leave their twelve-bedroomed home, but their designer image is all set to be exported to the mainland.'

There was a brief pause as their main courses were carried to the table, covered with brightly polished silver domes which their waiter removed with a flourish.

'God, I'm starving,' Martha said, but she was talking so hard that she couldn't bring herself to stop to eat and the chicken cooled in front of her. 'The business that will be carried on in the name of Mrs Candelle and Daughter will start off cushioned by Oliver's cash and backed by his shrewd business brain. What he's going to need' – Martha paused and at last tasted her food – 'is a chain of retail outlets. Suitable sites to sell Channel Island flowers – all fresh and dewy straight from the airport – as well as their spectacular dried arrangements, as designed by the afore-mentioned ladies. Actually, I might have sounded a bit bitchy, but it's quite a good idea. They'll go for franchiz-ing in a few years, of course. Oliver's got the money to sit out the high-street recession. I guess the old bastard will make a killing.' She sounded very cheerful despite her choice of words.

Marie glowed. She laid her fork down beside her untasted fish and just let the euphoria wash over her. 'You've found me a real live potential buyer – you're a genius.'

'Not so fast. I haven't done your deal. Just set up a meeting.'

'My God, I owe you, Martha.'

'No, no you don't.' Martha reached over and briefly squeezed Marie's hand. 'I've enjoyed myself more than I have in years setting this up. I'd lost the edge for a deal, not been hungry enough for a long time. Now I'm going to have myself fun watching you go for the jugular. Heck, this fizzy water is just so much piss. Waiter, champagne!'

Marie was suddenly hungry. She finished every piece of her fish and then set about demolishing a meringue glacé. She couldn't wait for the next part of her day.

The insistent ringing of a bell made Marie look around her in panic. There was a bicycle somewhere out there in the swirling, clinging mist. She was going to be knocked over, badly hurt. But she couldn't see where the sound was coming from.

She woke, sitting up suddenly, breathing hard and covered in sweat. The bell carried on ringing. She was at home; she stared down at the duvet cover, its richly flowered pattern reassuringly familiar.

Sarah had her finger pressed on the door bell and was leaning on it. It was ten o'clock and she had a meeting at eleven, but she was determined to see Marie first.

The door opened a fraction, restrained by the security catch. 'Oh,' Marie said. 'It's you.' Her movements were made clumsy by sleep, and she fumbled as she undid the chain.

Sarah walked briskly into the flat. She was wearing a short-cut swinging duster jacket in a vivid yellow over a sleeveless matching dress. Her legs, clad in flesh-coloured tights and low-heeled black patent shoes, looked young and long.

'You look like some kind of avenging Valkyrie.' Marie

237

walked over to the curtains and drew them back. 'You do know, I suppose, that I didn't get to bed until just over an hour ago. I'd only just got to sleep when you woke me. I was working up to the early hours this morning and then Martha wanted to go through everything before I caught my flight back. God knows, she deserved to hear all about it. But I didn't expect to see you this morning. I rang you from the airport, and left a message on your answerphone saying I'd got a buyer for another forty shops and that I'd fill you in this afternoon at the office.'

'I haven't been home to pick up any messages. I didn't get to bed at all last night.' Sarah turned round. The sunlight streaming through the windows was full on her face but she didn't look tired. Her skin was fresh and glowing. A small crease formed between her brows. 'Forty shops, you said? Presumably the next chunk down the list in desirability?'

'Absolutely. It means we're left with the dross. But the bank are just going to have to lump it for a while. I think we've done enough miracles for now.'

'Speak for yourself.' Sarah laughed. She looked inspired, full of life. 'Anyway, congrats. I won't say I'm surprised – you know I'm a believer.'

'Coffee?' Marie began shuffling through to the kitchen. She yawned and rubbed her hands over her face. She just couldn't seem to wake up. 'Sorry, I think it's jet-lag.'

'For heaven's sake, go and take a shower. I'll do the coffee. You look hysterical like that.'

Marie looked down at herself. She was wearing a jumbo-sized T-shirt. It was basically white, but on the front there was a highly coloured picture of a camel sitting in a deckchair. The camel was clutching a cocktail in one hand and sunglasses in the other. The caption was *It's tough in the Gulf*. She laughed and said 'Damion got it for me when he was in Kuwait.'

'You should frame it. Pre-Saddam Hussein ex-pat humour. Where do you keep your biscuits? I'm famished.'

Despite being short of time, Sarah couldn't bring herself to say what was on her mind. She kept prompting Marie to talk about the Guernsey trip, and she did want to know – saving the firm was important, now especially so.

'Where did you say you were going this morning?' Marie glanced down at the watch on her wrist. She was still disoriented. The dial had no numbers, and she had to concentrate to work out that the time it showed was twenty to eleven.

'I'm off to see a graphic artist, freelance. He's not long qualified. Ex-St Martin's, I saw his work at their show. It's fresh and crisp but somehow atmospheric, I think it will suit our stuff to a tee. And I can get a very nice two-page article out of *Vogue*. Ostensibly the piece is on him, but all the work they photograph will be ours.'

'That sounds useful.'

'All it'll cost is a few hundred for him to do some brochure work that we'll use anyway, and a really slap-up lunch at Brown's for the journalist. I trust that after your successful trip my expense account can stand it?'

'Why did you really come here this morning?' Marie's mind was clearing. It was no longer totally fogged by sleep. 'You're sitting there like a cat on a hot tin roof. And you've only half-listened to what I've said.'

Sarah quickly swallowed the last of her coffee and stood up. 'I've got to go, seriously. I don't want to miss out on this one.' She smiled and her lips curled up at the corners like a self-satisfied cat. 'I'll tell you everything this afternoon. But I'll give you a clue: we've all been busy on the company's account, and I do mean "all". So have the champers on ice.'

* * *

Larry Gold was a man at peace with his world. He was happy that he was chunky, flat bellied and deep chested. His physique, he reckoned, was excellent for a thirty-year-old high-flyer who took no exercise other than in bed, or – if inspired – in the shower, on the floor, or – if pushed – in the car. One of his favourite mannerisms was to run his manicured hand over his crisp dark hair that, to his delight, showed no signs of thinning.

He stood at the end of his immaculate suburban garden and looked back at the highly desirable four-bed, two-bath residence that had recently become his home. It was evening, and the lighted windows revealed tantalizing glimpses of opulence. He was delighted to see that the Czechoslovakian chandelier in the main bedroom was clearly visible. The name of his game was impressions, and first impressions underlined emphatically that he was a young man on his way to the top. He was in the travel trade, which was suffering along with every other high-street business, and the fact that he was prospering at all made him more than a success, it made him a miracle worker.

He watched as his wife Barbara crossed the patio en route from the American-style fitted kitchen to the built-in barbeque tucked in behind the carport. His wife was another proof of his affluence. She was expensively sun-tanned all year, her hair streaked with a dozen different shades of blonde. Three gold charm bracelets jangled as she walked, proclaiming her the spoilt daughter of a wealthy man – which she was. Her self-satisfied expression under the Elizabeth Arden mousse proclaimed her the darling wife of an admiring husband – which she wasn't. Fortunately for her peace of mind, she was too thick to know it.

The smell of spit-grilled jumbo prawns drifted up to the neon-tinted sky. A spotty young man dressed in red trousers, matching waistcoat and black-and-white striped shirt began noisily setting up a bar on a trestle table. The evening was beginning to roll. It would be a perfectly organized bout of showmanship, 1990s style. Larry took a last deep breath of solitary air and then started back towards the house. The fun was about to begin.

'Ladies and gentlemen,' the DJ drawled in a pseudo-transatlantic accent into his microphone. 'Pray silence for your host. I give you' – he dropped his hand to the turntable for a quick burst on the drum rolls – 'Larry, your golden boy!'

The assembled crowd cheered self-consciously. They all had to give it their best, every last one of them was dependent on their host's assorted talents. Larry liked things that way.

'Good evening, friends,' he bawled into the microphone. 'At least, I think you're all friends, I can't actually see any enemies lurking in the shrubbery!'

'Everybody here loves you, Larry.' The shout from the back was instantly recognizable to them all as Charlie, Larry's runaround, arse licker, picker up of loose ends, and tonight, as always, well-rehearsed assistant.

'Thanks, Charlie. Now, just in case any of you haven't read today's papers . . .'

There were more cheers.

'Well, just in case, and because I like to talk about my successes, here it comes again. As of yesterday, Cat Travel was sold, lock, stock and barrel to Shipping Inc. Every one of you here that works for the good old Pussy company will have had their letter setting out their new contract-of-employment details. And they're good, aren't they – very good.'

Over half the party gave a loud shout of agreement. The deal Larry had done had been amazing. He'd got out of a company he was convinced would go to the wall over the next few years, made a moderate fortune for himself, and the suckers buying the company had even taken on the existing staff. He was really enjoying playing at being the people's hero.

'Well, I'm sorry, fans, but you won't be seeing me at the good old Catford office any more.'

There were put-on groans. There were also a few tears from a couple of the women. But they needn't worry, Larry thought, some other guy would take over where he'd left off. They were the type of girl he really liked to have around the office – they didn't act coy and call it sexual harassment, they just enjoyed it.

'As for the rest of you . . .'

They were the also-rans in Larry's first stage of empire-building. They were contacts from companies he'd pulled into the Cat Travel group; a couple of seaside coach operators, a booking agency. They made up the rest of the party, except for the odd one out, a woman he'd met only recently. A slim blonde who'd made his wife's hackles rise.

'I hope you guys got the letters outlining the new contracts I got for you with Shipping Inc. I worked bloody hard getting those for you.'

His wife's harsh intake of breath at her husband's swearing was drowned by the burst of applause.

'Now the whole point of this evening is to eat, drink and be merry. And, of course, to tell you to remember who your friends are. I haven't yet decided what I'm going to do in the future, except for taking a long holiday with my dear wife. She's owed. I could tell you, the things she's put up with . . .' He let his voice trail off, wishing tears into his eyes. 'Anyway, you don't want to hear any more from me. The food's ready, the booze is on tap.

242

Don't forget, the day you hear it's Larry Gold calling you on the phone, you drop everything.'

'Three cheers for Larry.' It was Charlie again. 'Hip, hip.'

They all cheered, even Barbara, who found that kind of thing embarrassing. She was a bit worried that the noise might wake their children, Baby Larry and Samantha. They had their au pair within call, but she didn't think it would be the done thing for the guests to hear her children crying, not at ten o'clock at night. Barbara was very conscious of her own rules of social etiquette.

Larry was delighted. He was expanding in the praise he knew he deserved. He had positioned himself at the edge of the patio and his admirers came up to him, had their say and then drifted away as yet another came to ask a favour, or simply heap more praise. He was pleased he had decided to wear all white. It underlined his tan, and complemented the chunky gold necklet that lay so snugly on the curling hairs just visible above his shirt button. He always used his hands as he talked and it gave him the chance to show off the signet ring Barbara had given him to celebrate his success.

There had been some very good publicity about his sell-out, and he'd leaked the fact that he would be going back in again, right at the bottom of the market. He was convinced that was the way to go. Back into the coach trips, and the bucket-price seats. It was the C1s and below who weren't going to give up their cheap booze and their bit of sun. You couldn't frighten them off for long with a bit of scaremongering. That was why he had contacted Body Beautiful. He'd read in the tabloids they'd been zapped with their sun products, and he reckoned there had to be a whole load of tubes of sun cream lying around in some warehouse. He fancied himself a bit of an innovator. As of Christmas, anyone who paid their deposit on a holiday booked with him would get their sun oil by return of post.

'Larry.' It was luscious, lovely Brenda.

Perhaps it was something to do with her job, he thought, continually talking to the customers about the beds they wanted on their holidays, that made her think about it all the time. Bed, that is.

'Larry, couldn't we . . .?'

'Do me a favour, where the hell do you think we could?'

'I'll be at the end of the garden.' And she wafted off in a cloud of scent.

For another half an hour Larry stood, arms lightly folded, nodding, gesticulating with his hands, being the centre of the evening's revolutions. It gradually dawned on him that he was feeling restless. Perhaps, he thought, it was asking a lot of his lithe, fit body, to stand still for so long. Or perhaps the jumbo prawns had lived up to their reputation for being an aphrodisiac.

He escaped to the end of the garden, where, despite the damp of the evening, Brenda still waited. Within a couple of minutes he had her skirt up and his pants down. In a few more moments he was partaking of the pleasures that any potentate should – not that many eastern rulers have to do it standing up, balanced uncertainly to one side of a compost heap.

He shuffled them round so that he could see over Brenda's shoulder to the party. The blonde was walking across his patio. She moved slowly, swaying on her long legs like some exotic animal. He thrust harder. It could be her.

244

Chapter 18

Where beauty is, there will be love
ROBERT HEATH (fl. 1617)

Berry winked at Angelique as he walked through the door she was holding open for him and into Marie's office. Behind his back he held a jeroboam of champagne – Moët et Chandon, the secretary had told him it was her boss's favourite.

'I gather congratulations are in order, Marie.'

Marie raised her eyebrows in feigned surprise. 'However did you know that?' she asked.

'Intuition? Or maybe your tone on the phone was so friendly I knew that you thought you'd put one over on me.'

'Put one over on you?'

'I've spent a lot of time putting a package together that will bale you out totally, but you're still wasting your time running around trying to sell your sites off piecemeal. You should be concentrating on where your company goes from here. I've told you, you can trust me to dispose of your property interests. You should be using your energies to get your sales points established "in store" again. Just as we discussed the other evening.'

'Trust. That's a strange word coming from you.' Marie paused, her eyes narrowing. She was annoyed with herself – she was close to letting her personal feelings get in the way of what was, after all, strictly business. 'Talking about "strange", why have you got your hand hidden behind your back? I assume you're not carrying a sawn-off shotgun. I wouldn't like to think the bank has given you instructions to blow me away if I don't go along with your plans for me and my company.'

Berry displayed his bottle of champagne.

'How kind.' Marie smiled with her mouth, but her eyes remained hard. 'My cousins have been asking for contributions for the bottle stall at their village fête. I'm sure they'll be delighted. But then you probably knew all about the fête, didn't you? After all, you're buying their woodland.'

Berry ignored the reference to the Montfords and began peeling off the foil cap. He asked, 'Do you have any glasses?'

Marie shook her head. 'No, and I don't drink in the office during the day.'

'That's a shame.' Berry had the wire-caged cork exposed. 'And it's a pity about the glasses too. I'll just have to drink out of the bottle.'

Marie stood up and walked out from behind her desk. She was wearing a soft jersey dress. In shell pink, with a flattering scooped neck and cap sleeves, it draped tightly across her breasts and then fell in soft folds down to her knees.

Berry deliberately looked her up and down. 'You look delicious,' he said. The expression on his face was very serious. 'And you looked beautiful the other evening at Damion's.'

Marie stopped in front of him. 'I'm amazed you noticed.'

'I noticed, all right, as did that wimp Simeon.'

'Wimp? I don't know I'd agree with that. He was very charming.'

Berry stretched out a hand and placed it lightly on her

shoulder. 'I like the feel of that.' He stroked the fabric of the dress. 'And you smell wonderful.'

'What's brought all this on?' Marie forced her voice to stay level, to sound mocking. 'To what exactly do I owe being made flavour of the month?'

Berry pulled her gently towards him. She was yielding to his touch, tilting her face back to meet his, when she remembered the dinner party.

She stepped back abruptly. 'Save your champagne for your next horsey excursion. I'm sure the Vixen looks far better through an alcoholic haze.'

Berry laughed. 'Why, you are a scratchy little cat, after all.' He had one hand under the bottom of the bottle, the other holding the neck. He began shaking the bottle, slowly and deliberately to begin with and then faster and faster.

'What on earth are you doing that for?' Marie stepped back. She felt the edge of her desk against the back of her legs. 'Be careful it doesn't go off.'

'You don't like the horses, so I thought perhaps you went in for racing drivers. You know the good old victory ritual, don't you, Marie? Come on, join in, everyone loves to get wet, it brings you luck.' He was laughing out loud, shaking the bottle violently.

'You wouldn't dare.'

'Oh, but I would.' The cork popped, champagne foamed up, and a great stream of drenching liquid hit Marie in the chest, on her arms. She tried to escape, to get to the door, but Berry was in front of her, and there seemed to be no end to the bubbling drink.

'Wet T-shirt competition,' Berry laughed. 'You win hands down.' He was breathing heavily as if he'd been running.

Marie looked down in horror at her dress. It was

soaked, clinging to her. 'I could throttle you for that. Get out! Get out of my office! Get out of my life!'

'For God's sake.' He reached out and pulled her roughly towards him. 'Why the hell can't you understand . . .' His lips were on hers, kissing her hard, forcing his tongue between her teeth as he held her so tightly against him that the wet began soaking through his shirt.

Marie pushed against him. She had her hands on his chest, trying to get free, and all the time her body, her weak, treacherous body, wanted to yield.

'Don't fight it.' Berry was still holding her close. He was speaking softly, his breath warm on her ear.

'Let me go,' she whispered. She'd meant to sound strong, and yet she'd said the words softly, as if they were an endearment.

'I've wanted you since the first time I met you.' He was running his hands over her breasts, feeling the firmness of the nipples through the wet cloth.

Marie tipped her head back, moulded her body against his. She felt the strength, the hardness of him. A low moan came from deep in her throat.

The soft buzz of the intercom on her desk behind them sounded very loud.

'I have to answer that.' She could feel his lips at her throat, his broad hands caressing her. 'Please . . .' she stumbled away.

'Marie.' Angelique's voice was anxious. 'I have two men here from the VAT. They're insisting on seeing you.'

'I have someone with me.'

Berry had come up behind her. He put his hands round her waist, ran the flat of his hands down over her stomach. She breathed in sharply as his fingers paused. She wanted to lie down, to spread her legs wide in wanton ecstasy. 'Give me a couple of minutes,' she said into the receiver.

She turned in his hands and pressed herself fleetingly

against him then quickly backed away. 'So close.' She was laughing but she felt close to tears. 'Saved by the bell.'

'You can't leave me like this.'

'You certainly can't stay like that. You'd better go into my bathroom and cool down. You can leave by the other door. There's someone from the Customs and Excise outside. They've got right of entry – you know that.'

'Jesus.' Berry had his hand deep in his trouser pocket, he was desperately trying to adjust himself. 'Right of entry, that's just what I need right now.'

Marie didn't say any of the thoughts that quickly came to her. For a few moments she had wanted him more than anything else on earth. Everything seemed unreal, she felt shaken deep inside.

'I fly to Australia tonight.'

'Australia? But you never said . . .'

'I have to keep up some pretence of running my company.' He smiled, but it was lopsided. The heat in his eyes was cooling and he looked tired.

'When's your flight?' She couldn't believe what she was asking, but right then she would have met with him anywhere to finish what they'd started.

'I have to book in at six, I have a board meeting at four. Just how fast could you make it?' He laughed softly.

'The way I felt a few minutes ago it wouldn't take long at all.' She was blushing but smiling.

'I told you we were made for each other. I'll call you from the great land of Oz.' He stepped towards her and bent to kiss her gently on the cheek. 'Stay safe.'

She waited until he was turning the door handle, then she called, 'Berry!' He turned back. She looked very serious. 'I've already broken one rule in mixing business with pleasure, but I shan't break any more. I won't share a man with anyone.'

'You haven't met my dog yet.' He laughed. And then he was gone.

Marie sat cross-legged on a blue towelling exercise mat on the floor of her living room and stretched her arms towards the ceiling. What on earth had she got herself into?

Berry had phoned from his car on the way to the airport. He'd sounded abrupt. He would be away for ten days. His secretary had numbers where he could be reached if need be. By the tone of his voice he'd implied it would have to be a very important reason indeed to justify her calling.

Very slowly, keeping her spine at full stretch, she reached forward as far as she could and then bent until her hands touched the floor. She'd spoken very little on the phone, only when he'd said he was about to enter the airport had she said, quite softly, 'Take care.'

Berry's voice had altered, he'd suddenly sounded choked. 'Don't,' he'd said. And then he'd laughed. 'I could hardly walk when I left your office earlier. Just don't get me going again. You and I have some very unfinished business. This is going to be the longest ten days of my life.' With that, he'd hung up.

One, two, three, she was counting as she bent her forehead to her knees, straightened a little and then bent again. She had ten days to hone her body. Suddenly that didn't seem long at all. She wanted to lose at least four pounds. The recent trips had meant she'd been eating too much of the wrong things.

Her lime-green stretch leotard was cut high at the hips, and she ran her fingers over the smooth skin. She fairly regularly massaged her thighs and buttocks, exfoliated and moisturized them. So how come she could still feel cellulite? It was only with the very lightest pressure of the tips of her fingers that she could feel the minute ridges under the skin.

Damion had promised the earth with his massage kit but it couldn't have been effective. There was an Elancyl back at the office – the pack they'd bought to compare with their own product. Tomorrow she'd smuggle it out and bring it home. Meanwhile, what was it Sarah had suggested when they'd been planning the mitt? A loofah, that was what she'd said worked effectively – well she had one of those in the bathroom. But first – she stood up and stretched – she wanted to give herself a facial.

Rosemary and thyme, camomile and sea salt, she tipped generous handfuls of everything into the large, steaming bowl of water. The smell of sweet herbs filled the kitchen, reminding her that she was hungry. With luck, she thought, that meant she was losing weight.

Marie wrapped her hair in a towel, stripped out of her leotard and changed into a T-shirt. Calmly, she reminded herself; for beauty routines to work properly they must be undertaken calmly, and of course routinely. She'd given that pep talk more times than she cared to remember, but her own regime had still been the first thing to suffer when she'd hit problems at work.

Marie draped a towel over her head and the basin, enveloping herself in a thick, warm mist. For the first few minutes it was difficult to breathe in the scented steam, but after a while she became used to it. She could feel her skin hydrating. There was a dull ache of tension at the base of her neck that had been there for weeks. Gradually, she convinced herself, it was fading.

She began thinking about Berry. It couldn't all be due to him that she was looking forward to life again. In reality the biggest change was the fact that she had the offer from Guernsey, and now it was official. The fax had come through just before close of business. She would buy her flowers from Guernsey Belles for evermore out of gratitude.

Whatever Berry had said about letting him dispose of the properties, she had achieved what he apparently couldn't. And if Sarah's new contact came to anything, Body Beautiful was on the verge of a new success story.

She let her thoughts ramble. Berry was promiscuous; she knew for certain that he'd made love to Sarah, and to that foxy-haired bitch after the dinner party. She felt a pang of jealousy that tightened the muscles in her stomach. But as far as Sarah was concerned it was no more than par for the course; she thought that getting into bed with a man was the next form of greeting after shaking hands. And as for the Vixen – Damion had fixed that up.

Marie wriggled uncomfortably on the hard kitchen chair. She was still livid about the other women. But she knew that it was herself Berry really wanted, that for him she was special. It was all her fault for turning him down.

She opened her eyes in the steam and revelled in their stinging. It was a small pain compared to the mental anguish she was putting herself through. She was a highly intelligent, and thanks to God and the Guernsey Belles, a highly successful businesswoman, but she was acting like a teenager.

She began to sing. It was flat and out of tune but still recognizable, the words, muffled by the towel, floated out to compete with the clamour from the Garden below.

What do you get when you fall in love? You get enough germs to catch pneumonia, and when you do, he'll never phone you. I'll never fall in love again. It was what she used to sing in Peter's early days.

'It's no good,' Damion said to his unexpected visitor as he put down the bucket of oats he'd been carrying.

Tommy Docherty walked down the yard with a swagger. In the soft early evening light he was the picture of an Irish sporting gentleman from his Donegal tweed jacket to his shining brown brogues. The only incongruous item in his appearance was the briefcase he was carrying. Made from soft beige leather, it was too small to carry much more than a few letters and appeared more suited to a woman of leisure.

'Marie won't buy the shares off me at market price,' Damion continued. 'It doesn't matter what I say.'

'I thought as much. She's got a lot to learn, that sister of yours. Well, you've had a few months' grace, and a fat lot of good it's done you.' Tommy turned to stare into a loose box beside him where Beauty was standing in the shadows. 'What's this nag's form then?'

'It's nothing but a moderate point-to-pointer.'

The yard lights weren't on yet. Damion liked to play his cards close to his chest, especially if it might be a winning hand.

'I hear you've some likely animals about.'

'Only those in training for other owners. I've told you.' He let desperation creep into his voice – it seemed expected. 'I've got nothing, even the yard's rented. Nothing's gone as well as I hoped. I've been tied up, the baby came early and Rose still isn't right. You'll have to give me more time.'

'If it was left to me, you know you'd have as long as it takes,' Tommy said with obvious insincerity.

He had undone the top bolt on the outside of Beauty's stable door and lifted his foot ready to kick open the bottom bolt when he heard the clatter of approaching hooves. He looked quickly round at Damion. 'I don't want to be seen here.'

Damion ran up the yard towards the approaching riders. He stood in their way, laughing and joking for a

253

few minutes. It was an experiment he was trying, offering an escorted hack over the local downs. It was light work for Rose while the baby was sleeping. Its pram had been left close to the tack room, where one of the grooms was busy with the saddle soap.

The horses were ones Damion had hired in for the day. Later he'd turn them out in the paddock for the night, and then the youngsters from Sunnydale Stables would be over in the morning to take them back. If they got enough business he'd buy half a dozen hacks of his own. He was doing everything he could to keep the yard ticking over until interest rates dropped and the middle-range owners started to return.

Tommy had gone as efficiently as he'd arrived. Damion finished evening stables on his own. Rose had been feeling under the weather after her ride so he'd sent her in early to bed. The baby would keep them both awake later. It seemed to have its clock back to front, sleeping all day and awake all night. It bothered him that Tommy had been so concerned not to be seen. There was no reason for him to feel like that, unless something was going to happen – something to the stables, or to Damion – that he didn't want to be tied in to.

Horses were vulnerable. Dick Francis had made a fortune out of telling stories underlining that very fact. Another indisputable fact of the horsey world was that their owners were a strange, oversensitive breed of people. One whiff of bother and they'd be off to pastures greener. The thing Damion couldn't understand was what anyone could hope to gain by ruining his business. He kept working steadily at his chores as the problem revolved in his mind.

He was walking up the yard, in and out of the yellow pools of light beneath the wire-caged bulbs, when he understood. He stopped walking abruptly and the half-a-dozen sweet-smelling hay nets he was carrying jostled gently against him. Somewhere in the dusk a horse whickered for water. If Tommy and his associates thought violence was going to help, then they still hadn't appreciated the true situation of his shares in Body Beautiful.

The shares had no market value at all because Marie had the option to buy them for a pittance. It had seemed so logical at the beginning, but now it seemed grossly unfair. He'd worked for years to get the company off the ground. It had been his expertise that had produced the product range, the backbone of the business.

It was in Beauty's stable that he found the briefcase Tommy had carried into the yard. It contained photos, press shots by the look of them. All of the pictures were of fires, a lot of smoke, a lot of damage. There was something else, tucked in a flap designed for visiting cards. A book of matches from the Café Royal.

'Very funny,' Damion whispered as he pushed the photos back into the case.

Only it wasn't even vaguely amusing. He didn't have anything like enough insurance to cover what a major fire would do in his yard. The horses in training were covered, that was true, all except Beauty – being his own property, insurance on her had been an expendable luxury.

He'd kept the matches in his hand, and began tapping them thoughtfully against his teeth. He supposed he should have been scared. Tommy Docherty did some strange deals. If only Marie would show some interest in him, Damion reckoned he'd have some more time. And time could cure all, if Beauty could run herself into the money and him out of trouble.

'But it works both ways.' Marie's voice was insistent down the telephone. 'If I desperately wanted to sell out I'd have to offer my shares to you. And you'd pick up your option for a pittance, of course you would. Don't act as if I'm the ogre. If you wanted the cash for a good purpose and I had it spare then I wouldn't hesitate before buying you out at market value. But I don't have the money, and I know what you want it for. I wouldn't give you a penny to pay gambling debts. But it's all immaterial. Everything's in hock to the bank – you know that. I've agreed to put my flat in as collateral as well. I signed the papers last week. I had to buy some more time.'

'That's just what I need, time. And I'm afraid the only way I'm going to get it is if you talk to Tommy.'

'Never!'

'I've done things I didn't bloody enjoy doing for you and your precious company. I'm not asking you to sleep with the bastard, just buy me a few weeks more.'

'It's not just him, you know there are others involved.'

'Don't believe everything he says. He's worth a mint. You should know that if anyone does.'

All the times he'd tried to get her to agree to marry him, it was his wealth that he'd thought would swing the trick. The thousand or so acres he owned bordering the Sullivan estate, the thriving chain of bookmakers he'd built up.

'Look, just give him a call. That's not asking too much. Even of my holy Mary sister.'

'Just watch your tongue.'

They were shouting at each other, all the old jibes coming out, but Damion's face was calm. He was deliberately goading his sister. If he was lucky she'd end up feeling guilty for losing her temper and do what he wanted.

Chapter 19

Women . . .
   What is your sex's earliest, latest care?
   Your heart's supreme ambition?
   To be fair.
                        GEORGE LYTTELTON (1709–93)

'And I thought the beauty business was manic!' Sarah quickly moved to one side to avoid being knocked over by a rapidly moving donkey rail that was heavily loaded with suits and dresses.

The slightly built girl who was struggling to propel the metal contraption around all the obstructions in the cluttered, open-plan office gasped an apology.

Anne Barclay, five foot ten, eight stone, ex-fashion model, smiled smugly at Sarah. 'I told you that you'd be surprised by the action.'

In the eight years since she'd given up modelling, Anne had become a successful fashion journalist. Her appearance had hardly changed from the days when she'd featured on the front pages of the mass-market women's magazines. She still had ultra-short bobbed black hair; her blue eyes were still fringed with thickly mascara'd false eyelashes. She even still wore black crepe jersey all year round. It being autumn, her outfit had three-quarter-length sleeves, a high round neck and a straight tight skirt that barely reached to mid-thigh. She wore flesh-coloured tights and flat black patent pumps.

'I'm grateful for the chance to see the shop floor in action,' Sarah said. 'Sometimes I think I'm tucked up in my ivory tower, too far away from what's going on.'

'Your problem is too many long, long lunches. I thought I could detect a little softening in the outline.'

Sarah breathed in sharply. Just because the journalist was as thin as a rake she assumed no one else wanted a shape.

Anne gave a quick, practised smile to a short tubby man who was making his way purposefully towards them. 'Sam Wells,' she murmured. 'Groper of the first order.'

Sarah was introduced to Sam, head buyer of Anne Marie, the mid range of the high-street chain Elegance. He clasped her hand tightly as he said how delighted he was to meet her and then launched instantly into a hard sell on the benefits of his range. All the while he was looking Sarah up and down, apparently sizing her up as a future customer.

'Of course, you'd fit into our petite range,' he smiled. 'We do everything: coats, suits, dresses and separates, right down to the underwear. And that's where we really excel. Though I say it myself, I select a mean line in teddies.'

'Amazing.' Sarah wanted to giggle. Instead she managed to breathe the one word out seductively; she liked to stay in practice.

'Let's get on with it, shall we?' Anne said shortly. 'You roll out the dolly and we'll see how things go.'

They worked their way past a regiment of desks littered with computer screens and their attendant paraphernalia. On the way, the buyer effusively assured them that Sandra Selles was not a dolly. She was a very pretty girl, he said, who was doing very well for herself as a model. When Anne snorted her disgust loudly enough to be heard over the clamour around them, he hurried on to say that, of course, she was a photographic model, not fashion in the strictest sense. He paused and then added that, so far,

258

most of the coverage she'd got had been in the lower end of the tabloids.

The office that had been set aside for them contained a teak-topped table surrounded by eight beige tweed chairs. There were several white plastic planters overflowing with greenery.

Sam said, 'I'm sorry it's a bit of a crush.'

There were five donkey rails loaded with an assortment of multi-coloured garments filling most of the available floor space.

He moved a few chairs around as he asked, 'Tea, coffee, cold drinks?'

'Why the hell am I doing this?' Anne slumped down in a chair as Sam scuttled off to fetch her a Diet Coke. 'This little baggage is going to be way out of her league.'

Sarah began looking through the clothes on the racks. 'This is quite nice.' She pulled out a cream wool jacket. It was fitted in to the waist and softly shaped at the neck. 'I wouldn't mind wearing this myself.'

Anne snorted again.

'If you're so unhappy about doing this, then why are we here?' Sarah asked.

Anne had telephoned and asked if Body Beautiful would be interested in taking part in a promotional article she was doing for *Cosmopolitan*. Elegance was going to provide a whole new wardrobe – how would Sarah like to get her company involved in providing the skin care and selecting the make-up?

It had seemed an excellent idea, until the last moment. Elegance stipulated that the girl, Sandra, should be used because she had featured in some of their advertising. She wasn't the ideal role model for Body Beautiful. She was too chubby, and her skin wasn't all that good.

'I would have chosen some kind of sports personality.' Anne stood up and walked grudgingly towards the rails.

'I mean, just look at this. It would look great on a girl with a nice figure. Dorothy Perkins have done brilliantly with that snooker player Allison Fisher wearing their clothes. But on dear little Sandra these are going to look – ' She stopped abruptly as the door opened and half a dozen young women walked in.

From somewhere in the centre of the group a voice called out that she was Michelle, who would be running the morning's try-on session.

Michelle turned out to be a slim, energetic brunette with her long hair tied up in a froth of curls on top of her head. She wore sensible flat suede pumps and ankle-length black trousers, topped by a cream blouse that had obviously not been bought from her employers.

The other girls were all junior merchandisers, apart from a short, plump, sulky-faced twenty-year-old who was introduced as Sandra. She brightened a bit when she found out who Sarah was. She liked make-up, she explained, but on meeting Anne her sulk became even more pronounced. She was clearly suspicious of journalists, especially female ones.

'Well, ladies.' Michelle giggled self-consciously, coughed once and then adopted a teacher-like monotone. 'This morning we're going to select the clothes for Sandra to wear on the photo-shoot. Anne is going to be taking notes for her article, so mind the language please, girls.'

There was a subdued titter.

Michelle carried on, 'Sarah comes from the company which is going to do Sandra's make-over.'

'That's Body Beautiful,' Sarah said clearly. There was no point in wasting exposure, even on a limited scale.

'Let's start by making a temporary changing cubicle in the corner, shall we?'

Several of the girls got up and began pushing the

donkey rails around to make a screen at the end of the room.

Michelle paused until the commotion had died down, and then began to speak again.

'Elegance would like to feature its winter range. As you can see, I've brought a selection from Basics, Anne Marie and then finally Dinner Date. I thought Sandra would look best in our blues and reds, and possibly the grape for evening. I think the black's too harsh for her, and the classic autumn colours won't bring out her best points.'

Sarah wanted to yawn. It was hot and stuffy in the office. The girl, Sandra, was an ordinary-looking little baggage. She had a spot on her chin that she kept rubbing with her forefinger. She was going to photograph very badly indeed. The intention was to do full-length movement shots. They needed someone with Anne's figure for that, or at least someone slim and fit-looking.

They started with day wear. Sandra tried on a fitted pink suit. The size twelve skirt didn't stand a chance of doing up, and one of the girls was sent off to find a size fourteen. The jacket was fine across the shoulders but wouldn't do up across the bust. Sandra simpered at that, and said she always had trouble getting jackets and blouses to fit – jumpers, she confided, would stretch.

After nearly an hour, they had opened the windows to try and reduce the temperature, but still Sandra's face was red and puffy.

Michelle called out, 'Coffee, anyone?' and the atmosphere cooled marginally.

'This is not going to work.' Anne stood up slowly, unwinding her height from the chair to tower menacingly above everyone else in the room. 'I can tell you right now that this is not going to get into print. I know that my editor is keen on the project, but even she isn't going to put up with this. You can't photograph a five-foot three, size fourteen and not expect it to look like a baby elephant.'

'I'm not a fourteen,' Sandra snapped furiously. 'It's just their sizing that's all wrong.'

There was a sudden hush. As one person, the employees of Elegance rallied behind their products.

Michelle spoke for them all when she said, 'We should have checked your measurements ourselves, Sandra. I'm sorry we'd put the wrong size out to start with, but we only went by what your agent told us. The fourteens have fitted you very nicely. We're very well thought of in the trade for the accuracy of our sizing, despite buying in from several different manufacturers.'

'I've always worn twelves on the work I've done with you before,' Sandra said. Her voice had risen, and she was close to tears.

'We all put a bit of extra weight on at times. I gained three pounds on my holiday this year.' Michelle sounded worried. She'd spent a lot of time getting ready for this. She knew that she had to keep Sandra sweet, because the directors had said they would use her in the next campaign, but she also had to keep in with Anne.

'We'll have to scrub it,' Anne said firmly.

Sarah began gathering up her handbag and briefcase. She'd wasted most of a morning so she was feeling niggled. Just as she was standing up she remembered something Anne had said earlier.

'Did you have any specific sportswoman in mind?' she asked.

Anne turned away from Sandra. The journalist had been mesmerized by the amount of tears the girl was managing to produce. Great liquid globules were pouring in a steady stream down her already soaked cheeks. Michelle was ineffectively patting her shoulder and looking in irritation at the jumble of clothes the trying-on session had generated.

'Actually yes. That girl who's doing so well in the hundred metres – she's a Scot, I think. What's her name . . .?'

'Do you mean Tina MacAlister?' Michelle asked. 'She's very pretty, and slim and – '

'And a perfect size twelve, I should think,' Anne interrupted. 'Would you provide the gear for her?'

'I'd have to ask about that.' Michelle began picking up some of the suits lying on the table before her. 'It's not in my gift, so to speak, but I'll tell you one thing: there's going to be hell to pay if we don't get the piece you've said you'll do.'

'We'd be quite happy,' Sarah said. With a sportswoman using their products they could go much further, do a whole body regime, the works. 'What are the athletics governing body's rules about sponsorship, Anne, do you know?'

'I don't think we'll have any problems there. I'll have to get a percentage out of this.' Anne laughed. 'But seriously, folks, I'd be more than happy to go with MacAlister. See what you can do, will you, Michelle? And I don't think either Sarah or I need to turn up for the next try-on session. Just tell us when you're ready to go. I'll fudge something from what I've seen this morning about her choosing the outfits. The rest of the interview I'll do face to face somewhere less crowded.'

Sarah left as Michelle began explaining to Sandra that she couldn't actually have any of the items she'd tried on, since she wouldn't be modelling them on the shoot. The tears started anew.

'You can do this for me, my pretty baby. You can, can't you?' Damion's voice was thick with tears. They streamed unchecked down his face as he leaned close to the warm

263

flank of the creature he believed he loved most in the world.

The horse shifted its feet on the straw bedding. It was uneasy, unused to the uncertainty in Damion's voice.

'You know I wouldn't do this to us if there was any other way I could carry on.' Damion was using the palms of his hands to rub thick white cream in wide circles all over Beauty's coat.

The scent of flower oils in the emulsion almost covered the acrid smell as the mare spread her back legs and passed water. Damion kicked fresh straw on to the steaming dampness. Despite all his pleading, Marie had refused to help him deal with Tommy. He would never be able to get Rose to understand how the urge to gamble was stronger than any will-power he could summon up. He was on his own; the only hope he had was Beauty . . .

The mare was to race on the next day. She would be boxed up and driven a hundred miles to attend a meeting where the camel-coat brigade would have their cheque books ready and waiting. Beauty was entered in a selling race. She was at the peak of her fitness, ready to perform, all set to show her paces.

Damion had lavished all his abilities on her and she was far and away the best animal in his yard. He was convinced that Jopling wouldn't be able to resist the chance to buy her. He had made sure that the South African knew the score, and that Beauty would be up for grabs. He was convinced Jopling had instructed someone to buy for him in his absence in Australia. The opportunity to buy Beauty would be irresistible – it had to be.

In the cottage, propped up on the mantelpiece, was the last feed bill. Behind it was the letter from the corn chandlers that had arrived over a week ago. There were to be no more deliveries until Damion had cleared his debt. He owed them five thousand pounds. He also owed his landlords seven thousand; their solicitors were starting to talk about repossession.

His overdraft at the local bank was almost ten thousand pounds over his twenty-thousand limit. In an attempt to keep the manager happy he'd offered to lodge his shares in Body Beautiful with them, but the bank had seen that with the clause protecting Marie's interest they had no open market value. Beauty was his last chance. He had nothing else he owned that could bail him out.

His hands began to tingle as he massaged the creamy soap deep into the short brown hairs.

'You'll win for me, won't you, me darlin'.' His accent had thickened with emotion.

Rose paused outside the open stable door. She could hear the love in her husband's voice. Long ago he'd talked to her like that – before she'd fallen pregnant. In those days when they'd made love nothing else had mattered. Not even the fact that someone might come in and find them in the barn, not the fact that she knew he was too grand for her, not the fact that being on the pill had made her feel sick, so she'd stopped taking it.

She walked on slowly. Everything was so difficult. They weren't making a go of the yard, and just when they needed all their wits about them the baby kept waking them in the night. Perhaps it could still come right – they just needed a little luck. Perhaps selling Beauty would give them a fresh start. They could pay off their bills and maybe they could work things out between them. If only Damion would trust her a little more, talk to her when he worried instead of drinking himself to oblivion.

She was carrying two full buckets of water. Suddenly she was aware of how much they weighed. Her shoulders sagged and ached with the effort. Straw had found its way down the inside of her boot and her foot itched. It was almost time for her period and she felt swollen and heavy.

The waistband of her jodhpurs bit unmercifully into her soft skin.

The clatter of hooves behind her, and Damion's sudden swearing made Rose spin round. Inexplicably Beauty stood in the yard behind her. The horse's body was streaked with cream, her eyes rolling wildly. Then Rose saw the short, broken lead rein that dangled from the animal's head collar. The horse tossed its head, mucus dribbled down from its nostrils. The creature looked mad.

The baby began to cry. The small, high sound seemed piercingly loud in the silence as the animal stood, swaying, poised for flight. Rose turned round to look up at the pram. She took one small step towards it, away from the horse, and then she understood, and then she screamed. She dropped the buckets. The crash should have brought the other grooms running, but it didn't. The pram was at the end of the row of stables, outside the groom's small kitchenette on the corner of the brick-built block. It was in the way of anything leaving the yard. She'd never thought of that before.

Beauty's squeal of terror ricocheted off the sun-hot walls, and the wild clatter of her hooves as she started her bolt for freedom was deafening.

Rose ran. All conscious thought was wiped from her mind. Her baby was in danger, and her protective instincts gave her a speed she'd never known she possessed. Her arms were pumping, her head tipped back as she raced towards the fragile pale-grey carrycot that was rocking madly on its springs. Rose could hear her baby. She wanted picking up, she wanted feeding.

'Mummy's coming,' she was murmuring. 'Mummy's coming.' She could feel the horse so close behind her, sense the hot breath. There was so little time. She flung herself forward, her body draping over the snow-white blanket. The pink furry teddy hanging from the hood

266

jangled merrily and the baby stopped crying instantly, startled into silence by the gentle impact.

'Rose!' Damion shouted. He was running up the yard, his face contorted by pain, his hands clutched to his chest. 'Rose!'

It was all in slow motion. The water that had spilled from the buckets started Beauty sliding. Her legs thrashed out for a grip, and a cluster of orange sparks flew as her metal shoes scraped on the concrete. Struggling for balance, the animal pitched forward. It was as if she'd landed badly from some imaginary high jump.

Damion saw Rose reach the pram, she was cowering over it. Her face turned towards him, dead white, her mouth a scarlet gash, and still he was running – so close to the flashing hooves. He reached out. If he could only catch the rope . . .

Throwing her head up, Beauty screamed in panic. Her lips curled back, showing strong yellow teeth, her long pink tongue lolled, dripping saliva in thick white specks down her sweat-stained chest. With a final clatter her hooves slipped and her spindly legs shot sideways. Eel-like, her body twisted in a vain attempt to regain her balance. But nothing could save her now.

With all the impetus of her frantic dash up the yard she fell. The full weight of her shoulder struck Rose in the back. The woman's high-pitched cry of pain was cut almost instantaneously short as the whole weight of the animal fell down on her. The wheels of the pram crumpled slowly.

The doctor poured Damion a glass of his own brandy. 'If you won't have a sedative,' he said, 'at least drink that.'

The yard outside the cottage was full of people talking in whispers. There were a couple of vets, the girl grooms, several uniformed policemen and the firemen who'd provided the lifting tackle.

'There must be someone we can contact.' The doctor was young. He hadn't been a GP long.

He was a great believer in the power of relatives. Properly used, they could save the National Health Service a lot of man-hours. The baby was with its grand parents; that had saved calling in the social services.

Damion shook his head. He cradled the glass uneasily in his heavily bandaged hands, then uncertainly he put it up to his lips. He paused, and slowly he put the glass down, untasted.

It had been the cream that had sent Beauty mad. Even after they'd put her out of her misery from the broken leg, the cream had carried on eating into her skin. It was the cream that had burned Damion's hands. Numbed though he was by shock, the pain was still like a live thing.

'Who can I call?' The doctor paused, and looked encouragingly at his patient.

'We have to get hold of Marie,' Damion began.

The man of medicine nodded encouragingly.

'This was from our body shampoo. It came straight from the factory – I had it sent from Ireland.' Damion held his hands out, palms upwards as if in supplication, and the doctor began to look puzzled.

Damion struggled to stand. The strain in his back sent a fiery pain from his shoulderblade to the base of his spine.

'I told you, with a muscle tear like that you should be in bed.' The doctor hurried forward and firmly pushed Damion back into the chair. 'How you ever had the strength, I'll never know.'

Damion closed his eyes. He was fighting down the bile he tasted in his throat. He could still see it. Beauty lying

268

prone, only her eyes showing her pain. Beneath her heaving flanks, Rose lay, her dark hair fanned back over the horse's coat. She was utterly still. Beneath them both was the pram, squashed, misshapen. And then he'd heard the baby cry.

Superhuman strength, a policeman had said; he'd heard tales about it in the Force. Sometimes, inspired by love, a man could work miracles. Damion remembered grabbing at the twisted metal beneath his wife. Skin from his burning hands had stuck to the shining chrome.

Two of the girls had come at last. He remembered shouting at them, telling them to dial 999. His baby's crying was muffled – he could hear that she was being smothered. He'd pulled with all his strength, heaved so that he thought his arms would come out of their sockets. The horse whinnied pitifully and settled further down. The crying stopped.

That was when Damion pushed. He put his bleeding hands on his wife's still body and shoved. He was crying, shouting, praying. Suddenly, with no warning at all woman and horse slid forward. He snatched the baby from its contorted cradle. He heard the dull snap as his wife's spine broke; he twisted away, clutching his child to him.

Chapter 20

*The beauty of the world . . . all these things
are not merely accidental*

CICERO

A joyful peal of sound rang out from the church bells. It carried on the clear air to sound loud in the shadowy coolness of the buttery.

'Bloody bell-ringers,' Lucy muttered furiously. She had a splitting headache, her hands were covered in sticky pastry dough and now her nose was itching.

'They've got to practise sometime,' Honour said mildly.

She was sitting on a stool. For over an hour she had been stringing and then chopping runner beans that had been picked from the vegetable garden. A large heap, almost ten pounds, of prepared vegetables was in a colander beside her.

'You know,' she continued, 'sometimes I wonder if these executive lunches are such a good idea.'

They were preparing a meal for the next day. It was a booking that had come through Berry Jopling. One of his stipulations had been that a member of the family would be present at the drinks reception. Honour had drawn the short straw.

'I don't suppose for one minute Marie expected us to be doing the cooking ourselves.' Lucy slapped the dough out on to a floured board, sprinkled it liberally with flour and then began to roll it out. With swift, light strokes she quickly shaped a neat oblong. 'Mind you, I'm getting damned good at this, even though I do say it myself.'

'Your language is appalling, Lucy. I really think you should stop this swearing. You never used to do it.'

'I never used to bloody well spend my evenings up to my elbows in flour.' Lucy slammed a large Pyrex dish down noisily on the metalwork surface.

Honour stayed silent. Lucy had been so determined that the family should retain ownership of the Place. In all the arguments she'd been against Honour's wish to give the property to the National Trust.

'I know what you're thinking,' Lucy said. 'You said it would be hard work. Go on, say it. Say I told you so.'

'I have no intention of saying any such thing.' Honour stood up slowly. She put both her hands in the small of her back and straightened her spine. She was stiff and painful. 'If there hadn't been that row with Dibs then neither of us would be here now. I shall go down to the village myself.'

'Don't you dare.' Lucy put down the apple pie she had been about to put in the oven. 'If you go and apologize to that woman on my behalf . . .'

'I'm not going to do anything on your behalf. I'm not even going to see Dibs. I've heard that the people who took over the Inglenook Tea Rooms do a very good lunch. They paid rather over the odds for the property and will no doubt be grateful for some extra business. It's only twenty lunches here tomorrow, and you've already done the pudding. If you just blanch those beans they can go into the deep freeze.'

Lucy felt so angry she wanted to shout, to crash and bang, to tell her mother-in-law just what she thought of her. How could she leave it so late in the day to suggest what had obviously been on her mind all along. Timothy, their agent, would have gone to the concert on his own already. Or even worse . . . Lucy flushed as she thought

271

how bad it could really be. He might have taken the Vixen with him.

'I assume that's all right with you?' Honour asked as she undid her apron.

'Perfectly.' Lucy managed, with a struggle, to control her breathing. 'But I really think you should do it properly and ask them to prepare the dessert as well.'

She picked up the pie that had prevented her from going out with the man she loved so desperately and held it out in front of her. Quite deliberately she let it slip through her fingers so that it smashed down on to the hard stone floor. Amongst the debris the pastry lid stayed, almost undamaged, for a moment and then sagged and broke into a dozen pieces.

The chatter of girlish voices reached Fleur as she sat in the restaurant office. She was glad of the cheerful sound. Marie had been distraught when she'd called in on the way to her sister-in-law's funeral. It was as well that Sarah had been with her, because she had been in no fit state to drive. Fleur had overheard her cousin telling Honour that some of her products had been deliberately contaminated with acid and that that had been the cause of the accident.

The people from the tea rooms had taken over the kitchen to do lunch for the executives. There were outside caterers in the buttery preparing for an evening reception. The VAT returns for the restaurant had to be finished by that afternoon, and it had seemed only logical for her to work in the peace and quiet of the office. Only, it was no longer peaceful. She could hear what the girls were saying as they worked in the kitchen, and it was making it hard for her to concentrate on the figures in front of her.

'You're joking!' A girl's high voice giggled. 'How many times did you do it, Rita?'

'Don't make it sound like that.' Rita, the daughter of

272

the family who owned the Inglenook, tried to sound offended but couldn't. 'I only said a different fella every night for the first week, and then after that . . .'

'After that, you fell in love. Rita, you're a case all right. Go on, tell me again what it's like when you get there. That bit about the melon, on the beach.'

'Watermelon – you've got to get it right. It was a watermelon they got us girls to put between our knees, Beccy.'

Fleur found herself straining to listen. She'd gathered it was an eighteen-to-thirty holiday the girl was talking about. She'd been brought up never to eavesdrop, but the bit about the melon . . . Besides, she laid down her Biro, she was going to be a writer, she needed to listen to dialogue.

'I was just so glad it was a boy I fancied who went first. I mean, when he got down on his knees and took this great big bite I nearly died.'

There was a squeal of delight, before the friend pressed for more information. 'And then, after he'd had a bite, what then, Rita?'

'Well, then they all did. There was twenty of them, boys that is, and twenty of us girls. The boys queued up in a line, with us all lying on our backs in the sand. That's why it had to be a watermelon, see?' Rita laughed, and it was a low, conspiratorial sound, rich with meaning. 'If it had been any smaller to start with, well I would have been a naughty girl, 'specially since I didn't even know any of their names, not to start with.'

'Was he one of the five you actually did it with, then? The one you fancied right off, the one who went first?'

'Yeah. He went first then too, if you get my meaning.' They laughed together. 'But it got better. One of the others, he was amazing. I've never met anyone like him. He just went on and . . .'

273

There was a sudden silence, and then Fleur heard Rita's voice saying, 'Yes, Mum. We're nearly ready. No, no we haven't been goin' slow.'

Fleur picked up her pen and went back to her adding up. She'd never feel the same about watermelons again. The break from her work had done her good. She finished a good hour earlier than she'd expected. She didn't know if Marie would be calling in again later. In a way that she knew was selfish, she hoped not.

She decided to walk out through the restaurant kitchen. The two girls were dressed in white overalls. They didn't look up as she passed, so she couldn't see what they looked like. An older woman, presumably Rita's mother, was looking hot and bothered as she stirred a large pan on the stove. She said a hurried 'good morning' and quickly went back to looking at whatever was in the pan.

The girl Rita had said that in the second week she'd fallen in love. Perhaps, if the argument with Dibs continued, Fleur thought, she would have a chance to pick up on the second instalment later in the week. The regular Thursday lunch would need catering for.

She was smiling as she stepped out into the light rain that had sent the great yellow and pink flower heads nodding on the climbing roses that covered the stone walls around her.

Sarah slammed her foot down hard on the brake pedal, bringing her car to a shuddering halt, as a mud-splattered, green and black tractor lurched out of a field gate and on to the country lane in front of them.

'Damion shouldn't be left alone,' she said angrily.

'He's not alone.' Marie stared sightlessly out of the passenger window beside her. 'Rose's parents are staying with him tonight.'

'You know what I mean. He should have you there. You're his flesh and blood, you understand . . .'

'He didn't want me to stay,' Marie snapped. 'You heard me offer.'

Sarah tightened her grip on the steering wheel. She'd been there when Marie had made the suggestion to her brother. They'd all been at the graveyard, clustered around the raw, gaping hole in the ground. Damion had earth on his bandaged fingers; she'd watched him struggle to sprinkle the ritual handful.

For a few moments she concentrated on her driving, then said quietly, 'I still think we should have gone back to the stables with him.'

'He didn't want anybody.'

'That's not the point, though, is it? He was in shock. You don't ask someone in that state what they want, you do what you know is best for them.'

'Who the hell do you think you are?' Marie's face flushed with fury. She felt claustrophobic, restrained by her seat belt. She struggled against it so that she could turn to face Sarah. 'You don't have any standing in my family. I only accepted your offer to drive me down to the funeral today because I didn't feel up to it myself. It doesn't give you the right to go throwing your weight around in my life.'

The tractor in front of them pulled suddenly off to the left and into a farm driveway. The road ahead was clear.

'You're overwrought; understandable in the circumstances,' Sarah said. 'Do me a personal favour, and sit back in your seat. I want to get back to town.'

Marie laughed bitterly. 'Got some good-looking young man lined up for the evening, have you? I suppose I should say hooray for that. At least it'll stop you putting your nose in where it isn't wanted.'

Sarah could feel anger building inside her. There was a

275

lot she could have said, and only the thought of Damion stopped her. She wanted to get the conversation back to a civilized level. Tomorrow, she and Marie would have to work together again.

She coughed to clear her throat and then remarked, 'It's a pity Berry wasn't there.'

Marie almost choked. 'Pull over,' she said hoarsely. 'Stop here. Here!'

The car came swiftly to a halt. On either side of them, flat green fields stretched away to the damp, hazy distance.

Sarah reached down and turned off the key in the ignition, then sat back and folded her arms.

The metallic clicking of the engine cooling sounded very loud. It was warm inside the car, so Marie wound down the window beside her. Birds were twittering in the hedges and she could hear the far-off drone of a tractor working the fields.

'There's something I've been meaning to say to you for a long time,' Marie said. She was glad of the fury she felt, grateful for the brief, adrenalin surge of energy. 'You're very proficient at your job . . .'

'Thanks,' Sarah said drily.

'It wasn't a compliment, just a statement of fact. But in your private life you're a slut.'

'I'm so glad you don't feel you have to mince words, Marie. While we're in the "no holds barred" mode why don't you go on and tell me to keep away from Berry? Because that's what this is all about, isn't it? After all, I only had to mention his name just now and you blew your fuse.'

'I didn't blow anything.' Suddenly Marie felt an almost overwhelming exhaustion wash over her. She leaned back in her seat, tipping her head so that it was supported by the hard, unyielding headrest. 'You let yourself down by

276

sleeping around, and by implication you let Body Beautiful down too.'

'That sounds like one law for you and one for me. Only a few minutes ago you were telling me to keep out of your personal life – that cuts both ways.'

'It doesn't. When it comes to the good of the company what I say goes. And I don't like your morals – or rather lack of them.'

'I think you've said enough.'

'You'll toe the line?'

'What line? You're asking me to live by some antiquated set of rules just because you can't let yourself go to bed with a man you want? You're mad, Marie. Warped.'

Marie wanted to refute the accusation, to point out how close she and Berry had come, how much she wanted their relationship to be finally fulfilled. Only it wasn't true. She wasn't sure any more. The length of his absence and the shock of Rose's death had somehow combined. It had been a relief for her that Berry hadn't been at the funeral. That was why she'd hurried away: in case he'd somehow managed to make it back from Australia. As far as she was concerned, they were back to square one.

'I am concerned that your reputation might harm the company,' she said slowly, considering her words before speaking. 'I don't want to lose you, but you at least have to be discreet. Doesn't it worry you? Aren't you afraid you'll catch something?'

'Aids, you mean? You can say the word, you know. You don't catch it just by saying it out loud. Yes, I'm scared, who isn't? But I'm not paranoid.'

'Will you be more circumspect?'

Sarah smiled wryly, pleased that she hadn't allowed herself to lose her temper. 'I'll be the soul of discretion.'

There were reasons why she would be. Sarah had changed already, but Marie hadn't noticed.

'It had to be said.'

'If you say so.' Sarah reached forwards and turned on the ignition. It was time to get back on the road.

'It cleared the air.'

'I hope it made you feel better.'

It didn't. Marie felt worse. Her head was throbbing, and she was starting to feel sick. 'Damion says that the police are going to treat Rose's death as an accident. They don't see the connection with the doctored cream as being close enough to make a case.'

'But that's ridiculous.'

'They don't think so. The last thing they said was that when they find out who's been putting the stuff in the jars we might like to consider a private prosecution to link it with Rose, but they didn't hold out much hope that we'd win.'

'Well, I don't understand their attitude. It doesn't seem to me as if they're pulling out all the stops.'

'There's been no ransom demand, so far, and the only direct damage, as far as the law is concerned, is a few minor burns to a couple of people, and the effect on Beauty's skin. They even pointed out that the horse's actual death came as the result of a fall. They were full of assurances that they're doing their best. But they also pointed out how precious police resources are.'

'And what if it goes on? What if a customer buys a contaminated jar and gets seriously hurt?'

'Then I suppose it will be all hands to the pump. In the meantime, I'm going to have all the jars overwrapped with a tamper-proof seal and a warning not to use the product if the seal has been broken.'

'You could always get the press on your side. If the whole story about Rose got out . . .'

'We still wouldn't be able to say the tampering was directly responsible for her death. No, we'll go along with the official line while we think what to do next.'

They were silent for a while. The dampness in the air had become a drizzle, and the regular swishing of the windscreen wipers was almost hypnotic.

'I'm sorry,' Marie said, her voice muffled by the hand she'd clamped over her mouth. 'But you'll have to stop. I'm . . .'

She managed to throw the door open before being sick into the gutter.

Back at the flat, Sarah made coffee and brought it through to where Marie lay on the sofa. She put a cup down on the coffee table, and beside it a pink and white packet of contraceptive pills she'd found in the bathroom cupboard.

'Are you taking these?' she asked.

Marie nodded gingerly. Her headache was getting worse.

'Then I suggest you read the bit under "possible side-effects". They're the reason for all those aspirins you've been popping, and why half the time you only pick at your food. If you're not sleeping with anyone, why on earth were you taking them?'

'They made me more regular.' Marie sat up so that she could drink her coffee, and took the flimsy printed sheet of instructions Sarah was holding out to her.

'See what you make of what it says there, and then go and see your doctor. I reckon he'll say to pack them up right away.'

'He's a she.'

'All the better.' Sarah began walking towards the hall.

'Thanks,' Marie said. 'Thanks for driving me down today, and thanks for this.' She gestured to the packet on the table.

Sarah nodded an acknowledgement. Perhaps, she thought, she should put some of what she saw as Marie's unreasonableness down to how unwell she must have been feeling. She smiled as she reached her decision – no, she wasn't going to make any excuses for her boss.

She was laughing as she ran lightly down the stairs.

Men, she thought, would never stand a chance of understanding women. They just couldn't appreciate their multi-layered abilities.

Sarah's voice reverberated around Damion's cottage. 'What do you want me to say? That I'm sorry? All right, I'm sorry the poor little cow had to die like that. But I'm not sorry about us.'

'She knew,' Damion sobbed. He was curled in the old armchair, his arms round his shins, his face buried in his knees. 'Rose knew all about it. Jesus, she was so unhappy.'

'You're nothing but a bloody hypocrite.' Sarah stopped pacing the floor and looked round, seeing the room clearly for the first time. Everything was tatty. Now the girl was gone there was nothing, not even a few wild flowers in a jug, to add charm to the chaos.

'This place is a pigsty. And I can't stand men who cry.'

'You're a soulless bitch.'

'Oh, shut up.' She flopped down into an armchair and a cloud of dust made her cough. 'For Christ's sake, you're acting like a pauper. You could be back at Body Beautiful tomorrow. Just think about it, a lovely shiny office, someone to make your tea. You could even afford to have this tip cleared out.'

'I can't go back.'

'Why the hell not?'

'It's going down the pan.'

'Only because you won't pull your finger out and give Marie the help she needs.'

Damion felt cornered. 'There are the horses,' he said, although he knew it was hopeless.

'You're not the only trainer in Britain. What do you think you are, some kind of bloody Saint Francis of Assisi? Berry says you couldn't train your way out of a paper bag.'

There was a silence while Damion struggled to control the fury that had surfaced.

Eventually he said, 'I loved Rose. I couldn't go back to London now. It would be like pretending she never existed.'

'Please.' The sarcasm was heavy in Sarah's voice. 'You're making me want to weep with you. You've got to do something with yourself. And what about the baby?'

'The doctor said Rose's parents are doing fine.'

'They can't look after her for ever, Damion. You're going to have to earn enough to provide a nanny, and you're going to have to provide her and your kid with a decent home. Jesus.' She looked down at her white trainers in disgust. They were streaked with brown. 'There's horse shit on this floor. You could end up having the baby taken away from you. That would make good reading in the racing press, wouldn't it? That would show just how capable you are of looking after your precious animals.'

'I thought I'd send her over to Ireland, to my parents.'

Sarah stood up and walked over to where Damion sat. She seemed to tower above him. 'It's about time you grew up. Just start thinking about someone else for a change. You hate your parents.'

Damion started to speak but she just shouted over him.

'No, don't bother to try and contradict me. You're always going on about what a mean old bastard your father is. Marie even ran away from home to escape his discipline. And your mother's too weak to stand up to him. You can't send your child into that.'

'It's just . . .' Damion had put his hand up to his mouth, it was trembling.

He looked desperate, and he felt it. Tommy was pressurizing him more than ever. His eyes were red and two days' stubble grew on his chin, but Sarah knew with an awful certainty that he was the only man she could ever really fall in love with.

'I feel so bloody guilty. They've all said that I did the only thing I could – the doctor, the police, everybody. But when I pushed them off the pram . . .' His voice dropped to a whisper. 'I heard her back snap. It was as if everything I'd done to her – the cheating, the lying – it was as if all of it had led up to that moment, as if it had all been my fault. I didn't mean to hurt her.'

'I know that.' Sarah dropped to her knees beside his chair. She put her hand on his face. Gently, slowly, she began to stroke his cheek. 'You married her. No one else in your position would have done that. You stood by her when you could much more easily have walked away. I envied her. When she looked at you she had such a fierce glow of pride about her. You were her husband, the father of her child.'

'You envied her being married?' There was surprise in Damion's voice. He'd always thought Sarah was so independent.

Sarah bit her bottom lip. She who hesitates, she thought wildly, and then she said, 'I envied her you.'

Sarah stayed the night.

She vacuumed the sitting room as Damion checked the horses, then made an omelette with four eggs and a dried piece of bacon that she found in the fridge. They drank canned Heineken and watched a Miss Marple mystery on the TV.

Later they made love on the settee. Neither of them could face the empty double bed upstairs. Sarah kept touching him, stroking him. She couldn't stand the pain in his eyes. At last he fell asleep in the chair and she covered him with a blanket. After tidying up in the kitchen she went upstairs and tried to sleep on the hard, narrow bed in the baby's room.

She'd left the landing light on, and the cot bars made a shadow like a picket fence on the wall that Rose had wallpapered with Postman Pat.

A fox cried in the night, a vixen screaming with the strange pain of her mating. Sarah shivered despite the duvet that covered her. A horse coughed in the yard and there was a rustling in the roof. The country sounds seemed to pose a threat and yet there was a man asleep in the room beneath her. The man she wanted to be her man. She'd never felt so positive before.

Damion was weak. She lay, staring up at the ceiling, trying to convince herself of her folly. He was everything she'd ever despised in men. He was a chauvinist, a believer in one role for men, another for women. He was selfish, inconsiderate, and she knew from her own experience that he was unfaithful. But she thought he'd learned his lesson there – she was certain he would be faithful to her. Rose's death had been too hard a lesson to stand repeating.

She fell asleep as the first twitterings of the dawn chorus began in the sloe trees outside her window. There was talent in the man she loved. The ability to be a success in the world of business – her world. As for the horses, they were just the last of his toys. It was time they went out with the rest of his childhood.

* * *

'You look tired.' Meg Sullivan briefly held her daughter against her, cold cheek to warm.

Suddenly Marie did feel tired. The adrenaline flow that had kept her on a high for the flight into Dublin disappeared without trace. She said 'Hello, Mum,' in a listless voice.

Her father was nowhere to be seen. Her mother was too slight and feeble to help Marie with her luggage, and she'd brought far too much. Apart from the one containing her clothes there was a suitcase full of competitors' samples, items she'd selected for the factory to try and match up. As she struggled to get it on the airport trolley she thought how silly she'd been. She could have written a list, and someone from the factory could have bought everything in Dublin.

'We'll take a taxi,' her mother said. That meant her father hadn't come after all. After speaking to their parents on the telephone, Damion had implied that both of them would be there to meet her.

'It's nice to see you up and about,' Marie said. The last time she'd seen her mother she'd been bedridden, her hypochondria had convinced her she had a weak heart.

It was difficult manoeuvring through the crush.

'Ten years. You do realize it's ten years since you last visited us?' Meg's voice was a whine.

'It hasn't all been my choice. You know that.' For two years after she'd left, her father had refused to talk to her. He wouldn't come to the phone, he wouldn't write. The only message he'd sent was that she was banned from his door for ever. He had no daughter – that was what her mother had written. It was Damion who'd negotiated some kind of truce, but Marie had never been able to bring herself to go back, until now.

The taxi driver muttered about the amount of luggage. Meg got straight into the vehicle. She had her hand on her thin chest, her breathing seemed laboured, her mouth hung open. When Marie got in beside her, she turned away to look out of the window.

If only Damion had stayed with Body Beautiful, Marie thought, she would never have needed to come back.

The house was just as she'd remembered it, a rambling structure built from local grey stone. On the right was the ivy-clad castellated turret where she and Damion had played as children. Then it had seemed a fairytale fortress; now it looked like a prison.

Meg stepped out of the taxi and without looking back walked into the open front door. Marie paid the bill and the driver helped her get the bags out of the boot. The cab pulled away, the gravel crunched briefly, and then all was silent and still. Oppressive. She picked up the lightest case and began to walk towards the house. There was a movement in the shadow of the hall and she began to slow. Her father stood in the oak-framed doorway. He hadn't changed from the day she left. His face was still as stern, browned by the wind, his beard whitened by the sun, his thinning hair wiry grey. He wore a three-piece pale brown tweed suit, and the thick gold chain from his hunter hung across the flatness of his stomach.

She couldn't think what to say. She'd pictured the scene a thousand times, but now there were no words. He looked at her silently, giving no lead, and then abruptly he stepped to one side, staring down at the black and white tiled floor beneath his feet as he waited for her to enter.

The same red Turkey runner stretched the length of the limed oak-panelled hall. Marie glanced quickly at her reflection in the oblong mirror in the centre of the Art Nouveau hat stand. Her eyes seemed darker than ever, her face pale and pinched. She did indeed look tired, as her mother had said.

The door to the drawing room was open and Marie saw the back of her mother's head as she sat in a beige damask-covered armchair to the right of the empty marble fireplace.

There was sherry already poured, two small glasses on narrow stems for the women and a bigger one for the head of the family. It reminded her of Tommy. He had bought her a sherry that evening at the Café Royal without waiting to ask what she wanted.

'I don't drink sherry any more,' she said, and her voice sounded sharp, even to her.

'Ten years,' her father said. His voice was soft, mellifluous, the traditional accent of the country, and yet there was such an underlying hardness in it that Marie flinched.

'We have to start afresh,' she said.

'"Have to",' James Sullivan seemed to consider the words. He rolled them round his tongue with a mouthful of his sweet thick sherry.

'I rely on you to oversee the factory.' Marie had taken the opposite armchair to her mother. Her father sat on the matching sofa that faced the blackened grate. The room around them was chill. It was crowded with fine, large pieces of antique furniture, each of which would have looked beautiful in Marie's flat. En masse they were overpowering, funereal.

'The company relies on me, Marie. I have always been aware of that. The new security checks will mean there'll be no more "accidents".'

'Please.' Marie stood up abruptly, close to panic. 'Can't we just speak like normal human beings? It doesn't have to be so stilted, so difficult.' But she knew it did. It was just as she remembered, just as she'd feared.

286

James sipped his sherry again. 'You've met the Montfords, then?'

Meg gave a small sound, like a little animal in distress.

'I see a lot of them – at least, as much as I can. I'm very fond of them, of Lucy, of Fleur.'

'Of Honour?' James looked up sharply at his daughter. Seen through the overhanging fringe of his thick pepper-and-salt eyebrows, his eyes were a startling grey.

'Of course. Although she can be difficult. I admire her, she's a true matriarch.'

James laughed. It was a low, grumbling noise from deep in his throat. Marie looked at him, amazed. She couldn't remember when she'd ever heard him laugh before.

'She sent you greetings,' Marie said. 'I know we're distant cousins, but she's never told me about how you met. She said you'd understand that she didn't send her love.'

'So, she's a matriarch, is she? It's not surprising. All she's done is take after her mother. Isabella was a formidable woman.' He paused and then stood up and stepped closer to Marie. 'Family traits will out. In my early days I was determined to build an empire – Sullivan's stores. In my own way I've achieved fame, but it's taken the second generation to gain worldwide success. You and Damion. It took my issue to get where, all those years ago, I told Honour I would be. But I don't grudge you that.'

Slowly, hesitantly, Marie put her hand out and touched her father's arm. The rough texture of the tweed felt warm under her fingers. 'I've got an awful lot of problems with the company, Dad.'

'You won't find life smooth, not if you've got ambition. But it's worth it. I've never had such satisfaction in my life as when I was buying the stores. Building up the chain. It gave such a spice to life.'

Marie wanted to cry. She wanted to bury her face in the thick tweed jacket and sob with relief, only she knew she couldn't. To show weakness would be to leave herself open to attack. The one thing that worried her more even than the bank, was the possibility that her father could get himself into a position of power in the company. Then, the out-of-character gleam of humanity he'd just shown would disappear for ever in a great evangelical search for profit, for fame and glory. She knew it, she could recognize in her father the same all-consuming hunger for power that had been her own initial motivation.

'It's odd the way the grapes aren't ripening properly this year.' Meg stood beside the massive grape vine that covered almost a third of the south-facing wall of the west wing. It reached up some twelve feet. She could only reach the lower branches, but the trug hanging over her arm was already almost full of small bunches of vivid green fruit.

Marie picked one of them up to look more closely. It contained twenty or more grapes about the size of a one-penny piece, interspersed with dozens of tiny immature ones that would clearly never ripen. 'Won't these be all right?' She pointed to one of the larger fruits.

'It may well turn out sweet enough if left to its own devices, but I'm not having people think I can't grow a decent bunch. I'd rather not have any crop at all.' She turned her back on her daughter and carried on snipping.

Marie walked away, across the gravelled parterre, to the lichen-covered steps that led down to the pond. A leaden sky hung heavily overhead. Although there was no wind it was cold, a thick carpet of fallen leaves, the colour

288

of fire, littered the surface of the water. She pulled her cardigan more tightly around her. It was an Aran knit, one of her mother's, and it smelled of wool and lavender. It should have been comforting, but somehow it wasn't.

Autumn, season of mists and mellow fruitfulness. It wasn't like that in the world where Meg Sullivan lived, Marie suspected. It was a time of damp and decay. The almost mature fruit of the vine had somehow disappointed, therefore it was to be destroyed, harvested before its time. That was how it had been for Marie. Somehow, simply by growing up, she had been a disappointment to her mother. As soon as she'd become a teenager she'd felt she posed some kind of threat. She'd only just turned fifteen when her mother started talking about marriage.

She sat down on the grey stone bench that bordered the pond. The features of the tortuous dolphins that supported the vast slab beneath her had been almost worn away by time. But the surface under her hand was smooth and unmarked. Years ago, Tommy had sat here with her. She'd known him all her life. He was the farmer next door, but she'd felt he was a different generation, even though he was only some ten years her senior. He'd always been welcomed by her parents. After all, it was important that they should get on; neighbouring landowners could be a powerful force working together. And the traditional way to cement such a bond was marriage. It was all so carefully planned.

A solitary yellow leaf floated gently down beside her. She reached out to pick it up, feeling the cool of the green speckled surface. Damion had always been busy on his own pursuits; hunting, shooting, fishing, he'd crammed them all into his life, while at school his natural aptitude for chemistry had won him all the prizes, just as it had won him a place at university. Marie hadn't been interested in the subjects she studied – or at least in the way they were taught. She'd loved to spend hours looking at colour magazines, imagining herself in a world of high fashion and beauty, but her lack of drawing ability had ruled out the prospect of fashion college. More and more it had seemed she was destined for the role of wife and mother. And she might as well start young, her father had said. He'd felt the responsibility of a vulnerable young girl on his hands, especially one who would one day inherit a fair portion of the Sullivan estates and business.

Tommy. She'd always felt a bit awkward with him, despite the boisterous, roistering way he'd behaved towards her when she was small. She'd always felt it was somehow an act. On her fifteenth birthday he'd kissed her – on the lips. The family had been watching; after all, it had been at the dinner party in her honour, served on the long oval table watched over by the mediocre oil paintings of her ancestors. Tommy had brought her a present, a thin gold chain with a diamond-studded crucifix. He'd announced he was going to claim the privilege of her first 'grown-up' kiss and they'd all laughed, as inside she'd wanted to die of embarrassment. She could remember the taste, the stale, bitter cigar smoke on his mouth.

'Marie!' Her father's voice made her jump. Without thinking she crumpled the leaf she held in her hand.

'I was just going back.' She gestured vaguely towards the house. Somehow she felt guilty. She didn't belong, although it had been her childhood home.

'We have to talk.' James sat down beside his daughter. He'd been out at the Home Farm and was still wearing the immaculate brown duster coat he liked to affect on such occasions. Even his black mid-calf wellingtons were pristine. 'Damion has been telling me of his troubles.'

'You mean the gambling?'

'I mean his debt to Tommy. And, as far as I'm

290

concerned, they're one and the same. The reason for him owing the money is immaterial.'

'Not to me,' Marie said firmly. 'Damion can't go on like this. He would gamble his life away, given half a chance.'

'Don't talk rubbish, child. He's had a run of bad luck, that's all.'

'You can't possibly be defending him, not after all you've said against gambling. I can remember you going after him with a horse whip for betting at the Curragh.'

'He's a man now. I only chastised him when he was growing, when he could have had his habits formed. If he chooses to gamble on the horses now, it's his own affair. But the debt he owes to Tommy is more than that, it's family. It must be honoured.'

'Then you pay it.' Marie knew what her father was up to. He wanted her to cover the debt, to use Body Beautiful's money.

'Damion's given the best years of his life to you. He spent all that time in a laboratory that he would rather have spent in the open air.' He swept his arms out in an expansive gesture.

'He would never have worked these fields. You know that as well as I do. And he never wanted to train horses here in Ireland. He wanted to get right away, just as I did.'

'Damion would have stayed. If you'd married Tommy . . .'

'That's enough!' Marie jumped to her feet. 'I'll never marry him. Whatever happens. If he was the last man on this earth, if I'd starve if I didn't marry him, even then I wouldn't let him near me.'

'You're a strange girl, Marie, a strange, unnatural girl.'

'Strange? I'm not strange. It's you and my mother who are strange and unnatural. You know what that man did

291

to me, but you still won't see him for what he is. My God, any normal family would have called in the police. Instead you wanted to use it as a lever. He raped me, took me against my will. And I was a virgin. I never had the chance to give that to a man I wanted.'

James looked away in disgust.

'It's not a dirty subject. My virginity was a precious possession, something that should have been mine, in my gift, but that bastard stole it. If Damion didn't really ever understand, if we all chose to let him think it had been as much my fault as Tommy's, you at least knew different, and my mother did. She was with me at the doctor's. He'd hurt me, hurt me inside.'

James shouted, a harsh bark like an animal, to silence his daughter. He would listen to no more. He was a man of strong beliefs; lust was sinful, to be suppressed. To talk of the weakness of the flesh was a sin.

'But I'm not trying to undermine your authority, Father,' Marie said forcefully. 'Neither am I blaming you for what happened.'

James rested his elbows on the polished surface of his antique mahogany desk. Around him, the book-lined walls of his study provided evidence of solidarity, years of affluence. He had no intention of ever admitting he might have made a mistake. At the first hint of trouble, he had told the factory manager to tighten up security. Perhaps delegation had not been enough.

'Security has always been high on my list of priorities,' he said. 'There is no way a stranger could have got in unseen.'

'Then it must be someone already on the payroll.'

Even through her elegant tweed skirt, Marie could feel the chill of the leather-covered seat beneath. There was no heating in the room and the shining, blackened grate seemed to radiate cold.

'No.' James said the word strongly. He had been awake all night trying to work out who it could have been. His thoughts had gone round and round in meaningless circles, rebounding swiftly away from any unpleasant possibilities.

'You've had the police in?'

'Of course.' James had entertained his two visitors with good strong coffee and chocolate-covered digestive biscuits. He had known the detective sergeant, the more senior of the pair, for years; they were members of the same local rugby club.

'And?'

'And they questioned everybody who could have had access to the creams. They're satisfied that whatever happened didn't happen here.'

'But we know it did.' Marie's voice was rising. She was being hedged in. No one wanted the tampering to have happened on his 'patch'. 'Damion insists that the jar had come straight from the factory.'

James smiled, the corners of his lips lifting while his eyes remained fathomless. 'He's in no fit state to remember petty details. For all we know, the poor boy mixed the wrong stuff up himself. He's under such pressure, who could blame him?'

There was a pain under Marie's breastbone, a solid lump of stress. If she let herself, she could be thrown into total panic. That would be just what the perpetrator wanted.

'We're going to have to have sealed packaging,' she said. 'I've already talked to the suppliers. They've got a machine that seals around screw tops on both jars and tubes.'

'That'll be expensive.'

'And you think my going out of business won't be? I can't afford the kind of loss in sales that hit the baby food companies when they were the victims.'

'It'll mean taking on new staff.'

'That's up to you, as is the appointment of a security team. I want at least three full-time personnel, so they can work on shifts. Get some good people. I don't want this kind of thing happening again – ever.'

'Yes, ma'am.' James raised his hand to his temple in mock salute, his eyes glittered with sarcasm. He was glad there were no witnesses to the meeting. Damion had always known how to act, to defer to the older man in front of the employees. James would not be so certain of his daughter's behaviour.

They had supper in the dining room. Marie had laid the silver cutlery either side of the cork place mats. A thin vegetable soup served with bread was followed by scrambled eggs containing slivers of mushroom. There was shop-bought yoghurt as a dessert. The meal was eaten in silence. Marie had been hungry, but the atmosphere in the house was depressing. Now that she had spoken to her father, she had come to the decision that on this trip she wouldn't visit the factory. There was no real need; he would be capable of overseeing the implementation of the new machinery, and to go over his head would mean another scene. She just wanted to get back to London. To go home.

Marie's father drove her to the airport. Just as they were joining in the steady stream of traffic leading up to the departures point, he asked what she was going to do about Damion's debt.

'I can't do anything,' she replied. 'I've told you, the company is going through a difficult time. I've charged my own property to the bank. If you're so worried about it, you'll have to do something yourself.'

'They won't just let it lie,' he said, ignoring her reply. 'They will take some very unpleasant way of getting it out of him.'

'They? Who exactly is this "they" you're going on about? You said before that it was Tommy. Why can't you admit that it's he who's pressurizing your precious son. You won't tell Damion what a fool he's been and you won't bail him out. Don't think you can put it all in my lap.'

James drew up at the kerb. 'We'll say goodbye here,' he said.

'Won't you at least help me out with my luggage?'

'You'll have help enough.'

The door beside Marie opened suddenly. Tommy was there, smiling in at her, extending a hand to help her out of the car.

'Would you believe the luck? We're booked on the same flight,' he said. 'I've got a trolley ready and waiting. Come on, Marie, and I'll take you for a coffee while we wait for our call.'

She stepped out of the car in a daze. Her father had surrendered her to a man he knew she hated. 'Fuck off,' she said viciously, snatching her bag from Tommy's grip.

But she knew it was no use. She was going to have to deal with Damion's debt and she was going to have to deal permanently with Tommy Docherty.

Chapter 21

In beauty's course illustriously he fails
ALEXANDER POPE (1688–1744)

Peter liked Royal Tunbridge Wells. Its calm, respectable air invited the weary traveller to partake of rest and refreshment. And he was weary. He'd come over on the early ferry, Calais to Dover.

He couldn't stay cooped up in the South of France for ever. It was boring, and expensive. But at least there was the possibility of a nice bit of property development in the offing there. He thought he might well be able to interest Marie in coming in with him; that was the purpose of his trip. He'd hoped to catch her at Pencombe, because he thought London might be a bit dodgy for him.

He hadn't telephoned her first. There was a strong chance, he realized, that she might still be angry with him. Face to face, they'd make up their differences. He'd been missing her. It was a pity she hadn't been visiting the Montfords – he'd have to risk town after all. But it would be politic to wait till night.

He thought he'd take lunch at the elegant stone-faced Spa Hotel, which was bordered by the leafy common. Later, he'd stroll along the Pantiles – the Georgian paved walkway with its white colonnaded shops. If he'd been feeling a bit more flush, he might have picked up the odd antique.

He'd been having his post forwarded to a poste restante. There had been a non-stop stream of bills, and some of the chasing letters were offensive. He'd been quite amazed at the aggravation a finance company could get down on paper. It was a shame that he was a few months in arrears with his payments for the car, but he'd catch up with it sooner or later. Funnily enough, the finance company's head office was in Tunbridge Wells.

He kept a weather eye out for it as he drove through the town. It wouldn't be a good idea to drive his acid-yellow Porsche past their front door.

Lunch was first-rate. He had wafer-thin smoked salmon that he drenched with freshly squeezed lemon juice, followed by a ten-ounce steak, medium rare, served with straw potatoes and a green salad. The meal really perked him up. He finished with coffee and felt very noble – he'd only drunk Perrier water, no wine. Wandering out into the tree-lined car park he breathed in the fresh, country air.

It was coming up to three o'clock. There was time for a browse amongst the antiques before a pastry for tea – he was sure to find an olde worlde tea shoppe, it was that kind of place. Peter extricated his car from the close confines of a Volvo estate and a Peugeot 504, then made his way through the tortuous traffic, down the hill towards the Pantiles.

He drove around a miniature roundabout and, following blue arrows for parking, turned hard right beside an antique shop. He nosed his way slowly through a narrow lane to where, conveniently, there was one last space left in a minuscule car park.

He checked the car locks and set off. Meandering past Regency windows displaying aged oriental rugs, he loitered in front of another black-and-white-framed display area. A collection of respectably faded needlepoint cushions was spread over a pair of antique oak chairs and a small coffer. He was rather taken by a dark blue cushion with an ornate coat of arms. Eventually he managed to read the price on the tag that had not been completely turned around. It was one hundred and twenty-five pounds. He smiled. He was in the wrong business.

The tea shop was as he'd imagined. There were bottle-glass windows, mothers with small children, and elderly colonels and their ladies. He chose a florentine and an éclair from the assortment on display in the window. They were brought to him on a blue-and-white willow-pattern plate. With a pot of orange pekoe tea, he felt well provided for. The florentine was all it should be. It broke as he bit into it – the dark, toasted almonds crunching between his teeth. It was rich with Christmassy red and green chunks of glacé fruits and the bottom was thickly coated in dark chocolate.

In a few hours he would be with Marie again. He was sure they could patch things up. He'd never felt about anyone the way he felt about her. He admired her, but still wanted to boss her about. It made for a difficult relationship, but it made him feel good.

Marie was a real woman. The ones in France had been just so much window dressing. He bit into the éclair. It was light and insubstantial. That was how those French tarts had been. He smiled broadly. He didn't think Marie would like being compared to a florentine, but that's what she was. Sweet, with a hard crunch.

He walked back along the Pantiles in a benevolent mood. The shop windows were lighted now, and beck-oned invitingly. The car was waiting for him. He climbed in, feeling just slightly uncomfortable round his waist. It was as well he didn't succumb to pastries every day, he thought. He reversed effortlessly and rolled the car for-ward into the narrow lane leading back to the main road.

Some idiot in a red Fiesta pulled sharply across his front. He had to brake hard, and the lane ahead of him was now blocked. Peter lowered his window. He was about to shout out – and then somehow he realized. He sat very still, waiting.

The driver of the other car came round to his door. His passenger went to the far side.

'Mr Burnet? It is Mr Burnet, isn't it?' He was stocky, dark-haired, thirty something.

Peter nodded briefly.

'You've saved us a trip to town, Mr Burnet. We were going to come up this evening to collect this.' He tapped the car on the door frame. 'Only fortunately one of our staff saw you earlier, so we had a little cruise around. And here you are. Nice, bright motor you've got, Mr Burnet.'

'I'll give you a cheque.'

'Sorry, me old fruit. Cash or nothing. Coin of the realm. That's what the ticket's marked.'

'But it's gone four, the banks are closed . . .' It wouldn't have made a difference. Christ, what bad luck, he thought. He could hardly believe it. And they hadn't even realized he'd been out of the country – they'd been going to go up to his old address.

'You give us five grand, and we'll go on our merry way. We don't want to see you on foot, do we, Mr Burnet.'

Five thousand pounds.

'I'll have to make a phone call.'

The man by the passenger side of the car opened the door and handed him a mobile.

Marie wasn't there. She was away, out of town. They didn't expect her back for a couple of days. It was Angelique on the phone, he recognized her voice – and the way it cooled when she realized it was him.

There had to be someone else.

'Follow me up to town,' he said. 'I'll get it there.'

They hesitated for a moment, but he'd acted so confident, that maybe he did have the money. After all, he dressed expensively enough.

'You try and do a runner, Mr Burnet, and we'll give your number to the police. Now you're aware of the situation, it would be stealing for you to just drive off into the blue.'

Peter injected anger into his voice. 'Look,' he said, 'just because there's been some cock-up at the bank doesn't mean I'm some kind of criminal. Keep a civil tongue in your head. I'll pay you off in town, and that will be the end of this stupid aggravation.'

They went back to their car, smirking. The posh geezer wasn't so hard, after all. The minute they started to bluster, you knew you'd got under their skin.

The windows of the National Culture Club were a blaze of light. As Peter approached the prestigious Nash façade, he saw a liveried butler start drawing the heavy curtains to shut out the evening.

The two men had followed him up to town in their Fiesta, and now they were waiting, pulled up close behind where he'd parked in a nearby square. The only way he'd get to keep the car would be if Bowen-Smythe cooperated. He paused for a moment on the pavement, running his fingers through his hair, quickly straightening his tie. Squaring his shoulders, he walked purposefully up the wide stone steps and into the spacious maroon-carpeted vestibule.

All the noise of the streets was left behind as the heavy mahogany doors swung closed behind him. A porter stepped out from the small glass-windowed cubicle where he had been sitting. He had just settled down with a mug of tea, to read the *Daily Mirror*. Traditionally this was the quiet time for him. Members tended to come early and have a sherry before dinner. He didn't welcome the interruption.

'Bowen-Smythe in?' Peter demanded.

The porter was short, thin and old. He tilted his walnut-coloured head to one side and looked quizzically. Despite his age he was new at his job. The last 'boy' had died in harness, sitting in his cubby hole. He would have known who Peter was.

Peter could feel the stress washing over him in waves. He was suddenly aware that he was sweating. He felt damp under his arms; it was disgusting. 'I said, is Bowen-Smythe in?'

'Mr Bowen-Smythe is in the dining room.' The old man laid emphasis on the 'Mr'.

Peter took a step towards the great white marble staircase that led to the oak-panelled room his father had so enjoyed.

'Oh no you don't.'

The grip on Peter's arm was vicelike.

'More than my job's worth to let you up there.' There was a pause and then a grudging, 'Sir, if you'll just wait.'

Bowen-Smythe's office hadn't changed at all. Peter felt that, by rights, it should have. After all, his life had been turned upside down. He never saw his old pals any more, never saw Marie – if only he could have contacted her.

'You've got a damned cheek!' Gerry Bowen-Smythe stormed into his office and glowered at the visitor sitting on the green-hide member's chair and waiting for him. 'Of all places to show your face, I would have thought this was the least likely.'

'Hello, Gerry,' Peter said evenly. Now that the confrontation had come, he felt quite calm. He was sitting with his legs crossed, and he hitched his trouser leg up just a fraction, displaying a scant inch and a half of black sea-island-cotton sock.

The club secretary walked around his desk and sat down heavily in his elderly leather chair. He leaned

301

forward to scan the papers that he hadn't bothered to put away before going down to dinner. Slowly and deliberately he turned several of them face down. It was an insult that made Peter flush.

'So, have you come to return my investment?' Bowen-Smythe looked meaningfully towards the telephone. 'Or shall I tell the others you're here? We've got together, you know. We've got quite a useful team ranged up against you. You won't manage to slip out of the country so easily this time.'

'I'm not here to talk about your investment, Gerry. At least, not directly. I'm here to talk about our other unfinished business.'

'Unfinished . . . ?'

'The lodge.'

The secretary's florid complexion turned livid. 'We have no unfinished business. You have no standing here whatsoever. My God, your father would turn in his grave if he knew what you'd been up to.'

'What I was up to is one thing – I just made a bad business decision, that's all. What you've been up to is something else. You are in a position of trust, and you've abused it.'

'How dare you!' Bowen-Smythe was on his feet in an instant. 'A man like you, impugning my honour. God, it's a joke.'

Peter sat in silence. He felt in command now. He had only had the vaguest suspicion that Bowen-Smythe was on the fiddle. The man had reacted so violently that there must be some substance in it.

'Out with it, then. All these hints and accusations. Tell me what this is all about.'

'You must have had a nice time since I've been gone, Gerry. I should think that current account the committee set up has seen a fair bit of activity. What did you do about my signature? Any good at art, capable of a bit of forgery, are you, Gerry? Or did you pay someone to do it for you?'

'What do you want?'

'Five thousand, cash. And I want it now. Then I'll get out of your life, Gerry. And do us both a favour – don't tell any of your "team" about this little chat. If I'm squeezed over the avocado groves, I'll spill your little can of beans.'

'Five thousand pounds – but I can't get my hands on that kind of money.'

'You forget, my father was a member here. I know the ropes. That safe behind you will contain at least twenty grand.'

Bowen-Smythe slumped forward in his chair. He put his head in his hands. Peter felt the stress draining from him. When he'd paid the bastards off for the car, he'd find a hotel and get a bed for the night. Then, first thing in the morning, he'd go round to Marie's office and force Angelique to let him know where her boss was.

Marie. Peter closed his eyes briefly, thinking of her. He needed her, he wanted her with him for always. He'd clear up this mess, somehow, and then he'd ask her to marry him.

'The key is over the road.' Bowen-Smythe's voice was muffled – he spoke through his hands.

'I'll wait.'

'No, someone might find you here. That Harley Street doctor you took for a ride, he's a member, he might come in.'

Peter thought for a moment. He very much doubted if the urbane Dr Handley was in the habit of visiting the club secretary's office, but Bowen-Smythe was in a lather and he might as well humour him. He stood up and gestured towards the door.

* * *

The traffic had calmed, the commuter crush had thinned. The cars and taxis now passing the club were driving at speed. It was a fine evening. Peter felt the breath of air on his face. It was tainted with fumes, but cool. He was almost there. He walked beside the short, fat man, remembering the party he'd thrown to launch his scheme. Tansy, Claudia . . . He smiled reminiscently. He'd have to give up those games when he settled down with Marie. Kids would be nice, he thought. And a pony. They'd have to move out to the country.

'Over there.' Bowen-Smythe pointed to a small block of brick-built offices standing out like a sore thumb in a row of otherwise Regency splendour. 'We cross here.'

Peter nodded. He felt good. Within a few minutes he'd be master of the situation once again. He slipped his hand into his pocket and jangled the car keys. There were several taxis, a couple of cars, and then quite a decent gap before a red double-decker bus.

'Wait.' Bowen-Smythe gripped him fiercely by the arm. 'Can't you see?'

Peter looked puzzled. There was no reason why they couldn't cross the road. He looked down at the man so urgently holding him back. In a moment the bus would be too close.

'There!' cried Bowen-Smythe, flinging his arm out and pointing over the road. 'Look, there he is.'

Peter looked. There was nobody.

The sudden push between his shoulder blades sent him falling forward. He would smash his face, he thought fleetingly, probably break his nose. The pavement was hurtling up towards him. He threw his arms up to stop the road smashing into him. He had forgotten all about the bus.

* * *

Honour sat very upright. She was looking at the drawing room around her with new eyes.

It had hardly changed in over forty years. This was the cream and blue tapestry-covered chair where her mother had sat to receive James Sullivan. She, Honour, a girl of nineteen, had taken the lighter-weight white-and-gold-framed Hepplewhite lyre-back closer to the fireplace. How long ago it all was.

'He's here.' Fleur flung the door open with a crash as she hurried into the room.

Her grandmother's childhood sweetheart was visiting for the first time after almost half a century. She thought it was so exciting, so romantic.

'Calm down.' Honour sounded stern but she was smiling.

She almost wanted to giggle like a young girl herself. James had been so stuffy the first time they'd met, and she'd been full of her own importance. To begin with she'd looked down on his parochial manners and gaucherie, but she'd been wrong. James had been a success, just like his daughter Marie.

'Can I stay?' Fleur asked. She was dressed in a Laura Ashley print dress and matching jacket. The blues and pinks echoed the colour of her cheeks and eyes. 'I promise to be quiet. Just like a little mouse in the corner.'

'Don't be ridiculous. Get Dibs to show him up and you can go and sort out some tea. He'll be hungry, I expect. He's driven here straight from the airport.'

She had torn up his letters long ago. The pages covered in his neat, forceful writing. He'd been so concerned to justify himself against her criticisms. She'd been little more than a child when he'd left and she'd been foolish enough to think he had gone to escape the war. He hadn't, he'd left in order to take advantage of it.

He'd made his fortune in those years. A natural dealer

he'd shown himself to be, and she knew enough now to understand there was no shame in that. He'd just done what so many others had. It hadn't been profiteering, but profit-taking. So why did she still feel bitter?'

'Honour.' James Sullivan stopped just inside the doorway. 'Let me look at you.'

She stood up slowly, and he saw an old woman, but one with such an erect bearing and classic bone structure that she was still beautiful.

Honour had thought she'd be embarrassed to have aged, but she wasn't. Instead she felt proud, proud of her white hair, proud of having a grandchild, and over it all, a fierce burning pride of independence. She hadn't needed him, not ever.

'It's been a long time,' he said. 'Too long.'

'Certainly too long for you to stand there making speeches. Come and sit down. There's no point in standing too much at our age.'

His face showed the irritation he felt. He was fit and healthy. Wearing a dark-blue worsted suit and white shirt, he knew that he looked a fine figure of a man. He'd had his hair and beard trimmed before he left Ireland. He felt that Honour was determined to make him act older than he was.

'And how is your wife?' Honour settled herself comfortably.

Normally she would have sat ramrod straight; today she decided to sit more easily. She'd gathered from Marie that the atmosphere in her childhood home was an unhappy one. She didn't want James thinking she wasn't at ease in hers.

'Fine, fine. We're all fine.' He wasn't going to ask after her family. He had wanted to see her. What had inspired the visit had been nothing more than a whim, following

306

Marie's trip to Ireland, but it was one he was determined to pursue. The name Honour Montford had the power to create confusion in his home. Meg seemed to think of her as some kind of scarlet woman, and the notion amused and flattered him.

'You know we see Marie down here? We're well placed for her to come down from London. My daughter-in-law, Lucy, is very fond of her. We all are, come to that.'

Fleur knocked briskly on the door before coming in with the tea tray. She struggled not to smile. She'd had a vision of the two old dears cuddling up on the sofa. The reality was quite different. Her grandmother smiled at her. It was a sweet smile, the sort one might expect from a granny, but not from Gee.

'Tea, my dear. What a nice idea,' Honour said. 'I don't think you've met our cousin James.'

James stood up to shake hands with the girl. He had a sudden shock, and he knew instinctively that it was what Honour had intended. The girl's colouring was different, dark where Honour had been fair, but the structure of her face was identical to the girl he'd once kissed, once held in his arms.

'You're Marie's father,' Fleur said. Her eyes were bright with interest. 'I'm very pleased to meet you.' She wanted to stay and hear what they were saying to each other but Honour was looking meaningfully at the door.

The moment her granddaughter left the room, Honour laughed. 'That gave you a surprise. You should see your face. Just be careful you don't have a heart attack.'

'There's nothing wrong with my heart.'

'Really?' All the fury Honour had felt as a girl flashed suddenly in her eyes. 'There are some who might dispute that.'

'I only came because – ' James broke off. He wanted to say he came to heal old wounds. They shouldn't be enemies, they were family – although he didn't want to hark too heavily on the family connection. There was a thought he'd had on the flight over, a way to sort out several of the problems that were weighing on his mind. Since Marie's visit he had been unsettled and found his sleep disturbed.

'How do you like your tea?'

'No sugar, a little milk. Just as I always liked it. A man doesn't change that kind of habit.'

'You have to remember that for most of my life I have lived without a man, James.' The sarcasm in Honour's voice was lost on her visitor.

'It needn't have been like that. I offered you marriage.'

The teapot almost slipped from Honour's grip. She felt choked by anger, and when she managed to speak her voice was like ice. 'You and my aunt between you thought you had me trapped, didn't you? With me pregnant and Carl dead and then both my parents.'

'With you unmarried.' James's voice was hard.

'I didn't need you, I didn't need any man except Carl, ever.' Carl, her love, who had died before the twins were born . . .

'Commendable virtue, Honour. But surprising. As I remember, you were a hot-blooded little thing.' He was annoyed with himself for rising to her bait, but she had always had the power to irritate him – and to please him. His voice softened. 'So much water has gone under the bridge, and we were once friends, all else apart. That's what I would like to salvage, friendship.'

Honour held a tea cup out towards him. 'I think Marie must have had a difficult childhood,' she said. 'It explains why she's made such a go of things, I suppose. Many young women have gone off to achieve fame and fortune by running away from an oppressive home.'

'And many more achieved shame and degradation. I

308

was a strict father and I'm not ashamed of it. Spare the rod and spoil the child.'

Honour proffered cake, and James took it. If they had been twenty years younger he would have left by now, or Honour would have thrown him out. One thing that age had taught them both was to have their conversations out to the end.

Honour cleared her throat before speaking. 'Marie's not a child any more, and neither is your son Damion. I assume he thinks there is some kind of feud to continue between our families, because he's never come here with Marie. There isn't anything of the sort, of course, but I can't forgive you. I had thought that I could, but I'm too set in my ways. In any case, it isn't our relationship that's important, but I should like Damion to feel he can come here, to meet the others.'

'I will talk to my son.' James lowered his head over his tea cup.

He had at least achieved part of what he'd wanted. Damion would do as he was told and visit Pencombe. He was a natural charmer, and now that the girl Rose was out of the way, he could marry himself some money. Marie had told him all about the recent Montford tragedy, and he'd been able to see for himself that the girl Fleur had too much spirit to stay tied to a cripple. 'I'll have another piece of your delicious cake, Honour. Then if you've the energy, I'd welcome a stroll round the grounds. I've always remembered them with pleasure.'

'Poor Marie,' Fleur said to her mother. 'Her father looks ferocious, and he's got the shaggiest eyebrows you ever saw.' She kicked at a fir cone lying on the gravelled path. It was a delight to walk in the gardens now that they were closed to visitors. Although it was almost winter it wasn't too cold, as long as you were wrapped up in a thick cardigan.

Lucy laughed. 'At least she didn't inherit those. But perhaps her brother did, I wonder what Damion looks like.'

'If he's anything like his father, he'll have a Pilgrim Father's beard and piercing grey eyes.'

'That doesn't sound much like any of the trainers I've met.'

'I suppose not. So perhaps he'll wear appalling yellow waistcoats and pale-coloured socks, and' – she paused, working out something in really bad taste – 'worst of all, he could have hairs growing out of his nose. Long curly ones.'

'That's disgusting.'

They'd heard the scrunch of wheels on the gravel before rounding the corner. Benjy was coming towards them. He was wearing a green Barbour jacket and flat cap. He was also wearing long, leather riding boots. Fleur swallowed hard. It was the first time he'd worn those in the wheelchair.

'Skiving, Fleur?' he asked cheerfully. 'I was coming up to the office to see if you needed a bit of help, but I can see I shouldn't have bothered.'

'I've been helping Mummy with the accounts. We both felt we'd deserved a breath of fresh air. Isn't it glorious out here?'

The dove-grey sky was high and still, the last of the roses flowered on leafless branches. There was the subtle, bitter-sweet smell of freshly dug earth.

'A good day for cubbing,' Benjy said softly.

Lucy laid her hand on his shoulder. 'Come back up to the house with us. There are some figures I don't quite understand.'

He looked up at her searchingly. All he wanted was to

310

feel needed, but he suspected Lucy could manage perfectly well without him.

'I'd like to walk on a bit further,' Fleur said. 'I need the exercise. Benjy and I will come back together.' She'd almost said, 'I'll bring Benjy back with me.' It would have hurt him so much, and yet she wouldn't have meant it to.

They went silently between the almost empty flower beds. A robin jumped from its perch on the scallop-topped path edging on to a clod of rich earth. It studied them for a moment, head quizzically to one side, and then it flew, with three swift wing beats, to the comparative safety of an espalier pear.

'It didn't like the wheelchair,' Benjy said. 'There's no chance of my having a decent afternoon's sport with a gun any more. I can't get within a hundred yards of a pigeon without it jinking away. I've oiled everything that moves, but it still bloody squeaks.'

'Do you feel like spoiling me, Benjy?' Fleur asked. She was staring off into the middle distance, at the green fields stretching up the hill on the far side of the river ahead of them.

'That sounds ominous.'

'I suppose it is really, at least if by "ominous" you mean expensive. I don't have much money of my own, as you know. Not until I'm twenty-five, and I get the trust fund. I really don't want to wait.' She'd had an idea, worked out a scheme that she thought would give Benjy an interest.

'Don't beat about the bush, girl.' He reached out and took her hand, so that she turned to look down at him.

'I want to go into breeding.' She ignored Benjy's exaggeratedly raised eyebrows. 'I want to buy some brood mares, and breed from them, here at Pencombe. There are several fields that would be ideal to use for a stud, and the stable yard would benefit from being used again.

311

Gee is always saying that the buildings rot when they're empty. You know all about bloodstock, you could guide me.'

'You've never mentioned this before.' His face had closed down. She couldn't tell what he was thinking.

'I've just always been cagey about talking breeding in front of you – everyone knows what an expert you are on blood lines. But I realized the other day that it's silly. I've always been around horses and ponies, I'd like to have a go at producing my own, not to ride, so much as to race. I'd like to bring out a few decent point-to-pointers.' She paused.

Was it the right thing to say? So far Benjy had shied away from his past existence. All his land was sold now, he lived in a 'done-up' ex-farmhouse without outbuildings. It was, she felt, a sterile environment. This was a way he could be involved. Fleur was convinced it was a good idea.

'It's getting cold.' Benjy shivered suddenly. 'Let's get you back to the house.'

He was acting as if he hadn't heard her. He laughed as the robin fluttered away from the path again at their approach. He began talking about the garden he was planning for his new house – the house that would be their home. The lavender cuttings he would take from the Place gardens would be big enough to plant out next summer.

'I want to have a hand in planning our life too,' Fleur said. It probably sounded petulant, but she didn't care. He had to listen to her.

'But of course you have to.' Benjy slowed. He was talking down to her, humouring her as he would a dog, or a child. 'And you shall, only perhaps it's a bit soon for some things. You do understand, don't you?'

Fleur wanted to shout, to make Benjy agree with her.

312

She felt faced with the awful prospect of a future spent being painfully careful always to say the right thing, never to bring horses into the conversation, trying to pretend that nothing was missing from his life.

She was white-faced as she looked at him. 'I do try to understand.'

His grip on her hand was suddenly painfully hard as if he was punishing her for something she had done.

'It's not me I wanted it for,' she whispered.

'But I know that, Fleur. That's what makes it so bad.'

She'd said it all wrong, she'd meant it wasn't just for her. It was for him as well. That was naturally how it should have been, even if there had never been an accident.

'I'm going down to the village,' he said. 'Do you want anything?'

She shook her head. He hadn't been going to the village to begin with. He'd said he'd been coming up to the house to look for her.

A dog barked frantically far away on the footpath that ran beside the drive. It sounded desperate, trapped. That was how she felt. Trapped between the man she loved's intransigence and the overpowering bulk of the house beside her.

'Marie asked me up to London,' she said softly.

Benjy said nothing. He was watching her face as he would once have watched the actions of a wild animal.

'I thought I might go soon, this week. If there's nothing special on, nothing you want to do.'

'You go.' His voice sounded unnaturally hearty. 'Have a good time. All girls together – you'll both enjoy it.'

'I won't go if you don't want me to.' Ask me to stay, she was thinking. Please ask me to stay.

Lucy opened a casement window above them. 'Phone

call, Fleur,' she called. 'It's the man you wanted to speak to about the brochures.'

It was part of her job, her responsibilities. The pattern of her future would always be like that.

Benjy watched her go, her fine young figure so full of energy, the pleated skirt swinging as she walked. She was imprisoned like a bird in a cage, a cage made of his wheelchair. He pushed down hard on the wheels and they spun wildly on the gravel. He couldn't stand the thought of being near horses again. A sudden fear gripped him inside, and his stomach contracted sharply. The thought of the animals, so big and strong towering above him, made him desperate to flee. Fear – he had never known fear before. It was one more thing for him to hate the creatures for.

Berry rang as soon as he got back from Australia.

'Marie? I've just heard about Peter – are you OK?'

Marie clutched the receiver close to her ear. She nodded convulsively and then tried to say 'yes', but it came out as a muffled sob.

'I'll come straight over.'

'No!' The word exploded from her, surprising them both with its vehemence. 'Please don't.'

They were back to square one, Berry thought bitterly. He should have known better than to spend his precious spare time in Australia thinking about Marie, thinking about how it would be.

'Berry? Are you still there?'

Marie was sitting, hunched up, on her sofa. It was nearly lunch time, but she was still in her dressing gown. She couldn't get down to anything, it all seemed unreal. Peter had no living relatives. It had been her address that they'd found in his wallet. Her, they'd asked to identify the broken body.

'Is there anything I can do?' Berry asked.

He wanted to walk away, to slam the phone down in fury, but he knew he wouldn't feel that way later. So he'd do the right thing, back off, stay a friend – and get paid for it by the bank.

'There's been a lot happening at Body Beautiful.'

'Send me a fax.'

Marie slumped further. She could hear the bitterness in his tone. But what else could she do? She could remember Peter lying there, so still, so pale. They'd been very kind at the hospital – in the mortuary. They'd given her a cup of tea. The thought of the thick, sweet liquid almost made her vomit. She wasn't going to fall in love again. She was never going to let herself be that vulnerable.

'Please,' she whispered. 'Can't we still be friends?'

'Give me a call when you want to get on with things.' Berry's voice, like his face, was emotionless. 'Are you being looked after?'

'Fleur's here.' She's in no fit state to look after anyone, Marie thought. She was sleeping now, having kept Marie awake half the night talking about Benjy. Fleur was very young, very inexperienced at life.

'Have you got cover at the company?'

'Sarah's handling things for a couple of days.'

'You're lucky you've got her.'

With a sudden flare of jealousy Marie remembered Sarah looking up at Berry, the 'come-on' in her eyes. She struggled to control her feelings. He didn't matter to her. Not like that, not that much. She wasn't going to be hurt again.

'I had to identify his body,' she whispered.

There was silence. They both listened to the crackles on the line.

Finally Berry said, 'I'm here when you want me. Just

315

call the office. I'll tell them to make sure you get put through.'

Marie flinched at the loud click as he broke the connection between them. She sat for a long time, clutching the receiver in both her hands, holding it close to her body. Only when she put it back on its cradle did she start to cry again.

Chapter 22

Beauty has wings, and too hastily flies

'I've got a friend who's an interior designer.' Sarah looked critically around her. 'What you need is a whole new outlook on life, and you might as well start here.'

'I don't need an interior designer.' Marie sounded offended. 'I love my flat, I don't want to change it.'

'Well, at least I got a reaction.'

It was a week since Peter's cremation, the second time she'd been a mourner at a funeral service in only a matter of weeks, and Marie still felt numb. She tried, vainly, to summon some enthusiasm, and said, 'I might splash out on some new cushions.'

'If you let my friend have a free hand, you could well get it done for free, if I could get *Interiors* to do a piece.'

'Really, I don't need it revamped.'

Kit de Montmorency didn't look nearly as camp as his name. Prematurely white-haired, he was slim, elegantly tall, and had the features of a Roman senator. He was dressed conservatively, to Marie's surprise, in a double-breasted light grey suit and blue-and-white-striped shirt. Only his tie gave a clue that he was something artistic. It was hand-painted in several tones of blue that made up a clever abstract pattern, and the lightest shade of azure complemented his eyes.

'What a brilliant position.' He walked straight over to the window to look out on the scene below. 'How ever did you find it?'

'I had a friend in the business.'

'I'm sure *Interiors* will want to do a shot using these windows. That means the curtains will have to be something really special. And we'll have to make the most of the space.' He was looking around, searching for inspiration. 'But it would be hackneyed to go all white. Hockneyed to go all colour. Hey, that was good, don't you think? I'll have to use that again.'

Marie felt that her smile was strained. Sarah had convinced her it would be a good idea to change her surroundings, but there were things she loved. She didn't want to discard everything.

'There are some things I want to keep,' she said.

Kit looked distressed. 'But of course you do, my dear. I won't throw anything away that you want to hang on to. What have you got, a bijou weekend retreat, or something? It'll be fun changing that around with everything from here, won't it?'

'No, I didn't mean . . .' But she didn't quite know what she did mean.

Everything held some kind of memory. The years with Peter had had their problems, and after all they'd broken up months ago, but it seemed as if she'd lost something major in her life when he died. If she had the money, she would have liked a bolt-hole in the country.

She could have gone there now. To somewhere that was hers. She could imagine her furniture against the background of a whitewashed wall. And peace, she needed peace and quiet. Kit had opened the window and the sound of the Garden was suddenly irritating. She wanted calm and quiet. Pencombe would have been ideal, but she didn't want anyone around, not even Lucy or Fleur.

'Did you know these windows have a touch of rot? You want to get them looked at.' Kit pulled a car key out of

318

his pocket and jabbed aggressively into the wooden frame. 'It had better be done before my chaps get decorating. Now, as to colours. I think something strong and dominant set against cream for the walls – a sort of blazer stripe. Maroon, sage green? Or even navy blue. Let's see, what would sound nice in the article? It's just as important as the photos, after all.'

'I rather like the Swedish look,' Marie found herself saying.

She could remember something she'd seen about the interior of a museum in Sweden. There had been a lot of blue and white, and the wood had been a bleached grey.

'Much too "crafty",' Kit said with distaste. 'The sort of thing women decorators are heavily into *à ce moment*. No, no. We want a definite statement here. I mean, just think of the position you're in, absolutely the heart of town. So lucky.'

It was Honour who arranged the cottage. She understood perfectly Marie's need for somewhere of her own in the country, and thought it an excellent idea for her to take over one of the estate cottages. As she said, there would always be someone to pop in and check everything was all right if Marie couldn't get down.

It instantly solved the problem of what to do with her furniture. The cottage had two downstairs rooms, and a small kitchen in little more than an outhouse that had been built on at the back. Upstairs there was one good-sized bedroom and a boxroom and bathroom. There was even a small attic. The end-of-terrace cottage was built of grey stone with a grey slate roof and a tall Elizabethan brick chimney. The last tenant had fitted a Jotul wood-burning stove and the estate had bought it, in situ. It would be Honour's house-warming present. The property would cost sixty pounds a week. It was the going rate –

family didn't get a discount, but they did jump to the top of the queue.

Kit reckoned that the flat would be uninhabitable for three weeks. After that, he said, as long as Marie was prepared to put up with workmen turning up at eight in the morning and leaving at six in the evening, plus a fair degree of chaos, she could move back in. He stressed that he didn't want her coming back before the three weeks were up. That way, he said, she could just look forward to the finished creation, and not have to see the less than glamorous underpinnings.

Marie spent the weeks commuting from Pencombe. It was a ten-minute drive to the station, the train took forty-five minutes, and the journey to her office a further quarter of an hour. In the beginning, she couldn't get used to the routine. Even catching the seven o'clock train meant that she wasn't in the office until eight. She felt that she was spending half her life travelling. Things improved when she organized her day so that she could work on the train. Without the interruption of the telephone, she could get through a pile of paperwork.

Marie was excited as she climbed the stairs to her flat. She felt fit and well, she was managing to get out into the fresh air at the weekends, and she was beginning to feel she could see a new future for Body Beautiful.

Kit was waiting for her. He stepped back to let her walk round on her own. There were no builders, there was no mess, it was as if she'd stepped into the perfect home of a perfect stranger.

The one-time sitting room was now a drawing room of the first order. Thick, green, deckchair-striped wallpaper had been hung on all four walls. The window frames were sponge-painted in three tones of a similar green. The curtains, which matched the walls, contained a staggering amount of fabric. Thickly gathered, they hung from what appeared to be antique assegais. There were several generous fabric rosettes, and looped satin ropes adding to the opulence. The entire drapes system, which looked so heavy, could be drawn back with a delicate pull on a slender cream cord.

The grey stone fire surround had disappeared. In its place was a deeply carved pine mantelpiece, which had been decorated using a similar paint and technique as the windows. Standing in the grate, there was a pewter-coloured wrought-iron fire-basket overflowing with dried sedum and trailing ivy. On the mantelpiece, a single gilt obelisk was reflected in an antique rococo mirror. There were small side tables flanking the fireplace – only some two feet wide, they were of rosewood, banded with holly. Kit was effusive in describing them and their provenance. They were obviously to be a feature for the article.

There were half a dozen armchairs of various sorts, all of a good basic design. There were a couple with scrolled wooden arms, another one with deep buttoning; they were covered in what appeared to be thick silk. There were four rich burgundy velvet-seated side chairs, and two green. A multitude of tapestried cushions completed the effect.

A highly polished sofa table took pride of place in the centre of the room, between the windows and fireplace. It was honeyed gold, with claw feet. On top of it, slightly to one side, a blue and white bowl of orange chrysanthemums glowed softly; ranged around the bowl, several photos in silver frames added a touch of life.

It was beautiful, it was perfect. Marie sat cautiously on a chair. It wasn't her home.

The bedroom was very feminine. Two walls had been used for fitted wardrobes. Cream-painted doors had inset panels of fabric covered with what, on close inspection,

321

looked like chicken wire. The predominant theme was Sanderson cabbage roses. Pink and red against a white background, they rambled over the bedspread, on to the luxuriantly draped curtains, up the cupboard doors and finally all over the scatter cushions that were liberally sprinkled on the lime-green linen-covered sofa positioned at the end of the king-sized bed.

'No dressing table?' Marie asked. But she should have known better.

The bathroom had been completely renovated and there was now a dressing-room feel about it. Floor-length dark mahogany panels concealed shelves for towels; there was a fitted medicine cupboard, and a mini-gym that folded down off the wall. On the opposite side of the room, a six-foot-long slab of pink marble had been fitted in front of a vast mirror. Kit indicated it with a flick of his Ebel-watched wrist. '*Là-bas*,' he said.

Marie followed the designer back through the hall and into the sitting room.

'This has cost a fortune,' she said. 'It can't seriously be worth your while to have done all this just for an article in a magazine.'

Kit paused. He looked, for the first time since she'd met him, vaguely disconcerted. 'The article.' He paused. 'Well yes, it will be very nice. And it will have some value, certainly, in keeping my name in the public eye.'

'Then why?' Marie reached out and touched the silk-smooth surface of the circular dining room table that Kit had placed in the hall. Or rather, hall/diner as it would appear in a brochure.

'I suppose you might say it's been a bit of a scam. Not that you have to be alarmed. All you've done is profit by it. You do like it, don't you? I mean, the furniture alone is worth thousands.'

'I asked you why.'

'It was in part for the article. That's how I got the fabric, and the furniture too. Several pals of mine in the trade thought it would be a way to get their names out there, and they do mention them, you know. And of course, these dealers buy so cheap. You know the kind of thing, dear old lady hasn't got room for her dining-room table any more – they tell her it's not worth much, too big, or not the right fashion, all that sort of thing. So it's not really as much as it might look. And my contribution was the workmen, three of my chaps for a couple of weeks – that's not peanuts, but it was worth it. They did a beautiful job.'

Marie said nothing. She was annoyed now, and she wanted to know what her home had been used for.

Kit carried on. He seemed to be warming to his theme. 'It's so difficult to get the look one strives to attain when a client will keep putting their oar in. This way, I had the whole place vacant.'

'You could have offered to do up some developer's property.'

'No, no, that wouldn't have been at all nice. I wanted to decorate a home, somewhere that honestly existed.'

'You wanted to use my name.' Marie suddenly understood. 'This way you could show potential clients round and say this is what you did for me – that is what you did, isn't it?'

He flushed suddenly and nodded mutely.

'What a damned cheek. I'd never even seen it, but I bet you told them it was just what I wanted. Oh boy, I bet you went the whole hog. Exactly how delighted was I?'

His voice was little more than a whisper. 'Well, I did say we'd be doing your flat in Paris.'

'I don't have a flat in Paris.'

Kit shrugged. He seemed to relax now that the truth was out. 'In for a penny.'

323

'And I thought *I* was inventive.' Marie walked slowly through into the drawing room. She could look at it all with new eyes. 'The only things that don't fit in with your story are those side tables. Nobody in their right mind is going to accept that they're not fashionable. They're perfect little gems.'

'I was going to say . . .' Kit seemed, for a moment, lost for words.

'You are going to leave them where they are, aren't you?'

'I didn't exactly get them like the other stuff.'

'So.' Marie sat down on a long green footstool. 'What happens if the next journalist I have back here for an interview happens to get told I don't like it? After all, a woman's entitled to change her mind. I could say how quickly I got tired of the colour scheme, or I could say that the decorator didn't listen properly to my requirements. Or else, I could say how pleased I am and mention you by name, and when they come to take the photos, I might just like to sit on my cream leather sofa. I really think I'd like that back here. I can't see anything I can stretch out on in the evenings.'

'You wouldn't.'

'But I most certainly would. I don't owe you any favours. You've used my home, and my reputation, to sell your wares. I don't think I owe you anything.'

'All right. I'll leave them.'

Marie smiled. 'I thought you might.'

'You won't really bring that sofa back?' He was almost cringing at the thought of his perfect balance being ruined.

'I don't think I will. In fact, I think you've made up my mind for me. I don't suppose any of your clients fell seriously in love with this place, did they? For the right price I might be prepared to sell.'

'Lock, stock and barrel?' The decorator's eyes gleamed.

'Everything.' Then Marie paused. 'Except the side tables.' She had exactly the right place for them in her sitting room.

They'd look stunning against her whitewashed walls.

Marie looked down the boardroom table at Sarah. She then glanced to her right, where her brother Damion sat, and then to her left, at Berry. 'It's Moorman,' she said.

'You have proof?' Sarah asked.

'Not enough to take him to court.' Marie's voice was flat, expressionless.

There had been another 'doctoring' of Body Beautiful products. Acid in a jar of face cream. It had been done deliberately, and there had been a warning. By stripping all the jars off the shelves of her sixty remaining shops they'd found it.

'But why the hell won't the police act?' Damion exploded.

'Because they think it's just a business vendetta. They're going through the motions, but they're not really interested. No one's been hurt, and there have been no demands for a ransom or anything similar. The police think it's just wasting their time.' Marie spoke slowly. She had explained this to Damion before.

Damion's reply was the same as it always was. 'He killed Beauty. And in doing so killed my wife.'

Marie was looking at Sarah as her brother spoke and she saw the shadow pass over her face. She'd suspected as much.

'You must retaliate.' Berry leaned back in his chair. 'It's what they're trying to get you to do, but you have no choice. Otherwise this is going to go on and on, Marie.'

'I don't have time for all this, I want to get on with building the company up again.'

Berry shrugged. He'd said what he thought.

'Moorman is going around with St John Aldridge,' Sarah said. 'I'm not sure quite how far their relationship goes, but it's pretty close.'

Berry had walked over to the windows. He stood with his back to them as he said, 'Anyone fancy a party? I hear there's an interesting one next Friday night. Ex-love nest of the Prince Regent, on the way to Dover.'

'Dene Park?' Marie whispered the name, and then she repeated it louder. 'Dene Park. But of course, I thought I recognized the name when I saw the advertisement in *Vogue*. It's that place Aldridge took me to see. It's opening as a health hydro – they do all sorts of treatments. They're claiming miracle skin cures . . .' Her voice tailed off.

'Somehow I don't fancy Moorman's potions smeared all over me,' Sarah said. 'But I do fancy the party. I think we'd put the fear of God into them if we turned up mob-handed.'

'For Christ's sake, Sarah.' Damion was on his feet. 'Where on earth did you learn to speak like that?'

'In the course of business,' Marie said, and stood as well.

'What do you think Berry will do?' Sarah asked.

Marie smiled grimly. They were on their own now that the men had gone. It was six o'clock, so they shouldn't be disturbed. They could get through a lot of unfinished business. 'Something very unpleasant, I hope. In any case, he's said we don't have to do anything except get ourselves all dressed up for Friday evening, and that's fine by me. Now, let's get this last lot of properties under offer, shall we? You take your Larry the Lamb out for a long, leisurely lunch and see if you can't make him raise his offer.'

'I don't know about his offer, but I know something I

can make him raise.' Sarah grimaced. 'He thinks he's a real stud.'

'Then you should find convincing him easy.'

'That is a rotten thing to say.'

'But true.' Marie's face was set, her expression hard. 'You've never hidden what you're like from me, and it's too late to change now. My brother doesn't need you. He needs a woman with her feet on the ground, a realist, someone who'll work at marriage. He has a child. He needs someone else, not you, Sarah.'

'You're wrong.'

'No, I'm not. Do you know about his gambling?'

Sarah nodded briefly.

'All about it? Do you know how much he owes to Tommy Docherty?'

'Yes.'

'Then that should put you off, for a start. How's he going to pay?'

'Not by marrying Fleur.' Sarah almost spat the words out.

'Fleur? What on earth's she got to do with Damion?'

'It's your father's idea. He's met her, and he's got the idea that she and Damion would make the ideal pair. They both love horses, and she would be a great help to him with the county set and all that jazz. But best of all, when she's twenty-five she comes into money – serious money. Oh yes, Papa Sullivan has got it all worked out.' Sarah's pale cheeks were streaked with red. 'He's got everything planned except for the fact that I love Damion and he loves me, and it doesn't matter what any of you say, because that's how it is.'

'Fleur.' Marie whispered the name, but she wasn't really thinking of the girl. She was thinking about Sarah.

'I can get Damion to come back.'

'To Body Beautiful?'

'Yes.' Sarah nodded eagerly. 'He could be back here in a couple of weeks. We could all work together. Without the retail shops we could spend money on advertising – come and see the video producer I've found. He'd make beautiful ads.'

'We'd need money – more capital.'

'Berry has money.'

The silence lasted for almost a minute.

'I won't part with my shares.' Marie was staring abstractedly ahead of her.

'You wouldn't have to if you were married. He would be determined to make you a success.'

'I don't need anyone to make me a success.' Marie's eyes had narrowed in anger. 'I'm verging on the biggest company growth Body Beautiful has ever seen.'

'His money would be useful.'

'What the hell are you playing at?'

'I'm trying to give you a reason to let yourself fall for the guy you're mad about.'

'He . . .' Marie began to speak, but then found she couldn't. She swallowed hard before continuing, 'Berry doesn't want me – not any more.'

Sarah laughed.

'Seriously, it's just business between us now.'

'He's shit scared. Just like you are. He's serious, and it's frightening the hell out of him. You're going to have to make the next move. And while you're making it, just remember, his backing will be very, very useful in this family business we're creating.'

There was a long queue for taxis outside Charing Cross station. The rain that had been lashing the train windows all the way up from Kent was still coming down in torrents. Marie glanced at her watch. It was almost ten. She didn't have time to wait.

There were dozens of black taxi cabs driving slowly past her as she stood on the very edge of the pavement opposite the prestigious frontage of Coutts Bank, but all of them were full. She began to swear under her breath. She'd known she should have caught the earlier train. There was nothing she hated more than being late, especially when it was her own fault.

She jumped back too late to avoid her legs being soaked with dirty water that splashed up from the gutter as a taxi pulled in sharply beside her. Water was pouring from her shoes and she was just about to step out of them as she was pushed sideways. She wobbled for a moment, almost falling into the road, but then she caught hold of the bonnet of the taxi; she sensed rather than saw a man forcing his way behind the couple who were struggling to get out of the taxi.

'Sotheby's.' A high-pitched, autocratic male voice shouted instructions to the driver.

Marie straightened up, her face reflecting the fury she felt. But it was too late to assert herself. To her surprise, however, the taxi did not pull away from the kerb. It stayed where it was and the cabbie, a short, fat man with the flushed red face of a spirit drinker, laboriously got out from behind the steering wheel.

'Piss off!' he said loudly as he stood in the rain. 'I pulled in to let me passengers off and the lady in. Not you, you pushy sod, so piss off.'

For a second the man in the Wetherall mackintosh stayed where he was, clearly considering whether he could bluster his way through. Then he opened the door on the road side and stepped out, causing a double-decker bus to brake suddenly and the driver to shake his fist. Marie was grinning with satisfied revenge as she stepped into the cab. She'd been miserable about leaving Pencombe that morning, but when all was said and done, London was still her home ground. She settled back in her seat and tried to ignore the fact that her shoes were soaking. 'Maddox Street,' she said. 'The Bond Street end. And thanks very much for doing the Sir Galahad bit.'

The edit suite was on the first floor. The reception area was crammed with stacks of cardboard boxes, a pair of ultra-modern desks and half a dozen assorted 'bright young things'. One of them, a girl in orange and black designer T-shirt and charcoal leggings, showed Marie through to what she obviously considered the holy of holies, where a young producer who looked startlingly like a miniature Mel Gibson was holding court.

'Here you are at last.' Sarah unfolded her long legs and stretched herself out of a shell-shaped orange seat.

Behind her a machine-decked console was manned by the producer flanked by two young men in similar dark designer shirts. All three had their sleeves rolled up, two of them had long pony tails. 'Mel' as Marie mentally dubbed him, had short-cropped wavy hair.

'Marie,' he said, his voice warm and surprisingly deep for such a small man. 'You look so beautiful in that Armani outfit, darling. You've just made my day.'

Marie looked hard at Sarah. So this was the great Simon Dales, who, according to Sarah, would charm the underwear off any woman between seventeen and seventy.

'Can I get you anything else?' One of the girls from reception came in carrying a tray laden with small bottles of Perrier, glasses and lemon slices on a plate. 'I can do coffee, tea, fruit juices. Decaff if you want or . . .' Her voice trailed off in open admiration.

The producer stretched out a small, beautifully mani-cured hand to take a lemon slice. He put it into his mouth and chewed briefly whilst looking steadfastly at the battery of monitors ranged on the wall ahead of him.

'Not now, darling.' He almost whispered the words and the girl leaned forward to hear him.

Then she turned and reluctantly left, murmuring like an incantation, 'Fruit juices, tea, coffee . . .'

Marie started to laugh. She briefly put her hand up to her mouth, trying to stifle the sound, but then she just let herself go. 'Have you any idea' – she could hardly get the words out – 'of the effect you're having on that girl? My God, she probably has dreams about you ordering a coffee. Imagine it, you only have to say "a cappuccino" and it's heaven, ecstasy, a week of Sundays. You've got to admit it's funny.'

Sarah grimaced. The producer was staring fixedly at the monitors. Eventually he said, 'I think we should take this shot right out to the edges, get rid of the frame altogether, just until – that's it, perfect.' He let his breath out.

Marie suddenly realized that she too had stopped breathing for a moment. She shivered suddenly. Her wet feet were freezing.

'I think I'll have one of the coffees the girl was offering,' she said. 'And then perhaps you could show me the kind of thing you're envisaging, Simon.'

It had been a bad beginning to a relationship that Sarah had said might well prove fruitful. It was a pity, but then the situation wasn't irretrievable, Marie thought.

She spent the next half an hour looking at snatches of commercials. They were all well put together, their timing excellent, and although the products were very different – a dog food ad, one for disinfectant, then an announcement of a share opportunity in public utilities – there was still a strand of similarity running through them. The question was, would that same strand be beneficial to her products?

'Enough,' she said abruptly. 'I'm not taking it in any more. Thank you very much for the show, and your time.'

'I'd like your account,' Simon said. 'Sarah and I can work well together.' His tone didn't necessarily imply that Marie and he would find it difficult.

'I'll think about it.' Marie stood. 'Going into television advertising would be a big step, even if we are only talking satellite to start with. This set-up looks expensive. How much does it cost you to rent it?'

'Two hundred an hour.'

And he'd spent half an hour using it as nothing more than a glorified video to show her some of his samples.

As she walked downstairs with Sarah, Marie was wondering how she'd feel if she had to spend a hundred pounds every time she wanted to show off her wares.

Sarah paused as they stepped out on to the street. 'I've got another appointment and then I'm tied up for lunch. I'd like to talk, though. How about fourish?'

Marie shook her head. She had an important meeting with the suppliers of her plastic containers that afternoon. She expected it to go on until six at least. 'Pop in for a drink at the flat tonight,' she said.

Sarah held her hand out to hail a passing cab, and as it pulled up she called out over her shoulder, 'Sorry, I'm having supper with Damion. I'll catch you in the morning.'

The cab pulled away and Marie felt suddenly lonely. Supper. It was such an intimate word. She turned and began to walk quickly towards the office.

Chapter 23

Beauty when most unclothed is clothed best
PHINEAS FLETCHER (1582–1650)

A black Daimler limousine was pulled in tight to the kerb outside Body Beautiful's London office. It was seven in the evening, so the young, uniformed chauffeur thought there shouldn't be any problem with wardens.

He sat staring through the windscreen, rerunning in his mind every satisfactory stroke of his one hundred and two snooker break. It was the highest break of his life, and he'd made it less than a week ago. Since then he'd been working all hours with the cars and hadn't had a chance to get back to the table. He couldn't wait until next Monday when he'd got the day, and night, off. There was a tournament down at Tottenham; he'd scoop the jackpot, the way he was playing.

'Blimey,' the word slipped out inadvertently, and he coughed to cover it. The blonde walking purposefully towards his motor was a looker, and then some. She was slim but curvy, and she was dressed, or perhaps wrapped was the word, in a fuchsia-pink silk sheath. He jumped out of the car and made his way round to open the door for her. The bird in the back was a right cracker too, all done up in turquoise and gold, looking like a million dollars. It was his lucky night.

Sarah ducked her head to step into the leather-scented interior. She put her hand up to her chest, pressing the low, boned bodice against her front, and grinned at

333

Marie. 'Don't want to give the boy beautiful an eyeful,' she said.

'So, how was Larry?' Marie asked.

'Like a lamb to the slaughter.'

'Is he going to take the lot?'

'Absolutely – what do you take me for? And before you tell me, let me add that I did it all with a desk between us – and that's not some new kind of perversion.'

All the shops – Larry Gold was going to buy all the secondary locations. Marie closed her eyes and leaned back against the seat. She could feel tears stinging her throat. This was it, they were up and flying, on their way.

'And he'll take all the stock on the list that's stock-piled in the factory, everything. Plus, he'd like to put in a regular order for Sunkissed, as long as you carry on doing it in the shell-shaped bottles.'

'I could kiss him,' Marie whispered feelingly.

'I wouldn't bother, he's definitely the frog who doesn't turn into a prince.'

'Body Beautiful's out of UK property – I can hardly believe it. All that time, building up the chain, putting the pins in the map.' She sounded wistful.

Sarah looked at her sharply. 'It's too late to change your mind now. We're so nearly there. You'll have the capital in the bank from this deal and the regular orders from Larry that are just a nice manufacture-and-deliver job. He even wants to put a display up in each of the shops. He reckons he'll sell a fair bit. After all, as he says, they come in with sun, and suntans, on their minds. He's got some pushy woman called Brenda who's going to oversee that side of their business, I think she might do well. We clear the decks tonight and then it's all systems go.'

'Fleur,' Marie said. 'It's our future. The name of the scents. The name of the girl.'

334

'Thank Christ she agreed.'

Marie nodded. 'I almost didn't put it to her. It seemed such a gigantic step to ask her to take. But she was so desperate that time she came up to town. She needed something major to sort out her life.'

'You can't get much more major than spearheading a two-million-pound advertising campaign for body perfumes.'

'You can if you're Estée Lauder's Paulina Porizkova, she earns over the two million herself.'

'Yeah – the big-time girls. Paulina's the top earner. Then there's Calvin Klein's Christine Turlington – she's around the million and a half mark – and Revlon's Cindy Crawford at one million. You're going to have to watch out Fleur doesn't get ideas above her station.'

'The rate the product is going to go at, she will end up earning a fortune. But that's not what appealed to her. It was the freedom, the chance to do something completely different. It even gives her time to see her love for Benjy from a distance, and it'll give him a reason to respect her. When they got engaged he thought she was just a pretty little thing. Now he's going to have to face up to the fact that she's a woman, with character, and ability.'

'And when Fleur is established?'

'Then we go on to Beautiful People. That Julian Dodds at the advertising agency was right, the name says it all. It'll be interesting to see if they bill me for using it.'

'Just let them try. We'd give them a good run for their money.'

'I don't know, we might just do a bit of quid pro quo and use them when we need an agency.'

'Can this be the Marie I've come to know and admire?'

'No, probably not.' Marie laughed. 'I've changed a lot recently. I'm going to think even bigger. Now that Damion's coming back, and you're on board . . .'

'And Berry, what about him in your great scheme of things?'

'The wild card.' Marie paused. She screwed up her eyes as if she was trying to look into the future.

'I wouldn't do that. You'll give yourself wrinkles, never mind messing up your eye make-up.'

'The problem about Berry,' Marie continued, 'is the here and now. I can imagine a future, sometime a long way off, when everything's worked out. On the one hand, there will be you and Damion, with all your kids and horses, shouting at each other, loving each other. With me and Berry, it would be different. I think we'd be organized, each with our own lives, our own compartments – that's how I see us.'

'That doesn't sound much fun.'

'Doesn't it? I don't know. It's a question of my head ruling my heart. That's the way I think a marriage would have to work, for me.'

'No passion?'

'No, not too much passion. It gets in the way of things.'

Sarah leaned back against her seat and closed her eyes. For someone who could extricate herself from near bankruptcy to come out – literally – smelling of roses, Marie was a genius. But as far as affairs of the heart were concerned, she was nothing more than a babe in arms.

Dene Park sat serenely on its six acres of verdant lawns. In the kindly dusk of early evening, the many-paned windows shone like gunmetal in the white façade and the two stone lions guarding the front door appeared to yawn with ennui.

The freshly gravelled circle in front of the elegant central portico was littered with an assortment of vans. The caterers had two – both square and white, and very clean. There was also an elderly red Transit, from which

336

several earnest long-haired young men were unloading musical instruments; the cello came last.

St John Aldridge was in ecstasy. Around him his beloved mansion was coming to life. The formal rooms were full of flowers, log fires crackled in a dozen grates. The last of the books for the library had arrived that morning; Mark had finished putting them out on the shelves a couple of hours ago.

Mark. How St John's life had changed since they'd met. The future was now so exciting. Between them they had the knowledge to take the very cream of customers from the market. And the relationship worked so well, they were so alike, and yet so different. They each had their own room at Dene Park. St John had the Chinese boudoir. The massive, twenty-foot square room was decorated with rich blue and gold Chinese paper; blue brocade curtains hung at the floor-length windows; gold damask formed drapes for the bed. All the furniture in the room was dark mahogany, and the subtle scent of sandalwood perfumed the air.

It, like every other bedroom in the house, had its own en-suite bathroom, fully tiled and fitted with luxurious extras such as pulse shower and bidet. There was air conditioning in all the rooms too, as well as the inevitable concealed central heating. By pooling their resources, Mark and St John had managed to make Dene Park into the most beautiful and exclusive hydro in Britain.

Mark's taste had been a surprise. The cool greys and apricots he had chosen in sophisticated slub silks formed a perfect backdrop for the strangely haunting Scandinavian art that the chemist loved. There was a preponderance of seascapes in his collection, vistas of long, ash-blond beaches populated by one or sometimes two small figures. Women in Edwardian dress, perfect, insubstantial, untouchable creatures.

337

'Time to change, St John.' Mark came walking purposefully into the morning room. 'Stop fiddling with those flowers and get yourself ready. We don't want the guests arriving with you in that state.'

St John smiled guiltily. He had been rearranging a bowl full of exotic lilies. As soon as the flower arranger had left, his fingers had itched to encourage the blooms into a more perfect display. He was still wearing the soft corduroy trousers and cream polo-necked jumper that he'd put on that morning. Mark was right, the evening was a black-tie affair and it wouldn't do to get caught out. Besides, he wanted to go upstairs, he wanted to have one last look at the ballroom, all ready as it was to receive their expected one hundred guests.

'Come on, John-John.' Mark propelled him physically towards the wide, sweeping staircase. 'Up we go.'

They made their way up side by side, aglow with pride, eager for what was to be the culmination of their efforts.

Driving through Kent, at ease in the back of the limousine, Marie and Sarah worked on their strategy for the future. They were both convinced that they could mastermind the emergence of a completely new range of body perfumes.

The products would be based on the various moisturizers already made in the Irish plant, and they would add a complete range of deodorants. From top to toe – and, as Sarah put it, including the naughty bits in between – any woman could be soothed and pampered and made to smell of flowers.

Fleur would be the overall name. There would be four divisions: Summer; Autumn; Winter; Spring. And the packaging would be appropriately colour-coded. They were building on the groundwork already done by the rapidly growing numbers of colour counsellors.

338

A blonde with blue eyes, Sarah was a Spring person. Dark-haired, with green eyes, Marie was Autumn, as, too, was Fleur herself.

An illustrator had been given the brief to design four highly stylized bouquets that identified each individual range. The shape of the packs, once again, would be distinctive. Marie had taken inspiration from the Guernsey flower arrangers who'd bought her second tranche of shops. All the pots looked like miniature wickerwork baskets.

'Where are we meeting Damion?' Sarah asked. It was Marie who'd arranged the rendezvous.

'About five miles from Dene Park there's a pub called the Kentish Drover. We're to wait in the car park. I suppose we ought to start working out what we want to say to Moorman and Aldridge.'

Sarah smiled grimly. 'First word – four letters. Need any more clues?'

Damion flicked down the sun guard in front of him and checked his reflection in the vanity mirror. His immaculately tied black bow tie was straight, his shirt brilliant white, his face still lightly tanned from the summer.

'Don't forget the lipstick.' Berry laughed.

They were sitting in the Range Rover. The pub car park was almost deserted. If things went to plan, within the next half an hour it should fill up nicely, but the publican wouldn't pick up much trade.

'What are you going to do about Marie,' Damion asked, 'after this shindig's over.'

'What's this, the protective brother asking if my intentions are honourable?'

'You might put it like that.'

Berry looked up at the darkening sky. 'I've been given the hands-off routine. If she changes her mind, then I don't know. That's the truth. She's a strange lady, your sister.'

Damion thought, You can say that again, but he didn't say it out loud. He wouldn't mind seeing his sister married off – she'd be easier handled.

'There's the first of them,' Berry said, and excitement made his face predatory.

A middle-of-the-range BMW, in neutral grey, cruised into the space beside them. The man in the passenger seat raised his hand in a kind of salute.

'Jesus Christ,' Damion exploded. 'What the hell have you done?'

'I told you I was bringing along a bit of muscle.'

Having shown recognition to the man who was paying for his services and those of a few of his friends, Tommy Docherty turned to speak to his driver.

Damion stared despairingly at the back of his enemy's head. 'Why?' he whispered.

'Because Marie asked me to get you out of the shit you're in. Don't get it wrong, my getting involved in this isn't an answer to your earlier question. She's paying for all of this. Only I thought I might as well save her some money and kill two birds with one stone.'

'Here come your mobsters with a vengeance.'

Two more cars pulled off the main road. Again they were understated vehicles with power under their bonnets.

Berry turned to look fully at his passenger. 'Now,' he said, 'this is what I want you to do . . .'

Chamber music from the ballroom floated out into the garden. It swirled romantically around the yew walk, touched the lichen-garnished statue of Aphrodite in the centre of the great round rose bed, and faded away in the thick rhododendron hedge that bordered the tennis court.

'But you must do the guided tour,' St John gushed. 'My dear Ms Rendle, you, of all people, must see our beautiful house.'

'Anne, I told you to call me, Anne.' The tone of the journalist's voice was every bit as flat as when she had conducted the Sunkissed interview with Marie, but the expression on her face was very different. 'I'm just so pleased for you both. You deserve every success.'

'With you on our side, my dear Anne, I don't think we can fail.'

From across the highly polished, undersprung maple-wood floor, Mark Moorman watched his partner in action. The female journalist was a slag, but she'd been useful. There were others at the grand launch who had also played their part. A couple more journalists, a fashion model who'd done a little muck-spreading, and later there would come the final link. The one person without whom he could never have succeeded so well in getting his additional special ingredient into the Sullivan woman's creams.

The small orchestra was positioned in the wide bay window. They were playing loudly, with vigour, but a great deal of their sound found its way up to the ceiling some fifteen feet above them. The violinist was studying the cornicing, admiring the thick convoluted plasterwork. At a particularly surging passage, he gazed up at the vast circular design that formed a backdrop for the centrally hung crystal chandelier. One thousand shining droplets, the man Moorman had told them it contained, and seventy candle bulbs – two layers, one above the other. In the cavernous space of the great room, the light was as nothing. All around the oxblood walls gilt bracketed lights gleamed softly, and the room was still bathed in soft, flattering, scented dusk.

'Most of the guests have arrived,' St John whispered in Mark's ear. 'It's almost nine. We should start soon.'

There were to be speeches, toasts. A few suitably structured phrases to go out with the press release. They hadn't invited the television. They thought they were much too exclusive for that. For a moment, St John, looking at the beautiful people – the elegant men in their dinner jackets, the women with their lovely creamy shoulders – regretted the decision.

Disdaining the *No Entry* signs, Berry's convoy drove on, to pull to a gravel-scattering stop on the circle in front of the house. All down the drive, cars had been parked up on the verge, but they'd swept past, the Range Rover in the lead, Marie and Sarah in the limousine bringing up the rear.

'I'll go in first,' Tommy said. 'You follow in five minutes.'

'Don't trust him,' Marie said desperately, but no one paid any attention.

She couldn't understand why he was here. Berry had said that it was part of sorting out Damion, but she couldn't see how it was all going to happen.

'Tommy.' Mark Moorman pushed his way through his guests to greet the latest arrival. He shook him warmly by the hand, clasped him on the shoulder. 'I can't tell you how glad I am you've made it.'

'I wouldn't have missed this for the world,' Tommy said. The formal evening wear suited him. He looked bluff, hearty, and yet somehow sharp and astute. 'I'd love a quick look round before you get going with the speeches. Is there one of your people who could give me the five-bob tour?'

Moorman did it himself. Whisking Tommy past the

342

splendid array of downstairs facilities – the basin-decked hairdressing room, looking like something from the *QE2*. The dark-blue painted sound-proofed room for contemplation, bare as a monk's cell. There was a flotation suite, with four eight-foot-long tanks, each formed out of fibreglass, with lids that could be bolted down for complete silence. They looked like giant clams. The sea-shell shape reminded Tommy of Marie. That was something that still had to be sorted.

Further on, there were other treatment rooms. Areas with leather-covered tables, complete with wide restraining straps, hoses, and drainage holes sunk into the floor. These were, Moorman explained, for the hot mud treatments, to keep the patient perfectly still. Tommy was amused at the use of the word 'patient'. It was so hushed, so sterile, so far away from the luxurious reception rooms that, with the faint smell of antiseptic, it reminded him of a private hospital.

From the centre of the crowded room, St John watched Marie enter the ballroom. He had glanced over, his eye caught by a beautiful gold and turquoise dress, but quickly his admiration had turned to horror. He also recognized Sarah Hatherleigh. He'd seen her picture in the paper.

Accompanying the two women was Berry Jopling – he'd been sent an invitation. After all, his company had been involved in the property purchase. A crowd of other men entered the room behind the group that had so disturbed him. The final arrivals were all well-built, purposeful-looking. He knew at once that he should have spent the extra, as Mark had suggested, and employed security guards for the evening.

'Ladies and Gentlemen.' Mark swept into the room. There was a sea of faces in front of him, and he was so

343

excited that they registered as nothing more than a blur. 'Please, charge your glasses.'

Mark gripped St John by the arm. Typically, he thought, his friend was perturbed, concerned that the evening should be a great success. It wouldn't be long now, and they'd be surging on a wave of victory. Dear John-John, Mark thought, and gave him a quick squeeze as they hurried towards the microphones.

'What are you going to do?' St John asked anxiously. He couldn't get his voice to sound louder than a whisper.

The celebratory crowd had departed. The bright red brake lights of the white Cavalier driven by Anne Rendle, the last guest to leave, flashed on and off briefly in the ebony night.

'It was justified,' Moorman blustered. 'You insulted me . . .' He was talking to Marie, but it was Damion who answered him.

'You killed my wife.' His voice was low, his words considered, and they frightened Moorman far more than if the trainer had ranted and raved.

They were gathered in the elegant drawing room. The four sets of floor-length heavy pink silk curtains had been pulled tightly closed. The cream and green upholstered furniture gave the forty-foot room an atmosphere of lightness that was echoed by the delicate mahogany side tables and whatnots placed in front of the buttermilk damask-hung walls.

Berry coughed lightly into his clenched fist. As he began to speak, two of the men behind him slipped silently from the room.

'The interference with Body Beautiful's products has to stop,' he said.

'I promise . . .' St John began, but was swiftly silenced by the dismissive look on Berry's face.

'It will stop, because I have arranged things that way,' Berry continued. 'As you know, it was my company that did the overall purchase here. We bought the whole two thousand acres, and did the split-up. You, Moorman and Aldridge, jointly bought the freehold of Dene Park and the surrounding six acres.'

Moorman nodded, he felt that by being as agreeable as possible, he would alleviate whatever retribution was to come, and he was certain that there *would* be retribution. He felt as if Fate had been waiting to strike him a blow, a set-back when things were ready, at last, to go well. Just as when he'd had the accident in the lab, and his hands had been so badly burned.

'My company still owns the two hundred acres directly around this property. Including the farmhouse and out-buildings directly behind here. We also own the drive – all of it. The farmhouse has a right of way, as does the old dower house that has already been sold off, and the two lodge cottages. Just as far as their properties, and no further. Dene Park itself is another case entirely.'

Sarah took a few more steps into the room and sat down. After a few moments Marie did the same. It somehow seemed to make Berry more impressive.

'I had nothing to do with the acid,' St John said. His face was the colour of parchment. 'That was Mark's idea – as was his contact in Ireland. It was him who knew that man Docherty.'

Marie drew her breath in sharply. A flush of anger coloured her breast and Berry looked quickly at her. He didn't want dissension in their ranks.

Moorman threw himself down heavily into an over-stuffed button-back chair. 'Don't be a fool, St John,' he said. 'Don't give them the satisfaction of seeing that weak underbelly of yours, or that vivid yellow stripe down your back.'

St John burst into tears. He began gasping for breath, choking on his words. 'God damn you, Mark. I hate you,' he spluttered. 'I hate you, I hate you.'

Berry waited until the outburst had stopped, then he spoke directly to Moorman. 'At least I see now where the strength lies. You surprise me. I would have thought your friend Aldridge was the dominant partner.'

'Heterosexual instincts can be fallible.'

Berry bowed his head as if in agreement. 'Whatever you say. Shall we continue?'

No one broke the silence, they were all waiting on his words.

'The access way – that's the first thing. You should change your solicitor, find one more concerned with his client's welfare, and less concerned with his own status.'

'But Reginald's a friend!' St John burst out.

'And a fool. You have no legal right of access. Certainly if you take the matter to court, after a great deal of expense – and I do mean a great deal, counsel's fees don't come cheap – then you'll probably get reasonable vehicular access. What you won't get, of course, however much you spend, is anything that specifies the condition of the drive itself. Personally, I only require access for farm machinery – heavy farm machinery. The farmhouse will only be rented; so there will be no help for you from there. As to the dower house, it's been bought by a family of ecological enthusiasts. They're not going to want resources wasted on filling in pot-holes. Of course, you're a different case, you'll want a smooth, seamless surface. The kind of clients you want aren't going to arrive in Land Rovers.'

'Petty!' Moorman spat out the word.

'Agreed,' Berry said. 'But effective. Put together with the planning objection, I think you're going to find life a bit difficult in the near future.'

346

'Planning? There can't be any problem with planning. We've got permission . . .'

'Permission for a variety of uses. An old people's home, or even a private hotel – which is the one you think you're covered by, at least that's what your bank said. And you see, you're not a hotel, far from it. You're equipped to carry out all sorts of treatments – even, as far as I can understand, minor operations. That's the whole basis on which you're going out to the market.'

Marie stood suddenly. She felt empty. It was a hollow victory. The two men who'd been her enemies had shrunk before her eyes. She glanced at Sarah, who stood up beside her, and they left the room together.

They had travelled some twenty miles back towards London, scarcely talking, both looking out into the dark night, when the chauffeur called back, 'There's some bloke on a motorbike waving us down.'

Marie sat forward. She felt a sudden lurch of fear. It would be something to do with Tommy.

Sarah's voice startled her.

'Pull over,' she said firmly, and then to Marie she added, 'It's Berry.'

Damion slid the bolts himself. There was a satisfyingly final sound about it. Beneath the clam-shaped lid, St John floated – or rather, to be exact, thrashed, in a few inches of water. The dark would be absolute, and so would the silence. After a few hours, he might drift into a stupor. He wouldn't drown, not unless he turned over deliberately and sank his face in the salt-rich liquid. Damion didn't think he'd do that, but he didn't really care much, either way.

It was Tommy who did the straps up on the big man. With the help of one of his henchmen he fastened Moorman to the table. Then he slid on a pair of surgical gloves, and then he began smearing on the cream that Damion had brought. He rubbed it over everything: the man's face, the man's hair, his body and, very thoroughly, all over his genitals.

All the time, Damion watched. He kept his arms folded, his eyes on the chemist's face, watching the growing horror, the dreadful anticipation.

'I don't understand about Tommy,' Marie said.

The three of them were sitting in the back of the limo. They'd pulled into a lay-by, where Berry's bike was under the watchful eye of the chauffeur.

'He knows a lot of things, your man Docherty,' Berry said. 'But what he doesn't know is that as part of Aldridge and Moorman's schemes, they've had Dene Park completely wired for sound, and vision. Everything that is done there this evening, everything that was said earlier, has been filmed. I had one of my men in the control room from the start. He confirms that Docherty said enough to implicate himself in doctoring the cream at the factory. We have enough evidence now to bring a good case of wilful manslaughter against him. I shall present friend Tommy with a video – a copy of the original. There's enough on that to put him away for several years of Her Majesty's pleasure.'

'And he'll give up hounding Damion?'

'Give up the gambling debt? Oh no.' Berry laughed. 'That's one thing he'll never do. But he won't have to wait much longer. The sum I have in mind for Dene Park's right to access will cover that nicely, plus a little over for my expenses. And even when they've paid, they'll still be dependent on the kindness of my heart to allow them to resurface, as and when I see fit.'

Sarah kissed him on the cheek. 'You're a genius,' she said.

348

Berry laughed. He looked at Marie, into her eyes. She didn't say anything, didn't look anything. He stepped back out into the night and mounted his motorbike, gunning off down the motorway before the chauffeur even had the limo in drive.

Chapter 24

*The gods entrusted beauty to you and wealth,
and the capacity of enjoying it*

HORACE

It had taken Marie six months, over twenty-four weeks of flat-out effort, to get her product line launched and for the accolades to start piling in. The orders were flowing. Fleur's photo had appeared on dozens of magazine covers world-wide, and was set to appear on many more.

Sarah and Damion were to be married at Easter, less than five weeks away. The wedding itself would be a quiet affair. They planned to throw a big party when they came back from their honeymoon in America.

St John Aldridge had been seen at all the in night spots after his launch party at Dene Park. Brighter, more effusive than ever, in pursuit of business for his hydro, he had squired a succession of nubile young starlets to a succession of film premières and opening nights. At Christmas, he had disappeared suddenly from the social scene. After the holiday he featured in a spate of gossip-page articles, his name linked with the daughter of Giovanni Franchi, the wealthy Italian industrialist. At the same time, his business partner, Mark Moorman, was being photographed on the nudist beach of a private Caribbean island. Totally hairless from head to toe, his whale-like, golden-brown body made a brilliant shot for the sensation-seeking tabloids. With entrepreneurial genius, Larry Gold had the shot blown up and used it in his window, surrounded by tubes of Sunkissed. The bookings started rolling in.

Packaging. Marie kept turning the word over in her head. She pulled her coat more tightly over her knees as she sat in the taxi. The press were united in hailing her packaging as innovative, and exciting.

She leaned forward on her seat, looking out at the evening streets of Hampstead, checking that the cab was arriving at her destination.

Berry opened the door of his flat. He hadn't seen Marie in months. She looked well, wrapped in a cream velour coat, a coloured scarf worn round her shoulders. She was taller than he remembered, in high, slender-heeled, two-toned leather courts.

'May I come in?' she asked.

He stepped back and let her into the hall.

'I have something for you.' She handed him a small parcel, beautifully wrapped in cerise paper. 'But don't open it yet.'

'Shall I take your coat?'

She looked at him strangely. 'I'm not sure.'

'I won't eat you,' he said, and was surprised by her sudden laughter. 'I've missed you.'

'I've missed you, too. How're things?'

'How's business?' he asked, and then he laughed. 'And don't say you don't mix business with pleasure. We've been through too much together to go in for all that crap.'

Suddenly she was in his arms, and he was kissing her, holding her tightly.

'What the hell . . .?' He stepped back. 'What have you got on under there?'

She unbuttoned her coat slowly and then slipped it off. She was glad it was warm in the flat.

'Jesus,' he breathed. 'What a package.'

She was gift-wrapped. She'd nothing on but a wide band of wrapping paper printed with the symbols of Fleur.

There was a single piece of glittering string tied around her middle and Berry reached for it.

'Wait.' She laughed, and for the first time since he'd met her, there was sheer pleasure on her face, nothing held back. 'Open your other present first.'

He unwrapped it slowly, savouring the excitement – half a dozen individually wrapped condoms fell into his hand.

'Happy birthday.' She laughed again. 'Happy Christmas, happy everything.'

He was grinning as he pulled the string, took her into his arms, and into his life.